MURDER STACKS THE SHELVES, VOLUME 2

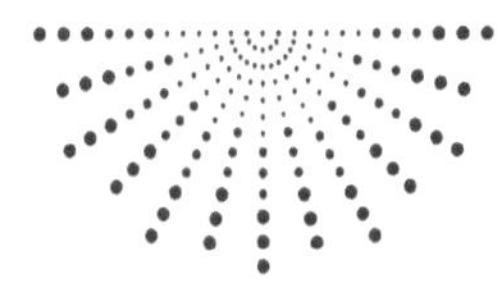

CHRISTY FIFIELD

A DAY IN THE LIFE

A message from Glory -

"Coffee."

My life seems to revolve around it.

That's what greets me every morning. When I come down to my store — Southern Treasures Gift Shop — from my apartment overhead, I carry my second, or sometimes third, cup of coffee because I need my caffeine.

And every morning Bluebeard begs for coffee. I have to tell him, every day, that parrots don't drink coffee. It's dangerous for them. But it doesn't stop him from asking. Thing is, I don't really think it's Bluebeard asking. Because lately I've been forced to admit I'm sharing my home with more than a parrot.

I have a ghost.

My great uncle Louis left me Southern Treasures, but I don't think he ever really left. Uncle Louis is still hanging around, talking to me, messing with stuff in the shop, and generally causing trouble. Part of it is his vocabulary, which is sometimes quite, um, colorful. And part of it is that he flirts with the pretty girls; Bluebeard has an impressive wolf whistle.

Coffee is part of another morning ritual. A couple years ago Jake Robinson bought Beach Books, across the main drag of Keyhole Bay from Southern Treasures. Jake is a bit of an attraction; tall, dark hair, and really smart (hey, he owns a book store, doesn't he?). Now, when we have a lull in customers, Jake and I meet at Lighthouse Coffee next door to me for lattes and scones. I've discovered Jake is a check-grabber, but I know there is a lot more I *don't* know about him.

Thing is, Bluebeard — well, Uncle Louis — thinks he needs to interfere where Jake is concerned. He always has to make some comment, every time I have coffee with Jake. And when he says "Pretty boy," you can bet he's not talking about himself.

There's a lot I don't know about Uncle Louis, too. He died when I was only ten, and my memories of him are jumbled. He seemed really old to me, but now I realize he was only in his sixties. I thought he was quite exotic; he served in Europe and the South Pacific during WWII. He was a single man in a small town where family was everything. Now I realize how little I know about him. Just like Jake.

Actually, Uncle Louis left me fifty-five percent of Southern Treasures. He left the other forty-five percent to my cousin Peter. Peter lives in Montgomery, and just because he has a Master's degree, he thinks he knows everything. His degree is in Engineering, but that doesn't stop him from sharing his wisdom about how to run Southern Treasures. Recently he tried to convince me to add a coffee bar, even though the best coffee shop in town is right next door. Believe me, I *know* where to get my coffee, and I know how to run my business.

My BFF, Karen Freed, can be counted on to know all the best drive-thru coffee in the county, since her job as a reporter for the local radio station takes her everywhere. She's always glad to introduce me to a new spot, and to help me out in whatever adventure comes our way.

See, my life really does revolve around coffee. But it also revolves around mystery.

Bluebeard got me involved with the mystery surrounding the death of local star quarterback Kevin Stanley. And somehow I have a hunch Bluebeard and Uncle Louis will see to it that I get involved in more mysteries in the future.

But there are other mysteries in my life, and I want to solve them, too. Uncle Louis and Jake are just the beginning. There's the SouthernTreasures website that needs work, and the mystery of what to do about Peter, oh, and just exactly what is my relationship with Jake.

Every day I face the mysteries in my life, and try to unravel them. It's what keep me going.

That, and a big dose of coffee.

MURDER SENDS A POSTCARD

"THOROUGHLY ENTERTAINING."
—JULIE HYZY, NEW YORK TIMES BESTSELLER

CHRISTY FIFIELD

NATIONAL BESTSELLING AUTHOR

MURDER SENDS A POSTCARD

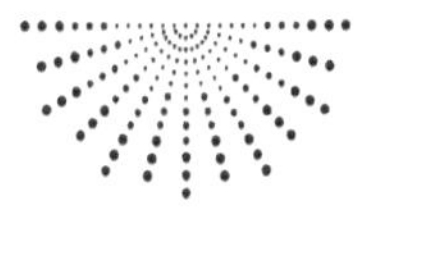

CHRISTY FIFIELD

ACKNOWLEDGMENTS

In a perfect world, a writer sits down in an immaculate garden full of unicorns and rainbows and creates a perfect book. Unfortunately, this writer lives in the real, far-from-perfect world. Fortunately, I have incredible people helping me navigate that world.

When I should have been in my perfect garden, I was instead learning firsthand the meaning of "Code 3." It really does mean the ambulance driver gets to use the lights and siren all the way to the hospital—even if it's ninety miles away. I also learned many new medical terms, and got up close and personal with amazing advances in medical technology.

I am indebted to the physicians, surgeons, nurses, and technicians at Oregon Health & Science University, especially Dr. Patrick Worth (my personal guardian angel), my amazing home health nurse Erik, and all the wound care staff. I cannot imagine the last months without your help.

My thanks, also, to everyone who helped at home: Sue and Sue (both of them!), Dan, Kris, Dean, and Debbie. And to the many people who provided much-needed support for my husband, especially Sean and Rose, Stephanie, Greg, Scott, Lynette, and Colleen.

And as always, I am grateful for the usual cast and crew:

Colleen (again), first reader, cheerleader, chauffeur;

the Oregon Writers Network crowd, especially Dean and Kris;

my sisters, Jan, Jeri, and Jeri (yep, there are two of them), who did more than I could have ever asked.

Most of all to Steve, who saved my life.

Literally this time.

CHAPTER ONE

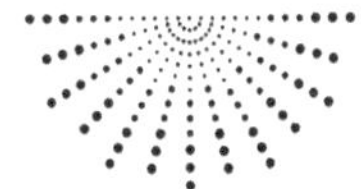

I knew who Bridget McKenna was the instant she stepped through the door of Southern Treasures. Not because she'd been in the gift shop I owned here in Keyhole Bay, Florida, but because she hadn't.

I'd only heard about her.

Our tourists usually fit in one of several categories: the young and single, the families, and the empty nesters, with the occasional girls'-weekend-without-the-husbands group.

Bridget was none of those. With her designer suits and stiletto heels, she appeared overdressed for the Florida panhandle. Careful makeup masked her age, though I suspected she was a few years north of my mid-thirties.

She looked good. Good enough to earn a wolf-whistle from Bluebeard, the parrot I'd inherited along with my 55 percent of Southern Treasures. My cousin Peter owned the other 45 percent, but he lived in Montgomery and didn't work in the store. He just meddled from a hundred miles away.

"Bluebeard!"

Harassing customers wasn't good for business, and he knew better.

To my relief, Bridget laughed, a clear, almost musical sound. "I'll take it as a compliment."

"Pretty girl," Bluebeard cooed, shooting me a triumphant look. He seemed so human sometimes. At least now I understood why.

"What's your name?" she asked, approaching his perch.

For one crazy moment I actually expected him to say "Louis," the name of my great-uncle, the previous owner of Southern Treasures—and the ghost who lived in the shop.

Uncle Louis used Bluebeard as a spokesbird, and I was never quite sure when he might decide he had something to say.

Fortunately, today Uncle Louis decided to stay quiet.

"Bluebeard," the parrot and I answered in unison.

"Well, I'm very glad to meet you, Bluebeard," she said, a smile in her voice. She turned around to face me. "And you, too."

She walked back across the shop to where I stood behind the counter, and stuck out her hand. "Bridget McKenna."

I shook her outstretched hand, answering her smile with one of my own. "Gloryanna," I said. "Gloryanna Martine, owner of this place and the rude parrot."

Up close, I could see my estimate of her age was at least five years low, maybe more. Her hair, expertly streaked dark honey-blond, hung low over her forehead, concealing the beginnings of frown lines between her perfectly arched eyebrows.

Her handshake was firm, and her friendly smile reached her eyes.

"Welcome to Keyhole Bay," I said.

She glanced down at her suit and shoes, so out of place in our little tourist town. "That obvious, huh?"

"Well," I admitted with a grin, "I already heard about you." I shrugged. "It's a small town."

It wasn't such a small town in the middle of summer, actually. Tourists swelled our population and a steady stream of people came through the door. Quiet, even just long enough to say hello, was rare.

Her expression sobered. "I'm not surprised. Big-city woman coming down from Minnesota to take over the local bank."

Candid *and* perceptive. I instantly liked Bridget McKenna.

I started to ask another question, but the bell over the door interrupted as a gaggle of youngsters poured in, followed by a harried-looking woman.

The gaggle surrounded the toy rack, the mass of sunburned arms and legs sorting themselves out into three kids: a boy about twelve, a girl of seven or eight, and a boy whose gap-toothed grin pegged him as five or six.

Their mother quickly took the two younger ones by the hand, pulling them back a step from the display. "Look with your eyes," she said. "Not with your hands."

It was a phrase Memaw used to use when she took me shopping, and I smiled at the memory.

I turned back to say something to Bridget, but she had walked over to the postcard spinner and was gazing at the offerings. She glanced up and smiled briefly, then went back to her perusal.

"Getting busy again?" a voice asked behind me.

I turned to see Julie Nelson, my part-time clerk, coming from the storage area behind the store. "Rose Ann's settled down, I can take over," she said.

Rose Ann was Julie's daughter, born just a few months earlier. In an effort to keep Julie working at the store, we had set up a small nursery—really little more than an alcove with partitions—for Rose Ann. The baby spent several days a week with her grandmother, but there was a place for her on the days Anita Nelson wasn't available.

"You sure?" I checked the time. Julie still had a couple hours on her shift.

She nodded.

I trudged up the stairs to my apartment over Southern Treasures. Summer had hit full force, and this morning's rain shower combined with the midday ninety-degree heat to drain all my energy.

Unfortunately, it was my turn to host our regular Thursday dinner. My three best friends would arrive at six thirty, expecting a traditional Southern meal, and it was too blasted hot even to think about cooking.

Fortunately, I had remembered something my mother used to make when I was a kid. *Cold supper*, she called it. A meal that involved very little actual cooking, all of it done in advance.

So while Julie watched the store, I was headed upstairs to put the finishing touches on tonight's meal.

I'd left the apartment closed and dark when I opened the store at nine, but by midafternoon the heat had seeped in around the tightly drawn drapes.

In an attempt to capture the afternoon breezes, I opened the windows overlooking the main drag in front of the store and the sliding door to my miniature balcony in back. From the balcony I could watch the boats in the tiny bay that gave Keyhole Bay its name.

The cross-ventilation helped, though the open windows also let in the traffic noise. A week before Fourth of July there was a lot of traffic.

I should be grateful, I told myself. It was exactly that traffic that kept me in business. Tourist season provided the revenue to keep our small town going through the quiet months.

We all complained about the traffic, and the noise, and the stupid tourist tricks, but we also knew they were the source of our income.

It was a love-hate relationship common to tourist towns everywhere, but most of the people who came through Southern Treasures were actually pretty nice. Like the woman downstairs with the three kids she kept from tearing up my display.

And at least the ones who weren't so nice made for funny stories later.

I checked the fresh peach ice cream in the freezer. It was set, ready to serve with the no-bake cookies I'd made the night before.

I turned up the volume on the intercom system I'd recently installed, in case Julie needed me. In three months, Rose Ann had settled into a routine, and she should sleep the rest of the afternoon. But as I was learning, babies didn't always do what they should.

The refrigerator was packed with an array of cold dishes: deviled eggs for an appetizer, chicken salad as the main course, potato salad, coleslaw, three-bean salad, and macaroni salad. I just needed to put together a fruit salad, and make a fresh batch of sweet tea.

I put a big jug of water on the balcony, and dropped in a half-dozen tea bags. Memaw would have pitched a fit about me not properly boiling water for the sweet tea. But Memaw passed many years ago, so I figured I was safe.

Then again, I knew there was at least one ghost in Southern Treasures. I hoped he was the only one.

I cut the chilled melons and popped fat green and red grapes off their stems. With the addition of sliced kiwi, an array of fresh berries, and slices of perfectly ripe peaches, the salad was ready to go back in the refrigerator to allow the flavors to mellow.

We could debate all evening whether it was traditional Southern cooking, but I had managed to avoid heating up the apartment, so I called it a win.

I was starting to set the table when I heard Rose Ann fussing. Her nursery was at the bottom of the stairs, just a few steps from the sales counter, where her mother worked.

I abandoned my preparations, grateful to have accomplished as much as I had, and hurried back downstairs to relieve Julie.

Glancing up at the black-and-white cartoon cat clock on the wall of the store, I realized Julie's shift had ended half an hour earlier. I felt a stab of guilt for keeping her past her quitting time.

"Sorry!" I said, sliding behind the counter. "You should have hollered."

Julie laughed. "And wake up the baby? Not a chance! I figure if she wants to sleep, I'll let her." She tucked a strand of long blond hair behind her ear and grinned at me.

From across the shop, a sharp whistle caught my attention. "Baby crying," Bluebeard said.

Julie shot him an amused glance. He turned into a real nag where Rose Ann's care was concerned. Like an indulgent old uncle.

"By the way," she said as she packed up her various bags, "your cousin called. He wanted to talk to you about something, but I didn't want to bother you while you were cooking. I told him I'd have you call back later."

"Thanks," I said. I was looking forward to a fun evening with my friends; there was no way I was going to call Peter tonight. Whatever he had to say, I wouldn't like it. It could wait until tomorrow. Or next week. Or next month. Heck, maybe I would just wait until he phoned me again.

A few minutes later Julie called out to tell me she was leaving. She went in and out the back door a couple times, carrying baby gear to her car before she liberated Rose Ann from her crib. With a final shouted "Bye!" they were gone. I listened to make sure the door locked behind them.

A late rush of customers kept me busy through the last couple hours and left a satisfying stack of bills in the cash drawer at the end of the day.

I locked the front door, flipped the sign from "Open" to "Closed," and emptied the cash drawer into the big safe under the stairs. I was still taking care of Bluebeard when I heard a knock at the front door.

I looked over to see my best friend, Karen Freed—otherwise known as "The Voice of the Shores" newscaster on local radio station WBBY.

With her shoulder-length auburn curls and a body that still fit into her high school jeans—though she wouldn't be caught dead in anything that out of style—she could have been a TV reporter. If she'd been willing to put up with the restrictions that went with the job. Instead she stayed at the local radio station, where she had a larger say in what stories she reported.

Bluebeard wolf-whistled when I let Karen in. She immediately went over and gave him a scratch on top of his head. He rubbed against her hand, enjoying the attention.

"You're only encouraging him," I complained as she talked softly to the bird. "I can't get him to stop whistling, and you just reinforce his bad behavior."

I relocked the door. Ernie and Felipe weren't due for another half hour. I signaled Karen to follow me and headed for the stairs. She gave Bluebeard a last pat and came up the stairs behind me.

While we waited, Karen finished setting the table while I added sugar to the tea and put it in a big spigot jar with lots and lots of ice.

"No Jake tonight?" she asked, counting the four places at the table.

"He's keeping the store open late," I answered. Jake Robinson owned Beach Books, across the street from Southern Treasures. We were edging closer to being a couple, although there were still a lot of unanswered questions. He'd been a frequent visitor at our Thursday dinners, but he wasn't a permanent member of the group. Yet.

"How about Riley?" I countered. Karen's ex-husband wasn't so *ex* lately, and he'd been to several of our dinners in recent weeks. "You said he couldn't make it tonight?"

"Family obligation," she said. "Bobby's birthday is Monday, so they're celebrating tonight, before the holiday weekend craziness."

I had to admit the Freeds had a lot to celebrate. Bobby, Riley's younger brother, had been accused of murdering a federal agent a few months earlier, and the Freeds were only now getting back to a semblance of normal family life.

"Too late," I said, thinking of the crowds I'd seen earlier in the day. "And you didn't go with him?"

She shook her head. "I didn't want to miss dinner. It's the only time I see Felipe and Ernie once summer starts."

Felipe Vargas and Ernie Jourdain owned Carousel Antiques. Once the summer crowds arrived, the two of them worked nearly every waking hour. The four of us rotated hosting duties every Thursday—had for several years— and it was the only night they closed early during the lucrative summer season.

The phone rang and I picked it up.

"Hello, darlin'," Ernie drawled. "We're running a few minutes late getting out of here, but we are on our way. Felipe is driving like a crazy man, so in two minutes we will either be at your door or we will be dead."

I laughed. "I'll open the door."

Karen started down the stairs before I could hang up the phone. "Got it," she called over her shoulder.

Minutes later I heard the three of them coming back up. Ernie looked elegant as always, the pale green of his crisp Oxford cloth shirt contrasting with his dark skin, his long legs covered with fashionably faded denim.

The man made blue jeans look like a tuxedo. I sighed. Some people just knew how to exude style, and I wasn't one of them. I kept my wardrobe simple—jeans and T-shirts mostly. I tried to look approachable when someone came in the store. That meant dressing just a step above the beachwear customers, with a casual hairstyle, light makeup, and minimal jewelry. Felipe was right behind his partner, carrying a six-pack of frosty longnecks, and Karen brought up the rear. Felipe immediately open four beers and passed them around as we all exchanged greetings.

Ernie instantly took in the lack of activity in the kitchen. "Where's the food?" he asked. "Did you give up and order out?"

I put the plate of deviled eggs on the table and planted my fists on my hips in mock outrage. "How dare you? I've been cooking for two days."

Behind me, Felipe swung open the refrigerator door to stash the last two beers. His startled "Wow" was all the corroboration I needed.

"How many people do you think you're feeding, girl?"

CHAPTER TWO

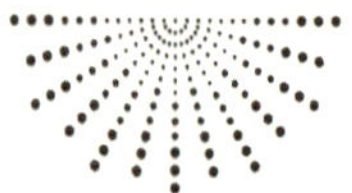

Ernie looked over my shoulder and let out a long, low whistle. "I take it all back. You *have* been cooking."

"Of course," I answered sweetly. "Would you care for an appetizer?" I gestured toward the eggs.

We nibbled on the eggs as we took the rest of the food from the refrigerator, arranged the unmatched bowls on the table, and sat down on an assortment of kitchen chairs.

Most of my apartment had been furnished with bits and pieces from my inventory downstairs. Searching the piney woods of north Florida and south Alabama for vintage furniture, kitchenware, and magazines was one of the best parts of running Southern Treasures. Occasionally I found a piece I couldn't bear to part with. At least until I found the next piece and had to move something out to make room.

As I expected, we spent the first hour debating the authenticity of a "cold supper."

"I really don't know," I finally admitted. "I have no idea how far back the idea goes. But my mother used to make cold meals when it got too hot to cook."

Karen admitted she remembered my mom's cold suppers when we were in high school. "She wasn't the only one either. Mrs. Freed used to do cold suppers sometimes."

The mention of Riley's mother snagged Felipe's attention. "Which reminds me, where is your *Mr.* Freed tonight?"

"He's not *my* Mr. Freed," Karen protested. Her red face contradicted her words as she repeated her earlier explanation, but we didn't bother to point it out.

"How is the shop doing?" she asked Ernie in an attempt to change the subject. "Are the tourists being good to you?"

"Pretty good," Ernie answered. "Good thing, too, since we've lost several of our best local customers."

"You mean the Andersons?" I asked, helping myself to another scoop of potato salad.

"Them," Ernie agreed, "and Lacey Simon. And Jennifer Marshall." He shook his head. "This bank mess is spilling over the whole town."

"That reminds me," I said, remembering my afternoon visitor. "I met the bank auditor, the McKenna woman. She came in the shop this afternoon."

My three dinner companions all stared at me for a silent moment, then everyone spoke at once.

"What's she like?"

"How old is she really?"

"How much did she spend?"

The last question made me laugh. Trust Felipe to cut to the heart of the matter.

"I don't know. I was upstairs fixing dinner when she left, and Julie would have taken care of her." I answered Felipe's query first, then I turned to Karen. "At least forty, I'd guess, maybe a little older." I told them about the careful makeup, the designer suit, and the stiletto heels. "Her haircut probably cost as much as any of us spends on haircuts in a year."

It was a pretty safe bet. Karen and I both visited the local beauty school a couple times a year, and the guys mostly cut each other's hair. In fact, Felipe had become a wizard with a pair of scissors.

"But what's she like?" Ernie repeated his question.

"Smart." I had only exchanged a few words with Bridget McKenna, but it was the one word that instantly came to mind. "Seems genuinely friendly, but she speaks her mind."

"That isn't exactly a news flash," Ernie said. "Last Merchants' Association meeting we got an earful from Andrew Marshall. Rumor has it his wife kicked him out, so maybe his views on women are a little skewed, but he was blaming the McKenna woman, and her bank, for everything that's happened."

"Marshall was a mess," Felipe said. "And I think he'd started happy hour a wee bit early, if you know what I mean."

Ernie nodded, and continued. "He acted like a guy who's lost everything. Which you would know if you'd been there."

He delivered the verbal jab with a resigned air. It was a ritual every Thursday, nagging me because I refused to join. But I wasn't one of the good ol' boys, and I didn't want to be.

"Marshall's already had a couple run-ins with her," Felipe added. "Said she has a bad temper, real short fuse, and a tongue sharp enough to slice bread."

"Well, he may have an attitude, too," Karen said. "After all, Bayvue Estates is the real reason she's here to begin with. If Marshall hadn't borrowed so much money from Back Bay for that development, the bank wouldn't be in trouble."

I shook my head. "You know it's more than that, Karen. Back Bay didn't have to lend that much to him. Or to anybody else. From what I hear, there were a lot of loans that were too big. Besides that, the Andersons treated the place like it was their own private piggy bank."

Felipe nodded, leaning back in his chair and clasping his hands over his stomach. "True that. Felicia Anderson never met an antique she didn't think she should have. Usually with some story about how it once belonged to old General Anderson, so we should give her a discount because it was really hers to begin with." He made a rude noise. "She only married into the family a couple years ago, but she acts like she's been here since plantation days."

It was a slight exaggeration. Billy Anderson had been a year ahead of Karen and me in school, and he'd married Felicia right out of college. So closer to fifteen years than just a couple.

The Andersons claimed they were descended from Civil War General Richard Anderson, based on evidence no one could confirm, and acted accordingly. To hear them tell it, we were all little more than sharecroppers and squatters on their ancestral estate.

Felipe's description wasn't far off. Felicia Anderson might have started out as a Yankee schoolgirl, but she quickly acquired a synthetic Southern drawl and the Andersons' superior attitude.

It was Karen's turn to sigh. "Billy's grandpa would just die to see what Billy's done to that bank. I remember the old man coming to school and starting us all on savings accounts when we were first-graders. Real proud of all the things he did for the community."

Karen stood up and waved away the topic of Billy and Felicia Anderson.

"Anything else about the bank woman?" she asked as she started gathering the dirty dishes.

I shook my head. "I only talked to her for a couple minutes. She did like Bluebeard, though."

"Everybody likes Bluebeard." Felipe laughed. "What's more important is whether he liked her. He thought for a second, then continued, "Or whether Louis did."

"Indeed," Ernie agreed. "What did Louis think?"

"Glory said she was attractive," Karen called over her shoulder from the counter, where she was stacking dishes. "Of course Louis liked her."

I laughed. "He is a sucker for a pretty face," I conceded, "but he still has his standards." *Was I actually defending the judgment of a ghost?* I guess I was. "She did get a whistle, so he at least approved that much."

We cleared the table quickly, stashing leftovers in the fridge. Ernie filled the sink with soapy water and washed the plates and silver—someday I'd get a dishwasher!—while I started a pot of coffee. It didn't matter if it was a hundred degrees out, Felipe would want coffee with his dessert.

I scooped ice cream into bowls and put a plate of cookies in the middle of the table. They looked like messy chocolate blobs, but I knew from my taste testing the night before that they would be good.

Karen eyed the plate, then looked up at me. "Are those what I think they are?"

I nodded.

She grabbed a cookie and took a bite. "I haven't had one of these in a million years!" she exclaimed around a mouthful of chocolate and oatmeal.

"What are they?" Felipe asked. He gave the brown blob a suspicious look.

"Lunchroom cookies," Karen and I answered in unison.

"What?"

As hostess, it was my job to explain. "I don't know what other people call them, although I'm sure they have a real name. We just call them lunchroom cookies because they used to have them in the school lunchroom when we were little kids."

Felipe didn't look like he was sold on the idea, but he took a tentative bite, chewing carefully. "Tastes kind of like fudge-coated oatmeal."

"You're pretty close," I agreed. "It's cocoa, sugar, butter, oatmeal, and peanut butter."

Felipe snapped his fingers. "Peanut butter! I knew there was something else. Just couldn't place it."

"The best part is they don't take much cooking. Cook the sugar, butter, and cocoa into a syrup, boil it for a minute, mix it with the oatmeal and peanut butter, and drop spoonfuls on waxed paper to cool."

Karen quizzed me about the recipe, and I fetched the copies I'd made for my guests. We always gave one another our recipes at the end of dinner. Over the years my Thursday notebook had grown fat with things I would cook someday.

"I haven't been able to come up with a definitive origin for the cookies," I admitted. "But I do have my own theory of why they were so common in the lunchroom."

My friends looked at me expectantly, and I explained. "When we were in grade school, there was a commodities program that provided food to the school lunch program. I don't know a lot about it, but I seem to remember a lot of peanut butter and butter in the cafeteria, and oatmeal. I'm guessing that most of the ingredients came from that program."

Karen nodded. "Keyhole Bay was definitely a rural school district back then," she told Felipe and Ernie. "We bused kids in from way out in the country."

As always, we talked far too late, catching up on the week's news and eventually circling back to the impending takeover of Back Bay Bank.

"Is it really that bad?" Ernie asked.

Karen nodded. As the lead reporter for WBBY, she took her news-gathering duties seriously, and usually had the inside track on whatever was happening in town. "I think it is," she said. "They sent down one of their big guns to run the audit, in the middle of the high season. Even at top rates they couldn't find her a hotel room."

"Then where is she staying?" I asked. "Pensacola's got to be worse."

"In one of the model homes," Karen answered. She yawned and stretched her arms over her head before standing up. "The bank owns the houses"—she shrugged—"so I guess it makes sense. Got some rental furniture out of one of those discount places over by Eglin, and moved in." She gathered up the over-sized bag she carried with her everywhere. "Early morning tomorrow. I need to be getting home."

Felipe and Ernie were on their feet, too. Ernie carried the ice cream bowls to the sink, but I waved him away. "You've done enough already," I said. "I can take care of the rest of this."

I walked them downstairs and said good night, carefully locking the door behind them and arming the alarm system. I'd become a fanatic about the alarm in the last year.

I checked on Bluebeard, giving him a shredded-wheat biscuit for a treat.

He nibbled the biscuit, then dropped the rest of it in his dish and hopped onto my arm. Bumping against my chin, he asked "Coffee?"

I shook my head. "You know the answer," I said, stroking his head. He leaned into me, as though the show of affection would change my mind.

I petted him for another minute or two, but I was already yawning, and it was time to go to bed.

I urged Bluebeard back into his cage, gave him a few seeds to assuage my guilt over the coffee, and made sure he was settled down for the night.

Through the wide front window I could see the lights still on across the street in Beach Books.

I made a quick mental calculation of the leftovers in the refrigerator. There were a *lot* of leftovers, I realized. I'd wanted to be sure I had enough of everything, but because I'd made so many dishes, I had ended up with a refrigerator full of food.

I picked up the phone and dialed Jake's cell number.

"Hi," I said when he answered. "You hungry?"

CHAPTER THREE

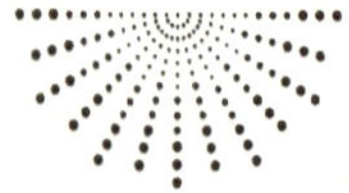

Five minutes after I hung up, the lights went out in Beach Books, and two minutes after that, Jake was at the front door.

I let him in, and Bluebeard squawked a greeting. Jake, understanding his duties as guest, went directly to the parrot to say hello.

"He's already had his biscuit," I warned Jake as he reached in his pocket. Jake often carried treats for the cantankerous bird.

"Not a @#%^$%#% biscuit," Bluebeard shot back, fixing me with a beady stare.

"Language!" I cautioned. Bluebeard could swear like, well, like a pirate, and I hadn't had much luck breaking him of his lifelong habit.

He muttered for a minute, the words indistinguishable but the tone crystal clear, then turned back to Jake. "Pretty boy," he cooed and quickly exited his cage.

Jake looked at me, his glance quizzical. I shook my head in resignation. The two of them had started ganging up on me lately, and I knew I didn't stand a chance.

Privately I was pleased with the turn of events. Bluebeard—and Uncle Louis—were the only blood family I had left, if you didn't count my annoying cousin Peter and his parents, which I usually didn't.

Whether Jake and I were actually a couple was still up for debate, but neither of us was seeing anyone else. So the apparent approval of my great-uncle, even when it came via his spokesbird, was treasured.

I watched Jake pull out a small plastic bag of plump green grapes and put them in Bluebeard's dish. He was rewarded with a quick head butt and another cooed "Pretty boy" before Bluebeard hopped over to the dish and greedily consumed the grapes.

When he had devoured his second treat, Bluebeard went back into his large cage and settled on his perch for the night. I left the door open, which we both preferred, but I draped the cage with a blanket to block the street-lights coming through the big front windows.

"'Night," I whispered.

Bluebeard murmured something soft and indistinct, already on his way to parrot dreamland. I wondered if parrots dreamed. And if Bluebeard didn't dream, did Uncle Louis? I still had no idea what the rules were for ghosts, and Uncle Louis had done very little to enlighten me. Mostly he flirted with customers and swore a lot.

Having given Bluebeard his due, Jake turned his attention back to me, giving me a hug and a quick kiss. As we climbed the stairs to my apartment, I told him about dinner and asked him what he'd like to eat.

"How am I supposed to choose? It all sounds good!"

I gesture to the table. "Sit down, I'll fix you a plate."

Jake protested, but I shook my head. "I had plenty of help with cleanup, and you were stuck working. I'll get it."

"It's not like I was that stuck," he said. But he settled for getting himself some silverware before he sat and watched me put samples of several salads on a plate. I put the plate on the table, along with a tall glass of sweet tea for each of us.

While Jake ate, making appreciative noises with each bite, I filled him in on everything I'd learned over dinner.

He shook his head at my description of Felicia Anderson. "Fifteen years, and she's still a Yankee?" He lifted his hands in a gesture of surrender that was marred by the potato salad that fell off his fork and plopped back onto his plate. "There's no hope for me then, is there?"

"Probably not," I agreed. "But you're at least a Westerner, not a true Yankee." Though Jake's background was still a bit sketchy, I knew he'd grown up on the West Coast. "Felicia's from somewhere in Connecticut, and even Mark Twain said people from there were Yankees."

"Two points," Jake said, "for a literary reference. Very good."

"But it's all about family," I continued. "Who your family is, who you're related to, how long you've lived here."

Families in Keyhole Bay measured their residence in generations, not years. I knew people whose families had lived in the area for more than two centuries. Family history was a popular topic of conversation, always had been. Which meant I knew hours' worth of stories about families like the Andersons.

"Felicia will always be a Yankee in the eyes of the old families around here." I shrugged. "You will, too—not that it matters to me."

I grinned at him. "Think you can live with that?"

Jake returned my grin. "I guess I can manage," he said. He scraped up the last bite of coleslaw. "Do I get dessert, since I ate all my dinner?" he asked with mock innocence. He already knew there were cookies and homemade peach ice cream, and I knew he had a sweet tooth.

I snagged another cookie for myself when I brought Jake his dessert. He looked askance at the cookies, and I had to explain their history.

"I don't think they're exactly traditional," I admitted. "But I loved them when I was a kid."

While Jake finished dessert, I tried unsuccessfully to stifle a yawn.

"You're tired," he said. "I need to get out of here and let you get some sleep."

I didn't argue. We weren't at the staying-over stage, still far from it, and I wasn't in any hurry to get there.

I let Jake out the front door, and watched as he loped across the deserted street to the front door of his shop before I trudged back upstairs and fell into bed.

It was nearly closing time on Friday when Bridget McKenna came back in the shop. She went straight to Bluebeard's perch and said hello, even remembering to use his name.

A few minutes later, after making a circuit of the shop, inspecting the handmade quilts and thumbing through the vintage magazines, she came to the counter with a couple postcards and a garish T-shirt in a size small. "I should have packed some weekend clothes," she said, handing me the T-shirt. "Usually I plan better than this."

"You travel a lot?" I asked, ringing up her purchases.

She nodded. "It used to be long-term assignments, but over the last few months it's been every other week, with a week at home in between. This time"—she paused to dig in her wallet for a credit card—"it's going to take a little longer than expected, so I'm stuck here over the weekend."

I took the postcards and turned them over to scan the price codes. "I'd swear I bought postcards when I was in here yesterday," she said. "But when I got home, they were nowhere to be found."

I vaguely remembered seeing her standing at the spinner rack the afternoon before when I had gone upstairs to fix dinner. I thought she'd had postcards in her hand, though I couldn't be sure.

It might not be our mistake, but I bought the cards by the hundreds, and they didn't cost a lot. Call it a gesture of goodwill, I could afford to give away a few postcards.

"These are on me," I said as I slipped the postcards into a small bag. "You want to put these in your purse?"

She took the small bag and slid it into a side pocket of her purse.

"Thank you," she said. "If I find the others, I will be sure to return them to you."

"Not necessary. Consider it a gift," I said as I handed her the large bag with the T-shirt.

She glanced around, as though making sure there weren't any other customers in the store. "So what's to do on the weekends around here?"

"Depends on what you like," I replied. "Boat tours, museums, beaches if you can stand the crowds." I ignored the shudder that passed through me at the thought and added, "Lots of scuba diving in the Gulf.

"You have a car, right?"

She nodded.

"Biloxi's just a couple hours west, if you want a casino. Another hour or so to New Orleans, a couple more and you're in Cajun country, if you want to do some driving. There are some lovely places in southern Louisiana: bayous, plantations, there's even a couple places that have sternwheeler cruises. And there's always a festival or something."

She thought for a moment, then asked, "Where would you go?"

"Biloxi, I guess, because I haven't been there in a while," I answered. "I usually go over a couple times a year with friends. Catch a show, gamble a little, maybe stay over one night. But mostly I can't be gone longer than a day," I said, glancing around the shop.

I also couldn't afford to gamble if I wanted to continue saving for my secret goal: to buy out my annoying cousin Peter. Which reminded me he had called the day before. My mother would be scandalized that I was ignoring the social obligation of returning his call, but my mother hadn't had to deal with Peter the way I did.

"One more question. Where around here is good for dinner? I've been living on takeout all week."

I shook my head. "Wish I had a good answer to that one. There are a couple great places, but everything's packed on a Friday night in the summer."

She sighed. "Guess it's another evening of fish and chips, or burgers. I am so not ready to fight crowds." She glanced around again. "Besides, I know I'm not exactly welcome around here."

The ghost of a grin played around her mouth. "Not like that's anything new."

I don't know what possessed me, but before I could stop myself, I blurted out, "If you don't mind leftovers, I've got plenty to share."

CHAPTER FOUR

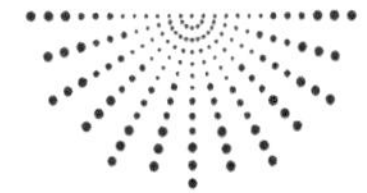

Bridget—after my hasty invitation, I had to start thinking of her on a first-name basis—considered my offer for several seconds, but she answered before I could rescind it.

"That's very generous, but I wouldn't want to put you out. Are you sure you want to do this?"

My brain was screaming "No!" but the manners drilled into me by generations of Martine and Beaumont women wouldn't let me take back an offer of hospitality.

"Of course," I lied, smiling in what I hoped was a sincere way. "I'll just need to tidy up a little." I frantically tried to remember if I had made the bed that morning, or washed the rest of last night's dishes.

"Are those leftovers portable?" she asked.

"Uh, yeah, I guess so. Why?"

"Why don't you bring them out to Bayvue, and we can eat there? I have a huge house all to myself. Besides"—she lowered her voice conspiratorially—"I know everybody around here wants to see what those houses look like. Unless you've been out there already?"

I shook my head. The houses had been completed just as Marshall Development cratered. Nobody from Keyhole Bay got a chance to see the models before they were locked up tight. Since then, only the bank examiners had been allowed on the property.

"I have to admit I'm curious," I said. I knew that my curiosity sometimes got me into trouble, but I couldn't see any harm in getting a tour of the notorious model home. "Why don't I give you a call when I'm ready to drive out?"

There wasn't any way I could get in trouble just going out to see those houses, was there? And how could I resist the opportunity to get a close-up look at the development that was causing so much debate?

As soon as Bridget was out the door, I grabbed the phone and called Karen. The call went to voice mail, and I instinctively checked the time; it was five minutes past the hour, time for Karen's local news segment on WBBY.

While I turned on the radio to catch her broadcast, I left a message. "Call me ASAP."

For the next ten minutes, I listened to Karen. She interviewed a local author who just happened to have a signing scheduled at Beach Books on Saturday, reported on the fresh catch at the fishing piers, and presented a recorded segment of her ongoing coverage of Keyhole Bay history.

Karen kept her boss happy by doing the stories he wanted, the ones that cast his advertisers and listeners in a good light. But she also liked to do what she called *real reporting*. Digging into stories with an edge energized her more than a triple espresso, and she managed to get them on the air even when the portrayal was less than flattering.

It took her another fifteen minutes to return my call. "Only have a few minutes," she said without preamble. "Meeting with the station manager in five."

"Well, whatever plans you had for tonight, cancel them."

She didn't argue. We'd been best friends for decades, and she knew I would have a good reason. But that didn't stop her from asking, "Why?"

"You want to see the inside of one of the Bayvue Estates model homes." It wasn't a question; I knew she'd want to go. The fact that I needed some moral support had nothing to do with anything. Much.

"When?"

"Soon as you're off. We're taking the leftovers from last night. Oh, and we'll need a main dish to fill out the menu. There isn't much chicken salad left. 'Bye!" I broke the connection, knowing she wouldn't delay her meeting to call me back.

I could deal with the fallout while we got ready to go out to Bayvue Estates. Besides, I was the one with the invitation. She wouldn't get to see the house without me.

My hands shook as I put the phone back in place. I didn't spontaneously invite strangers to dinner, or boss Karen around. If anything, Karen bossed *me* around. And everyone else. It was one of the main reasons she and Riley couldn't seem to live together. Riley owned his own fishing boat, and he was used to being the boss. Having two bosses in one house had led to some interesting times. And a divorce.

So where did all this gumption come from?

That was the exact question Karen asked when she showed up at my door an hour later.

I was just closing up for the night when her SUV slid in next to the curb. How *did* she manage to find the exact perfect parking spot, no matter where she went? It was as if the universe acknowledged that she was in a hurry and it catered to her needs. It was part of her charm that she simply accepted her good fortune as her due.

She came through the front door with a grocery bag in her hand, her giant shoulder bag slung over her shoulder, and a bemused look on her face.

"Who was that strange woman who called me an hour ago and started giving orders?" she asked with a laugh in her voice as she locked the door behind her. "I don't believe I know her."

"I don't either," I admitted. "But I need your help, and I knew you'd want to go with me."

"With you where?" She shook her head. "You can explain while we take care of this." She waved the grocery bag in my direction. "An extra pound of chicken salad from the deli at Frank's. We'll mix it with whatever's left of yours and no one's the wiser."

She was halfway up the stairs before I caught up with her.

I pulled the leftovers out of the refrigerator, gauging whether there was enough food for three people. I decided it was probably fine. Bridget wasn't tiny, but she was slender, and I would bet she wasn't a big eater.

I don't know what I was concerned about. Last night I had a refrigerator so full I didn't know what to do. And now I was worrying over how much Bridget would eat, in case I didn't have enough. But a good Southern hostess always served way more food than her guests would eat.

Karen took my bowl of chicken salad and added in her contribution from Frank's Foods. She mixed the two together and tasted, then transferred it to a clean bowl. I debated doing the same with the other salads, but they were all in refrigerator containers with secure lids, and they would travel better that way.

I tried not to imagine what Memaw would have said about serving food from a plastic box. It simply wouldn't have happened in her house.

As we worked, I explained to Karen how the invitation had come about. "She sounded kind of lonely," I said, "and the idea of take-out burgers, even good ones, every night?" It didn't appeal to me, and I was certain it hadn't appealed to Bridget. Why else would she have said yes to an invitation from a complete stranger?

"Did you tell her I was coming with you?" Karen asked. The challenge in her voice told me she already knew the answer.

"I will," I said, trying not to sound defensive.

Karen was packing the boxes and bowls into a couple canvas shopping bags. "Well, you better get on that, since we're about ready to leave."

We were ready, but I suddenly felt hesitant about the whole enterprise. What were we doing, really?

I shoved aside my trepidation and picked up the phone. It rang twice, then I heard Bridget say, "Hello."

"Hi, Ms. McKenna. This is Glory Martine from Southern Treasures. I'm just closing up the shop. We still on for dinner?"

"Of course. And please call me Bridget. I'm only Ms. McKenna to clients and my boss."

"Okay," I said. "Just one thing. I forgot I was going to see a friend tonight. Do you mind if I bring her along? I think you'll like her."

"I'm sure I will." I could hear Bridget's smile, and an undertone of something—relief?—in her voice. "Do you need directions?"

I told her no, and said we'd see her in a few minutes.

Bayvue Estates was a couple miles beyond the city limits, but nowhere in Keyhole Bay was much more than five minutes from anywhere else.

Except in summer traffic.

Karen offered to drive her SUV, but I wanted to take my truck and she agreed to ride with me. The truck was my pride and joy, purchased a few months earlier from my friend Sly.

It was really more of a gift, though Sly would insist I had paid a fair price. The 1949 Ford pickup had belonged to Uncle Louis before Sly bought it, and he'd sold it to me for what he'd spent on it. It had just come back from the lettering shop with the name and number of my store emblazoned in old-fashioned gold script on the dark forest green paint. According to Sly, it was just the way it had been when Uncle Louis owned it.

I thought it was the most beautiful truck in the South.

CHAPTER FIVE

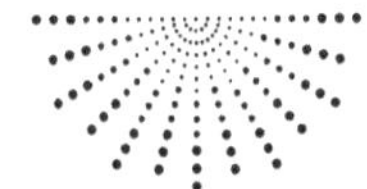

We crept through the early evening traffic with the windows rolled down. Auto air-conditioning was unheard of in 1949, and in spite of the Florida heat, I couldn't bear the idea of adding it. The truck was completely original and I wanted to keep it that way. So we drove with the windows open.

"Thanks for coming with me," I said to Karen. "This could be really awkward, just the two of us. But you can talk to anyone anytime."

"I can ask nosy questions, you mean."

"That, too," I answered. "But I think you'll like Bridget. Besides, you might get something that will make a good news story down the road."

Traffic thinned as we moved away from the crush of motels, restaurants, and souvenir shops. Most people never got off the main drag, never saw the homes and schools that made Keyhole Bay a real town.

We passed the city limit, turned north on a county road, and spotted the brick gateposts that marked the entrance to Bayvue Estates. They guarded the entrance to an unfenced swath of bare land with a single paved road leading away from the highway.

There weren't many estates, just two model homes surrounded by empty lots. And there wasn't a view of the bay either.

A tall magnolia tree, its base hidden beneath fallen leaves and waxy white blossoms, stood in front of one house. The rest of the front yard, overgrown with tall grass, gave the new construction an air of defeat and abandonment.

The only sign of human occupation was a midsize sedan parked in the driveway.

The paving petered out a few yards beyond the model homes, the remainder of the streets in the development nothing more than graded dirt paths wandering between the vacant lots.

I pulled the truck up next to the sedan, and we clambered out with the bags of food. As we approached the front door, it swung open and Bridget called out a greeting, as though she had been listening for our arrival. She had changed from her suit and stilettos into a pair of fashionable jeans and a casual tank top that probably cost more than my entire wardrobe.

"Hi," I answered. "We brought a cold supper, since it's too hot to cook." I nodded to Karen. "Bridget, this is my best friend, Karen Freed. If you've listened to WBBY since you've been here, you've probably heard her newscasts.

"Karen, this is Bridget McKenna."

Karen managed to shift the grocery bag to her left hand and extended her right hand to Bridget.

"I'm that evil woman from up North," Bridget said with the same warm smile I'd seen the day before. "Glad to meet you." She glanced over at me. "And yes, I have heard her on the radio." She held the door for us. "Come on in."

I waved away Bridget's offer to take my bag and followed her toward the kitchen with Karen right behind me. As we crossed the two-story-tall entry, I took in the marble floor and the view across the broad living room to the backyard.

Without landscaping, the backyard looked even more desolate than the front. I could imagine what it might look like if a professional landscape architect had been able to finish the job with native grasses, flowering bushes, and tropical plants.

Bridget led us through the empty dining room and into the kitchen. Speckled black granite counters topped honey-colored wood cabinets. Glass doors, meant to display china and crystal, exposed empty shelves. A six-burner gas range under a top-of-the-line microwave–range hood combination dominated one wall, and a three-door refrigerator stood within easy reach of the butcher-block-topped central island. I could see where a big chunk of Back Bay's money had gone.

Next to the deep farmhouse sink, a roll of paper towels stood on end by a cheap toaster and coffeemaker, which seemed out of place in the high-end kitchen. They were the only things that looked as though they had been used.

"Cold supper sounds like an excellent idea," Bridget said as we unpacked the bags and laid out plastic boxes and bowls on the island next to a collection of plates and silverware. "Food first?" she asked. "Or would you rather have the grand tour?"

I didn't wait for Karen's answer. "Tour first."

We stuffed the food into the nearly empty refrigerator, battling the door that closed on us the minute we let go of it.

"It needs to be leveled," Bridget said. "It's on my to-do list."

Karen shot her a quizzical glance.

"The bank wants to liquidate as soon as possible, to get our money back out. They asked me to evaluate the property—get an appraisal if I need to—and see what it will take to unload the houses and the empty lots."

Bridget led us through the house. Upstairs, a huge master suite opened to an expansive balcony running along the entire back of the house, and over-looking the barren backyard. Windows in the master bathroom surrounded the jetted tub set on a ceramic-tiled pedestal, and shared the same view.

Karen let out a low whistle. "Could have been gorgeous," she said, "if the yard was finished."

We saw two smaller bedrooms on the second floor with a Jack-and-Jill bathroom between them. In the shared bathroom there were no faucets or towel bars, and the vessel sinks still had manufacturer's stickers on the outside.

In the closet of the back bedroom, one wall had been lined in cedar, and a stack of planks on the floor looked as though the carpenter had left at the end of the workday and never come back. Which, I suppose, was pretty close to the truth.

Back in the central hallway, the door to the hall cabinet sagged open. Karen had pushed it closed as we walked past, but it had swung open again. Either the house had a ghost, or the cabinet door had been hung improperly. I suspected the latter. On the other hand, I had some firsthand experience with ghosts. I was convinced Uncle Louis sometimes did things like that just to mess with me.

Back downstairs Bridget showed us the home office with its own entrance around the corner of the house from the front door. It was a room full of built-in dark oak cabinets and bookcases, tucked behind the soaring entry.

Karen eyed the office appraisingly. "Nice setup for someone who works from home," she said. "A lawyer, or an architect. Something like that."

In contrast to the open plan, huge windows, and light colors of the rest of the house, this room had a cozy, private feel to it. It was my favorite room in the house, one where I could have happily settled down and filled the shelves with books. But as we left the room, I noticed how uneven the textured finish of the walls looked.

The house was a study in contradictions. The kitchen was completely finished, filled with custom cabinets and high-end appliances befitting a sales display for expensive homes, the beautiful office storage units were clearly custom-fitted to the room, and the smell of new carpet still permeated the entire structure. But the upstairs hadn't been completed, and in several places work had been done in such a hurry that it wasn't properly finished, like the sagging closet door and faulty texturing.

As we trooped back down the stairs, the doorbell rang. Bridget shot us a questioning glance. We both shook our heads and followed her to the door.

It couldn't be anyone from Keyhole Bay; no one was that ill-mannered, not even Felicia Anderson. Showing up at someone's home—if you weren't family, or as good as—without an invitation was considered rude, but without even calling first was ever so much worse.

Before we reached the bottom of the stairs, the bell rang again. A fist pounded against the door, and from outside a deep voice yelled, "Marshall, are you in there? I want to talk to you!"

The three of us exchanged a quick look. "You know who he's looking for, right?" I asked Bridget.

She nodded. "The developer, Andrew Marshall. But he's never lived here. Nobody has."

"Yeah," Karen said as we crossed the entry hall, "I thought they just used it as the sales model."

"That's right," Bridget answered. "They had a construction trailer out here when they started. Moved it when they had these places close to finished. That was about a week before the hammer fell."

She stopped at the door and took a moment to draw a deep breath. In an instant she transformed from the relaxed and friendly woman we'd been talking to into an executive with a commanding air of authority.

All the while the pounding and screaming continued, with the addition of some rather inventive cursing that would have impressed even Bluebeard.

Bridget took one last deep breath and opened the door.

"Can I help you?" she asked in a tone that implied she probably couldn't. Or wouldn't.

The man paused for a second, then yelled, "Where is that thieving SOB?"

I had been right. He definitely wasn't from Keyhole Bay. Sixtysomething, with the ruddy face and veined nose of a longtime drinker, his pale skin branded him as a Northerner as surely as his bad manners did. He wore custom-tailored white slacks and a pastel golf shirt that strained across his beer belly, with an expensive and ostentatious watch clasped around his wrist.

He stood on the porch, his head thrust forward in the challenging posture of a lifelong bully. A man with a lot of money, very little class, and no tact at all.

I stood back and watched as Bridget carefully dismantled his air of superiority.

"I'm afraid I have no idea where Mr. Marshall is," she said calmly, as though she hadn't heard his outburst. "He has no interest in this property. There is no reason for him to be here."

Somehow, despite the fact that the man was at least six inches taller, she appeared to look down her nose at him. "Will there be anything else?"

"There damn well will be!" he shouted. Like most bullies, volume was one of his favorite weapons.

"And that is?" Bridget made a show of suppressing a sigh, as though her boredom threshold had long been passed. She turned and looked at us, the gesture broad and theatrical. Taking the cue, we both shrugged elaborately.

"I want my damned house! If he's not here, then maybe you better be turning it over to me, honey."

I saw Bridget's spine stiffen at the casual condescension in his tone, and the familiarity of his words. But she didn't let him see it.

"Well," she said, her voice still controlled, her posture deliberately relaxed, and her tone deceptively cheery, "since I don't know who you are, or why I should give you anything, particularly the house where I am currently residing, I don't see how that is going to happen."

"I gave that SOB a hefty deposit on this house." He had stopped screaming, though he was still loud. "He said it'd be ready for us to move in by the first of July. Now I get here and I find you living in my house, Marshall's nowhere to be found, and my wife is raising hell." He gestured toward the expensive sedan parked in the road in front of the house.

I assumed his wife was in the car, though the tinted windows obscured any view of his passenger.

Bridget shook her head. "You did not put a deposit on this house. This house was never for sale. You put a deposit on a house in this development. *This* house"—she waved her arm as though displaying a prize on a TV game show—"belongs to the bank that financed Mr. Marshall's venture. And so does the rest of the development."

She stared him down. "If you have any other questions, I suggest you make an appointment to see me in my office at Back Bay Bank. You can call my secretary on Monday morning. Bring your receipts and contracts. And maybe your lawyer.

"In the meantime, I suggest you get off my porch and out of my yard. You're trespassing."

She didn't wait for his answer.

She shut the door in his face. She didn't slam it, just closed it swiftly and firmly, and shot the dead bolt as soon as the latch clicked into place.

From the porch we could hear the man continuing to yell. He pounded on the door and leaned on the doorbell for several minutes at a time.

Bridget waited until he was getting hoarse from the shouting, and the pounding grew weaker. Whoever her visitor was, he wasn't a young man, and he didn't have the stamina for a sustained attack.

As he started another round of pounding, she whipped the door open. His arm was in mid-strike, and without the solid surface of the door, the momentum of his swing threw him off balance.

For long seconds he flailed around, nearly falling in a heap on the doorstep. She just stared at him as he struggled to stay on his feet.

Once he was stable, she looked him up and down, then spoke. "By the way, can I get your name? For my report?"

His answer would have made Bluebeard blush, and contained several suggestions that I didn't think were physically possible. He finally turned to leave, but stopped long enough to stare back at her.

"You'll pay for that."

For the first time since he'd appeared, I was frightened.

Bridget didn't appear the least bit afraid, but fury bubbled in her every word and gesture. "The worst part is, I have no idea if he's the only one, or how many there might be. Three? Five? A dozen? Back Bay doesn't have a record of how many deposits Marshall took, or how much they were." She slammed her fist against the door, an echo of the man's tantrum on the porch.

"Dammit! I do not want to have to hire security guards again."

Karen looked startled. "Again?"

Bridget sighed, and I could see her anger ebbing. "Yeah. It's one of the hazards of the job. You're messing with people's money and their lives.

"Desperate people sometimes do desperate things. Once in a while I've needed a little extra help getting through some of the worst situations."

"Come on," she said, waving toward the kitchen. "Let's see what you brought. Confrontations make me hungry."

She laughed, her tone and attitude dismissing the angry bully who never did give her his name, and she led the way through the house.

Back in the kitchen, we retrieved the food and spread it across the butcher block. As we filled our plates, I explained the various dishes to Bridget, which led to a discussion of our Thursday night dinner.

"It started out as a way to keep in touch during the summer, when we were all really busy," Karen said after we were settled at the small dining table tucked into a corner of the kitchen. "And then we just kept going. After a while it kind of became a tradition, and now we can't stop."

Bridget looked wistful. "Sounds great to me. I travel so much I could never keep up with a schedule like that."

"Well, we do sometimes miss a week, if someone's on vacation or something," I said.

"Like you ever take a vacation," Karen said.

"I do. But when you work for yourself, the boss won't give you much time off."

"A real slave driver, eh?" Bridget asked.

"Sure is," Karen answered before I could. "She never really takes a day for herself."

"Not true," I said. "We went to De Funiak—"

"A year ago," Karen interrupted. "And even then it wasn't a day off. It was a treasure-hunting expedition and you bought a bunch of inventory for the store."

"But that's fun for me," I protested.

"So, Bridget," I said, trying to steer the conversation away from my supposed obsession with work, "did you decide what you're going to do with your days off?"

Bridget hesitated, as though reconsidering her options. "I think," she said finally, "I may go over to Biloxi for the day, maybe even stay over one night." She glanced around the sparsely furnished house. "It might be good to get away from here, especially after my visitor. At least for a few hours."

She had a point. The house might someday be a lovely home, but right now it was downright depressing. The rental furniture was low-end commercial: a basic bedroom set, a bare-bones living room set, and the dining table and chairs. I didn't like a lot of clutter—my apartment was far too small for tons of knickknacks or mementos—but I had books in my bookcases, pictures on the walls, and canisters on my kitchen counter.

Even a hotel room would feel homier than Bayvue Estates.

CHAPTER SIX

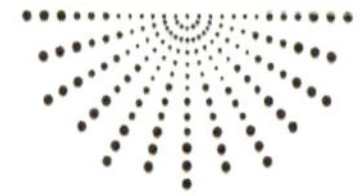

"Biloxi sounds like fun," Karen said when we pulled out of Bridget's driveway. "We ought to go again soon."

"Yeah, right," I answered dryly. "In my copious free time."

"You have Julie," she countered. "I know you can't go in the summer, but September's only a couple months away."

I pulled out of the deserted development past the brick gateposts, turning south onto the county road. Far behind me I saw a pair of headlights, the only other vehicle on what most tourists would consider a back road. Once you got off the highway, you could travel for miles without seeing another car.

We turned onto the highway, heading back into the center of town. The midsummer sun was just setting, and waiting crowds spilled out of restaurants onto the sidewalk, a reminder of what Bridget would have encountered in her search for dinner.

As we drove through, I mentally tallied the number of hotels and motels with red neon signs blazing "No Vacancy." It was a good indication of what to expect for the weekend. Near as I could tell, the town was 100 percent full.

Tomorrow should be a busy day. Biloxi was sounding better all the time, but I'd be wishing for the crowds when business dropped off at the end of the summer and I still had bills to pay.

It was my constant balancing act. I'd been orphaned by a hit-and-run driver at seventeen, and I felt like I'd been pretty much on my own since then. Paying the bills and taking care of myself topped my list of priorities, and had for over fifteen years. It often didn't leave a lot of time for other things.

I had accepted the responsibility long ago. I'd chosen to run Southern Treasures myself, and I usually preferred it that way. But it didn't stop me from occasionally chafing under my self-imposed restrictions.

I pulled into the parking area behind the shop and shut off the engine. "Wine?" I asked Karen as we climbed out of the truck.

She shook her head. "After I ditched Riley to go with you, I better not," she said. "I promised him I'd be home before it got too late."

I stopped at the back door, key in hand. "Home? He's checking up on you?"

She hesitated, and I prodded some more. "What's really going on with you two? *Really?*"

"It's complicated," she answered.

I shook my head. "That's not an answer, Freed." As I said it, I realized something that had somehow eluded me for years. Karen had divorced Riley, but she had kept his name. At the time she had claimed it was for professional reasons: she was known on air as Karen Freed and she didn't want to lose that identity. Now I wasn't sure I completely believed her.

"And don't tell me you're 'taking it slow' again. That isn't an answer either."

Karen's unhappy frown didn't deflect my question. I stood my ground, not yet unlocking the door while I waited for an answer.

Finally she sighed and looked away. "We're not together, if that's what you're asking," she said without looking at me. "But we are seeing a lot of each other, and we aren't seeing anyone else."

She hesitated and took another deep breath. "And he's stayed at the house a few times. *That* was never a problem."

"Are you crazy?" I asked. I kept my voice low, concerned, not challenging. "You divorced him once, and now you're going right back into"—I struggled for the right word—"into whatever this is. You two keep splitting up and getting back together, and now he's staying over? Do you not remember how upset he got when you went to Jacksonville alone?"

I reached out, put my hand on her arm. "You got hurt bad the first time, hon. Can you handle that again when you break up for good?"

"*If,*" she insisted. "*If* we break up, not when. We're adults this time. Sure, Riley got upset when I went to Jacksonville, but we talked it out instead of fighting. That's progress, isn't it?

"We know where the pitfalls are, Glory, and we're trying to find ways around them. So we *are* taking it slow, even if you don't think that's an answer."

I squeezed her arm. There wasn't anything I could say that was going to change her mind, and she knew full well the risk she was taking. And maybe they could make it work. I hoped so, for both their sakes.

"Okay," I said. "I'll be here if you need me." As if there was any question. We'd always been there for each other, ever since grade school.

I unlocked the door.

I followed Karen inside, stopping to double-check the locks on the back door, then moving through the storage room to let her out the front, where her SUV waited at the curb.

"Thanks again for going with me," I said.

"Glad to," she answered with a grin. "You were right, you know. I did like her. Too bad she'll be gone again in a couple weeks."

"Who knows?" I answered. "Maybe she'll come back and work here when the sale goes through. We could start a girls' network, have our own answer to the good ol' boys."

"Yeah, sure." Sarcasm dripped from her words. "I won't hold my breath."

I laughed. "Someday."

I locked the door behind her, and went to check on Bluebeard.

I changed his water and fed him a shredded-wheat biscuit from the can underneath his cage.

"Coffee?" he asked hopefully.

"No, Bluebeard, parrots do not get coffee. *I* don't even get coffee at this hour." I gave him a couple scritches, checked the locks again, and headed upstairs.

I was downstairs working on a T-shirt order when Julie arrived the next morning. She let herself in and turned over the "Closed" sign.

"Morning, boss," she said, sliding behind the counter next to me. She pointed to an image on the computer screen. "That one's been really popular this summer," she said. "You might want to order a few extra in kid sizes. For some reason, that's one they want to buy as matching mother-daughter sets."

"Thanks," I said, clicking back on the design and adding two dozen in mixed sizes before checking the totals and clicking on the "Order" button.

"There was one other thing," Julie said. "I've been getting a lot of people asking about stuff with Bluebeard on it. T-shirts, shot glasses, postcards, stuff like that. Some of them say they saw him on the website and they are disappointed we don't have anything."

I'd spent months learning about websites, working for hours experimenting with ways to display my merchandise and promote the store. Adding Bluebeard's picture to the pages had been Jake's suggestion, a good one.

Now Julie offered a way to take it a step further.

"I'll give Mandy a call, if you'd like," Julie said.

"Mandy?"

"A friend of mine. She works over at Coast Custom Printers. They do the shirts for Mermaid Grotto. Started out as a uniform for the staff, but customers kept asking if they could buy them. They put a stack at the register and she says their order gets bigger every month."

She started to say more, but the bell over the door rang as a tourist couple came in. She gave them her dazzling, cheerleader smile and called out, "Hi, y'all! Can I help you find something special?"

They shook their heads. "Just looking," the wife said.

"Sure thing," Julie said, still smiling. "Let me know if there's anything you need."

She made a show of going back to straightening the shelves behind the counter. She'd learned quickly that the fastest way to drive a customer out the door was to hover, to make them feel like they were being watched, even when they were.

Across the street, Jake's "Closed" sign still hung in the front window. He'd changed his hours, opening later in the morning and staying open later at night every Saturday, and he said the new hours had boosted sales.

Jake emerged from his front door and crossed the street to my front door. He glanced around, spotting the one couple flipping through the vintage magazine rack against the back wall. "Got time for coffee?" he asked.

I looked at Julie, who nodded. "I'll call if it gets busy," she said.

I made sure I had my cell phone, and followed Jake next door to Lighthouse Coffee.

Chloe put out two vanilla lattes and two lemon scones as soon as we reached the counter. "The usual," she said. "Saw you coming." She grinned.

Jake tossed a twenty on the counter. "Keep it," he said, waving away the change she offered him. "I had a good day yesterday. Besides"—he grinned back at her—"come winter, there may be no tips at all."

Chloe shook her head. "I don't think that's even possible for you," she said. "You're far too nice to stiff the barista."

"You'd be surprised," he teased her, but I knew she was right. Jake was one of the most considerate people I'd ever known.

Out of habit, we sat by the front window, where Jake could watch the front door of Beach Books, even though the "Closed" sign was still up.

I took a sip of the sweet coffee. "Thanks. A good day yesterday, huh?"

Jake nodded. "I don't know why, but the store was busy from open to close. You?"

I shrugged. "Good. Not a blockbuster, but a good day. The evening got a little strange, though."

"Oh?" Jake cocked an eyebrow. "What happened?"

I told him about Bridget coming back into the shop, and my impulsive invitation.

"You had her over for dinner?" he asked, surprised.

I shook my head. "Not exactly."

Jake listened while I gave him a quick summary of the previous night's adventure. He looked alarmed when I told him about the guy pounding on the door.

"You didn't call the cops?" he asked.

I shook my head. "Bridget chased him off, and he left. There wasn't much they could have done anyway. Warned him, maybe, or cited him for trespassing. But the property isn't marked, so I don't know if they could even charge him with trespassing unless he came back after she told him to go away."

Jake looked thoughtful. "I don't know. I guess it depends on what the law is. I don't even know if that's a local ordinance or a state law."

"I don't know either." I ate the last bite of my scone, and took a sip of lukewarm latte. "I've never had to worry about it, but I bet Karen knows. I'll have to ask her. Not that it matters, but now I am curious."

Jake drained his coffee cup and glanced at his watch. "Time to go open up," he said, gathering his trash.

I looked up, intending to answer, and saw Bridget coming through the door. Dressed in the gaudy T-shirt she'd bought the day before, she had on a pair of jeans that looked like they'd been custom-made for her. Judging by what I'd seen of her wardrobe, maybe they had been.

She spotted me and waved, heading for our table.

"Hi, Glory," she said. She turned to Jake, who had started to stand. "Don't get up on my account," she said with a smile. "I'm on my way out of town, just stopped to return Glory's dishes."

She turned back to me. "I took them to the shop, and that sweet girl said you were over here having coffee. I just wanted to say thanks again for the meal, and the company."

"You're welcome," I said. I gestured to Jake. "Bridget, this is Jake Robinson. He owns the bookstore across the street. Jake, this is Bridget McKenna."

I didn't bother to explain Bridget's position. Jake, like everyone else in town, knew *exactly* who she was.

Jake was already on his feet, and shook her outstretched hand. "Glad to meet you, Ms. McKenna. Don't mean to be rude, but I really was on my way out. Time to open up."

"Not at all," she answered. "I'm actually heading out myself. Taking Glory's suggestion and going over to Biloxi for a little R and R."

Jake nodded. "Have fun," he said. "Glory"—he looked at me—"talk to you later." He turned and waved over his shoulder as he walked out the door.

I gestured to the empty chair across from me. "I need to get back, but I have a minute if you want."

Bridget shook her head. "I should get on the road, I think. How about a rain check? One morning next week?"

She glanced out the window, watching Jake stride across the street, and smiled back at me. "That one looks like a keeper."

I felt a blush creep up my face. "Yeah. Maybe."

Bridget laughed. "See you next week."

I followed her out the door and went back to Southern Treasures.

More customers came in as the morning wore on. Julie and I handled questions, sales, and special requests. Bluebeard whistled and squawked and was rewarded with giggles, finger-pointing, and occasional shrieks from teenaged girls.

He had his picture taken with a steady stream of visitors, flirted with every woman, and only had to be reprimanded for his vocabulary a couple times.

The foot traffic thinned in the early afternoon as the temperature climbed and the tourists retreated to swimming pools and air-conditioned hotel rooms, or prostrated themselves on the blistering sand. Julie came back from her break, and I was free for a few minutes.

I stuck my cell phone in my pocket and headed for the front door. "Call if you need me," I said as I went out. "Otherwise I'll be back in twenty minutes or so."

My first stop was back to Lighthouse, for a trio of frozen mochas. Then I walked past Southern Treasures on my way to the Grog Shop.

I tried to check in with Linda, the owner, every couple days. Linda had been a friend of my mother's and was like the older sister I never had. She and her husband, Guy, had taken me in when my parents were killed, and she was the person I turned to when I needed advice.

Linda was at the register, ringing up a sale. I put two drinks on the counter, and wandered into the back looking for Guy. I found him checking off delivery sheets and hoisting cases of beer onto racks in their small warehouse space.

I put my drink down and started stacking cases as he marked them off. "Yours is up front, if Linda doesn't drink both of them before you claim it."

"She wouldn't dare," he growled.

I didn't believe his act for a minute. He and Linda were as devoted a couple as I had ever seen, a relationship I both envied and aspired to. If and when I found the right man. The image of Jake, grinning as he handed me my latte, flashed through my memory. I shoved the idea into the back closet of my mind and slammed the door. Too soon. Way too soon.

"How's it going?" I asked.

"Doing good," he replied. "Definitely beer weather."

I looked around, taking in the nearly empty shelves. "Looks like it."

Guy kept working as he talked. "Would you believe I already had two deliveries this week, and I had to call for another one this morning?" He ticked off the last case and I put it on the shelf. "Not that I'm complaining, mind you. Always good when people are buying."

Guy maneuvered a hand truck loaded with more cases toward the door. "Get that for me, would you?" he asked.

I grabbed my coffee and held the door while he steered the load through it and toward the giant walk-in cooler at the back of the store. I opened the cooler door, and he pushed the hand truck through, letting the door close behind him.

Linda was alone at the counter, and I walked behind it to give her a hug.

"Thanks for the mocha," she said.

We talked for a couple minutes, catching up on what we'd been doing the last few days. I told her about our Thursday dinner, and about taking the leftovers out to Bayvue Estates the night before.

"You went out there with that woman?" She sounded shocked. "What made you go all the way out there, all alone with a total stranger?"

"She seems really nice." Okay, that sounded lame, even to me. "I took Karen with me. And we got to see one of the model homes."

"Was it as deluxe as everybody said it was?"

I hated to disappoint her, but I had to say no. "Oh, they tried," I told her. "But the work wasn't done right. A lot of stuff looked like it was done in a hurry, or just not finished at all. It was sad, and kind of creepy.

"Like something had died out there."

CHAPTER SEVEN

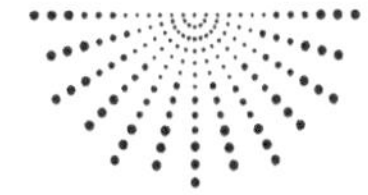

I wanted to talk to Linda about Karen and Riley, to have her reassure me that my best friend wasn't heading for a fall. It was the kind of conversation I imagined most women had with their mothers or sisters, and Linda was the closest thing I had to either one. But a steady stream of customers cut our visit short. That conversation would have to wait until we both closed for the night, or for another day.

I waved good-bye and went back to work. At least I got a cold drink, a jolt of caffeine, and a change of scenery for a few minutes.

By the time we closed up for the day, I was too tired to talk to anybody. It took me another couple hours to close out the register, balance the books, and get the store ready for the next day. When I was through, all I wanted to do was crawl upstairs and collapse in a heap. Even fixing dinner sounded like too much work.

And I wasn't the only one. As I was checking the locks and setting the alarm, the store phone rang. I ignored it, letting it go to voice mail. I'd check the message before I went upstairs and decide if it could wait until morning.

A few seconds later my cell phone rang.

"Hello?"

"Pizza's on the way," Jake said. "Want some?"

"Thank you, yes. I was just thinking I was too tired to cook, so it was going to be corn flakes for dinner."

"Neil's said they'd have it here in half an hour, if that works for you." There was a pause, then he continued. "I gave them your address for the delivery."

"That's some nerve, Mr. Robinson. What if I'd had other plans? It's Saturday night. I might have had a date," I teased.

"Saturday night in July," he answered. "You never go out on the weekends in the summer. That was one of the first rules you taught me about being a local."

"Got me," I said. "I'll unlock the door, if you're coming over soon."

"On my way," he replied.

True to his word, I saw him emerge from his door onto the sidewalk, heading for the crosswalk in front of his store.

I dropped the phone in my pocket and went to take care of Bluebeard. He'd had a long day of customers, and he was as tuckered out as I was.

Bluebeard spotted Jake through the big front windows, approaching my door. "Pretty boy," he said, in a voice eerily like that of my great-uncle Louis Georges. I hadn't heard Uncle Louis since he passed away when I was ten, but I recognized his voice coming from Bluebeard, and I knew he wasn't talking about himself.

"Hush!" I said. "You keep your nose out of my business. Or your beak. Whatever. Just butt out, okay?"

Bluebeard cast a beady eye around the shop before glaring at me and uttering a clear profanity.

"Language, Bluebeard!"

He quieted to a low mutter, but I'd known this parrot a long time. Other people might not hear it, but I could make out several words he knew he wasn't supposed to use. I guess I should be glad he chose to wait until there were no customers in the store.

Jake locked the door behind himself and made his way between the display racks to where I stood.

"Arguing with Bluebeard again?" he asked, slipping an arm around my shoulders for a quick hug. He seemed to hesitate about any display of affection in front of Bluebeard.

I wanted to deny it, but he was right. I was arguing. *With a bird.* Okay, it was a bird who occasionally channeled the ghost of Uncle Louis, but it was still ridiculous.

"Bluebeard's misbehaving again, if that's what you mean," I said, sidestepping any admission of guilt. "He needs to learn to mind his own business."

Jake cocked an eyebrow at Bluebeard. "Trying to keep her out of trouble?"

Jake knew about Uncle Louis, and it amused him to think my great-uncle chose to meddle in my life. I wondered if he would think it was so funny if he knew Bluebeard was talking about him.

"Mostly he's tired and cranky," I said. "He's had a long hard day of being a celebrity." I remembered Julie's suggestion from that morning. "Speaking of which, what would you think about shirts and postcards with Bluebeard on them? We could use the same pictures we used for the website. It was Julie's idea," I added, not wanting to take credit that wasn't mine.

"Brilliant! Those oughta sell like crazy, if you can make the numbers work out."

"I don't know about the costs yet," I said. "Julie said she had a friend at a print shop where they do the shirts for Mermaid Grotto."

Jake's eyes widened for a moment. "Of course. I saw those at the hostess stand the night we were there. Don't know why I didn't think of doing them for Southern Treasures."

"You were busy taking in the atmosphere." Mermaid Grotto was all about the atmosphere. A giant fish tank separated the restaurant from the bar. The tank was home to a live mermaid show when I was a kid; now it held tropical fish and aquatic plants.

It had also had one very unwilling swimmer. I'd become far too familiar with that tank a few months earlier when I'd been shoved into it, and a shudder passed over me at the memory.

Jake put a comforting arm around me and drew me close to his side. Clearly he was remembering my visit to the mermaid tank, too.

I shook off the memory, refusing to dwell on an unhappy might-have-been.

"What kind of pizza did you order?"

"Pepperoni and tomato with extra onion and bell pepper. Right?"

I was impressed. Jake had clearly been paying attention.

In a few minutes Neil's delivery van pulled up in front and a kid jumped out holding an insulated carrier. Jake met him at the door with his wallet in hand.

Soon we were upstairs with hot pizza and cold beer. A far better end to the day than I had imagined possible.

We talked about watching a movie, but neither of us could work up enough enthusiasm to actually pick out something and put it in the player.

Instead we hung out eating pizza and talking about putting Bluebeard's image on T-shirts and postcards.

"You could also do mugs," Jake said. "See what other things the printer has, and what they cost."

"I wonder what Mermaid Grotto sells their shirts for," I said.

The question began to eat at me, and I had to get up and find my laptop. "Maybe they have them on their website."

"If they have a website," Jake said.

"Everybody has a website, according to you," I said. "You said I had to have one, because everyone else did. So they better have something."

It took me a couple minutes of searching, but I finally connected to the Mermaid Grotto site. "Look," I said, briefly turning the screen so he could see it, "here's their page. Lunch menus, dinner menus, entertainment . . ."

I ran the cursor along the tabs at the top of the page, stopping over the one that said *Merchandise*. I clicked and a new page loaded showing shirts, mugs, decals, and calendars.

Jake moved to share the display, coming close enough that I could feel the warmth of his shoulder pressed against mine. I liked the feeling.

We checked out the prices on the shirts. They were comparable to the graphic shirts I already sold at Southern Treasures. Definitely something I should look into.

But it would have to wait for Monday when Julie came back to work. I shut the laptop and leaned against Jake's shoulder, stifling a yawn.

"I saw that," he said, kissing me gently. "You need to get some sleep, and I need to get home."

I kissed him back, tempted to ask him to stay, but the reality of our respective responsibilities quickly drove the idea from my mind.

"I'll walk you down."

"You don't have to come downstairs," Jake replied, closing the pizza box and taking it to the refrigerator. "I can lock up."

I shook my head. Even though I'd given him the alarm codes, I couldn't relax without my daily ritual. "You know I have to check the locks and alarms for myself."

I followed him down. We checked the back door and the alarms, and kissed good night at the bottom of the stairs. We walked silently to the front door so as not to wake Bluebeard. I locked the door and watched Jake lope across the street and around the building to where he parked his car.

Bluebeard, however, wasn't nearly as cooperative. He stuck his head out of his cage and glared through the dim light.

"Trying to $&#$&$% sleep here."

I took the hint and went back upstairs.

CHAPTER EIGHT

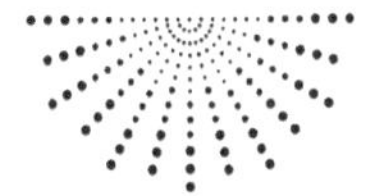

A freak Sunday morning thunderstorm chased the tourists off the beach and into coffee shops and stores like mine. As soon as the sun broke through, though, the shop emptied as the crowds headed for the water.

In the lull that followed, I straightened and restocked the shelves, filling in the bare spots with merchandise from the warehouse. The shirts were stacked, the mugs and glassware lined up, and I was refilling the postcard rack when I heard Bluebeard mutter, "Uh-oh."

I glanced at him, realized he was staring at the door, and turned to see what caused his distress.

Peter.

Peter was coming through the front door, with his family close behind. Peggy waved at me, a harried look on her face as she headed directly for the back of the shop, seven-year-old Matthew clinging to her hand. Judging from Matthew's awkward gait, I suspected they were headed for the small bathroom tucked into a corner of the warehouse. Eleven-year-old Melissa followed at a more leisurely pace, her expression making it quite clear that she considered her brother's distress an affront to proper etiquette.

"Peter?" My voice came out with a quaver. I swallowed hard and tried again. "Peter, what a surprise! What brings you here?"

Peter shrugged, not meeting my eye. "We were visiting the folks for the weekend, and the kids wanted to come to the beach, so we figured we'd come down for the day."

There was more to it than that, I was sure, but I knew Peter—and he would take his time getting around to the real reason for his visit. Meanwhile, I was stuck with him, Peggy, Matthew, and Melissa in the store.

I asked Peter how he'd been, and let him rattle on about his job while I worked on the postcard rack. I wasn't listening carefully, but I gathered his success was just beginning and he would undoubtedly be running the company soon.

After a few minutes of Peter's chatter, Peggy returned from the bathroom with Matthew still in tow.

Melissa trailed behind, as though trying to keep as much distance between herself and the rest of the family as possible without risking a public scolding. Clearly, adolescence had hit full force. Going to the beach was good. Going with your parents was barely tolerable. Going with your little brother was clearly unacceptable.

I'd always gotten on well with Melissa when she was younger and I was the cool independent auntie with an apartment, a store, and a parrot. But I hadn't seen her in nearly a year, and it looked like I had joined the ranks of the other adults in her life.

The verdict was crystal clear when she greeted me with "Hello, Aunt Gloryanna. It's good to see you." Gone were the excited hugs, the "Auntie Glory," the begging to feed Bluebeard. I bit back a sigh. Most kids went through this stage; I had just hoped it would be different for Melissa and me.

"Good to see you, too"—I hesitated—"Melissa." Somehow, calling her Mel, which I had always done, felt wrong. She gave me a perfunctory hug, immediately pulling away as though anxious that someone might see her. With a shock I realized she was nearly as tall as me. When did that happen?

When you were busy avoiding her father, Martine.

Fortunately for my bruised ego, Matthew still thought I was cool. He waited impatiently until I released Melissa, then charged up and grabbed me around the waist. "Hi, Glory!"

Peter cleared his throat and looked hard at Matthew. His smile slipped and he released me. "Hello, Aunt Gloryanna," he said.

Ignoring Peter, I crouched down to Matthew's eye level and gave him a quick hug. "Hi, Matthew. I'm very glad to see you."

I stood back up and patted his mop of unruly sun-bleached hair. "How are you?"

"Good. Can I feed your bird?"

Bluebeard muttered again. I think Melissa had hurt his feelings, and I was grateful for Matthew's little-boy enthusiasm.

I led Matthew to the biscuit tin and let him extract a couple of the shredded-wheat squares that were Bluebeard's usual treat. Looking at the parrot, I said, "If he behaves himself, I'll let you give him some banana a little later."

His grin told me I had scored some important auntie points.

Peggy hadn't spoken a word since she'd emerged from the back of the shop. In fact, she didn't seem able to even look me in the eye. Her gaze seemed rooted somewhere around my navel, her brow furrowed as though she was trying to unravel a particularly puzzling problem.

"Peggy?" I said.

Her eyes flickered to my face and then back down.

"Honey?" Even Peter, oblivious as ever, had noticed her concern. "Is something wrong?"

Peggy pulled her lips in, biting them as if to prevent her thoughts from spilling out. She shook her head slightly and unclenched her lips. "No," she said, but she didn't sound convinced.

Matthew was feeding Bluebeard, ignoring the grown-up drama taking place a few feet behind his back, and Melissa had moved several paces away as though once again putting as much distance as possible between herself and the adults.

Silence stretched as we waited for Peggy to continue. Something was clearly bothering her, but I didn't know what, and Peter, as always, didn't have a clue.

Finally Melissa broke the uncomfortable silence with a dramatic sigh. "Mom, just *ask*, for God's sake!"

"Melissa! Do not take the Lord's name in vain!" Peter seized on his daughter's expression as a way to extract himself from whatever was upsetting his wife. But Melissa wasn't having any of it.

"Oh, Dad," she said in her most disgusted almost-a-teenager tone. "Really? Mom is about to lose it, and you're worried about my language?" She shook her head, clearly incredulous that her parents could be so clueless.

Peggy, meanwhile, still hadn't spoken, and didn't look as though she was going to.

Melissa tossed her long dark hair over her shoulder with a flip of her head, dismissing her father. "Mom, if you won't ask, I will."

Peggy didn't respond. Melissa turned and looked at me. Something in her expression told me I was being tested. I hoped I wouldn't fail.

"Aunt Gloryanna, why is there a baby crib in your back room?"

It took a few seconds for her question, and the meaning of Peggy's stare, to sink in. I started to laugh, but before I could explain, Peter broke in angrily.

"Is that why you wouldn't come visit Mother and Dad? Why you've been avoiding us? Glory, what were you *thinking?*"

I stopped laughing, anger bubbling in my stomach like a cup of bad coffee. I felt my face flush and my hands clenched into fists.

"Oh, no," Bluebeard said softly.

I had to control my temper.

One.

Two.

Three.

I couldn't punch Peter in front of his wife and kids, much as I wanted to.

Four.

Five.

I would not swear at him with Melissa and Matthew listening.

Six.

Seven.

Eight.

Even if he was being a judgmental asshat.

Nine.

Ten.

Like hell I wouldn't.

"What the hell?" My voice was loud, but I didn't scream, and my language was milder than it might have been. I'd had Bluebeard as an example, after all. But I got my point across.

"A—a crib?" Peter stammered.

"So what if there is?" I shot back. "Would you just hold off on your judgmental BS for a minute?"

I turned my back on Peter and addressed Melissa. "Yes, there's a baby crib back there. And a changing table, a rocking chair, and a chest full of diapers. They are for my friend Julie who works here part-time, so she can bring her baby with her when she doesn't have a babysitter."

I felt a hand on my arm. I turned and found Peggy standing at my side. "Sorry," she said, a blush in her cheeks. "I just saw the crib, and I thought . . ." She hesitated, then shook her head. "I didn't know quite what I thought, or how to ask about it. I'm sorry."

Melissa's attitude relented. "That is so cool, Aunt Glory! You really let your employee bring her baby to work?"

I nodded. "Rose Ann usually stays with her grandma, but some days her grandma can't keep her and she comes here. She's a very good baby."

I turned to Peter. "Do you have any other questions?"

Peter didn't answer. Not that I expected him to.

In a too-bright voice, Peggy tried to change the subject. "Have you been busy, Glory? There was a lot of traffic on the way down."

"It was a pretty good morning," I answered. She was trying desperately to ignore the tension that remained after her husband's outburst, and I went along. But in the back of my mind another strike was added to Peter's list of offenses. It was growing into a long list. "You're getting your reports and checks all right every month, aren't you?"

"Of course we are." Peter spoke up again, now that his wife had smoothed things over. "In fact, that was one of the things I wanted to talk to you about." He looked at Peggy, a clear reminder that she had a specific role to play in his little performance.

She looked relieved, and called to the children. "Let's go!" She turned back to me, her cool, impassive mask back in place. "I promised the children ice cream when we got here. We'll be back in a jiffy," she said with an insincere smile.

Obviously, her moment of embarrassment had passed. She took Matthew by the hand and led the way back to the sidewalk, Melissa trailing along in her wake.

Melissa looked at her father and me over her shoulder, her expression telling me quite clearly that she would rather listen in on our conversation than hang out at the ice cream shop with her mother and little brother.

A rush of warm air flowed through the door, then the three of them were outside and the door closed behind them.

The old air conditioner droned on, battling against the heat, its constant whirring the only sound in the shop. Even Bluebeard remained silent, waiting to see what fool thing would come out of Peter's mouth next.

But I didn't get a chance to find out why Peter had dropped in. He got as far as "I wanted to talk to you," when the bell sounded over the door and a trio of thirtysomething women came in.

I smiled at the new arrivals. "Can I help you find something?" I asked in a friendly voice. Even if Peter had angered me beyond endurance, I couldn't let it change the way I treated my customers.

"Thanks," said a leggy blonde, clearly the alpha of their little group. "Just looking for some souvenirs for the family before we have to head back."

The other two giggled in a way that said "girls' weekend" more clearly than their sunburns and the slight air of one-too-many umbrella drinks last night that clung to them.

"Anything in particular?" I asked, stepping closer. "Kid stuff, or something for the men in your life?" I had stopped using *husband* and *boyfriend* a few years back, in a moment of extreme caution, and the habit had stuck.

"Kids," the blonde's companions said in unison, and burst into giggles again, which the blonde didn't share. I revised the umbrella drink hypothesis to mimosas with brunch, with the blonde as designated driver.

I moved to the spinner rack full of T-shirts and hoodies with garish slogans emblazoned across them. I was already wishing I had Bluebeard T-shirts. These women would have snatched them up. "Boys or girls?"

Before the giggling women had a chance to answer, Peter clamped his hand on my arm. "We need to talk," he said. "But this isn't the time. Let's have dinner together. I'll call and tell you where to meet us."

Without waiting for an answer, he hurried out onto the sidewalk just as Peggy and the kids approached from down the block.

I turned back to my customers, wondering just what it was we had to talk about.

CHAPTER NINE

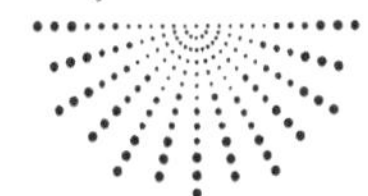

True to his word, Peter called just before I closed up for the night.

"We have reservations at Mermaid Grotto in an hour," he said. "Can you meet us there, or do we need to pick you up?"

How did he do that? Somehow, in his own bumbling way, Peter had managed to choose the one place in Keyhole Bay where I never wanted to go again. Even without knowing about my adventure, he'd zeroed in on the worst possible choice. And unless I wanted to tell him why, there wasn't any easy way around it.

"We loved going there when we were kids, remember, Glory?" he went on. "I thought it would be great to go again, and to introduce Matthew and Melissa to one of our favorite places. They don't have mermaids anymore, of course."

If you only knew!

"I'll meet you there," I told Peter. If I had to go to Mermaid Grotto, I at least wanted to have my own car with me.

And I didn't really want to go alone. Not when I would be facing Peter and Peggy and both kids.

I could call Karen, but I'd already intruded on her Friday night, and there were limits to what I could ask, even from my best friend. My gaze went to the shop across the street, as it did more and more lately. Jake knew about Peter, and about my secret plan to buy him out. But Beach Books still had an "Open" sign in the front window, and there were people in the store.

I thought about asking Felipe, or Ernie, but Sunday night was their time to relax and regroup after the weekend. Same for Linda and Guy. Although I knew Linda would drop whatever she was doing to go with me if I needed her, it wasn't fair of me to ask.

I locked the store, and went to take care of Bluebeard. "Looks like I'm going to have to face him alone," I said as I filled his water and checked his food dish. "Not that I can't do it, but I hate being outnumbered."

I put a few grapes and a piece of banana in Bluebeard's dish. He'd had a long weekend, too, and he deserved a treat.

"Won't be the first time," I continued.

Bluebeard cocked his head and looked at me with his beady black eyes. He looked so human when he did that, as though he was thinking hard about his response. But it wasn't the parrot who answered.

"Sylvester." The name came from the bird, but the voice was Uncle Louis's. "Sylvester," he repeated.

I felt a slow smile spread across my face as I considered his suggestion. Sly was the one person I knew who had known my great-uncle well. Though I had only met him recently, he felt like a long-lost uncle. He wasn't blood, but I trusted and respected Sly a lot more than Peter, who was.

"Perfect!" I said. I gave Bluebeard another piece of banana. "Good boy!"

I called Sly and asked him if he'd like to have dinner with me. His enthusiasm dimmed somewhat when I explained about Peter and his family, but he agreed to be my date. I said I'd pick him up in half an hour.

Then I called Peter back. "Hope you don't mind," I said in a rushed tone. "I'm bringing a friend along to dinner. I had plans with him," I lied, "so I'll just bring him with. I'm sure there isn't anything you need to tell me that he can't hear."

I didn't wait for Peter to break his stunned silence. "Gotta run. See you in a little bit." I broke the connection and charged upstairs to change. My phone rang as I reached the top of the stairs and the caller ID said it was Peter.

I didn't answer.

Twenty minutes later, showered and wearing a cool cotton dress and a pair of flat sandals, my hair pulled into a loose ponytail that kept it off my neck, I ran back downstairs. I said good-bye to Bluebeard, checked the locks and alarms, and hurried out the back door to where my truck was parked behind the shop.

Five minutes later I pulled into the junkyard behind Fowler's Auto Sales. I congratualted myself on knowing all the back roads, and avoiding the parking lot that Main Street became on a summer weekend. One of the benefits of living in Keyhole Bay all my life.

A grin split Sly's face when he saw the truck gleaming in the late afternoon sun. He may have sold her to me, but I knew she held a special place in his heart.

I tossed him the keys. "Want to drive?"

He snatched the keys out of the air with the dexterity of a man forty years younger, and the grin grew wider.

"Guess I could do that for you, girl," he said. But the joy in his voice belied the casual words, and made me smile.

"By the way, if Peter asks, we had plans."

He nodded.

Sly slid behind the big steering wheel and started the engine. He cocked his head, listening carefully to the muted rumble. After a minute of concentration he nodded, as though satisfied the truck was performing properly, and expertly released the clutch.

I watched his face as he drove the few blocks to Mermaid Grotto. His delight in driving the old truck was evident, and I felt a lump in my throat as I realized how much the old man had come to mean to me.

He pulled into the far corner of the lot, as far from other vehicles as possible, and parked protectively next to a curb. It was exactly what I would have done.

We climbed out of the cab, and I caught Sly patting the hood when he thought I wasn't looking. "Just making sure she isn't running too hot," he said. I didn't believe it for a second.

I walked across the parking lot, through the shimmering waves of heat rising from the blacktop. As we neared the front door, my steps slowed.

Facing Peter was bad enough, but I hadn't been through the front door of Mermaid Grotto since the afternoon Sly had sold me the truck. Since that afternoon in the old mermaid tank that had nearly been my last.

"You have to face it sometime," Sly said, offering me his arm. "But it don't have to be today. Up to you, girl."

I took his arm with my left hand and straightened my slumping shoulders. "No, you're right. And today's as good a day as any." I patted his arm with my right hand. "Thanks for being here," I said softly.

"Any time you need me," he answered. "Now let's go meet that cousin of yours and see what damn fool scheme he's got in his head this time."

I grinned. Trust Sly to cut to the heart of the matter.

But even with Sly at my side, walking into Mermaid Grotto turned my stomach and weakened my knees. I stopped just inside the door, unable to take another step for fear my legs would give out and send me tumbling to the floor.

"It don't have to be today," Sly repeated in a whisper.

I closed my eyes for a second and took a deep breath, steeling myself against the sight of the mermaid tank. "Yes, it does," I whispered back, opening my eyes and looking around. "Or I have to explain to Peter why not. And I do not want to discuss my swim in that tank with him. Ever."

"Up to you," Sly replied.

I stood my ground, and Sly stayed at my side.

After a few seconds I felt stronger, and we moved toward the hostess stand. I distracted myself by examining the T-shirts on display. The graphics were excellent, and the shirts appeared to be high quality.

"Did I tell you we might be doing T-shirts with Bluebeard on them?" I asked Sly.

He shook his head. "You didn't, but it sounds like a great idea. Heck, you might even get me to wear one."

The idea made me smile. Sly may have worn coveralls in the junkyard, but they always looked as though they had started the day clean and freshly pressed. When he wasn't working, he wore sharply creased khakis and long-sleeved sport shirts with the sleeves rolled up to expose his sinewy forearms.

I had never seen him in anything as casual as a T-shirt. Especially one with a parrot on the front.

"I'll give you one, if you promise to wear it," I teased.

"You got a deal," he answered.

The hostess gave me an inquiring glance, and I told her we had a reservation.

"Name?" she asked, looking at her list.

I realized belatedly that Peter hadn't told me what name he'd given them. I gave her Peter's name, but there wasn't anything. I tried Peggy. It would be just like my cousin to delegate the actual work to his wife. No joy.

I was about to abandon my quest and just wait for Peter and his family to arrive when I had one more idea. "Southern Treasures?" I asked.

The girl glanced down at her list and back up with a polite smile. "That's it," she said, as though I was a small child that had finally given the correct answer to a question. A frown creased her perfect brow. "But it says three adults and two children?"

"Actually there are four adults," I said, returning her false smile. "The others should be along any minute. We're just a little early."

She eyed me for a moment longer, than motioned us to follow her. I gripped Sly's arm tighter, and kept my gaze on the hostess's back as she led us to a large round table near the enormous fish tank.

Sly immediately pulled out the chair that faced away from the tank and held it for me. "We should let the guests watch the tank, don't you think?" he said, taking the chair next to mine.

I nodded, but couldn't find my voice to answer. I could feel the mass of water at my back, and I shivered with a chill that had nothing to do with the temperature of the room.

Within seconds ice water appeared, and a young man took our order for sweet tea. After he left to fetch the drinks, Sly gave me a concerned look. "Sure you're okay? You look like you seen a ghost."

I laughed, or at least I tried. What came out of my throat was closer to a gargle. "No, I only talk to a ghost."

"You know what I mean."

"I do, Sly," I croaked. I took a long drink of water and tried again. "Really, I'll be fine."

To distract us both from our surroundings, I began to tell Sly about Peter and Peggy's visit to the shop. I got as far as Peggy's return from the restroom when Sly shook his head slightly and looked over my shoulder.

I turned to follow his glance, and saw the hostess approaching our table with Peter, Peggy, Melissa, and Matthew trailing along behind her.

The next few minutes were a chaos of introductions and musical chairs, as the kids jockeyed for the seats facing the fish tank, and Peter tried to control everyone's movements.

Sly acknowledged the children with the courtly manners of an earlier generation, and practically bowed over Peggy's hand when she offered it to him.

Peter maneuvered himself into the chair on my left. He leaned close as the kids and Peggy were exclaiming over the fish tank and took advantage of the hubbub to whisper, "Don't you think we should talk about our business in private, Gloryanna?"

I forced an innocent smile onto my face. "Whatever do you mean, Peter? You said you wanted to talk, but you never actually said it was about business."

He glared, but I wasn't finished. "You know, Sly is an old friend of Uncle Louis, and he's kind of taken to looking out for me, since I'm alone down here."

I stopped and bit my lip, trying to look sincere. It wasn't exactly a lie; Sly did kind of look out for me. Not because I was alone, or because I needed looking after, but because he was my friend.

"You know we wanted to have you move up closer to your family," he said. "You could have come and stayed with Mom and Dad when your folks . . ." He left the rest of the sentence dangling, as though he was too considerate to actually say something indelicate.

"No, I couldn't have, Peter. We've had that conversation a million times. But that's ancient history. Sly is here, and there isn't anything you can say that you can't say in front of him."

"You're sure you want our family business discussed in front of *him?*" Peter's voice rose slightly, and he clamped his mouth shut as though trying to stop the flow of words.

"It won't bother me," I said, maintaining my innocent tone. Truth be told, I kind of wanted a witness to whatever Peter had planned, and I trusted Sly to be objective. Even though he'd called Peter's ideas "damn fool schemes."

Some things were just self-evident.

Peter, as usual, had to stall for a while before he could actually get to his point. He made a show of examining the menu, and asked me a series of questions about the offerings. Had I tried a particular dish? Did I remember if that was on the menu when we were kids? Had I been here lately?

It was the one question I hoped he wouldn't ask but knew he would. Like his choice of restaurant, he'd managed to find the most inane question with the most painful associations.

"I was here for dinner a few months back," I answered. "Before spring break. But I avoid places like this during the tourist season, they're usually very crowded." I neglected to mention my subsequent visit, and tried to deflect further questions. "Which reminds me, how in heaven's name did you manage to wrangle an actual reservation? Usually they don't take them; it's first come, first served, and the lines are monstrous on the weekends."

It worked. Peter launched into a long-winded explanation about how he'd impressed the hostess and the manager and talked them into allowing him to put his name on the list and arrange to return at a particular time. "You can usually get what you want," he said smugly, "if you know how to play the game."

He smiled knowingly. "That's how it works in the city."

I turned my head and caught Sly's eye. His warning frown kept me from bursting into hysterical laughter. It was the standard procedure at the Grotto during the summer, when their clientele tended toward families with children, who couldn't wait in the bar. It wasn't a reservation exactly, but it let them manage the waiting crowd a little better.

While I tried to figure out how to answer Peter's arrogance, the waitress appeared to take our orders. I was grateful for the interruption.

Peter, naturally, had to modify everything he selected for his dinner, so it took several minutes to get the order exactly to his specifications. Eventually, though, he was satisfied and the waitress left.

She returned in a couple minutes with a glass of white wine for Peggy and sodas for the rest of the family. I envied Peggy; if I had to spend much longer around Peter, I'd need something a lot stronger than wine.

But that would have to wait until I got home.

For the next few minutes, Peter held court, explaining the fish tank and its history to his family. I could see the kids rapidly losing interest, until Peter started talking about the mermaids that used to swim in the tank.

"Real mermaids? Really?" Matthew asked, his eyes alight with the prospect.

"There's no such thing as a mermaid," Melissa said, with barely concealed contempt. "Everybody knows that."

"They were real enough," Peter said. "Ladies with tails and long hair. They swam around the tank in a kind of slow dance, and they did flips and loops and all sorts of things. They were all really beautiful, and really amazing swimmers, and they did a show every half hour, I think it was, all day and all night. It was really something to see." He turned and looked at me. "You remember that, don't you, Glory? Way back, when there were people swimming in the tank?"

For one insane second I considered telling him it had only been a few months since someone went swimming in the tank, but the impulse passed.

So I nodded in agreement, and motioned for him to go on.

Peter chattered on about the mermaids, and how their show was famous all along the Gulf. I sat with my back to the tank and let his voice wash over me, wondering when he would finally get to the point of his visit.

Dinner arrived, fish and chips for the kids, grilled shrimp for Sly, salads for Peggy and me, and a highly modified sampler platter for Peter. Everything looked and smelled good, and the conversation died away quickly as we tucked into the meal.

Peter ate quickly, nodding appreciatively. "It's as good as I remember," he said when he pushed the empty platter away with a contented sigh.

"When was the last time you were here?" I asked, searching for some way to restart the conversation.

"Not since I was a teenager," Peter said. He stared off into space, as though trying to remember. But the details didn't come, and he shrugged. "A long time anyway."

Peter drew a deep breath and turned in his chair to look at me. "I want to talk to you about the store."

"I presumed as much," I said dryly. "Especially when you made the reservation in the name of the store."

Peter shrugged. "It just seemed appropriate. Anyway," he went on, "I thought I'd talk to you while we were down here, and after our visit to the shop, well . . ." His voice trailed off, as though I should know what he meant.

"Well, what?" I played dumb. I wasn't sure what he had in mind, but I suspected it had to do with Rose Ann's nursery. I wasn't wrong.

"I think we need more merchandise," Peter said. "Revenue is up a little, but it could be better. Have you thought about expanding?"

"There isn't any space. The places on either side of me have been there for years, they're doing well, and neither one is going anywhere. I can't expand." I dismissed his suggestion. "Maybe someday, but not right now."

Peter shook his head. "I thought about that, but after I looked the place over again today, I think there's room to bring in more merchandise.

"If you don't need the space in the back for warehouse space, if you can waste that area, and our money, on a nursery for a part-time employee, you can use it for more displays and more merchandise."

Even though I was expecting him to say something along these lines, his pronouncement stunned me into silence. Wrong in so many ways. I felt anger start to bubble, but I forced it back. I'd already yelled at Peter once today, with no apparent affect. It was time for a different approach. "I understand that you aren't around the store much," I said. Beneath the table I clenched my hands into fists, my fingernails digging into my palms in an effort to control my temper. "You have no way of knowing what works and what doesn't. And you have no way of knowing how that nursery came to be. But believe me, there is no waste of 'our' space, and I did not spend any of the store's money."

He started to speak, but I cut him off. "The nursery was a gift from many of Julie's friends, a way to allow her to keep her job. Which, I want to point out, she is very, *very* good at, though you have no way of knowing that either."

Ignoring most of what I said, Peter shot back, "Well, maybe I need to be more involved then. Maybe I should spend some time here, see what works. I'm sure you could profit from a fresh pair of eyes on the operation." He sniffed indignantly. "Of course, I have a very important job that keeps me busy."

He shook his head. "There isn't any way I can personally supervise your operation."

He cocked his head to the side and tried to pretend he'd just had an idea. I knew we were finally getting to his real mission. And I knew I wasn't going to like it.

CHAPTER TEN

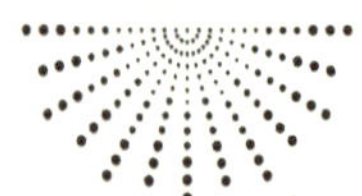

"Since I can't be here myself," he continued, "maybe I can get someone else to take a look at the operation. A consultant maybe?"

I controlled my mounting anger. Peter's interference had reached a new height. He had always worked for a large corporation, and he had trouble translating what was appropriate for a big company into what worked for a small store. I had to keep that in mind, or I would explode.

"We've talked about consultants before, Peter," I reminded him. "The expense far outweighs anything they could do for a company this small."

"But there must be something," Peter replied.

I should have come up with an alternative, but I couldn't think of anything that would pacify Peter. Which gave him time to come up with something on his own.

I could see the wheels turning as he searched for another plan. Clearly he hadn't been prepared to discuss other ideas, and didn't have a Plan B. But that didn't stop him from saying the first thing that popped into his head.

"What if Peggy comes down for a few weeks? While the kids are out of school."

"What?" Peggy clearly hadn't heard this idea before, and judging from her tone, she wasn't on board with it. "I can't possibly be away from the children."

Peter glanced over at her. "You could bring them with you. It would be like an extended vacation for all of you."

I glanced at Peggy, assuring myself she would be my ally in shooting down this latest scheme.

"There are about a million reasons that is not a good idea," I said. "It's obvious Peggy has a few of her own, and I could give you a long list. Starting with, where will they stay? Summer rentals are completely booked, and even if you found a cancellation, the rates are massively expensive."

Before I could offer any other arguments, Peggy spoke up again. "Peter, there is no way I am going to spend the rest of the summer down here with the children, staying Lord-knows-where, and leaving them alone while I work in some tacky shop."

She tossed me an apologetic glance. "Not that *your* shop is really tacky, Glory, but it's the idea of the place."

She turned her attention back to Peter. "That is not a good idea, and you should have at least talked to me first."

She looked toward the children, then back at her husband. "We can talk about this. Later. But spending the summer down here simply isn't going to work."

Sly had held his tongue all through the conversation, though his presence had helped calm me. Now he spoke up. "I knew your uncle, Mr. Peter," he said quietly. "He was a good man, but he knew his limits. That's why he never made that store no bigger. Kept it small enough to run by hisself; or with his little sister helping." He nodded in answer to the question he saw on my face. "That was your granny. But he never did hire anyone else."

Peter tried to interrupt, but Sly waved him to silence. "Mr. Louis was plenty smart. Knew what he was about, all the time. And he made a success of that little shop. Still in business all these years later, isn't it?

"So you might want to think real careful before you go messing with what Mr. Louis started. You know the old saying, 'If it ain't broke, don't fix it.'"

Sly sat back and fell silent. He'd spoken his piece, and he was done. He pulled a worn leather wallet from his pants pocket, counted out some bills, and left them on the table.

"I believe I'll wait in the car, Miss Glory. If that's okay with you?"

I nodded, ignoring Peter. "I'll be right along, Sylvester. Just let me say good night to my family."

Peter tried to draw me into another discussion after Sly walked away, but I had nothing more to say. "I understand that you want the shop to grow," I said. "But there isn't a good way to do it, and this isn't the time. Maybe in the future, if Pansy decides to close up Lighthouse, or Guy and Linda want to retire, then we can talk about it. But not right now."

I added some bills to the stack Sly had left by his plate. "It was good to see all of you, but I have to be up early tomorrow."

I turned to Peter with a sober expression. "You have a demanding job. So do I. I have not had a day off since before summer started. And I won't have one until at least September or October. That's what keeps your earnings checks coming every month. I love it, and I'm darned good at it.

"Just trust me, Peter. I know what I'm doing."

With that I turned my back and walked toward the door. I had held my temper in check for as long as I possibly could. If I didn't get away from Peter —and out of the restaurant crowded with bad memories—I was going to explode.

When I got to the truck, Sly had the doors open, letting the evening breeze cool off the interior. I ducked my head into the cab and quickly popped back out. It would be a few more minutes before we'd be going anywhere.

"You did good, Miss Glory," Sly said. "Mr. Louis would be proud of you."

"Thanks. You didn't do so bad yourself."

"Just speakin' the truth. A man's got to know his limits, that's all."

We climbed in the truck, Sly behind the wheel, and he started the engine. Peter and his family hadn't come out of the restaurant when we pulled out into traffic and started back to Sly's cottage in the junkyard.

"There is one thing I still don't understand," I said as Sly expertly maneuvered through the crowded streets. "Uncle Louis left the store to Peter and me instead of our parents, his niece and nephew. And he didn't leave us equal shares. That's never made any sense to me."

Sly didn't answer right away. He finessed his way between two carloads of way-lost tourists, one trying to turn left across the steady stream of traffic and the other waiting to turn right while a gaggle of teenagers straggled across the street in front of them, oblivious to the traffic.

We turned into the lot at Fowler's Auto Sales and drove around back to the fenced-off junkyard before Sly finally answered me.

"It was because of the tuition," he said, as though that explained everything. It explained nothing.

"What tuition?" I asked.

"Your Uncle Andrew's."

"Peter's dad?" I asked. "What does his tuition have to do with anything?" I paused and thought for a minute. "He didn't even go to college, did he?"

"Nope."

Sly parked the truck outside the gate and jumped down out of the cab. He walked up to the gate and dragged a key ring from his pocket. Selecting a key, he opened the padlock that held the gate closed.

At the sound of the key, Bobo came running from somewhere deep in the shadows of the junkyard. Even though I knew and loved Sly's dog, I had to admit he looked pretty intimidating coming at us out of the dark. If I didn't have any good reason to be in that yard, I would have been running. Fast.

Sly climbed back in the truck and pulled into the yard, leaving the gate open behind us. He knew I wouldn't be staying long.

"So," I said once the truck stopped inside the gate, "what about Uncle Andrew's tuition? What has that got to do with Southern Treasures?"

Sly stared into the darkness, as though looking at something only he could see. In a way that was true; he was looking at memories from before I was born.

"Mr. Andrew took a long time figuring out what he wanted to do with hisself. He tried a couple things around here, even thought about lettin' me teach him mechanicing." He grinned as though remembering an old joke. "Bet you can just imagine how popular *that* idea would have been."

He shook his head and went back to his story. "But nothing ever quite took. Not until he started messing with that old aeroplane. Pretty soon he was out at the airfield every spare minute. It was real clear that boy purely loved planes, and there weren't nothing else he wanted to do."

"I know he works on planes," I said. "But I always thought he was kind of an airplane mechanic. Isn't it all the same thing?"

"Yes and no," Sly answered. "The engines work the same way. Sort of. But they're more different than they are the same. At least according to Mr. Andrew.

"Anyway, when he put his mind to a thing, that was the end of it, and he decided he wanted to work on planes. But to do that, he had to go to school, and school cost money."

"Which Uncle Andrew didn't have?" I guessed aloud.

"Which Mr. Andrew didn't have," Sly agreed. "And his daddy didn't have it, neither. So he went looking for some way to come up with the money."

"And Uncle Louis had something to do with it?"

"You're right smart, girl." Sly chuckled. "Yep, Mr. Louis helped him out with the schooling. Lent him money and didn't pester him about paying it back.

"Your mama, though, didn't borrow anything from Mr. Louis. Mr. Andrew did fine; he got married, then your mama got married, and Peter came along and then you."

"Uncle Andrew still owed Uncle Louis the money?" I asked.

"Yep, but he didn't forget about it. The two of them worked out a deal when Mr. Louis went to do his will: everything would be divided between you two, but you got a bigger share to make up for the tuition money."

He turned and looked at me. "So you can stop feeling guilty about getting more than Peter. The fact is, Peter got a lot more than you in the long run. And he keeps getting it without doing any work."

Sly's explanation made a lot of pieces fall into place. Things that had bothered me since I was a kid suddenly made sense. As I thought about it, I realized something else.

"Peter doesn't know, does he?"

"I doubt it," Sly answered. "Mr. Andrew kept things pretty close to his chest. Doubt he would have told the boy."

"Thanks, Sly," I said. "It helps a lot to know why things happened the way they did."

"Don't you let Mr. Louis know I told you," he said. "I don't know as he'd want me to be talkin' about all this."

I promised, and pulled out of the junkyard with my head spinning. I was more determined than ever to buy out Peter's share of Southern Treasures.

CHAPTER ELEVEN

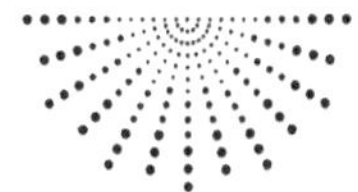

It was Wednesday before I talked to Karen again. The store was busy, as it always was the week of the Fourth; busy enough I hadn't had time to worry about her.

I was working alone near closing time when she showed up. The sight of her SUV reminded me of the situation with her and Riley. I hoped everything was okay.

She sat in the car for a minute, and I realized she was listening to the police scanner. She kept one in the car, one at the station, and one in her house—all in case a story broke.

As I watched, she gestured impatiently at the machine, then jerked it free of the power connection and burst out of the car carrying the scanner, now running on battery power.

She slammed through the front door, tossed her bag on the counter, and hushed me when I tried to say hello. "Something's up," she said. "Don't know what, but something, and I want to hear it."

The scanner was quiet as we waited in silence. I had learned a long time ago to hold my tongue when Karen was listening to the scanner.

The tiny speaker buzzed and crackled with static, then a voice came through clearly. We listened as Boomer Hardy, the police chief, finally responded to the dispatcher.

"Keep your britches on, Travis. I was in the head. What's so dang important?"

"Just had a phone call from a guy up in Minnesota, works for that bank?"

Boomer—his name was Barclay, but no one ever called him that—didn't need to ask which bank. Everyone in town knew which bank had taken an interest in Keyhole Bay.

"What did he want that was so important you had to keep calling me?" Boomer's impatience came clearly through the transmission.

"He asked us to check up on that Yankee gal, the one's down here snooping around Back Bay. Says she hasn't checked in since Friday and she's not answering her phone."

Boomer snorted. "So he's got his panties in a bunch 'cause she hasn't called in a couple days? Tell him to call her at work; she's at the bank before they open and there 'til after they close."

"Well, that's just it, Boomer. He did try calling the bank. They said she hadn't been in all week. He sure didn't like the sound of that, acted like they should've let him know she hadn't shown up."

I wondered if something had happened on Bridget's trip to Biloxi. Car trouble maybe, or she could be sick in her hotel. There had to be a reasonable explanation.

There wasn't anything to worry about.

I caught Karen's eye; she was thinking the same thing I was, and we both had the same sick feeling.

Something had gone badly wrong.

"I'll go take a look, if it'll make him feel better," Boomer agreed, annoyance clear in his voice. "Can't have those Yankees worryin' about their little gal down here. Give me the location."

The dispatcher reeled off the address where Karen and I had been on Friday, and the image of the deserted subdivision full of empty and abandoned lots flashed in my mind. A chill passed through me, making me shiver.

I locked up while we waited, mentally ticking off the minutes until Boomer would reach Bayvue Estates.

"She's probably stuck in Biloxi," I said.

"Probably," Karen agreed. "But you'd think she'd at least call and let somebody know where she was."

"Who would she call?" I asked. "Nobody here would give a flip, probably just as glad she wasn't at the bank digging into their records."

"Still, you'd think there would be somebody."

I shrugged. "You'd think."

I wondered who would miss me if I didn't check in for a few days. Julie would notice on the days she was in the shop, but she only worked three days a week. I talked to Karen and Jake almost every day, but if they were busy, it might take a couple days before anyone realized I was gone.

It was a creepy thought.

The scanner crackled to life with Boomer's voice. "Travis, I'm out at the location you gave me. There's a car in the driveway, but no sign of anyone." He described Bridget's rental car and recited a license number. "Verify the renter on that, would you?"

"Roger that."

Another minute of silence, and then Travis confirmed what Karen and I already knew: The car had been rented by Bridget. She'd used a company credit card.

"Maybe she wasn't supposed to use the company car for a personal trip?" I said.

Karen shrugged. "That could be." She went into what I called her reporter mode, a distance that shielded against emotional distress. "After all the scrutiny banks have been under, a lot of them have adopted very stringent rules to avoid looking like anybody's getting away with anything."

"Call that guy up North," Boomer instructed over the radio. "Ask him what he wants us to do. It's his house, and his gal. In the meantime I'll take a look around."

Karen and I made small talk while we waited, not sure what we were waiting for. The scanner sputtered to life occasionally with routine business: patrol officers checking licenses and issuing warnings or citations, reports of shoplifting and noisy neighbors. All the usual summer calls.

Travis finally came back, calling for Boomer. "Chief Hardy? I talked to the guy in Minnesota. He said to go in and take a look around."

Boomer's reply was an unintelligible mutter, reminding me of Bluebeard. The words might not be clear, but the meaning was. He wasn't happy.

"Place is locked up," Boomer answered. "What does he want me to do about that?"

"He said if you couldn't get in, to do—I am quoting here—whatever is necessary."

"Got it," Boomer answered. He didn't sound any happier.

He sounded even less happy when he called back a few minutes later. "Travis, send a wagon and Dr. Frazier. I think I found her."

"Roger," Travis answered.

Karen and I stared wordlessly, hoping it wasn't Bridget. Not if Boomer was calling for Marlon Frazier. Dr. Frazier was the county coroner.

Whoever Boomer had found was dead.

CHAPTER TWELVE

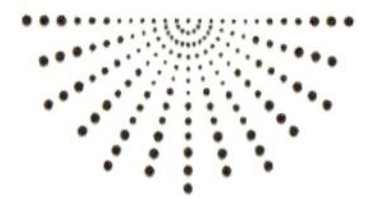

"I'm heading out there," Karen said, gathering up her scanner and bag. "I'll call you when I know something more."

"I'll go with you," I offered.

"No. Stay here. This could be a long night, and I don't know where I'll end up. I promise I'll call."

I reluctantly agreed; there was a part of me that didn't want to see what was out at Bayvue Estates. Besides, Boomer might tolerate Karen doing her job, but he wouldn't be thrilled to see me with her.

"Please do," I said. "It's got to be some kind of mistake, or it's somebody else. Or something."

"I don't think it's a mistake; Boomer doesn't make very many. But I'll keep you posted."

I followed Karen out onto the sidewalk. She jumped into her SUV and pulled into traffic.

I didn't want to be alone quite yet, and I realized I was staring across the street again, looking for Jake. Since when did I think of him first when I needed company?

I didn't stop to consider the answer to that question. I made sure the door was locked, and seeing a break in traffic, I hurried across.

The door was locked, but I could see Jake inside, counting the register and checking it against his computer screen. I tapped on the window and he looked up with an annoyed frown, which disappeared as soon as he recognized me.

His welcoming smile faded, though, the minute he opened the door and saw my face. "Glory, what's wrong?"

I blurted out the news.

"Karen and I were out there on Friday night," I reminded him. "She seemed fine. Said she might go over to Biloxi for the day on Saturday. That's where she was headed when you and I saw her on Saturday morning. She didn't stay long after you left; she seemed to be ready to be on the road."

"Let me finish up here," he said. "We can talk while I work." He offered me a chair behind the counter and went back to closing out his register. "Do you know anything more?"

I shook my head. "Just what we heard on the scanner. Boomer was out there, said it was her, but that was all. Karen's gone to chase down the story and she promised to let me know what she finds out."

Jake tapped the computer keys, the printer whirred and spat out a few pages, and he shut down the machine. "Let's get out of here," he suggested. "We can pick up some burgers at Curly's and figure out what to do from there."

Jake drove. We considered and rejected a dozen places to eat as we drove toward Curly's. "We could just eat there," I said, unable to come up with a better idea.

But when we pulled in, the parking lot was packed and we knew the small dining room would be even worse. We pulled into the line of cars at the drive-through, still trying to come up with a place to take our burgers.

Jake handed me the bag after we reached the window, and pulled out of the lot. "How about we take them to my place?" he asked without looking at me.

He'd never invited me to his place before. We went out or he joined the Thursday dinner crew, and my place was convenient after work. But tonight was different.

"I think I'd like that," I said quietly. I didn't want to be out in a crowd, and I didn't want to go home.

Jake's small rental house was only a few blocks from Beach Books, on a dead end in a maze of narrow residential streets. The pale green single-story cottage with a covered carport sat only a few feet from the street, a white board fence defining the perimeter of the postage-stamp lot. Native grass filled the front yard, trimmed precisely around the cobblestone walkway and the fence line.

Jake pulled into the carport and unlocked a side door that led directly into an immaculate kitchen as tiny as Bridget's had been spacious. The counters were clear of clutter, the sink empty and scrubbed until it shone, and the tile countertops gleamed in the light from the overhead fixture.

On one side of the room sat a small wooden table painted a soft blue, and two dark blue kitchen chairs. I put the bag of burgers on the table as Jake pulled colorful pottery plates out of the cupboard and filled tall glasses with ice.

"Sweet tea?" he asked, taking a pitcher from the refrigerator. He filled the glasses without waiting for an answer.

We made small talk while we ate, and when we were done, Jake offered me a tour of his house. "There isn't much to it," he said, leading me through into the living room.

It was no surprise to find every inch of wall space covered with packed bookcases. "You know, Jake, you have an entire store full of books," I said, gesturing to the bulging shelves. "Isn't that enough?"

He grinned sheepishly. "These are just the keepers," he explained. "The books I want to have around forever."

I stepped close to the nearest shelf, reading titles. "I'll have to check this out, see what it is you can't live without." I stopped as I read a string of titles shelved together.

"You're really taking this volunteer fire department thing seriously!" I ran my finger along the spines neatly lined up together. Firefighting equipment. Fire investigation. Arson. At least a dozen titles.

Jake's laugh sounded forced. "Yeah, I guess." He nodded toward the hallway off the living room. "Want to see the rest of the house?" he said, moving in that direction.

Clearly this topic was closed for the moment, but I guessed we'd come back to it eventually. Why else would he have let me see that row of books?

Down the short hallway were a single bedroom and a small bath, both as tidy as the kitchen. The real surprise, though, was at the end of the hall, where a pair of multipaned glass doors led to a screened patio.

We sat down on the patio chairs, watching the light slowly fade from the sky. A soft breeze blew through, carrying the scent of roses from an unseen bush in a nearby yard.

The neighborhood was quiet. "Your neighbors must not be home," I said.

Jake shook his head. "May not be home from work yet," he said, "but even when they are, it's pretty quiet around here. No vacation rentals, just a few weekenders, but mostly they're all permanent residents."

"No wonder you like it here," I replied, "if it's this peaceful all the time."

"Pretty much," he said. "Makes it a good place to live. I'm kind of hoping the landlord will consider selling the house. I think I could stay right here for a good long time."

I struggled to find an opening to bring up the firefighting books again. They appeared to be older editions, not what a newly minted volunteer would read, and they were important to Jake. I wanted to know why.

From inside the house I heard the faint ringing of my cell phone. I had left it in my purse, hanging from the back of a kitchen chair.

I got up quickly and hurried back down the hallway and through the living room, but by the time I reached my purse, the phone had stopped ringing.

Jake shot me a questioning glance as I checked the call log. "It was Karen," I said, quickly redialing her number.

She answered on the second ring. "I was just leaving you a voice mail," she said. "Are you okay? It surprised me when you didn't answer."

"I left the phone in the other room," I explained, without giving her any details. "So what did you find out?"

Her voice shook a little as she answered me. "It's Bridget, for sure. Boomer recognized her, and he had her driver's license for confirmation."

She paused, and I could imagine her slipping into reporter mode, distancing herself from what she had seen. "They're trying to reach her next of kin, but no luck so far, so Boomer hasn't officially released her name."

"What happened?" I asked. "She seemed fine on Saturday when she stopped by on her way to Biloxi."

"She stopped by Saturday?"

"Just returning my food containers," I answered. "But what's going on out there? What happened to Bridget?"

"I don't know. Dr. Frazier's here, but he's not saying anything yet." Karen's façade slipped, and stress pushed her voice into a higher register. "I have to go, but I promised to call, so I did. I'll call you back as soon as I know anything more."

CHAPTER THIRTEEN

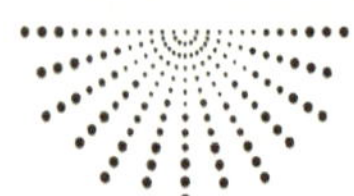

"I heard," Jake said, his hand resting lightly on my shoulder. "Are you okay?"

"Not really," I answered, leaning against him. "I didn't know her very well —really just met her a couple times—but she seemed nice, and a little lonely. I thought maybe we could be friends while she was here. Felt like she could use someone to talk to."

I stood for several minutes with my head resting against Jake's chest, feeling the warmth of his arms around me. He didn't speak, and I was grateful for his quiet strength, for the patience to let me deal with things in my own way.

Outside, the sunset had faded to full dark. The kitchen light turned the windows to shadowy mirrors, reflecting the image of Jake and me standing with our arms around each other.

I really didn't know why Bridget's death affected me so strongly. I didn't know her for very long. We didn't have a lot in common, as far as I could tell. There was just something about her that had clicked, and now she was gone.

From a distance we heard the whine and boom of fireworks as night fell. The Fourth was still a day away, but legions of visiting children couldn't wait another minute. Tomorrow there would be a professional display at the football stadium, but tonight was strictly amateur hour. It reminded me why I didn't go out much this time of year.

I knew I should get home, but I wasn't ready to leave just yet. My internal debate was short-circuited by the squawk of Jake's radio. I hadn't noticed it before, silent on a shelf in the corner of the kitchen, but now it crackled to life and the voice of the dispatcher filled the room.

"Station Three, Engine One. Grass fire reported at Anderson Park. Engine One respond, Code Two."

Answers poured in almost before the dispatcher had finished the call. Volunteers at the station radioed they were on the way, and several others responded they would meet the unit on-site.

Jake released me and reached for the microphone. "Robinson, on call," he said. "Will report to station."

He turned back to me. "Time to go. I'm on call to cover the station in case of a call out."

I didn't need any more of an explanation. I threw my purse over my shoulder and followed him to the car.

He pulled out of the carport, and propped a portable flasher in the window. "With the holiday traffic, I may need this."

He was right. Getting onto the highway would have been nearly impossible without the red and blue strobes clearing the way. As he turned onto the main drag, he glanced at me. "I can drop you at home, or you can come with me. But you have about twenty seconds to decide."

I didn't hesitate. "I'm going with you."

Jake threaded his way through the evening traffic to the low brick building that housed the volunteer fire department. Keyhole Bay could call for help and support from Pensacola, if needed, but mostly our own volunteers handled our emergencies, large and small.

The station was empty, the pumper truck and medical unit already calling in from Anderson Park. "Small grass fire," a voice reported. "Under control. No injuries. Medical unit returning to station."

"Roger," the dispatcher answered.

"I have to stay until they get back," Jake said. He led the way to the small kitchen behind the truck bays. "You want something while we wait?"

I accepted his offer of a bottle of water. I swallowed, and felt the cold slide down my throat, still tight with emotion.

I looked at Jake. He looked so at home in the station, as though he belonged there. I remembered the volumes on his living room shelf, and wondered again what they might reveal about him.

Whatever that was, though, I wasn't going to find out tonight. While we waited for the medical unit to return, the radio continued to broadcast one call after another.

The pumper rolled in, the crew sweating in their heavy turnouts. Jake handed me his keys with an apologetic shrug. "Looks like a busy night," he said. "They're going to need me. Take my car. Drop the keys through the mail slot and I'll pick it up later, or in the morning." He gave me a quick kiss and sprinted for the truck.

I watched the activity in the station for a few minutes, flattening myself against the brick wall and trying to stay out of the way. It quickly became clear that Jake was right: the station was a buzz of activity, and he was needed.

I don't think he even noticed when I left.

I parked Jake's car behind the bookstore and crossed the street to the front door of Southern Treasures. In spite of all that had happened, it wasn't that late and I realized Linda and Guy were still open.

I walked past my front door and into the Grog Shop.

Guy waved a greeting from the back of the shop, where he was filling a shelf with giant bottles of daiquiri and margarita mix. Based on past history, those shelves would be bare before noon tomorrow.

Linda was behind the counter, ringing up a steady stream of customers preparing for their holiday celebrations. I walked back and gave Guy a hand with the stocking.

It was a job I'd done every weekend my last year of high school, when I had lived with Guy and Linda after my parents died, and in a strange way it comforted me.

A few minutes later the clock hit closing time. Linda checked out the last customers and locked the front door behind them before coming over to check on our progress.

"Haven't lost your touch," she said, admiring the neat rows of bottles.

Guy snagged three bottles of soda from the cooler, twisting off the caps and giving one to each of us, keeping one for himself. "Stocking is thirsty work," he proclaimed.

It was a little ritual we'd observed since I first started helping him when I was just a bored little kid who thought his store was a cool place to hang out. I didn't realize back then just how lucky I was to have Guy and Linda.

Linda gave me a questioning look. "Something wrong, Glory? You look upset."

I told her the same thing I'd told Jake. "Nobody knows what happened," I said before she could ask. "Boomer went out on a welfare check and he found her body."

"It's just sad, thinking of her out there all alone," I said, shrugging off any further discussion.

"I did have something I wanted to ask you about," I said to Linda, trying to change the subject.

Guy gave us a lopsided grin. "I know girl talk when I see it coming," he said. "I'm pretty sure I have some work to do in the back."

He moved quickly, as though we might be contagious. Linda watched him go, an affectionate grin lighting her face. I envied her.

"What's up, Glory?" Linda asked as soon as Guy was out of earshot. "You looked like you had something on your mind when you were here over the weekend, but we didn't get a chance to talk."

"It's Karen and Riley."

Linda rolled her eyes. "Those two! Glory, whatever is going on between them, there is nothing you can do to change it. You're just going to have to let them do whatever they do."

"I know," I said. "But I still worry about Karen."

Linda put an arm around me. "That's what friends are for. We worry about the people we care about, even if there isn't anything we can do." She gave my shoulders a squeeze. "Who knows? They just might surprise you."

I hoped she was right. They had been spectacularly unsuccessful at actually living together so far, but maybe Karen was right and things were different this time. I allowed myself a glimmer of hope that they would get it right this time.

We talked a few minutes longer, carefully avoiding the subject of Bridget. The whole time a part of me was waiting for the phone to ring, with an update from Karen.

I left Linda with a promise to keep her posted on whatever I heard, and went home to take care of Bluebeard.

And wait.

CHAPTER FOURTEEN

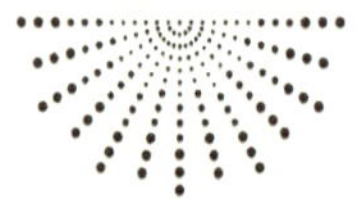

I had gone to bed with the phone close at hand, but it was nearly midnight when Karen finally called. I picked it up on the first ring.

"It's not too late, is it?"

"No, I couldn't sleep," I admitted, tucking a bookmark into the paperback I'd been reading. "Where have you been?"

"I went out to Bayvue, which I told you. Stayed there until Boomer chased everyone out and sealed the place. It'll stay closed up until he has a preliminary cause of death."

"That sounds ominous."

"He swears it's just precautionary. Any unattended death requires an autopsy. Anyway, nobody is in any hurry to get into the house, so he's just covering his butt. No sense making the bankers think he isn't doing his job."

"Which bankers? The Andersons? Or the Yankees?"

"Either one," Karen shot back. "Dr. Frazier is supposed to do an autopsy tomorrow, so we should know more then."

"On the holiday? That ought to make him super happy."

"Like I said, Boomer wants to keep everybody off his back, much as he can. No sense picking a fight with anybody."

"What about Bridget's family?" It was the question that had lingered in the back of my mind ever since that first dispatch call. *Who would miss her?*

"According to what her boss told the dispatcher, there's a brother in

Minneapolis. Boomer called the local police department, asked them to contact him."

I didn't have to imagine what that visit would be like. I knew. I'd experienced the knock on the door, the wall of uniforms on the porch asking if I was Gloryanna Martine, asking if they could come in, telling me to sit down. It was a memory that would never go away.

I shoved those thoughts into a deep corner of my mind, slamming a mental door on the pain. I hoped Bridget's brother had someone to help him through the coming weeks.

"I guess that's all we're going to get for tonight, huh?"

"Think so," Karen answered. "I'll see you tomorrow at dinner."

In all the stress of the evening, I had forgotten tomorrow was Thursday. Another late night.

Julie had just returned from a break when Jake came into Southern Treasures the next morning with two cups from Lighthouse. He nodded to me, and stopped to greet Bluebeard.

"Coffee?" Bluebeard asked, hopeful. He bobbed his head in excitement. I'd been told parrots didn't have much sense of smell, but he clearly knew what was in those cups.

"Sorry, buddy," Jake said. "We both know you're not supposed to have coffee. And you wouldn't want me to argue with the boss over there, would you?"

Bluebeard eyed me as though I might weaken. I shook my head. Coffee was dangerous for several reasons and I wouldn't take any risks where my parrot was concerned.

"Told you," Jake said. He reached under Bluebeard's cage and took a shredded-wheat biscuit from the can. "This is the best I can do right now."

Having paid his respects, Jake came back across the shop to where I stood behind the counter. "Vanilla latte," he said as he handed me one of the cups. "By way of apology and thanks."

"Apology? For what?"

Julie moved discreetly away and began dusting and straightening shelves.

"For dumping you last night," he said, looking away. "You wanted some company and I bailed on you."

"You were needed at the station. I understood."

He shook his head. "Don't let me off that easy," he said with an embarrassed laugh. "*You* needed me. I should have stayed with you."

I put my hand on his arm and squeezed gently. "I'm a big girl," I said. "I can take care of myself. I appreciate that you were there while you could be. That's enough for me."

Jake hesitated, as though there was more to say.

"Now, it's the middle of a holiday, and you have a business to run," I reminded him with a smile. "Thanks for the coffee, even if it wasn't necessary."

His look told me the subject wasn't closed, but he let it drop. "The other reason I came over was to let you know Felipe called and invited me to dinner tonight, if that's okay with you?"

"Of course it is. Felipe doesn't need my permission to include you."

"That wasn't him asking, it was me," Jake explained.

"Either way," I said. "It'll be fun to have you there."

"Good." He hesitated. "Will you ride with me? I promise not to abandon you this time."

"Don't promise," I warned him. "This could be another busy night for the department. Besides, if you have to leave, I can always ride home with Karen."

We agreed to meet at Beach Books at six, and Jake headed back to his store.

Julie came back behind the counter without a word, but her look said a lot.

"It wasn't anything, really," I said. "I just wanted somebody to talk to. We got burgers from Curly's and then he got called out."

Julie already knew what I had wanted to talk to Jake about. The news of Bridget's death was all over town; gossip was an industry second only to tourism in our small town, and we were good at it.

"They called the fire department out there?" Julie asked, puzzled. "Why would they do that if she was dead?"

"No, they got called to Anderson Park. A grass fire. But there were a bunch of calls just after dark, when the tourists started setting off their fireworks."

Julie's confused expression cleared. "Oh. That makes more sense."

A steady stream of customers kept us busy until closing time, and beyond. It was nearly six when the last ones straggled out the door with their T-shirts and postcards.

As the last group of customers milled around the entrance, holding the door open, an orange cat slipped in. Sydney, who lived a couple blocks over, the official greeter at Molly Young's B and B.

Sydney was supposed to be an indoor cat, but she sometimes managed to escape. And when she did, she went exploring.

The door closed. I quickly turned the lock, trapping Sydney inside the shop, and reached for the phone to call Molly.

"Molly's Magnolia Bed and Breakfast," Molly answered. "How can I help you?"

"Hey, Molly," I said. "How are you?" Even if I was rescuing her cat, good manners dictated that I at least ask after her.

"Doing fine, Glory," she said. "How about you?"

"Can't complain. The tourists are spending, and the weather's not too hot."

"I hear that," she chuckled. "What can I do for you, sugar?"

"Well, I thought I ought to let you know, Sydney's come calling. I locked the door behind her, but I know you'll be wanting to get her back home."

"I'll be there quick as I can," she said.

Before I could say good-bye properly, Bluebeard let out a shriek.

I turned around just in time to see him half jump, half fly toward one of the hanging light fixtures. The shop wasn't really big enough for him to fly, but he was clearly agitated and trying to get to as high a perch as he could.

The fluorescent lamp swung wildly, and Bluebeard slipped from his precarious spot, losing his footing.

"@&%&%%^* cat!" he screeched. "Cat here!"

He flapped his wings wildly, managing to slow his fall somewhat, and he landed clumsily on a stack of T-shirts, sending several of them cascading to the floor.

Sydney, curious about the commotion, jumped onto the lower shelf and batted at Bluebeard with one paw, as though playing with a particularly noisy toy.

Bluebeard leaped away, cursing nonstop, his outburst punctuated every few seconds with the phrase "$%^#%& cat."

Sydney followed her new prey across the shop, crouched low, tail twitching. She'd gone from curious to hunting, and while Bluebeard was bigger, stronger, and a lot more aggressive when he wanted to be, he wasn't a predator by nature.

Bluebeard lit on top of the postcard spinner, and Sydney leaped up against the rack, trying to claw her way up the slippery chrome rungs.

The spinner teetered, spilling cards out of the pockets, and unseating Bluebeard. He slipped off the rack and onto another display table, hopping quickly across the shop and into the relative safety of his cage.

I moved faster that I thought possible, beating Sydney to the cage, and closing the door before she could follow Bluebeard inside.

She glared up at me, like I had interrupted an especially amusing game, then lay down and started grooming herself as though nothing had happened.

In the cage I could hear Bluebeard cursing and ranting. I reached over and rattled the cage door gently. "It's closed," I told him. "No one can bother you. Even the cat."

The cursing grew softer, more like his usual muttering, but it didn't stop and I didn't argue with him about it. This was the first time I'd seen him encounter a cat, and his obvious distress was far beyond anything I would have imagined. I wondered what had happened to make him react so badly, but that was a question for later.

Right now I had to deal with Miss Sydney.

I managed to pick the cat up and carry her back to the counter, where I'd left the phone. The line was dead, which didn't surprise me, though I had to wonder what Molly had heard before she hung up.

I put Sydney on the counter, holding her in place with one arm while I picked up the phone and called Molly again.

I identified myself, and Molly immediately asked, "What happened, sugar? You were talking, and then there was a terrible commotion and the call dropped. I was about to send Ronnie over to make sure you were okay!"

I thanked her for her concern, and reassured her that I was fine. "But Bluebeard apparently has a serious issue with cats. He pitched a huge fit when he saw Sydney. He's in his cage now, and she's just sitting here like nothing happened."

"I am leaving right this minute," she said. I heard her holler for Ronnie, and tell him she had to go out. She turned back to the phone and said she would be right over.

True to her word, she was at my door in about three minutes, her plump cheeks bright red, and huffing and puffing like she'd run the three blocks. In her hand was a cat carrier with "Sydney" written on it in marking pen.

Sydney wasn't happy about getting in the carrier, but Molly wrestled her in and slammed the door shut, scolding the cat in a singsong voice the entire time.

"She knows she's not supposed to go out," she said. "But since when does a cat care what she's supposed to do?"

I shook my head. I had no idea what a cat cared about. I'd never had a cat, and judging by Bluebeard's reaction, I never would.

I thanked Molly for coming so quickly, and she apologized for upsetting Bluebeard.

I shrugged. "I had no idea," I told her. "I don't know why he got so freaked out. But now I know to watch out for cats."

Molly left with Sydney in the carrier, her plaintive yowls clearly indicating her indignation at her treatment.

When they were gone, I opened Bluebeard's cage. I never closed it, giving him the freedom of the store, but this had been an emergency.

I reached my hand in. He came close enough for me to scratch his head, but he refused to leave the cage. The encounter had upset him badly, and he just needed to be left alone to recover. I retreated, and began repairing the damage to the displays. There were a few shirts to fold, but not much else.

Except for the postcards.

The postcard spinner rack was a disaster area, but I didn't have time to straighten and stock it before dinner; it would have to wait for tomorrow morning.

I groaned at the thought of having to get up early to take care of it, but it was one of the delights of running my own business. In the end, it was all up to me.

CHAPTER FIFTEEN

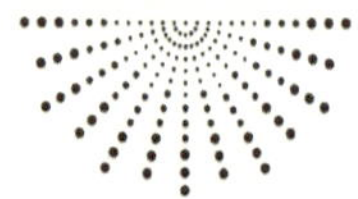

Jake was waiting at the front door when I crossed the street. On the drive to Felipe and Ernie's, Jake asked if I'd heard anything more from Karen.

"She didn't learn much. They were trying to reach Bridget's brother in Minneapolis, and Dr. Frazier was supposed to do the autopsy today."

We threaded our way slowly through the crush of tourist traffic, my usual back-road routes blocked. Normally the drive would take five minutes, but with the holiday swelling our population tenfold, we crawled along for closer to twenty.

I chuckled as we waited for yet another knot of visitors to dash across the street in the middle of the block, on their way to who-knows-where.

"What's so funny?" Jake asked, glaring impatiently as the last straggler passed in front of us.

"Those are the same people who were in the shop earlier today, asking how I could stand to live here with all this traffic." I chuckled again at the memory. "I didn't tell them it was only like this when they're here."

I shook my head at the scowl on his face. "Come on, you've been here long enough to know that. You've seen what it's like in the winter. These people go home, and we still live here.

"It's worth putting up with the traffic for a few weeks out of the year."

Jake crept forward with the slow-moving traffic. He glanced over and gave me a wry smile. "I suppose you're right," he said, turning back to watch the road. "But traffic has always been one of my hot buttons."

Hard to imagine that Jake, one of the calmest people I knew, even had hot buttons. Most people do, sure, but I hadn't seen anything upset him. Worried, yeah, like after my little adventure in the mermaid tank. But not upset or angry.

Then again, how much did I really know about Jake? He'd been in town a couple years, but I didn't know exactly where he came from, or what he did before he bought Beach Books. In many ways he was still a mystery.

We pulled up in front of Felipe and Ernie's tidy house, parking on the street behind Riley Freed's pickup. Looked like tonight was going to be a full house.

Ernie greeted us at the door in sharply creased khaki shorts and a garish Hawaiian shirt. No one should be able to make that outfit look elegant, but somehow he pulled it off.

On the patio out back, Felipe was hard at work over a top-of-the-line gas grill, his naturally olive complexion flushed with the heat and a bandanna tied jauntily around his brow to keep the sweat out of his eyes.

He waved a pair of grill tongs in our direction. "Hi! There's beer in the cooler. Help yourself!"

Before we could make a move, Riley grabbed a couple bottles from the bed of ice in the vintage metal cooler. He popped the tops and offered them to us.

"Thanks." Jake accepted the bottle, and clapped his other hand on Riley's shoulder. "Good to see you."

I thanked Riley for my beer with a hug. "How was Bobby's birthday party?"

"Great. Great," Riley answered, returning my hug. "You probably should have been there."

"No, it was a family time. You didn't need any outsiders."

His voice grew serious. "Glory, you'll always be family to us."

I gave him a last squeeze and pulled away. "Thanks for that. But there are times . . ."

I let my voice trail off. He knew what I meant.

"Speaking of family," I resumed, "wait 'til you hear what my cousin pulled this last weekend." I gave them a greatly abbreviated version of my Sunday encounter with Peter and his family.

"They thought the crib was for you?" Karen laughed.

I nodded.

"I'm trying to imagine the look on his face," Karen said between bursts of hilarity. "And you actually stood up to him? Good for you!"

Peter's scheme seemed forgotten in the midst of Karen's amusement. Just another of his crazy ideas.

Jake and I walked over to the grill to inspect Felipe's work. Chicken sizzled softly above the gas flame, glistening with a clear glaze.

Looking closer, I was able to identify the long needles of rosemary. I glanced back at Felipe. "Rosemary? Since when is that traditional Southern?"

"It's Independence Day, Glory. I am declaring myself independent of dinner rules for the day. We're having a grilled feast. Besides, you bent the rules last week. Or have you forgotten?"

"Bent, not broke," I argued. "It was something I remembered from my childhood. My *Southern* childhood," I added pointedly.

"Puerto Rico is south of here, *amiga*," he shot back. "And it is still too hot to cook inside."

"And New York is way north." I raised a hand in surrender. "But it *is* too hot," I agreed. "So what else is for dinner?"

Felipe pointed to a foil-covered baking dish tucked to one side of the grill. "Baked beans and"—he gestured at a tray of filled skewers waiting on the table beside the grill—"lots of vegetables. Grilled tomatoes. Tortillas." He held up a hand. "I *know* those aren't Southern, but they're good with the chicken."

Ernie appeared at my side with a plate of cocktail shrimp in tiny lettuce leaf bowls, topped with a spicy dressing. "Not traditional either," he said. "But tasty!"

I laughed and relaxed. The boys had invited Jake and Riley, and they had discarded our recent tradition for a far older one: the Fourth of July backyard barbeque. This was a night for a celebration with friends.

So be it.

We settled around a rustic picnic table on the screened porch, leaving the formal dining room and its mid-century modern furnishings for another night. And just like most Thursdays, we spent the first part of the meal talking about the food.

"The sauce is simple," Felipe said, passing the platter of juicy chicken pieces. "White wine, butter, rosemary, a little lemon juice. Careful grilling so it doesn't dry out, and you're done."

I helped myself to a skewer of vegetables from the pile on the tray in front of me. It held colorful peppers, onions, broccoli, mushrooms, several kinds of squash, and cherry tomatoes. Next to the tray of skewers were plates of grilled eggplant and grilled tomatoes.

"Delicious," Jake said, taking another piece of chicken and more tomatoes. He scooped part of the tomato into a tortilla, added chicken he'd pulled from the bone, and rolled it into a sort of taco.

I had to admit, traditional Southern or not, the food was sensational.

Across from me, Karen and Riley sat close together on the wooden bench, their shoulders touching. They giggled as they occasionally stole bits of food from each other's plates.

When we had finished eating and I'd helped Ernie clear away the leftovers, we moved to the cushioned patio chairs clustered at one end of the porch. In an hour or so we would move outside, where we could watch the fireworks from the high school stadium as they exploded over the heads of the crowd. We were all content to watch from a distance, avoiding the crush of people and vehicles that filled the stadium.

Karen hadn't mentioned Bridget during dinner, but I had waited as long as I could. "Did you find out anything more about Bridget?" I asked her once we were seated.

"Not a lot. Boomer has finally released her name, now that he's talked to her brother."

Felipe and Ernie both sat forward. "So it was her? We'd heard rumors, but you can't always believe everything you hear," Ernie said.

"Even from the Merchants' Association?" I asked with false innocence. "I thought they had all the latest news."

He shot me a withering glance. "I trust what I hear officially at the meetings. Not so much what I hear fourth-hand from an individual with an agenda."

"Agenda?" Karen responded to the whiff of gossip. She always said that gossip meant a story, just like smoke meant fire.

"He means Felicia Anderson," Felipe cut in. "That woman was in the shop already today, nosing around some of the merchandise."

"But she can't really be planning any shopping," I blurted out. "Just because Bridget's"—I hesitated—"gone doesn't mean the bank won't send somebody else down here."

"Oh, she made all the right noises about 'that poor woman,'" Felipe said, his words dripping with contempt. "Not that I believed her for a minute. But she was right there, trying to talk me down on the price of an old chest that she was just *sure* used to belong to her husband's dear uncle, the General."

"You know, General Anderson never even lived in this area," I said. "I looked him up after we got to talking about Felicia the other day. He commanded the troops when they attacked Fort Pickens, but he was only here for a short while. He never really lived here, and his wife and family were all in South Carolina."

Karen laughed out loud. "You know, I always just took their stories at face value," she said. "Never thought about checking them out. You know how it is down here"—she waved her arm, encompassing the entire region—"you measure your time by generations, and we all knew the Andersons had been here forever.

"I wonder who started that story," she said quietly. I could see the wheels already turning on the piece she'd write.

"But Felicia can't possibly think this ends here, can she?" I asked Ernie. "I mean, the bank is sure to send another auditor."

"I don't know what that"—Ernie paused, and I could see him struggle with the word he wanted to use—"that *witch* thinks. If she thinks at all. She just assumes she will get everything she wants because she always has."

"Oh, there will be another auditor," Karen said. The note of certainty in her voice told us there was more to the story. We all turned and looked at her expectantly.

She let the silence stretch out, taunting us with the hint of news to come. I let her have her moment, but impatience soon got the better of me. "Spill, Freed! I've been waiting all day to hear what you found out."

"Like I said, Boomer talked to her brother. He's on his way down. Apparently he works for the same bank, and he'll report to her manager about everything he finds down here."

She sat back with a sad little smile, and I knew she still hadn't told us everything.

"And?" I prompted.

"And," she said at last, "Dr. Frazier wouldn't give Boomer a definite cause of death until he gets the lab results. He hand-carried the samples to Pensacola for analysis.

"He said it looked like a drug overdose."

CHAPTER SIXTEEN

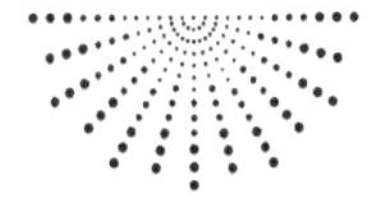

I shook my head, refusing to believe what she'd said. "Are you kidding? She wasn't taking drugs."

"Depends on what drugs," Jake said. "*Drug overdose* covers a lot of different possibilities."

"Glory's right, though," Karen said. "I was out there. I saw her and I saw that house. I've talked to a lot of people over the past few years, and I think I've seen about every kind of drug use around. She didn't have any of the signs."

"But it might have been something you *haven't* seen," Ernie said. "Maybe something that isn't common around here."

Karen shook her head, her expression stubborn. "I don't think that's likely, Ernie. Remember, we had a steroid problem here just last year." She shot me a sympathetic glance. I'd learned far more than I had ever wanted to know about 'roid rage, dealing with Julie's ex-husband.

"And this is a tourist town," she went on. "We get everything around here. Besides, she just wasn't the type."

"Type?" Felipe laughed, not an amused sound but a harsh bark. "There's no type. Not everybody who uses drugs is a meth head with their teeth falling out."

"He's right," Jake said. "And a drug overdose doesn't mean she was even doing anything illegal. People overdose on legal drugs. They take the wrong prescription, or they combine things they shouldn't. They forget they took their pills and take them again. Saying it looked like an overdose can mean a lot of things." He put his arm around me and patted my shoulder. "We won't really know until they get the lab results."

"Wouldn't Felicia Anderson just love that?" Ernie said. "Get rid of the auditor and discredit her all at once."

"You don't really think . . ." Riley's unfinished question, the same one that had occurred to me, hung in the air.

Ernie waved a dismissive hand. "Not really. Felicia wouldn't dirty her hands. But it sure wouldn't break her heart either."

"I still can't believe it was drugs," I muttered.

"Let's wait and see," Jake said softly, so close to my ear I could feel the warmth of his breath against my cheek. "The doctor could be wrong, too."

I nodded, just a slight brush of my face against his.

"Did you find out anything else about the brother?" I asked Karen, pushing the topic of drugs out of my mind. "Like when he'll get here, or what he does for the bank?"

Karen shook her head. "Boomer is being pretty closemouthed about the whole thing."

"Then he's the only one," Ernie drawled. "Everyone else is certainly quacking their fool heads off about it."

Felipe nodded. "While Felicia was in the store today, she must have had a dozen calls. The rumor mill was working overtime, I can tell you that."

"Did you hear anything interesting?" Karen asked.

"Not much," Felipe said slowly as he stopped to think about it. "I tried not to eavesdrop, but it isn't easy when she's screeching away."

Ernie reached over to pat his partner's knee. "You could hear her all over the store," he said. "A lot of people noticed. You couldn't help hearing her entire conversation."

Felipe nodded at Ernie, grateful for his loyal defense. "She kept talking to people about how she'd heard that Bridget was on drugs. She was convinced that Bridget had gone to Biloxi because she certainly couldn't have bought anything like that here, in our fair city."

"Yeah, right." Ernie muttered.

Karen's derisive whoop of laughter interrupted Felipe's story. "Is she crazy?" She turned to me. "You remember a couple years ago, when Boomer had to shut down a party at the pool house? Right in the development where she made Billy build her that big new house? There were plenty of pills and powders and Lord knows what else out there that night, practically next door to her!"

I had to think for a minute, but I remembered the incident she was talking about. "I think it was more like four years," I said. "They built that house out there about the time I took over Southern Treasures completely. I remember because Shandra—my old manager?—she went to work at the bank just in time to be invited to the housewarming."

"You sure?" Karen said.

"Yep. She bought the housewarming gift from me. Some old chamber pot I found up near Campground."

"Campground?" Jake asked. "What campground?"

"Not *a* campground," I explained. "Campground. It's a little town a ways north of here."

Felipe broke out laughing. "She gave them a *chamber pot* for a house-warming gift?"

I nodded. "She said she'd put flowers in it and Felicia wouldn't know the difference. And she was going to tell her she thought it had belonged to the General."

Jake whistled softly. "Wow! Apparently her employees don't like her very much."

Karen and I launched into an explanation of Felicia, and the Anderson family history, starting with the General. After a couple minutes, Jake held up his hand. "Much as I love your stories about everyone's family," he said, "if you don't skip a few generations, I will still be sitting here when the sun comes up."

"Okay. Fast-forward about a hundred years. Billy returns from college with a girlfriend. They announce their engagement at Christmas, and get married a year after Billy finishes grad school.

"Billy comes home and settles down to doing not much of anything, except collecting—and spending—dividend checks. His granddaddy had just passed —" The look on Jake's face stopped me in midsentence. "Sorry. Fast-forward another ten years. Felicia wants a new house, so Billy gets the bank board— basically his parents, him, and his younger sister—to raise the dividends. And he borrows a pot of money, too, if what I hear is right."

I explained about Felicia's fake drawl, her constant references to "the General," and how she put on airs around town. "Memaw always said, 'Pretty is as pretty does,'" I told him. "And by that standard, all the beauty salons in the world couldn't help that woman."

"So that's how the dreaded Felicia came to town," he said dryly. "I can see why she's so popular."

Karen picked up the story, telling Jake how Billy's ambition and greed had got him into some risky business ventures, culminating with the Bayvue Estates development.

"They got a couple model homes up, sold a bunch that weren't built yet, and then the bottom dropped out. They held on for a bit, but there was no way they could recover. So now we have this auditor for the new owners, and no one's happy."

Jake sighed. "What a mess."

"Oh, that's not all," Felipe said. "Not only are there people who bought houses that were never built—"

"We met one of them," I interjected. "Sort of. Friday night when we were out at Bayvue. Some man showed up looking for Andrew Marshall, and when he couldn't find him, he started yelling at us. He never did tell us his name, but he said he wanted his house and he made some pretty direct threats."

"I doubt seriously if he's the only one," Karen added.

"Exactly," Felipe said. "And there's a developer who's out of business, construction crews thrown out of work, a bank manager who lost his job—"

"And his house," Riley added.

"Really? How awful!" Karen's concern was genuine. We all knew Francis Simon had been fired over the Back Bay scandal, but we hadn't heard about the house.

Riley nodded. "My mom works with his wife at the drugstore. She heard the Simons have to move this month, that since Francis got fired, the bank is calling in their loans, and taking over their house."

Jake looked from one person to another around the room.

"This is more than just a mess," he said. "That development is jinxed for sure."

CHAPTER SEVENTEEN

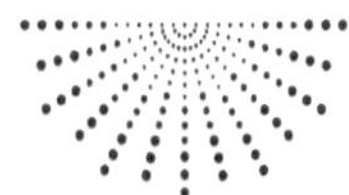

We let the squeal and boom of fireworks draw us out of the screened porch and into the backyard, leaving behind the discussion of Bridget, Back Bay, and the Andersons.

We stood there, three couples watching a visual display that we had each contributed to. Although the city collected a "donation" from those sitting in the stands, the majority of the cost was underwritten by the annual arm-twisting of the Merchants' Association. Members put donation jars on their counters for months beforehand, and we all tossed something in.

I had my differences with the Merchants' Association, but I still supported the fireworks. There was something about the scream and thunder, the shower of glittering lights, and the multicolor explosions that reminded me how much I loved this holiday.

In spite of the grown-up problems of traffic and crowds, noisy neighbors with too much beer, and the inevitable mess the morning after, on the Fourth I was nine years old again, sitting in the stadium with Mom and Dad, watching the fireworks.

The final volley launched into the sky with clusters of brilliant light and color. We stood transfixed, listening to the growing quiet as the final sparkles faded from view.

After a moment, Felipe broke the silence. "Dessert?"

Everyone agreed it sounded like a great idea.

Felipe disappeared into the kitchen and emerged seconds later with a shallow bowl full of halved peaches. I had almost expected watermelon to top his grilled meal, but he had a bigger surprise in store.

With a flourish he raised the lid on the grill he'd heated while we were watching the fireworks, and laid the glistening peach halves on the rack.

He turned them once, the aroma of caramelizing sugar and pungent cinnamon teasing our noses as we watched. Within minutes he dished the halves onto elegant dessert plates, topping each with a dollop of sweet whipped cream.

For the next few minutes, conversation stopped except for an occasional question about his recipe. We were all too busy eating and murmuring approval to actually speak.

Finally, when the last plate had been scraped clean, Riley stood and stretched. "Wonderful meal, Felipe. A perfect Fourth of July." He reached for Karen's hand and pulled her up off the turquoise cushions of the sofa they had shared. "But some of us have to get up early."

Karen sighed and nodded. "Unfortunately." She made the rounds, saying good night with hugs. When she got to me, she gave me an extra squeeze. "I'll let you know if I hear anything," she promised.

Jake and I soon followed their lead. It was getting late—the fireworks hadn't started until well after dark—and we both had to work in the morning. At least we had waited out most of the traffic from the stadium.

"Just be patient," Jake said when he parked in front of my store. "Boomer isn't a fool. He'll get to the truth."

"I hope so," I answered with a sigh.

"He will." Jake came around and opened my door, taking my hand to help me out of the car. I was perfectly capable of getting out of the car on my own, but I appreciated his gesture and liked letting him act the gentleman.

He waited while I unlocked my front door, and he followed me inside. It was a habit he'd developed after my break-in last year. I'd installed an alarm system, but Jake still wanted to check for himself, and I had to admit it was kind of nice to have someone looking out for me.

"Trying to #$$^$%$ sleep here!" Bluebeard hollered, sticking his head out of his cage.

"Just checking the alarm, Bluebeard," I said as I walked through to the storeroom, where the alarm lights glowed green. Set and secure.

I was about to head upstairs after saying good night to Jake when I remembered the postcard spinner. It had been a mess before I left, and I should go clean it up and restock it. But I was exhausted, and it was already way past my bedtime. I told myself the tourists would be getting a late start tomorrow after tonight's celebration. The postcards could wait until morning.

Morning came far too early. I woke before dawn from a fitful sleep filled with unpleasant dreams, and couldn't stop thinking about Bridget. How long had she been alone in that house, in the middle of an abandoned construction site? Did she suffer? Couldn't she have called for help?

Questions chased each other around my brain in the gray light until I gave up and crawled out of bed. I was still tired, but I knew I wouldn't get back to sleep.

If I had to be awake, I should do something constructive with the time. I promised myself a latte from Lighthouse, and maybe even one of Pansy's muffins, while I worked.

With that incentive, I was showered and dressed in just a few minutes. Lighthouse didn't open for another half hour, but Pansy, the eighty-one-year-old owner, came in every morning at three thirty to do the baking. Chloe, the barista, often came in early to help, in the hopes of someday prying Pansy's recipes out of her. So far she hadn't succeeded, but Chloe was ever optimistic.

Sure enough, when I went out my back door, I could smell the heady aroma of fresh cinnamon rolls wafting from Lighthouse.

I tapped on the open back door and stuck my head in. Chloe was just taking a tray of scones from the oven and sliding them into the cooling rack. She nodded at me to come in.

"You're up early," she said. "Need coffee?"

Pansy, all four-feet-nine of her, glanced over from the industrial mixer that was nearly as tall as she was. Dough hooks the size of cantaloupes slowly turned and stretched a batch of sweet dough that would become trays of sticky pecan buns. "Good morning, Gloryanna," she called cheerfully, waving a hand gnarled with arthritis as though being up before the sun was cause for celebration.

"Morning, Miss Pansy."

Chloe disappeared to the front and returned a minute later with a vanilla latte. She handed me the coffee, and a sample-sized scone. "We're trying out a new recipe," she explained. "Florida citrus is what Miss Pansy calls it, but she won't tell me exactly what's in it."

"Take two," Pansy said, hobbling over with another tiny pastry resting on her palm. "One for that handsome fella of yours. I'd like to know what he thinks, too."

I shook my head. "He's not my *fella*. He's just a friend," I lied. I had begun to secretly hope he was my fella, but I wasn't about to admit it. Especially to Pansy, who guarded her recipes like a dragon guards its treasure, but thrived on local gossip.

Pansy arched an eyebrow and made a disbelieving face. "Oh, he is. Don't you think for a minute you can tell me otherwise. I see the two of you in here, looking all googly-eyed at each other. I might have been born in the morning, but it wasn't *this* morning."

She went back to her mixer, throwing her last words over her bony shoulder. "You mark my words, girl! He's your fella."

Chloe just shrugged. "She's never wrong."

"Googly-eyed? Did she really say that?"

"Well . . ." Chloe drew the word out, as though hesitant to answer. "You *do* pay a lot of attention to each other."

"I may have to start getting my coffee somewhere else," I said darkly.

Chloe laughed. "We're the best, and you know it. Besides, it's the most convenient place for you and"—she drew a deep breath—"where else can you get a free latte before six A.M.?"

She had me and she knew it. "You win," I laughed. "But I'll have to be more careful about how I look at Jake from now on. And thanks for the coffee."

I went back to Southern Treasures and let myself in the back door. I still had to face the postcard mess, and get ready for what I hoped would be a busy Friday.

On my way through the storage area, I filled a box with postcards and note cards to restock the spinner and carried it out front.

"Coffee?" I don't know how Bluebeard knew I had coffee. No, I did know. I *always* had coffee first thing in the morning, although it was usually a mug from my French press upstairs, not a paper cup from Lighthouse. Generally, my latte intake began later in the day.

"No coffee," I answered. "But I will give you a treat."

I set my cup on the counter with the box of cards and broke off a small piece of my scone. Parrots shouldn't have much fat, and no sugar, but it wasn't toxic like coffee. I offered him the crumb of pastry, followed by his usual shredded-wheat biscuit.

The tiny treat earned me a head bump.

I pulled the spinning rack across the shop so I could spread the cards out on the counter—another reason to do this before the customers arrived.

Several of the wire pockets were empty, and a couple more had no postcards, only note cards without envelopes, which was odd. I was used to a few of the cards going missing each time I filled the rack. People picked up the cards, admired the pictures on the front, and walked out with them, leaving the empty envelope on the rack. And sometimes I found note cards mixed in with postcards in other pockets.

But I didn't usually find cards without envelopes. Who would take an empty envelope?

CHAPTER EIGHTEEN

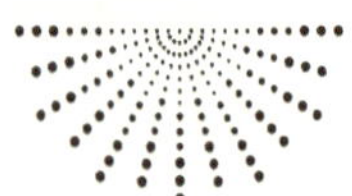

I emptied all the pockets, sorting cards and stacking them across the counter. Pictures of boats and beaches, silly sayings, tropical flowers, and vintage photos of Keyhole Bay.

I didn't find the missing envelopes, but by the time Julie arrived, the store was tidy, the postcard rack was fully stocked, and I was ready for a break. Not that I was going to get one. Not on the Friday of a holiday weekend, which was why Julie was working an extra day this week. I needed to take care of some errands, and I didn't dare close, even long enough to go to the bank.

I opened the safe to stock the till and was reminded that I had no reason to complain. It had been a good week so far, and the weekend looked promising. I made up a bank deposit, wrote a list of necessary errands, and stuck my wallet in my pocket with my driver's license.

I called Jake before I ducked out the back door. "You have a bank deposit?" I asked. "Or a change order? I'm heading over, be glad to take care of yours, too."

"Would you?" Jake sounded relieved. "I was already short of change, and the first customer through the door this morning spent ten bucks and gave me a hundred."

"Call in the order and I'll pick it up."

I hung up, told Julie what I was doing, and trotted across the street to pick up Jake's bank bag, and drop off Pansy's scone. *Not because he was my fella*, I told myself. *Just doing a favor for a friend.*

But as I came back across, I caught Chloe grinning at me through the big front window at Lighthouse and felt like I'd been caught. Doing what? I wasn't sure. I just knew I felt guilty.

I steered the Southern Treasures truck down back streets, avoiding the main drag as long as possible. I finally turned into traffic and crept the last few blocks to Back Bay Bank. As I parked the truck, I realized with a start that soon the signs would change and Back Bay would cease to exist.

I waited behind two other local merchants as Barbara counted their deposits and stamped their receipts. Everyone wanted to talk about the dead auditor and what it would mean for the transition.

"I really don't know yet," Barbara said to Cheryl Beauford. "There's supposed to be somebody from the bank coming down today, but who knows when he'll actually get here. You know what it's like trying to get a flight this time of year."

Cheryl nodded. "We don't travel during the summer, but we've had friends *try* to get here. It's ridiculous."

Cheryl stuffed her receipts in her bag and turned to leave.

"Hi, Glory," she said as she headed for the door. "How you doing?"

"Can't complain." I wiggled my zippered deposit bag. "Been a decent summer so far. How about you?"

"The Fourth's always good," she laughed. "Lots of cookouts and beer."

"Tell Frank I said hey," I told her, moving up as the person in front of me finished at the teller window. "I'll be by a little later, my cupboards are pretty bare."

"We'll be there," Cheryl said with an eye roll.

I laughed. Running the main grocery store in town meant they were there all day every day.

I stepped to the counter and handed over my deposits to Barbara. "Any word about Bridget?" I asked as she emptied the bag and started checking off the totals.

"Bridget?" Her head shot up and she gave me a puzzled look. "Did you know her?"

"A little," I said. "She came in the shop a couple times and we had dinner together the Friday before she died. Seemed like a nice gal."

Barbara shook her head. "I thought so, too."

She lowered her voice to a whisper. "Until I heard she was doing drugs out there. Is that true?"

She looked stricken as she realized what she'd just said. "Not that I thought you—I mean, you talked to her, maybe you got an impression or something."

"I did," I said, trying to contain the shock I felt. I knew the rumors were flying, but I hadn't heard them firsthand until now, and I certainly hadn't heard them associated with me. "To tell the truth, I don't believe it. She just didn't seem like that kind of person, and I didn't notice anything in the way she acted that made me think any different."

Barbara straightened up and went back to counting. I suspected my tone had been harsher than I'd intended, and she hadn't meant to accuse me of hanging out with a drug user. Still, her words stung.

I took my receipts and Jake's change order, and hurried back out to the truck. Traffic was already heavy, I absolutely had to go by Frank's Foods, and I needed to get the oil changed in the truck—though that would have to wait until next week.

On impulse, I pulled into Fowler's Auto Sales on my way to the grocery store. Not that I'd let any of those clowns touch my baby. Instead, I pulled around to the back of the lot and through the chain-link fence that marked the end of Fowler's property and the beginning of Sly's. I knew Fowler had his eye on the junkyard with the small cinderblock house in the middle, but Sly had said many times that he'd never get his hands on it. Sly didn't have much use for Matt Fowler, and neither did I.

Bobo, his teeth bared in a slobbery doggy grin, loped out from between the rows of trucks parked against the fence. I reached into the glove box of the pickup and retrieved a treat for him before I climbed out of the cab.

As I alighted, he sat expectantly, trying to control his excited wiggling. I remembered the first time I'd encountered Bobo, when I'd walked into the junkyard not knowing he, and Sly, lived there. All I saw that day was a head the size of a basketball, if basketballs had rows of large pointy teeth.

Since then I'd been accepted as part of his pack, and he treated me with affection and deference.

A few steps behind Bobo was Sly, his dark face split by a wide grin that exposed the gaps where several teeth used to be.

"Miz Glory! Didn't expect to see you again so soon."

"Hello, Sly." Anyone else I'd have greeted with a hug, but I wouldn't presume to violate his dignity. Sly was nearly seventy, after all, and had the courtly manners of a true Southern gentleman. Although he treated me with the affection of family, I still felt like I needed to maintain some reserve.

"What brings you here this morning?" he asked. "Seems like you ought to be pretty busy with your store."

"Julie's there, and Rose Ann is with her grandma. I had to go to the bank and stop at Frank's—Bluebeard is out of bananas and apples, and that's a crisis."

"He always was set in his ways," Sly said. I knew he wasn't talking about the parrot. Sly had been as close to a friend as Uncle Louis had in his later years.

"Anyway, I need an oil change, and since I was driving right by, I figured I'd stop and see when would be a good time for you."

"Any time. I could do it right now, if you like. Take me about twenty minutes."

I hesitated. I would love to stay and visit with Sly, but I'd promised Julie I'd be back quickly.

"Wish I could, Sly. I'd enjoy spending a little time with you and Bobo." I patted the patient hound and he rewarded my attention with a wag of his tail. "But I still need to get groceries, and I have to get back to the store."

"Well then, why don't you come back next time Julie's there to mind the store?"

I smiled. "She'll be in all day Monday. How about I bring lunch? Say, around noon?"

Sly nodded his agreement.

I headed back to the truck, but his voice stopped me. "Miz Glory? I don't mean to pry, but you look mighty down. Are you needin' something more than an oil change?"

The concern in his voice was what broke me. I couldn't bear to have Sly worrying about me.

I gave him a condensed version of the last few days, ending with my encounter at the bank. "I just can't believe she was doing drugs," I repeated for about the millionth time, "and I know I certainly wasn't! But now it looks like I could end up with the same things being said about me."

CHAPTER NINETEEN

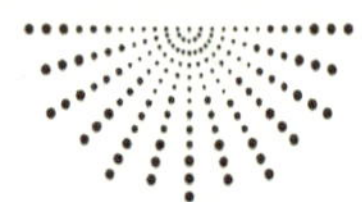

Sly scowled. "They better not say anything like that where I can hear. Bobo neither."

Beside me Bobo rose to his feet and growled, as though he knew exactly what Sly had said.

The two of them coming to my defense reassured me. No one who knew me, even slightly, would have any doubt of my innocence. And everyone in town knew me.

"Thanks, Sly," I said. "And Bobo," I added with a pat on his broad head. "I know it will all get straightened out when they get the tests back from the lab."

I wished I felt as confident as I sounded.

"I'll bring the truck in on Monday," I said, climbing back in the cab. "Thanks!"

I waved at Sly through the windshield and put the truck into gear, backing out through the gate. I turned around and headed onto the road, in the direction of Frank's Foods.

The parking lot was busy, but not as jammed as it would be later in the day. I grabbed a couple cloth bags from behind the seat and hurried inside. I'd spent longer than I'd intended talking with Sly, and I needed to get back to the shop.

But in Keyhole Bay—like all small towns—nothing ever gets done fast. I ran into two different people in the bread aisle who wanted to talk about Back

Bay and its troubles, and by the time I got to the produce section, I was beginning to regret my decision. Surely Bluebeard could have managed another day without a banana.

I quickly piled fruit and vegetables into my cart, anxious to get through with my shopping.

Frank appeared from the back, pushing a cart piled with melons, and called my name. "Just got a shipment of watermelon in," he said, "but one of 'em broke, and we can't eat it all. Would Bluebeard like some melon?"

"You know he would, Frank."

"Hang on." He ran into the storeroom and came running back a few seconds later with a plastic zip-seal bag from the fish counter. I could see chunks of bright red watermelon with juice puddling in the bag.

"Here you go."

"I owe you," I said as he scrawled his initials and the words *No Charge* across the heavy plastic.

He handed me the bag with a shrug. "No you don't."

Cheryl was ringing up another customer when I got in line, and a few minutes later I was handing her a check in exchange for my two bags of groceries.

"I know this is good," she joked as she slid the check in the bottom of the cash register. "Since I just saw you in the bank."

"Yeah. It's going to be strange, isn't it, when they take down the Back Bay signs."

"Sure is. Too bad about Francis and Lacey, too. He did what his bosses told him, and they just threw him to the wolves.

"Which reminds me," she went on, "have you heard anything about what they're going to do with Bayvue Estates? I know there are a bunch of the construction guys who are anxious to get in line if there's going to be work."

I slung the sacks over my shoulder and picked up the plastic bag of watermelon. "Wish I knew, Cheryl. It's terrible about all the people thrown out of work by this mess."

"You know, Frank and I actually thought about buying a lot out there. Maybe put up a place where we could retire one of these days," Cheryl said, shaking her head. "But then we went out and took a good look around. We knew we'd never be happy out there, not with what they had planned."

I hesitated. I should get home, but there was nobody in line, and I wanted to hear more. "What were they planning?"

"A bunch of patio homes. You know, big houses on lots so tiny that there's only room for a patio, with your neighbors living practically in your hip pocket. And a bunch of community stuff, like a pool and clubhouse, and eventually a golf course." She gave a little laugh. "Even if we could have afforded one of those overbuilt places—which we couldn't—we would have never fit in. It just felt cold and plastic and like it could be anywhere."

I couldn't imagine Frank and Cheryl in the kind of neighborhood she described. Nor could I picture the two of them, with their adored nephews and nieces who traipsed in and out of their home constantly, in the house I'd visited just a week ago.

"I can't even imagine y'all retiring," I told her. "Much less moving away from your family."

"Well, Glory, it's not like Bayvue Estates is that far away. It's just a few miles from where we are now."

"And your sister and her kids are right next door to where you are now."

She chuckled. "Got me."

I wanted to ask her who had showed her the development and talked to her about the plans, but just then a couple in shorts and loud shirts wheeled a cart up to the check stand. A quick glance at their cart loaded with wine, ice, and snack food pegged them as tourists.

I waved good-bye to Cheryl and went back to the truck. It was way past time I got back to the store.

I checked in with Julie, who assured me she had things under control, before I ran across the street to deliver Jake's change.

"Sorry it took so long," I said. "Long story, and neither of us has time for it right now."

"Tell me over dinner," he said, "once we're closed."

I accepted his invitation along with a promise to call a little later with dinner details.

Bluebeard gobbled down the watermelon when I put it in his dish, much to the delight of a couple little boys who were in the shop. Somehow the idea that the parrot was eating watermelon was one of the most entertaining things they had seen all day, and they begged to be able to feed him.

"I'm really sorry," I told them. "But he doesn't have very good table manners sometimes, and he might hurt your fingers."

Bluebeard cursed softly behind my back, but fortunately he was quiet enough that I was the only one who heard him. Then he squawked loudly. "Good Bluebeard!"

The boys dissolved into fresh giggles and went running for their parents.

As they were leaving, the father asked in a tone that was only half joking if I would ever consider selling the bird.

I shook my head. "There isn't anyone I dislike that much," I said with a lighthearted laugh. "Parrots can be a handful, especially one like Bluebeard."

I didn't tell him about the ghost that came along with the bird, and made it impossible for me to part with him. I doubt he would have believed me.

A tall woman with cropped red hair came through the door, eliciting a wolf-whistle from Bluebeard.

Julie was around the counter, giving our visitor a warm hug, by the time I had admonished Bluebeard. It was a lost cause, I knew, but I still tried to curb his flirtatious behavior. Not everyone thought it was cute.

Our new arrival, though, didn't seem to notice. She was engaged in a rapid-fire conversation with Julie, and it was clear the two were old friends.

"Mandy," she said, pulling her friend over to where I stood behind the counter, "this is my boss, Gloryanna Martine. She owns this awesome place. Miss Glory, this is my friend Mandy Price. She works for Coast Custom Printers. You know, the place that does Mermaid Grotto's T-shirts."

"Glad to meet you, Miss Glory." Mandy handed me a business card. "Julie told me you might be interested in some T-shirts?"

"We did talk a little about that," I said. I didn't tell her I'd forgotten we'd scheduled a meeting this afternoon. "Julie thought shirts with Bluebeard on them would sell well in the store."

"Pretty boy!" Bluebeard yelled.

Mandy noticed him this time. She turned and looked at the parrot across the shop. "May I?" she asked before she approached him.

"He's bad-mannered," I said. "But I couldn't have him in the store if he wasn't okay around the customers."

Julie led her friend across the shop and showed her where to find the shredded-wheat biscuits that he loved. One treat from an attractive lady and he practically melted.

Mandy gingerly touched his head and he rubbed against her hand. "Pretty girl."

"You're not too bad yourself, Bluebeard," she said.

"He likes pretty girls," Julie told her. "Especially the ones that give him treats," she added dryly.

Mandy laughed and came back to me. "So that's your star. I can see why Julie thinks he'd sell on a shirt. She's absolutely right. Mascots sell well, especially when it's one with a personality, and that he has in spades.

"So what did you have in mind?"

CHAPTER TWENTY

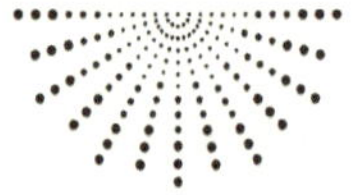

I had to hand it to Mandy. She was one heck of a saleswoman. By the time she left, she had an order for five dozen shirts, a case of mugs, and several hundred postcards—all with full-color images of Bluebeard. And a deposit check for an amount that made me swallow hard.

She promised me that everything could be in the store in a week. Plenty of time, in her words, to "sell out and reorder before the end of the summer."

I truly hoped she was right. It was a gamble that would limit the money I could put in my Buy-Out-Peter Fund. On the other hand, if it was as successful as she expected, I would have a lot more in the Peter Fund at the end of the year.

That alone made it worth the risk.

While we were finalizing the order, a man walked through the door. He didn't fit in, just as Bridget hadn't a week earlier. Didn't seem interested in the merchandise exactly, just wandered around while I talked to Mandy and Julie waited on the customers who lined up at the register.

Julie walked Mandy out to her car, chattering about Rose Ann. I made a mental note that if the experiment was successful, she deserved a bonus for her idea, and a single mom could use all the help she could get.

The man who'd been wandering around finally approached me once we were alone. "Are you Miss Martine?" he asked.

His flat, Midwestern accent had a vaguely familiar tone. Lots of people come through Southern Treasures in the summer, and I'd probably talked to someone from his region recently. But he sounded exhausted, as though he hadn't slept in several days, and his manner was hesitant, almost deferential.

"Yes, I am."

"I, uh, I just wanted to thank you. My sister mentioned you and your parrot. She said he was quite flirty, but really sweet."

I must have looked puzzled, which I certainly was. What was this stranger thanking me for? And who was his sis—

"I'm so sorry—" I began as the pieces finally fell in place.

"I'm sorry," he said at the same time. "I should have introduced—"

We both stopped in one of those awkward conversational pauses, started to speak again, and stopped again. After a few seconds I rushed ahead.

"You're Bridget's brother." It was a statement, not a question. I could see a family resemblance. "I heard you were coming down. I'm so, so sorry. I really liked your sister."

He nodded and offered his hand. "Bradford McKenna—people call me Buddy."

I shook his hand. "Gloryanna Martine. Please call me Glory. And again, I am so sorry for your loss."

"Thank you," he said. He looked around the shop as if he didn't know quite what to say next. "She said it was a fun place," he continued, more to himself than to me. "Now I see what she meant."

From his perch, Bluebeard followed Buddy's movements with bright eyes. Did he see the same resemblance I did? Or was there more to his interest? I never knew when Uncle Louis would offer an opinion on something. Or someone.

Julie came back in, setting off the bell over the front door. At one time I had considered disabling that bell during the busy season, but I'd never got around to it. Right now, as the silence became uncomfortable, the interruption was welcome.

"Bridget told me about you." Buddy spoke suddenly, as though the words had escaped from his thoughts. "She said you and your friend were the first people that didn't treat her like she was trying to kill the town."

"She had a job to do," I answered, keeping my voice carefully neutral. Caution had returned when he mentioned Bridget's introduction to Keyhole Bay—his motives for coming in to Southern Treasures might not be as innocent as he claimed.

"It was more than that."

Silence stretched again. Julie fiddled casually with a display, her back to us, but I saw her fingering her cell phone in her pocket and I understood the gesture. She had my back in case of a confrontation.

"She got that a lot," Buddy continued. "And she understood it. When the big guns from out of town arrived, people got nervous and scared. They didn't know what the outcome of the audit might be, they felt threatened, and they wanted to protect themselves. That made sense to her."

I wasn't sure how to respond, so I waited to see what he would say next.

"She always sent me postcards," he said, turning to look at the spinner.

It was still tidy from my restock; was that only this morning? It seemed like a world away.

He ran a finger along the pockets, as though looking for something. He paused over a card of a fishing boat, then shook his head and continued his examination.

"This one," he said, picking up a shot of the tiny bay that gave the town its name. "This is the one she would have sent."

He turned back to me, his eyes clouded. "She knew I liked boats. It's the one she would have chosen. "

He carefully slid the card back into the rack, squaring up the corners as though trying to impose order on a world that had suddenly turned chaotic.

He was stalling. I was sure of it. There was something on his mind, something he had wanted to say from the moment he first walked in the door, but he couldn't bring himself to do it.

"She seemed like a nice person," I said. "I only just met her, but Karen and I both liked her. We hoped we could be friends while she was here."

"She hoped that, too," he answered without turning back to face me. "She texted me on Saturday morning, from Biloxi. Said you'd recommended the trip. She was having fun, she said, and thought she might go on over to New Orleans before heading back."

His hung his head and his voice dropped to a whisper. "That was the last time I heard from her."

He finally turned to look at me. His pain was clear on his face. "Miss Martine, Gloryanna, I just came from the police station. They said they had the results of the tests they ran, but I don't believe them. They're wrong. They have to be.

"They said she died of a self-inflicted drug overdose."

CHAPTER TWENTY-ONE

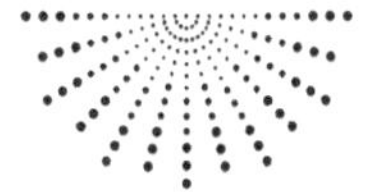

"They actually *said* it was self-inflicted?"

"Not in so many words," he admitted. "They said she overdosed. No signs of foul play. It sounded to me like there wasn't going to be much of an investigation."

"Who did you talk to?" I asked.

"A detective, I think. His name was Sherman." He fished in his pocket and came up with a business card. "Gregory Sherman. Yeah, he's a detective. But he didn't seem especially interested in doing anything about Bridget."

"They're pretty busy this time of year," I said. "Maybe he was just in a hurry and didn't express himself very well."

"I don't know. I got the impression there are a lot of people around here that would like this audit to just go away. She said she had the same impression, said you and your friend were about the only people who didn't treat her like some kind of pariah."

"But just because Bridget is"—he struggled for a moment—"*gone*, it doesn't change anything. That's part of why I'm here. Bridget and I worked in the same department. She was a senior auditor—one of the best. I'm just a staff auditor. So far." He added that last bit with a touch of defiance.

"They'll send another senior person," he continued. "But there wasn't anyone else available on a holiday weekend, so they sent me. They knew I'd come anyway."

"They let you work with your sister?" I was surprised. I thought most big companies had lots of rules about family members working together.

"Half sister," he admitted with a shrug. "Our dad married my mom when Bridget was six or seven, I think. By the time I came along, she was ten and her mom had moved her to Chicago. We didn't see that much of each other when we were growing up.

"I didn't even know she was in the department when I started there. We weren't that close, really, though we were beginning to build a relationship."

I tried to imagine how anyone could not be close to their sibling. As an only child, I had longed desperately for a little brother or sister. In my early teens I had fantasized about an older brother. Especially an older brother with lots of cute friends. Instead I had Peter. Not a winner in the sibling-substitute sweepstakes.

But my folks never had any other children, and I never knew why. I had been too polite to ask my mother, too well behaved to question her about something so personal. After she was gone, I could have asked Linda. She might know. Heck, she probably *did* know; she and my mother had been good friends. But even if she would tell me, was I ready to know the answer, to know the intimate details of my mother's life?

I'd filled the family places in my life with friends: my foster parents, Guy and Linda; and Karen and Riley, the siblings I never had. And now I had Uncle Louis. Sort of.

Buddy's sigh brought me back to the present. "I guess there was more to my coming in here than just wanting to thank you," he admitted. "I think I wanted to talk to someone who knew her. Someone who would believe me when I said she wouldn't ever do drugs."

"But if you weren't that close, how could you be sure? Really?"

"There was an incident I heard about, right after I started at the bank. A couple of the junior accounting guys were getting high on the weekends, and word got back to the bank. They were gone within days. Turns out she was their supervisor, and she made it exceedingly clear that when she said she had a zero tolerance policy, she meant it."

I was still struggling with something he had mentioned earlier.

"How could you not know she worked in your department?"

He shrugged. "She was ten years older than me. I hadn't seen her in years, and I always figured she'd gotten married and changed her name. Bridget isn't that unusual a name. I knew there was a Bridget McKenna in the department, but I assumed it was her married name. She was out of the office a lot on travel assignments, and I'd been there several months before we actually met."

The bell over the door jingled and a trio of twentysomething women in tank tops and shorts wafted in on a cloud of coconut-scented sunscreen. Julie moved quickly to intercept them and offer her help.

Buddy, seeing the new arrivals, shifted gears. "Thanks for your time, Miss Martine. I really appreciate it. I'll be in town for a few more days, at least until we get another auditor down from Minneapolis." He drew a business card from his pocket and scribbled something on the back before handing it to me. "My cell number," he explained. "If you think of anything that might help, please give me a call. I know my sister didn't take her own life, accidentally or otherwise."

I remembered the trouble his sister had had finding a place to stay. Curious, I asked, "Where are you staying?"

"The other model home," he replied. He lowered his voice to a discreet whisper. "The police haven't released the house where, uh, it happened. But the bank owns both of the houses out there, and they arranged for me to get the keys to the other one."

He thanked me again for my time, and headed out the door.

A few minutes later, Julie rang up the purchases for the three young women and locked the door behind them.

"Thanks," I said to her as she came back across the shop.

"What was that all about?" she asked. "I tried to give you some space, but he seemed pretty intense."

"Bridget McKenna's half brother. The one the bank sent down here to take over for her. Temporarily."

"But what did he want here? I mean, why did he want to talk to you? And what did he want you to help with?"

"Nothing really. A detective, somebody named Gregory Sherman—ever heard of him?—told him it was a drug overdose, and gave him the impression they were blaming Bridget. He thought . . . I don't know what he thought. He wanted someone to listen to him mostly. Someone to believe Bridget wasn't responsible for her own death."

"And do you? Believe him, I mean?"

"I do, but not because anything he said changed my mind. I already agreed with him before he walked through the door."

But now I had to wonder if anyone else shared my opinion.

I was still debating the question when Jake called about dinner plans. "I have fixings for chicken tacos," I volunteered. "And there's plenty for two. Why don't you just come over here?"

"You don't want to cook chicken."

"It's already cooked. We just have to nuke it."

"Sounds like a plan then. Need anything more?"

"I've got sweet tea," I answered. That should be no surprise. There was always a jug of sweet tea in my refrigerator. "If you want something else to drink, you should bring it."

He chuckled. "I will be there with a six-pack of microbrew as soon as I see what your friend Linda has cold."

I promised I'd leave the door open, said good night to Julie, and went to settle Bluebeard for the evening. He'd already had watermelon for a treat, and several of the shop's customers had been allowed to feed him unsalted wheat crackers and shredded-wheat biscuits. I checked his food dish, added a couple apple slices, and gave him clean water.

Jake had just stepped through the front door when Bluebeard shook off his end-of-day lethargy and began squawking loudly. Jake hastily locked the door behind him and hurried to my side, where I was trying to calm the agitated bird.

Fixing Jake with a beady-eyed stare, Bluebeard ceased his squawking. The sudden silence was even more unnerving than the shrill noise had been.

Then he spoke, clearly and in Uncle Louis's voice.

"Find the postcards, buddy boy."

CHAPTER TWENTY-TWO

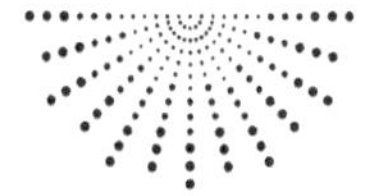

I thought I was used to Uncle Louis using Bluebeard to issue cryptic clues and veiled warnings. But this was the first time he'd tried to give orders. And as always, he said something that didn't make much sense.

"What postcards?" Jake asked.

But Bluebeard didn't reply. He ruffled his feathers as though shrugging off our puzzlement, and retreated to his cage.

"What postcards?" I repeated Jake's question, but I didn't get an answer either. Not that I really expected one.

What I did get was a string of curses, and a final announcement of "Trying to @^@$^%* sleep here!"

Bluebeard was quite clearly done talking.

Jake and I took the hint and retreated upstairs.

"Any idea what that was about?" Jake asked.

"Not a clue," I answered. "In fact, I cleaned up all the postcards this morning. Oh! And I ordered Bluebeard postcards this afternoon! Julie's friend Mandy was here from the print shop."

I launched into an explanation of Mandy's visit, talking about the designs we'd chosen and what merchandise I'd finally settled on for my first order. Soon Bluebeard's outburst was forgotten in the excitement over my new venture.

"It's still a big gamble," I said. "And I'm a little scared at the amount of money I've committed to this. But Julie and Mandy are confident it will work."

Jake watched me pull ingredients from the refrigerator. "What can I do to help?"

I pointed to the domed plastic cover over the whole roasted chicken. "How about shredding the chicken?"

Jake nodded and took a pair of forks out of the drawer. He set to work removing the meat from the bones and using the forks to separate it into shreds. The man had some definite kitchen skills.

"Have you been watching the Cooking Channel?" I asked lightly. He had to have acquired the know-how somewhere.

"I used to, back in California. I did a fair amount of cooking for a crowd, once upon a time."

"Restaurant?"

"Naw." He tossed a handful of expertly shredded chicken in a ceramic bowl, ready for the microwave. "Just friends." His tone said the subject was closed for now.

I pulled on a pair of latex gloves to protect me from the peppers, and set to work on the salsa. With a sharp knife I slit open a couple jalapeños and carefully removed the seeds and membranes. Then I removed the stems from a handful of tomatoes, quartered and peeled an onion, and washed a bunch of cilantro.

I tossed it all in the food processor with garlic, salt, and pepper, and pulsed it a few times, just until the vegetables were chopped.

Jake's California roots weren't really a secret; I'd known all along he was from the West Coast, and I'd learned several months ago that he was from California specifically.

So far I had resisted the temptation to try digging into his history online, even though I knew with Karen's help I could probably find out anything I wanted to know. It was up to Jake to decide what he was willing to share, and I told myself I had to trust him just as I wanted him to trust me.

One thing I did know was how much he loved avocados. I started peeling and mashing the bright green flesh for guacamole and was rewarded with a broad smile.

"You better eat this," I joked. "Because this is one leftover Bluebeard can't have. Avocados are right up there with coffee on the bad list."

"I'll make that sacrifice," he said. "I wouldn't want him to get sick, after all."

We finished the dinner prep, heated the chicken in the microwave, and sat down at the table with our plates and beers.

"So how was your day?" Jake asked. "You said you had a story when you came back this morning. Oh, thanks for the change run, by the way. Good thing, too. I got two more big bills this afternoon."

I had to stop and think. This morning seemed a long time ago. "Well," I said, trying to reconstruct the day, "it started way too early."

I told him about the delays at the bank, and the grocery store, and the visit to Sly in between.

"I agree with him," Jake said, his voice somber. "That's an awful thing to say about anyone. And in your case, it's absolutely ridiculous."

"Thank you. But how do you know about anybody?" I asked. "How can you tell? I mean, I still don't want to believe that Bridget had anything to do with drugs, but how else do you explain what happened?"

He shook his head. "Who knows? Maybe she got involved with something over in Biloxi."

"Her brother did say she texted him from there," I said, thinking out loud.

"Her brother? When did you talk to her brother?"

"Half brother," I corrected. "He came into the store just before closing."

I repeated the story Bridget's brother had told me, emphasizing the part about the lab results. "They told him she died of an overdose, and there was no sign of foul play. What else could it be?" I still didn't want to think it was true, but I was having trouble coming up with any other explanation.

"I don't know, Glory."

I helped myself to another tortilla and carefully assembled a second taco. "I need to change the subject," I said. "This is just too depressing."

Jake nodded. But try as we might, every conversation seemed to circle back around and trip over the one topic we were trying to avoid, and we lapsed into silence.

"How's the website going?" Jake asked.

"Slowly. I'm making progress, but it takes time I usually don't have in the summer."

"For sure," Jake answered. "Did that last book help?"

In answer I got up and went to get my laptop. Setting it on the table between us, I navigated to the Southern Treasures page and showed him the latest additions.

"You should put up an announcement about the new T-shirts," he suggested.

"Good idea." I opened my to-do file and made a note.

As I was closing the file, my phone rang. Distracted, I didn't check the caller ID before I answered.

I wished I had.

"Glory?"

My cousin Peter's drawl leaned dangerously close to a whine, and I scowled at the phone.

"Yes, Peter."

Jake rolled his eyes. He knew how annoying Peter could be, how much I resented his intrusions into the running of Southern Treasures, and how crazy his suggestions were. Just because he had a lot of schooling didn't mean he understood a thing about running a retail business, and his visit on Sunday had just reinforced that. I guess he was a good engineer—he held a high-level job doing something that I didn't understand—but a master's degree in engineering had nothing to do with a souvenir shop.

"Glory, I was thinking."

That was a bad sign. It meant he was about to suggest some dang fool scheme again. It also meant I had to count to ten before I could speak, or risk using words I'd learned from Bluebeard.

"What, Peter?"

"Do you think we ought to consider branching out? Maybe finding another location?"

I held my tongue between my teeth for several seconds as I did a quick ten count, then took a deep breath.

"I don't think we're in a position to do that, Peter."

"But I've been hearing that the Gulf Coast is making an economic recovery, that tourists are back and spending like they used to, before Katrina and the oil spill. We should position ourselves to take advantage of that."

I tried to imagine where he was getting his information. I got to six before I blurted out, "Where did you hear that?"

"One of the guys at work. He showed me an article in U.S. News that said tourism spending is growing every year, and I keep hearing how the hotels down there are filling up every weekend. You told me the same thing when I was there on Sunday." His voice dropped into a lower register, as though he was trying to sound more authoritative. "The indicators are for improved cash flow in the second half of this year."

What? That sentence didn't even make sense.

"What indicators? Where did that information come from? Who's making these predictions?"

"Now, Glory," he said, his voice dripping with condescension. "It's all very complex economics. Very complex. I don't expect you to be able to—"

This time I didn't even try to count.

"Peter, I don't know who you are listening to, but for right now, you listen to this.

"I am on the ground here, and I see *exactly* how the economics are working in my town. I know how much money is being spent, where, and how. I take care of the sales and the expenses for Southern Treasures, and I send you your share of the profits every month. Take a look at those checks, and you tell me if there's enough there to consider opening another store."

I drew a ragged breath, fighting to control the adrenaline rush brought on by anger. "Have you looked, really looked, at those checks, Peter? Or do you just hand them to your wife to put in the bank?"

"Now, Glory—"

"Don't." The word came out quietly. "If you want to open another store, if you want to take on that expense and that risk, you can. Don't let me stop you. But don't expect to use the Southern Treasures name, and don't expect me to assume any responsibility for it. I have more than enough on my plate here, and like I told you Sunday, this is not the time to consider expansion."

I took another gulp of air, and tried to calm down. "Peter, you're my family, and I don't mean to yell at you. But you have to trust me on this. I am here twenty-four/seven, and I know what is best for Southern Treasures. Believe me when I say I want the shop to succeed; it's how I pay my bills. But you need to give me credit for knowing my business, just like I give you credit for knowing yours."

Okay, that last part was only kind of true. Right now I didn't give him credit for knowing a blasted thing.

Peter stammered a sort-of apology, promising to trust my judgment, and hung up.

I couldn't look at Jake, ashamed of my outburst. I had overreacted to Peter's suggestion and taken my frustration out on him.

It wasn't his fault that Bridget died, or that I was having trouble accepting the fact.

CHAPTER TWENTY-THREE

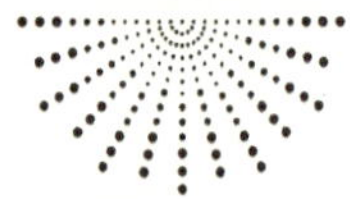

I had to do something. Shouting at Peter was a clue I was far too stressed out, and my usual treatment for stress was activity.

I patted my pocket, checking for keys. "Want to go for a ride?" I asked Jake. "I promise not to drive like a crazy woman. Honest."

He shoved the last of the leftovers in the refrigerator, a task he'd started while I was on the phone. "Where we going?"

It was all the answer I needed.

"I want you to meet Bridget's brother." It was only part of the reason. I also wanted to take a look at the house where I'd been just a week ago.

The house where Bridget died.

We were already in the traffic of the main drag when I realized I hadn't called Bradford McKenna to tell him we were coming. I dug in my pocket for his card and handed it to Jake, along with my phone. "Can you dial this for me?"

I spoke briefly with Bridget's brother, and he said he'd be glad to have some company. Who wouldn't, stuck out there in an empty subdivision with no one else around? I wasn't exactly a city girl—Keyhole Bay wasn't exactly a city, just a small town—but just being out there for a couple hours had given me the heebie-jeebies. And that was when Bridget was still alive.

On the drive out to Bayvue, I distracted myself from thoughts of Bridget by filling Jake in on Peter's latest scheme. "I can barely keep up with one store. How am I supposed to take on a second one?"

"He has no idea how much work is involved," Jake agreed. "And you really would be better off to buy him out." He stopped, as though deep in thought. "Have you ever considered," he continued, "getting a different partner? One that actually understands what you're doing?"

"Sure. And I also wanted a pet unicorn. I think I'm just as likely to find one of those. I mean, who do you trust? Where do you even look?"

I turned off the highway onto the county road.

"Right here," Jake said quietly. "I might be looking for another investment, and Southern Treasures has a lot going for it. Including a really good manager."

The offer, and the compliment, stunned me. Jake wanted to invest in Southern Treasures? He was willing to help me buy out Peter?

"You, uh, well, um. It's a lot of money," I stammered. "Not that I mean to say you can't do it. I have no idea what your situation is, and, well, it's none of my business how much money you have and what you do with it."

I was handling this badly, and I couldn't seem to find a way out of the corner I'd put myself in.

I turned off the county road, driving between the brick gateposts, lonely sentinels with nothing to guard but bare land scraped clear of any sign of life.

I pulled up in front of the model home where a single light shone in the kitchen window. The house next door where Bridget had stayed loomed in the dark, a menacing presence in a deserted landscape.

It was like the setting for a slasher movie. I just hoped there wasn't a guy with a hockey mask lurking somewhere.

Before I got out of the truck, I turned to Jake. "Thank you for the vote of confidence. I appreciate it. Truly. But I don't want you taking any chances on account of me."

"Like I said, I may be looking for another investment." He held up his hand and ticked off his points on his fingers as he continued. "The bookstore is doing okay, I've discovered I like what I'm doing, I've got some money, and I think Southern Treasures is a good bet. So can we talk about me helping you buy out Peter?"

I nodded, then realized he might not be able to see the gesture clearly in the darkened truck cab. "We can talk," I said. "No promises. But we'll talk."

He shook my hand, a move that felt somehow more trusting and intimate at that point than a kiss. We had crossed some kind of invisible line, as though much more than a simple financial conversation was promised by our decision.

No porch light illuminated the front door. I leaned across, opened the glove box, and took out a sturdy flashlight. I did a lot of treasure hunting in old barns and storage sheds without enough light to see what I was buying. I needed—and always had on hand—a good flashlight.

The bright beam lighted our way across the hard-packed dirt of the front yard.

The door opened, faint light spilling out. "Miss Martine, Glory, it's good to see you." Bradford invited us in.

"I haven't had time to make the place habitable," he said, leading us into the kitchen. A coffeemaker and toaster that matched the cheap ones I'd seen at Bridget's rested on an identical granite counter. The layout was different, but the atmosphere was the same: an open floor plan with lots of space, high-end appliances and cabinetry, everything finished in stone and natural wood.

That is, everything that was visible. Papers were scattered across most of the flat surfaces, and two laptops sat open on the far end of the counter.

I introduced the two men and they shook hands.

"Buddy to my friends," Bridget's brother reminded us. "So what can I do for you?" He looked at me, curiosity clear in his expression.

I hesitated. Why had I decided to come out here? What had I hoped to accomplish with this sudden excursion?

When in doubt, stick as close to the truth as possible.

"I don't really know," I admitted in what I hoped was a lighter tone than I felt. "It just felt like there was more you wanted to tell me this afternoon, and I cut you off."

"Not at all," he said. He bustled around, starting a pot of coffee, as though anxious for something to do. "Not at all," he repeated. "You had work to do. Actually I owe you an apology for the interruption."

"Oh no! It was sweet of you to even think of coming to thank me at a time like this. You have so many more important things on your mind right now."

Buddy's visit to Southern Treasures hadn't bothered me, but I had been a little freaked out by his intensity. Under the circumstances, though, I could understand. Memaw would have been proud of my graciousness. My mother probably wouldn't have believed me capable of it, but her early training had taken hold far deeper than she ever knew. I liked to think I had outgrown the surly teenager who refused to write thank-you notes.

"But yes, there was something more," Buddy admitted. "Bridget said she thought you might be a good source of background information."

"Don't sugarcoat it," I said. "You mean she thought I knew the local gossip."

He winced at the blunt description, but a tiny twinkle lit his eyes. "You sound like her," he said. "She was direct, said what she thought. You do that, too."

I blushed. "Sorry, I shouldn't have said that. It wasn't very nice of me."

"Actually, it's refreshing. It reminds me of Bridget. In a good way." His voice broke but he quickly regained control.

The coffeepot hissed, signaling the end of the brewing cycle. Without asking, Jake took three foam cups out of a package on the counter, filled them with steaming liquid, and handed one to each of us.

"Thanks," I said, touching his hand.

Buddy nodded his thanks, too, and continued. "Bridget did a lot of audits, and she specialized in small-town, family-owned institutions. A lot of times the personal background of the people involved told her more than the paperwork."

He sipped his coffee and winced at the near scalding temperature. "This wasn't her first rodeo, Miss—Glory. She had a regular routine when it came to her investigations. She did her formal job, and did it well. But she also tried to make friends with someone she could count on for reliable information about the community.

"She generally looked for a woman without a close connection to the bank. An independent. A woman, in her words, who was too smart for her own good. I'm afraid," Buddy said, "that three marriages left her with a pretty low opinion of men."

He glanced from me to Jake and back again as though assessing our relationship. I wondered what he concluded, since I wasn't sure myself.

"I'm not sure how to take that," I said slowly.

"I assure you, Glory, it's a compliment. Bridget said understanding the community was good for business, and her track record speaks for itself. But she never thought she knew everything. She wanted to be sure she got it right. Having someone she could trust helped."

He shrugged. "I'm probably putting it badly. And for that I apologize. But the bottom line was that she liked you and thought you were smart. That's a pretty big plus in my book."

CHAPTER TWENTY-FOUR

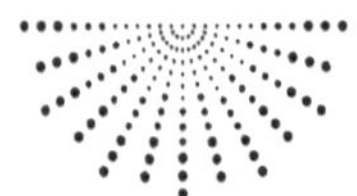

I sipped my coffee and tried to swallow past the lump in my throat. Bridget's good opinion of me shouldn't really matter. I had barely known her. Still, I was touched by her brother's words.

And more determined than ever to find out what really happened to her.

"What do we know?" I asked him. "Was she on some medication she could have mixed up, or taken wrong?"

Buddy reached for a large sealed envelope off one of the piles on the island counter. "I don't think so," he said. "The bank pulled some strings and got a copy of her medical records before I flew down here, in case the faxed copies didn't get to the medical examiner." He held up the envelope, wide tape with large red letters reading CONFIDENTIAL stretched across both sides. "But the doctor said he had everything he needed, and I honestly forgot I had these until I was going through the records tonight. I just don't know if I can make sense of them."

Jake reached for the envelope, holding it for a moment before handing it back.

"She's dead," I said. "It can't hurt for us to look at these now, if you agree?"

Buddy put the envelope back on the counter and slowly pushed it toward me. "I have no idea what's in there, and I'm not sure I want to know. But if there's something in there that could help..." His voice trailed off, but his meaning was clear.

I picked up the envelope, carefully removed the tape, broke the seal and pulled out the papers inside.

I skimmed the pages, grateful for modern technology. Instead of a cramped illegible doctor's scrawl, there were neat lines of computer printing detailing the notes from each medical interaction. There weren't very many.

Jake relented and moved to look over my shoulder. As I turned the pages, I could feel him leaning closer, his interest engaged in spite of himself.

As we turned the final page, he stepped back. "Nothing," he said with authority.

I shot him a questioning look, but I had to admit I agreed with him. "I didn't see anything either."

"So it wasn't an accident with a prescription," Buddy said. "Not that I expected it to be.

"And there's no indication in her records of any recreational drug use? Not that people don't lie about that," he added hastily. "But they usually don't lie to their doctor."

"No. Which means," I said, "she got something accidentally, maybe in her food or something."

"That isn't likely either," Buddy said. "The doctor told me it was an injection. It hit her fast, and she fell and banged her head."

"There's nothing accidental about an injection," Jake said. "You don't trip and fall on a needle."

"Where . . ." I stopped and swallowed hard, then tried again. "Where did they find her?"

"She was in the kitchen. She'd hit her head on the edge of the island. The detective told me the kitchen was a mess, but they could recommend someone to do the cleanup. Said they should be able to release the scene of the accident over the weekend and I could get started."

"I want to go look."

"Glory," Jake said warningly. "It's dark out, and there aren't any streetlights around, in case you hadn't noticed."

"I know. But I have a good flashlight, and there's another one still in the truck. I want to see where they found her."

I couldn't explain exactly why; I just knew I had to look. And none of Jake's arguments were going to change my mind.

"The house is locked," Buddy warned. "And there are seals on all the doors and windows."

"I won't go inside," I promised. "There are big windows in the back, just like this place. I won't touch anything, and I won't open any of the doors or windows." I remembered Memaw's saying I'd heard a few days ago. "I will look with my eyes," I said, "and not with my hands."

"If you're going, I'm going," Buddy said. "Let's go get that other flashlight."

Jake wasn't happy with my decision, but he insisted on coming with me. "I don't want you out there wandering around alone," he said as the three of us went out to the truck for my second flashlight. I resisted the temptation to remind him that Buddy had already said he was coming with me.

We worked our way around the side of the house, using the twin beams of the two flashlights to illuminate the occasional clumps of spindly grass and the sticker bushes that brushed against our legs.

In the dark, the flashlight beams sent shadows dancing across the barren yard. The light caught in the glass of the back doors and reflected into the inky black of the night.

I swept the beam across the yard and into the emptiness beyond, the light fading by the time it reached the tree line at the edge of the development. I had flashlights designed for seeing into tight corners of crowded buildings, not illuminating a wide landscape or the distant trees.

I caught the flash of eyes in the distance. There were lots of nocturnal animals in the panhandle. It could be a fox, or a possum, a coyote, or a raccoon. But whatever it was, it hurried away from the light.

We moved carefully, trying to avoid the potholes and divots left by the construction equipment. At the back of the house, an excavation marked the position of a planned patio, or perhaps a screened porch—what the developer would call a Florida room.

A snort of disgust escaped my lips before I was able to stop it.

"Glory?" Jake's voice was loud in the surrounding silence. He lowered it to a whisper and continued, "Are you okay?"

I played the flashlight beam around the hole in the ground. "Looks like they were planning to add another slab," I said, illuminating the initial construction of the forms for the concrete. "Probably screen it in and call it a Florida room. Like that makes it so much better than a screened porch, and they can charge three prices for it."

"I've never heard that expression before," Buddy said. "What does it mean?"

"It just means charging a lot," I answered. "Paying three times what something is worth."

Our conversation felt like nervous chatter designed to take our minds off what we were doing.

We stepped over the concrete forms and into the shallow hole where the patio was supposed to go. At least this small portion of the yard was reasonably level, as opposed to the lumps and holes we'd been walking through.

Ahead of us, yellow tape printed with the words CRIME SCENE looped across the glass doors and through the handles. Wide tape covered the gaps where the doors met the frames, and a large notice on the door informed us that we were not to enter the building or disturb the seal.

I had no intention of doing either one.

CHAPTER TWENTY-FIVE

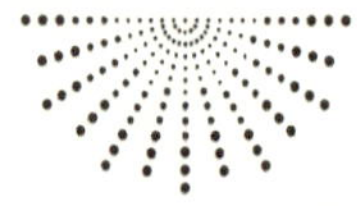

All I wanted to do was take a look.

I put my face to the glass next to the warning notice. I placed the flashlight lens close to the door, and slowly swung the beam over the kitchen.

The coffeemaker and toaster stood in the same place on the counter, and dishes were stacked neatly on the far side of the sink. Nothing appeared to be out of place.

I don't know what I expected. Chaos, maybe. Dishes and silverware strewn around the kitchen, the toaster ripped from the outlet and smashed on the floor. A shattered coffeepot.

Something.

Some sign that this was anything other than what the police had concluded. Some piece or part that I could point to and say, "There's your evidence."

Buddy lingered at the edge of the excavation, obviously not wanting to get any closer to the spot where his sister had died.

Jake moved to the far side of the back wall, where he could use his flashlight to illuminate things from a different angle. I watched him slowly pass the beam over the same counters and cupboards I had just covered, but from several feet to the side.

I still didn't see what I wanted.

As he passed the light over the butcher block on the island, I noticed a dark stain on one corner of the counter. With a sickening lurch, my stomach recognized what my brain had registered: this was the place where Bridget had hit her head.

I recoiled, stepping back from the window and dropping my flashlight.

I remembered what Buddy had said about getting cleaners in after the police released the scene. That corner of the counter was only part of what was in that house, and I didn't want to see any more.

I battled with my stomach as I crawled after my flashlight. The last thing I wanted to do right now was lose my dinner all over the backyard.

I picked up the flashlight and aimed it toward the house next door, where the faint light still shone in the kitchen window.

"Let's go," I said. My voice sounded funny, pinched and tight, but at least I had regained control. For the moment.

I walked slowly across the shallow hole to where Buddy waited. Jake followed a couple steps behind me.

No one spoke as we retraced our steps to the front of the house and across the yards to Buddy's front door.

We shuffled into the house and went directly to the kitchen. We retrieved our coffee cups and refreshed them from the pot. I shouldn't drink coffee this late, but something told me I wouldn't be sleeping much tonight anyway.

Buddy moved aimlessly around the room, fiddling with the papers. He picked up a stack of printouts, then set them back down on another stack without so much as a glance.

"What did Bridget say she wanted from me?" I asked Buddy, trying to get his focus back on our previous conversation. "You said she wanted to be sure she really understood the local community. What did she want to know?"

He moved another stack of papers, but didn't respond. I silently repeated every word I'd learned from Bluebeard, angry with myself for letting him go over there with us. I'd been so carried away with my own concerns I hadn't thought about how it might make Buddy feel.

"I'm sorry, Buddy," I said, taking his arm and forcing him to stop and look at me. "I should never have suggested we go over there. You didn't need to see any of that."

He shook his head, gazing out the dark windows with a faraway look. "I didn't really see anything." He brushed my hand away. "I'm sad that she's gone, and I really liked her, as much as I knew her. But she was just a friend, barely more than an acquaintance so far. And now she'll never be anything more than that." He stared into the dark, as though the answers he needed were hidden somewhere in the shadows. "That's the real loss," he said softly. "That I don't miss her more. Everyone deserves to be mourned."

He sighed deeply and squared his shoulders, bringing himself back from whatever dark place he had been.

He gestured to me and Jake to join him at the island counter, where he laid out several stacks of papers. "If you can help me through this," he said, his voice firmer than I'd ever heard it, "maybe we can figure out what she found. *I* know she didn't overdose, so what did *she* know that got her in trouble?"

"Aren't those records confidential?" Jake asked. "Maybe we shouldn't be looking at them."

"They are," Buddy conceded. "At least the customers' financial records are. But so were the medical records. A lot of this is Bridget's own assessments. Those are the bank's property, and I think I can trust the two of you to be discreet."

Discreet didn't begin to describe Jake Robinson. The man was a sphinx when it came to keeping secrets. He certainly kept plenty from me.

"Sounds like a good plan," I said.

Buddy flipped through the pages of notes. He began sorting them into several stacks. He moved with efficiency, deciding at a glance which pile a particular piece belonged in and putting it there without hesitation.

Watching him work, he hardly seemed like the same tentative and confused man who had come through my door that morning. He was clearly in his element, examining the information in front of him, making judgments and acting on them. He really was a lot like the sister he barely knew.

It took him only a minute to collect the pages he wanted. Shoving the rest of the stacks to the far side of the counter, he spread the pages in front of us.

"She's listed the primary players here." He indicated a short list of names, most of them Andersons. "This sheet has the major investors in Bayvue, and this one"—he pointed at the longest list—"is a list of Back Bay employees."

Bridget had printed each name in block letters, leaving several blank lines beneath each one. Some of them had additional information written beneath them in cramped but precise script. Others had only a printed word or two, and several were blank.

"Where do you want to start?" I asked.

Buddy scanned the lists. "Let's wait on the employees," he decided. "I'll have access to personnel files and employment records to fill them in." He pushed the employee list away and looked at the remaining two.

"Wait a minute." Jake pulled the employee list back from where Buddy had put it and placed it next to the investors list. Several of the names were on both lists.

"That doesn't seem right," Jake said. "Should the employees of the bank be investing in a development they were financing?"

"It's a small town," I said, coming to the defense of my friends whose names showed up on both lists. "You get these kinds of overlaps all the time."

"It still seems kind of sketchy to me," Jake said. "If they're involved in lending money to the development, they shouldn't be investors, too."

"Jake, these people are employees. Look." I pointed to Barbara's name. "She's a teller. She makes change, takes deposits, and cashes checks. She isn't involved in any loans."

"No," Buddy said slowly, pointing to a name on the list. "But he is."

It was Francis Simon, the recently fired manager of the bank. And right below his name on the investor list was Melanie Randall, the chief loan officer.

"And so is she," Jake said, pointing to her name. "She set up my line of credit when I opened Beach Books. She's definitely involved in making loans."

Buddy made a star next to the employee names on the investor list. There were several. "I'm sure Bridget already noticed the duplication," he said. "I'll have to find her notes on that." He looked up at Jake. "Good catch, though. A lot will depend on how, and how much, these people invested. We're not going to get too excited over a teller putting a few hundred dollars from her savings account into a multimillion-dollar construction project."

He looked back at the two lists, lying side by side on the counter. "But if there's someone with a sizable investment, or who went into unreasonable debt, that's somebody we'll look at a lot closer."

He pushed the employee list back across the counter, starting a new pile. He took a blank sheet of paper, wrote a giant "1" on it, and put it on top.

"How about the Board of Directors?" Buddy asked, pulling that sheet over where we could all see it. "She started making notes on them. Maybe you can tell me if her impressions are correct."

The names on the list were familiar. William and Felicia Anderson. His little sister, Pearl. Their parents, Willa and Richard. There were a couple other names that weren't familiar, and Bridget had noted they were partners of a law firm in Pensacola. But five of the seven names were Andersons. A big enough majority to do as they pleased, with other people's money.

CHAPTER TWENTY-SIX

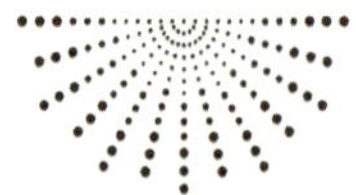

Outside the glass wall of the kitchen, a dog barked, startling all of us.

I jostled my coffee cup and barely managed to grab it and prevent it from spilling all over the papers on the counter. I carried the foam cup to the sink and carefully poured the cold contents down the drain. I clearly didn't need any more caffeine.

The dog continued barking. The sound was nearby, seeming to come from the darkened backyard.

Jake grabbed a flashlight and opened the French doors, playing the light across the bare dirt. His light caught the dog, a dark hound, standing next to a man sitting in the dirt.

The man on the ground shielded his eyes as the beam of light caught his face. He looked familiar as I moved closer to Jake, though I couldn't see him clearly.

"Cut it out," he whined. His words slurred, and I realized he was undoubtedly drunk.

I also recognized him as someone we had just been talking about: Andrew Marshall, the high-flying developer of Bayvue Estates. It looked like he'd been brought back down to Earth, and he'd made a hard landing.

"Andy?"

"Who's asking?"

I suppose the question was meant to be challenging, but his drunken slur reduced it to a pathetic whine.

"It's Glory, Andy. Glory Martine."

"Little Glory? Is that really you? What're you doin' all the way out here?"

Andy was a few years older than me, closer to Linda's age than mine. I suppose he did still think of me as a little girl, though I had passed that stage a long time ago.

"It's me," I answered. "Do you need a hand?"

"Naw." He waved his hand in front of his face. "I can manage. Just get that light out of my eyes."

Jake moved the beam aside, lighting up the dirt a few feet in front of Andy and his dog. In the shadow left behind, I saw Andy struggle to his feet and stagger toward the house, his hound dog sticking by his side.

Jake tensed, and I put my hand on his arm.

Andy stumbled over the concrete forms that defined the patio space, but he managed to stay upright. Judging by the miasma of unwashed clothes and spilled liquor that floated ahead of him, it was nothing short of a miracle.

He reached the back door, but didn't seem capable of navigating the tall step up out of the excavation into the kitchen.

I struggled to reconcile the successful developer I knew with the man standing in front of me, swaying like he was on the deck of a ship. Andy Marshall took chances, but most of them paid off handsomely. He dressed well, visited his personal barber for a shave every day, indulged in the best food and drink, and collected rich man's toys. The man I faced was an emaciated drunk who hadn't had a shower or a shave in weeks.

I stepped down next to him. Jake and Buddy followed. I silently gave thanks for the evening breeze that allowed me to move slightly upwind of Andy. I tried not to think about what he would have smelled like in the confines of the kitchen. There wasn't a floor plan open enough to make it bearable.

Behind me I heard Buddy gasp as the stench hit him. He quickly closed the door behind him, trying not to let the stink invade the house.

"Andy, what are *you* doing out here, just you and Bear?" I asked.

"Just takin' a little stroll after dinner," he answered, as though that explained everything. He'd lost the genteel accent and precise diction he used with his customers, reverting to the cracker drawl of his childhood.

"But your house is way the other side of town." True, that meant it was only a few minutes' drive from where we stood, but I prayed he hadn't been driving in his condition.

"Not no more."

"Sure it is. You and Jen have a gorgeous house. I was just there."

That was an exaggeration. I'd been there six months earlier, for about five minutes. I'd let Felipe and Ernie talk me into contributing to some charity fund-raiser—I think it was for the "clean and sober" grad night—and we'd been invited to a cocktail party hosted by Jen Anderson, the committee chair.

One ginger ale and I'd been out the door. It was a beautiful house all right, but it wasn't my kind of party. I'd promised myself the next time I'd just send a check.

"Oh, Jen and the girls are still there. She swears she's gonna keep that house, though I don't see how. The bank's gonna take it, just like they took everything else I own."

It obviously wasn't the time to introduce Buddy. I glanced over and caught his eye, nodding slightly toward the darkened corner of the house. He caught my hint and faded back into the shadows, out of sight.

I reached for Jake's arm and pulled him a little closer to me, trying to keep Andy focused on the two of us.

"Andy, have you met Jake Robinson? He bought Beach Books a couple years ago." I held my breath and leaned in a little. "He's from California, but he's okay."

I laughed and leaned back toward Jake, sucking in a breath of marginally cleaner air.

"Glad to meet ya," Andy said, sticking out a grimy hand.

Jake didn't flinch. He took Andy's hand. "Same here," he said. "Any friend of Glory's, and all that."

Andy cocked his head and looked at me. "She is a purty little thing, isn't she? Always was."

"Andy, if Jen's still in the house, why are you out here? It's a long way from home."

"Not my home anymore," he whined. "Threw me out. Called me everything but a gentleman and said to get out and stay out."

He turned in an unsteady circle, his gaze taking in the entire development, hidden in the dark beyond the faint light spilling from the house. "This place took everything from me, Glory. Took my job, took my family, took every last cent I had in the world.

"All I got left's the trailer. Hauled it out in the woods so the bank won't find it." His voice grew bitter and angry. "They'd take it, too, if they could find it, the bastards."

His voice grew louder as he continued to rant about how the bank had taken everything. He cursed the Andersons and Francis Simon. He called Melanie Randall a couple names that even Bluebeard didn't use.

Jake put his arm around me and whispered in my ear, "I'll take care of this."

I shook my head. "Let it go. He's always been a bit of a hothead, but it never lasts long."

I hoped I was right.

Andy's tirade petered out into mutters and self-pity within a few minutes. Tears began to run down his face as he launched into a litany of excuses.

As hard as it was to watch him unravel, I could only imagine the pain he must feel.

"Can I give you a lift somewhere?" I asked as Andy sank into silence, an occasional sniffle the only sound he made.

He shook his head. "Me 'n' Bear, we're good. We got the trailer out there, out where nobody will find us. We'll be just fine." His eyes glowed with anger for an instant. "We know how to take care of things."

The anger faded, and Andy gave a deep sigh. "C'mon, Bear," he said. The hound, who had waited patiently through his master's ranting, stood up and nudged Andy's hand.

The two of them turned their backs on us and faded into the dark.

"Nice seeing you, Glory," he called as he walked away. "You take care now, y'hear?"

CHAPTER TWENTY-SEVEN

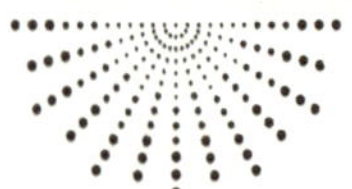

Buddy stayed in the shadows as we listened to Andy and Bear make their way to the edge of the woods. Bear barked again, a lonely, mournful sound, in the distance.

Jake pointed his flashlight in the direction they'd gone, but the light faded before it reached the tree line, and I couldn't see anyone.

I heard the door open and turned around. Buddy stood with the knob in one hand, waving us back inside.

Back in the kitchen with the lights on, I suddenly felt very exposed. The few low-watt bulbs hadn't seemed very bright before we went outside. But now I realized it was the only light around, and it felt like we were a target, shining in the dark.

Clearly, Buddy and Jake had the same feeling. Buddy shut down the laptops and closed them. He stacked the two computers with several bunches of paper, and put them next to the doorway.

"Maybe I'll work in the study. There are blinds on those windows." He sounded sheepish, as though embarrassed by his decision to hide behind the covered windows, but I didn't blame him. I wouldn't want to be on display either.

We went back to the lists on the counter, but we had all been unnerved by the encounter with Andy Marshall. We tried to concentrate on the names in front of us, but it was no use.

"I tell you what," I said to Buddy. "I have to work tomorrow; we both do." I gestured at Jake. "I wish I could help more, but I am going to have to get home."

"No problem," Buddy said. "I need to spend some time going over Bridget's notes. Maybe I can come up with some specific questions, things I need to verify."

He walked us to the door, apologizing all the while for taking up our evening with his problems, as though he'd forgotten it was us who had come to see him.

We were standing in the entry when his phone rang. He pulled it off his belt and looked at the display.

"I had no idea it was this late," he said. "I better get this. Time to say good night to the kids." He chuckled self-consciously. "My wife lets them call me before bed every night if I'm not home. Kind of a little family ritual."

We waved our good-byes and let ourselves out as he answered the phone. We heard him greet his wife, and promise her that everything was just fine.

As I dug out my keys and followed the beam of Jake's flashlight toward the truck, I sincerely hoped it was true.

We stowed the flashlights back in the glove box. "You might want to change those batteries," Jake said, closing the door. "It was getting kind of weak near the end there."

"I will. And thank you for everything you did tonight."

"I didn't do much."

"No, you did." I pulled away from the model homes, one dark, the other with a faint light coming from the back of the house. "You put up with my lousy mood, cleaned up my kitchen, and came with me out here.

"And you didn't overreact when Andy got a little crazy," I added. "A lot of people would have."

I couldn't see Jake's expression in the dark. "That was easy," he said. "You've known the people around here your whole life. You said to trust him, that he'd run down, and you were right."

I pulled onto the empty county road, our headlights the only bright spots visible. "I hope he doesn't come back," I said. "He seemed pretty angry at the bank. What if he decided to do something stupid?"

"Do you really think he would?" Jake asked.

I thought about it for a minute as we neared the highway. I stopped at the intersection, waiting for traffic to clear so I could turn.

"I wouldn't think so," I answered. "But I didn't think Bridget would take drugs. So what do I know?"

The thought that I had been wrong about Bridget bothered me. But what other explanation was there? Jake was right. She didn't accidentally fall on a hypodermic full of drugs.

What bothered me even more were all the unanswered questions.

"I wish we knew more about the medical examiner's report, like what drug actually killed her. And if she was using, were there other needle marks? And if she wasn't, then how else would they get in her system? You don't just sit there and let somebody shoot you full of something that kills you."

"I agree," Jake said.

"Then how?" I persisted. "Either she did it herself, or someone did it to her. And if someone tried to inject her and she didn't want them to, she would have fought with them."

"And the police said no signs of foul play, right?"

"Right," I said. "So we're right back where we started."

I turned off the highway and made my way along the back streets to the lot where Jake had parked his car. It was the least I could do after dragging him out to Bayvue.

"Will you be okay?" he asked before climbing out of the truck.

I assured him I would, and kissed him good night. I bit my lip as he closed the door, fighting the impulse to invite him back to my place.

I drove home thinking about Jake, and about Bridget. Buddy said she'd been married three times, but he didn't mention children. And he was the person taking care of everything—a half brother she barely knew. I remembered thinking she seemed lonely, and I wondered if there had been anyone else in her life, anyone she was close to.

I was afraid I already knew the answer.

There wasn't.

I unlocked the back door and reset the alarm. Through the doorway I could see the streetlights casting soft shadows in the front of the store, but I didn't see the night-lights I usually left burning.

I'd better go check them.

But when I stepped into the front, I discovered that the problem wasn't just the night-lights.

Bluebeard had gone on one of his rampages. Either that or I'd been vandalized.

No broken windows. No tripped alarms. The register stood open and empty, just as I'd left it.

Nope. This was all on Bluebeard.

I turned on the overhead lights to examine the shop and assess the damage. Piles of T-shirts littered the floor, postcards spilled from the spinner, and plastic water bottles had fallen from the shelves and rolled away into all the nooks and crannies.

As the lights revealed the extent of the mess and the work I had ahead of me, Bluebeard stuck his head out of his cage.

"Find the postcards," he said.

He glared up at the overhead fixtures, with all the fluorescent tubes burning brightly. "#%&$%#$^ lights! Trying to $#%#&# sleep!"

He stomped back into his cage and refused to come out or to say anything more. He didn't respond when I asked him about the postcards, and he even ignored the offer of a banana. He was done talking for the night, and there was nothing I could do to change that.

I started picking up the shirts, inspecting them for dust or tears, but Julie had swept the floors at the end of the day and all the shirts were clean and intact. I had to marvel at how Bluebeard had managed to completely destroy the display, strew merchandise around the shop, and create havoc—all without actually damaging any of the inventory.

I told myself it was part of his charm, and set to work cleaning up the mess he'd made.

I piled shirts on the front counter to be folded and tracked down the water bottles. As I placed them back on the shelves, I straightened the rows. It reminded me of helping Guy stock shelves at the Grog Shop, and made me smile. I'd been training to take over Southern Treasures since I was a kid.

I gathered up the postcards and put them in a box. They would have to be sorted, *again*, and put back in the proper slots on the spinner rack. That much, at least, could wait until morning.

I sorted the shirts by design, turning the big pile into several smaller ones. It was tedious work, and my mind wandered as I set about refolding each shirt and putting the sizes in order.

I thought about Buddy, talking to his kids every night before bed. I'd heard his warm, happy tone when he answered his wife's call. He had people in his life, people who would know if something was wrong. People who would notice and care.

I remembered what he had said about Bridget, that the saddest part was that he didn't miss her more. That everyone deserved to be mourned.

Was that why I'd thought about inviting Jake back here?

I pushed the thought aside. The answer was simpler than that, if I was honest about it. Jake was gorgeous and smart, a rare combination in my experience. Of course I was attracted to him. Any woman with two eyes and a brain would be.

Simple.

I finished folding shirts and carried the tidy stacks to the shelves, filling in the bare spaces where Bluebeard had emptied the display.

As I reached to slide a stack of back-stock shirts into the bottom shelf, something caught my eye.

I reached into the space between the stacks and felt around. My fingers closed around a piece of stiff paper, and I pulled it out into the light, where I could examine it.

The address side of the postcard had just a city and state, like somebody had started to write the address and had been distracted. Edina, MN, and the message side had only part of one word, as though the writer had been interrupted before she could finish. I had no idea what she meant to write.

The handwriting, though, was perfectly clear.

And it matched Bridget McKenna's precise block printing on the lists I'd looked at earlier in the evening.

CHAPTER TWENTY-EIGHT

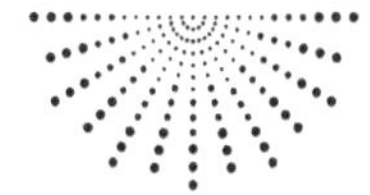

The postcard mess was waiting for me when I came downstairs the next morning with my coffee. I brought Bluebeard's breakfast down, but I wasn't quite ready to forgive him for trashing the shop while I was gone.

"Was that really necessary?" I grumbled as I cleaned his dish and changed his water.

"Find the postcards," he said, as though that explained everything. As far as I was concerned, it explained nothing. I'd found one postcard that had fallen behind a T-shirt display, and despite being possibly written by Bridget, it didn't have anything useful on it.

"You were just being cranky," I told him. "You think you have the right to trash the place and waste my time cleaning up after you."

He didn't answer me, just turned his back and pouted.

I swear, sometimes that bird was more trouble than a two-year-old. Of course I'd never had a two-year-old, but I'd heard stories about the Terrible Twos.

Those kids had nothing on a parrot in a foul mood.

Bluebeard was still ignoring me when Julie and Rose Ann came in. Someday Rose Ann would be a Terrible Two, but right now she was only a few months old.

She looked adorable in a ruffled sunsuit and a tiny bonnet, with a light flannel blanket covering her bare arms and legs.

I worried aloud that she might be cold without a sweater.

"It's seventy degrees outside." Julie laughed. "And it'll be ninety-five by noon. She's fine." She carried Rose Ann and her diaper bag through to the back. "She's had breakfast already," Julie called from the nursery area. "Let me put her down for a nap and I'll be right out."

It took her about ten minutes to get Rose Ann settled, while I started sorting the postcards that I'd left on the counter the night before.

"Didn't you just do that?" Julie asked, slipping behind the counter and taking a handful of the jumbled cards.

"Yes, I did. But *someone* decided they had to mess up the rack again last night."

"I see," she said. She quickly shuffled cards onto the stacks I'd started and took another handful. "And do I need to guess who that might have been?"

"I think you know."

I didn't tell her what he'd said, or what I'd found. Julie might have her suspicions about Bluebeard, although we had never actually discussed Uncle Louis. I didn't know how much longer I could put off telling her, but today wasn't the day for that conversation.

We got enough of the cards sorted to refill the rack before it was time to unlock the front doors. I stashed the box of unsorted cards under the counter. If there was time later in the day, I would finish the task. If not, it could wait until after closing.

The morning started with a steady stream of customers, and they continued coming well into the afternoon. Somewhere around noon I managed to slip upstairs and throw together a ham sandwich, but Julie called from downstairs before I took the first bite.

"There's someone here who wants to talk to you," she said over the intercom. "Can you come down, please?"

Her manner was in such sharp contrast to her usual friendly chatter that I didn't stop to ask questions. I slipped the sandwich into a plastic bag and tossed it into the refrigerator.

The shop was quiet when I got downstairs, with a few tourists milling around the souvenir racks.

A woman waited at the counter, fiddling with her cell phone and glancing up at the clock every few seconds. Her curly, dishwater blond hair had turned into a frizzy halo in the humidity, and a deep tan branded her as a local who spent a lot of time in the sun.

It took me a minute to place her. She worked someplace with a uniform, but in jeans and double-layered white tank tops, she wasn't familiar. I was used to seeing her in a lab coat. At first I thought she might be from my dentist's office, but then something clicked. The pharmacy. Lacey Simon.

"Lacey," I said, approaching the counter with my hand out.

She took my hand and leaned in with an air kiss. It wasn't my style, but I'd learned long ago to tolerate the familiarity.

"Good to see you. How are you and Francis doing?"

Not that I really needed to ask. From her appearance, it was clear they weren't doing well.

Lacey had a reputation as a health nut, finishing first in every local walk-a-thon and leading beach runs for visiting snow birds during the winter.

No wonder I hadn't recognized her. Dark bags under her eyes spoke of sleepless nights, and the muffin top that spilled over the waist of her jeans and strained at her shirt told me she hadn't been eating right. Or exercising.

"Can I talk to you?" she asked, looking around the store at the scattering of customers. Clearly she meant privately.

"Sure," I said. "Come on back."

I led her into my storage area, putting a finger to my lips as we passed the slumbering Rose Ann. Lacey glanced at the baby in her crib and attempted a smile, but it didn't reach her eyes.

We moved past the partition that marked Rose Ann's nursery, and stopped a few feet beyond. "She's a sound sleeper," I said softly. "But I'd still hate to disturb her."

Lacey nodded her understanding. "Sure thing," she whispered.

"So what can I do for you, Lacey?"

"I, uh . . ." She gave an embarrassed laugh and tried again. "I need to, well, to sell some stuff. We're moving to a smaller place, and I need to get rid of some of the clutter."

I didn't let on that I already knew she was losing the house. Let her keep some shred of dignity for as long as possible. "What kind of stuff?" I asked.

"Some knickknacks. A few of the larger pieces of furniture." She swallowed hard and I could see her pulse pounding in the hollow of her throat. "I've got some antique quilts that I'm ready to let go," she continued, "and some Fiesta ware. Oh, and a big collection of Bakelite, including some jewelry."

I knew I would take the Fiesta ware, if I could get it at a reasonable price, but I struggled with the idea of benefitting from Lacey's troubles. On the other hand, I couldn't overpay for merchandise I was going to resell; if I wanted to stay in business, I needed to turn a profit.

"I might be interested in some of that. But this is a small shop; I don't have room for furniture, especially if it's very big."

She rolled her eyes. "The dining room set seats a dozen," she said. "And there's a grandfather clock that's about eight feet tall."

"Have you thought about an auction house? I can help you find a reputable one."

She shook her head. "They take forever. Weeks to set things up and advertise, and then a month or more before they actually *do* anything. And I don't have enough to justify doing a private sale, so I'd have to wait until they got enough sellers together to make it worthwhile.

"Besides, they charge a fortune, and they add more fees and charges for every little thing. It's worse than the airlines."

Since I hadn't flown anywhere in many years, I had no idea how bad the airlines were, but the rest of her arguments were valid. An auction house couldn't afford to stage a sale for a few pieces of furniture. Not unless they were from Versailles, or Buckingham Palace. She would have to wait and be one of a group of sellers, and I knew why she was in a hurry. She had to move next month, and she didn't have the luxury of waiting.

"I can't handle the big stuff," I repeated. "But Felipe Vargas, over at Carousel Antiques, specializes in that kind of thing. He loves dining room sets. Does yours have a china hutch? Felipe's a sucker for china hutches."

Lacey lifted the corners of her mouth in another attempt at a smile, only slightly more successful than the last one. "It does. It's monstrous, takes up an entire wall of the dining room. And there's a sideboard that goes with it."

I tried to imagine how big her dining room must be to hold the massive pieces she described. Bigger than my entire apartment, I'd bet. They didn't support a place like that on the salary of a bank manager and a pharmacy tech. Not unless the pharmacy paid a lot better than I thought. ·

Or Francis had some income on the side. Like investing heavily in real estate developments. If he'd been riding Andrew Marshall's coattails, he could have afforded a great house. Right up until he couldn't.

His name had been on the investor list, after all.

All of which led to a desperate attempt to liquidate what they could, before their creditors came calling.

"Let me call Felipe and see if he's available. And come back with the Fiesta ware and the quilts and let's see if we can work something out."

I called Felipe. I filled him in, choosing my words carefully. He said to send her over, and I saw the relief in her eyes when I told her he was interested in the furniture. Desperation like hers was not pretty.

I felt like a fraud accepting Lacey's thanks. I'd buy the quilts and kitchen-ware at a fair price, and I knew Felipe would take the furniture, but we wouldn't do her any favors.

Deep down I didn't think she, or Francis, deserved any. They'd done plenty for themselves.

I watched Lacey leave, trying to hold her head up and pretend her life was still somewhere near normal. I knew the truth was far different that the image she wanted to preserve.

The phone in my hand buzzed, and I pushed the answer button without looking. Probably Felipe calling back after he figured Lacey was gone.

"Good afternoon, Southern Treasures. How can I help you?" I almost said, "Hi, Felipe," but I stopped myself at the last second.

"Miss Gloryanna, is that you?" The voice wasn't Felipe, and I was glad I had used our standard greeting. It sounded a lot like Peter's nasal-y whine, but it wasn't him, either. Thank heavens.

"This is Gloryanna," I replied. "How can I help you?"

"It's Francis Simon. I, uh, well, I was looking for Lacey." He sounded almost scared, like a kid looking for his missing mom. "She said she was coming by your place, and I, um, need to talk to her. Is she still there?"

"I'm sorry, Francis," I said. "She just left. I think she's going to down Carousel, to talk to Felipe. Maybe you can catch her there. Do you need the number?"

He declined my offer, mumbling that he was sure he had the number, and hung up. As I put the phone back in its base, I wondered why he hadn't called Lacey on her cell phone. Were things so bad she didn't even have a working phone?

CHAPTER TWENTY-NINE

I didn't get back to sorting the postcard mess until late in the afternoon. Bluebeard was still pouting in the corner, and I told myself I really didn't care. Whatever he was trying to tell me, he didn't need to trash the shop and make extra work for me in the process.

I didn't want the stacks spread across the counter, so I sat in the tall chair at the register and flipped through the jumble in the box, pulling out one design at a time. It was slow-going, but at least I was able to work in between customers without cluttering up the counter.

The bell rang over the front door and I looked up from my sorting. Buddy McKenna, a zippered leather portfolio tucked under his arm, walked in. He hesitated as though he was intruding, then made a slow circuit of the store.

He took his time, examining each T-shirt and souvenir, and he went back to the postcard spinner several times. When he finally approached the counter, he was carrying a handful of trinkets and a couple colorful T-shirts.

"I haven't got this packing thing down quite yet," he said with a nod to the T-shirts. Just like his sister.

"The department manager called a little bit ago," he continued as I rang up his purchases. "He verified that he wouldn't be able to get anyone down here until the middle of next week. Asked me to stay on and continue Bridget's work."

"That sounds like a compliment," I said.

"Backhanded, I'm afraid. Like I said, they still plan to send a senior auditor next week. But yeah, still something of a compliment, I guess."

He paid for his purchases, and lingered at the counter. He laid his portfolio down and put his hand on top of it. "I wondered if you might have some time this afternoon. To go over the notes we talked about. I found some things I'd like you to look at."

I glanced up at the clock. Nearly closing time. The postcards could wait. I was intensely curious about what Bridget might have uncovered, and I thought it would be interesting to hear her impressions of Keyhole Bay and its inhabitants. The prospect of seeing my hometown through the eyes of an outsider enticed me. Especially an outsider who didn't expect anyone in town to read what she thought.

"I close in a few minutes. How about I meet you next door at Lighthouse?"

Buddy accepted my suggestion, and we agreed to meet for coffee as soon as I could get closed up. He was about to say something else when we were interrupted by a wail from the back room. He gave me a startled look and turned in the direction of the noise.

"Rose Ann," I said. I told him about setting up the nursery and having the baby in the shop when her grandma wasn't available. "Anita'd rather have the baby with her, of course. But she can't keep her every day, so we found a way for Rose Ann to come to work with her mom.

"I know it won't last forever, but it works for now."

"It's a great idea. I wish the bank had something similar; it would make life easier for my wife and me.

"How about you, Glory?" he asked. "Any kids?"

I shook my head. "Not me," I answered. "Just a business that takes all my time, and a badly behaved parrot."

From his perch on the other side of the shop, Bluebeard squawked a mild curse, then settled into a litany of muttered complaints.

"Language, Bluebeard."

The muttering became quieter, but I knew what he was saying, even if Buddy couldn't understand it.

"He's having a bad day," I said. "He's sort of like a cranky baby sometimes. Probably just needs a nap."

Buddy laughed politely at my lame joke, and said he'd wait for me at Lighthouse. I promised to meet him as soon as I could.

A few minutes later I flipped the sign on the door from "Open" to "Closed" and went next door. As soon as Chloe spotted me, she started a vanilla latte. "Hot or iced?" she asked when I reached the counter.

"Hot, I think."

A minute later she handed me a cup in a paper sleeve. I reached in my pocket but she refused my payment. "Your friend already took care of it."

Buddy had a table against the wall, where he had unloaded the contents of his portfolio, and he sat studying the pages spread in front of him.

I took the seat across from him and sipped my drink. "Thank you," I said.

"My pleasure. But the bank's paying for this one. It's part of the job."

"Either way, I'm grateful." The caffeine and sugar were giving me a pleasant buzz after a long day in the shop. And it was only July. There were several weeks of summer yet to go.

"So what have you got for me?" I asked Buddy. "How can I help?"

"Well, I went back to the lists from last night, and looked at all of Bridget's notes. I found a couple files on her laptop, too. Some of it is confidential, but there are some things that I'd like you to confirm if you can."

He looked at the top page and ran his finger along the list. "Jennifer Marshall, for example. You mentioned her when you were talking to her husband. Does she really have the resources to hang on to their house?"

I thought for a minute before I answered. Memaw would be horrified to hear me gossip about my neighbors with a Yankee. On the other hand, I really didn't know anything I could tell him that wasn't common knowledge. Besides, I had promised to help him, and it was for a good cause. We both wanted Bridget's killer found.

"Good question," I said. "I'm really not sure. When Andy said the bank was going to take it—"

"Thanks, by the way," Buddy interrupted, "for not giving me away to Marshall. I don't know if he's violent, but I really didn't want to find out."

"Got in a few fights when he was a kid, from what I'm told. Nothing serious." I shrugged. "Anyway, that's all ancient history. He's mostly the kind of guy who blows up and gets over it pretty quick. Like he did last night."

"Still, I appreciate that you didn't tell him who I was."

"You're welcome." I went back to his original question. "Jen's folks have money, and I believe she had an inheritance from her grandparents, but I don't know how much. You're more likely to be able to find that out for yourself, in the bank records.

"People around here don't talk about money a whole lot. It's just not something you share with everyone. Like—" I stopped myself before I said what I was thinking, searching instead for an overly polite euphemism. "Like, you know, your private life."

Buddy blinked in confusion a couple times, then a faint blush crept up his pale face. He got my meaning.

"And I don't know if she still has it," I continued. "Her grandmother passed away right after their second daughter was born, and that's been probably ten years."

I stopped and took another sip of coffee, letting the sweetness fill my mouth and slide down my throat.

"She and Andy may have spent it. On the business, or the girls, or a vacation. Or on that house."

"You said you were just out there. What's it like?"

I explained how I'd come to be in Jen Marshall's house, however briefly. "It was lovely, in a new-money kind of way. Jen came from money, but Andy didn't. You saw him."

"I saw a man who'd lost everything," Buddy said. "He looked like he'd started drinking on New Year's Eve and hadn't stopped. But with the pressure he's been under, well"—he shrugged—"I try not to judge too harshly."

"Memaw used to say, 'Don't marry a boy from a dirt road,' and Andrew Marshall could have been exactly the kind of boy she was talking about. No education, no prospects, and a taste for hard liquor. Except Andrew was stubborn and he worked hard. He's one of those up-by-his-bootstraps success stories."

"And he married into money," Buddy added.

"Yeah. He was the local boy who made good and swept Daddy's Little Princess off her feet. I remember their wedding, even though I was just a kid. It took the entire front page of the 'Society' section in the *News and Times*. They called it the wedding of the year."

"Sounds like a proper Horatio Alger story," Buddy said.

"It was. Andy purely wore himself out, the number of hours he'd work. He was used to living poor, and he managed to put a lot by to start his own construction company.

"I think Bayvue was supposed to be his big score, the one that finally set him up for life."

"I'm not telling you anything you don't already know when I say he was overextended," Buddy said. "He'd leveraged everything he had to buy the land and start construction. And he sank every penny into what's out there right now. Which isn't that much."

It didn't surprise me. "I'd heard rumors for years about how Andy Marshall kept plowing money back into Marshall Development. Each time he pulled out a win, he'd turn around and pour it all into the next project, culminating in Bayvue Estates."

"That ties in with what Bridget found," Buddy said. He made an X next to Marshall's name on his list. "I don't think he defrauded the bank exactly," he explained. "Poor judgment, yes. But I don't think there was anything criminal in his handling of the loans."

We talked about the Andersons. Bridget had pegged them accurately as clueless and entitled. I told him about Felicia's visit to Carousel Antiques right after Bridget's death.

"My friend Felipe said she acted as though she was immune to what was going on. Like she'd get her way, like she always does. If Bridget described her as entitled, that's pretty accurate. And Billy is the same way."

I thought about the difference between the two couples. "Jen and Andy took their money seriously," I said. "Jen always supported local charities, and Andy supported Jen. They would open their house for every good cause that came along.

"Billy and Felicia had a party for their employees once a year, at Christmas. They served a lavish buffet, and handed out holiday bonus checks. But the checks came from the bank, not the Andersons."

Buddy made a note under Billy Anderson's name, and slid his finger along the list. "Pearl Anderson. It's still Anderson on all our records. She is single, right?"

I nodded. "I don't know much about her. She's a couple years younger than me, but she didn't go to school here. Her parents sent her away to some exclusive boarding school, and she was only home for short periods. She travels a lot, like a lady of leisure out of a nineteenth-century novel, but she shows up for every meeting of the board and—according to people who work at the bank—votes the way her brother and father tell her to."

"Bridget seemed to think she might be, um, challenged in some way. Had you heard anything like that?"

I considered the question. "The family does seem to keep her out of the public eye. Just never thought about why. That would explain a whole lot."

Buddy put a question mark next to Pearl's name.

"Sorry I wasn't more help on that one."

He drained his coffee cup and set it aside. "I can't expect you to do *all* my work for me," he said lightly. "Especially when I'm only paying you in coffee."

A shadow fell across the table and I looked up to find that Jake had come in while we were talking. Buddy jumped to his feet, greeting Jake warmly.

"Good to see you, and thanks for your help last night."

"Thanks for letting me tag along," Jake replied.

"Please, sit down. Join us." Buddy pulled another chair over and placed it next to me. "Can I get you something?"

Jake shook his head. "I was just heading home and I spotted Glory sitting here. Thought I'd come across and say hello before I left."

I patted the chair and Jake sat down, though he didn't relax. He looked tired and he was probably anxious to get home after I'd dragged him out last night.

We talked for another few minutes, but I realized Chloe was hovering nearby, clearly ready to close up herself.

"We better get going," I said. "I'd be glad to talk some more, Buddy. Why don't you give me a call if you need more information?"

I scribbled my cell number on my business card and handed it to him. "Holler if you need me."

Buddy thanked me and excused himself, saying he had a lot more work to do tonight. Jake and I followed him out, and said good night as he walked away toward the city parking lot.

"I better get going, too," Jake said. "I'd love to take you to dinner, if it wasn't a Saturday night." He laughed. "See? I'll turn into a local yet."

I smiled up at him. "And I'd love to go. But not on a Saturday night. Besides, I am beat and tomorrow's going to be another long day. I think I'll go upstairs, have a bowl of cereal, and collapse."

"Cereal? For dinner?"

"That's the joy of being a grown-up," I said, rising up on my tiptoes to give him a quick kiss. "If I want cereal for dinner, nobody can tell me not to."

CHAPTER THIRTY

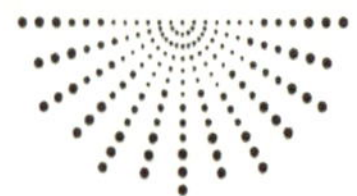

Jake paused at the crosswalk, waiting for traffic to clear. "How about tomorrow night? I'll cook."

"Deal." Never turn down a meal when someone else volunteers to cook.

I let myself in the shop, prepared to spend the next hour getting ready for the Sunday summer rush. But Julie had already straightened and restocked. The shelves were dusted and the floors swept.

All I had to do was take myself upstairs and relax.

Which I did.

Late Sunday afternoon Jake called me. "I'm having car trouble," he said. "I called Sly, and he offered to come by the house in about an hour. But I didn't want to upset our dinner plans."

"Tell him to come ahead. I know what a pain it is to be without a car." Jake knew, too. I'd had to borrow his car a couple times when my old car had been out of commission.

"It might be a good thing to cook enough to share," I said. "It'd be the polite thing to offer him dinner."

"You sure this is okay?" he asked again.

"It's fine. I'll see you in an hour."

When I pulled up in front of Jake's, there was a vintage Thunderbird already parked at the curb. The chrome gleamed in the late afternoon sunshine, and the turquoise paint was buffed until it gleamed. No need to wonder whose car it was.

I started up the walk, but Jake called to me from the carport. I walked around the corner of the house and spotted Jake and Sly up to their elbows in the engine of Jake's car.

"Sly thinks it's probably just a spark plug," Jake said. "I'll take it over later this week."

"Hey, Miss Glory," Sly said, smiling broadly. "Mr. Jake says he's fixing to feed us." He wiped his hands on a shop towel and tossed it in his toolbox.

I started to answer, but the ringing of my cell phone interrupted me. I pulled out the phone and checked the number before I answered. No sense having another argument with Peter when I could let it go to voice mail.

"Karen," I said. "I was beginning to wonder where she is. Excuse me for a minute."

I hit the "Answer" key and said hello.

"Where have you been?" I asked her. "I haven't talked to you in forever!"

"It's been three days," she said. "Don't exaggerate. And a holiday weekend besides. Figured you'd be too exhausted to do anything but sleep."

She had me there.

"Anyway, I thought I'd check in, see what you were up to."

Jake moved close to me and signaled for my attention. I muted the phone. "Yes?"

"There's plenty of food," he said. "Tell her to join us."

"Sure?"

"Why not?" He grinned at me. "Let's make it a party!"

I went back to Karen. "Hey, I'm at Jake's, and Sly's here. We were just getting ready to eat. Why don't you join us?"

It was my turn to wait while she turned to someone else. I heard a soft conversation in the background, then she came back to the phone. "Riley's here, too. Does the invitation include both of us?"

I looked at Jake, who was standing close enough to hear what she said. He nodded and I relayed the expanded invitation.

"All right," she said. "Give me the address."

Sly and Jake went to wash up, and Jake said he needed to check on dinner. I waited in the carport, watching for Karen and Riley.

I did wonder where Karen had been. I hadn't talked to her since our dinner on the Fourth, and as I thought about it, I realized I hadn't heard her on the radio all weekend. She hadn't said anything about being gone, but it seemed like the logical explanation.

In just a couple minutes, Riley's pickup rolled up across the street from

Sly's T-Bird and the two of them climbed out. I greeted them with hugs and took them into the kitchen through the side door.

Inside, the tang of tomato and the musky fragrance of oregano mingled with onion and garlic into a heady promise of Italian delights.

Jake stood at the counter, stirring a dark red sauce in the Crock-Pot. "Spaghetti," he said unnecessarily. The smell had already given it away.

"Smells divine," Karen said. She spoke for us all.

Dinner turned into the usual group effort. I made garlic bread, Sly put together a salad, and Jake boiled the pasta.

Karen and Riley volunteered to set the table, but Jake suggested we eat on the screened patio. He showed them the way, and the two of them disappeared with a stack of plates and silverware.

They came back several times for things like glasses and napkins. Both of them. As though they couldn't stay apart for long enough to walk from one room to another. And each time they seemed deep in a private conversation. They hardly noticed that the rest of us were there.

Jake drained the pasta and tossed it with a small scoop of the sauce to keep it from sticking. I sliced garlic bread and piled it on a platter, and Sly tossed the salad with a dressing of olive oil, wine vinegar, and assorted herbs.

Riley carried the crock of sauce, and the food procession made its way down the hall and out to the porch.

Even without the usual Thursday group, the conversation followed our normal pattern: We spent the first half of the meal quizzing Jake about his sauce and sharing our own personal takes on the art of spaghetti. Everyone had their own recipe, and we all had our own take on what was essential.

When we had exhausted that topic, Jake asked me about my meeting with Buddy McKenzie. "What did he want to know?"

"The kind of thing we talked about on Friday night," I said. "Did I agree with what Bridget said in her notes. Did I have something to add that wasn't there. He was very careful not to tell me anything he didn't think I already knew, but he did confirm that Andy Marshall had sunk everything into Bayvue, and then gone into debt so deep he couldn't get out."

I told Jake what Buddy had said about Andy's behavior, and about not judging too harshly.

"Wait a minute," Karen said. "Let's back up a little, shall we? When did you see Andy Marshall? And for that matter, when did you spend all this time with Mr. McKenna?"

Jake and I took turns filling the three of them in on the adventures of the weekend. Riley looked especially upset as we described Andy's appearance and behavior.

"He was a few years ahead of us, wasn't he?" I said. "How did you know him?"

"I didn't know him very well, but my older brother did. Well enough to get in a couple fights with him," Riley said. "They played football together, and didn't always see eye-to-eye on things. Andy was rough around the edges, and he was a fierce competitor. Hated to lose. Just purely hated it. Once in a while they disagreed about tactics; what was okay and what wasn't."

"I remember one time," Karen said. "Tom had a knot on his head for a week. Was that from Andy?"

"Sure was. Andy didn't think Tom had hit an opposing lineman hard enough, and he showed Tom exactly what he thought he should have done. Tom said his ears rang for days."

"Sounds like a dangerous guy," Jake said, his brow furrowing in concern. He turned to me. "You sure Buddy's safe out there with that guy stumbling around?"

"Andy's broken," Sly cut in. "He's done lost everything he worked for, and it broke something inside him. Seen it happen before. Makes a man weak, or it makes him mean." He turned to look at me. "Which do you think he is, Glory?"

I shook my head. "I couldn't say, Sly. But I don't think I saw mean in that man out there.

"I sure hope I'm right," I added softly.

"So anyway, after our talk on Friday night, Buddy stopped by the store on Saturday and wanted to ask me some questions. I met him at Lighthouse and had a cup of coffee, Jake dropped by and joined us for a few minutes, and that was the end of it.

"Which, by the way, you would have heard about if you'd been around this weekend." I glared at Karen and Riley. "Now give. Just where were the two of you the last three days? 'Cause I am convinced you weren't in town."

Karen reached for Riley's hand and held it so tightly her knuckles turned white. "We went away for the weekend."

Clearly there was more to the story. "And?" I prodded.

She looked around the table. "You all have to swear you will not repeat a word of this. Not a word.

"Swear."

We nodded but that wasn't enough for her. "Say it!"

Sly, Jake, and I each promised, but she had me really worried. I had asked Linda what to do about Karen and Riley and she'd told me to just be supportive, but now I wondered exactly what I was supporting.

"We went to a couples retreat."

"A retreat? You mean like a church camp or something?"

Karen shook her head. "No. It was just something our counselor recommended. A few days away, concentrating on the two of us."

"Your counselor? Since when do you have a counselor? And why do you need a counselor anyway? You're divorced!"

"Because," Riley explained, "if we're going to get married again, we want to do it right this time."

My gaze shot to Karen's left hand. Bare. So it hadn't happened yet. Maybe.

I thought I'd lost my mind. "You're getting married again, and you're seeing a counselor to help you do it right, *and* you went to a retreat—and you haven't mentioned a word about this to me? Did I hear all that right?"

"It's only been the last couple weeks," Karen said. "And you've been so worried about Riley and me getting back together that I didn't want to say anything until we were sure."

"So it isn't really *if* you get married again, it's *when*."

Karen nodded.

Jake got up from his chair and walked around the table. He shook Riley's hand, a huge grin on his face. "Congratulations, man! That's great news."

Riley grinned back. "Yeah, I think it is."

Jake reached down to hug Karen. "You'll be great," he said. "Just great."

By that time I was out of my seat and around the table. I threw my arms around Riley, unsure whether to laugh or cry. "Do it right this time. Or there will be hell to pay."

Karen stood up and I wrapped my arms around her. "If this is what you want, then I'm happy for you," I said, and I meant it. I never doubted for a minute that they loved each other. They just needed to learn how to live together. And maybe they had matured enough to make it work.

"Have you told your families yet?" I asked when we had settled in lounge chairs with refilled glasses a few minutes later. "Does Bobby know?"

"Nobody knows," Riley said. "They didn't even know we were spending the weekend together. Like Karen said, we didn't want to say anything until we were sure."

"And if you'll notice," Karen added, "you were the first person we called when we got back."

"I'm so sorry," I said. "I should have thought of that before I shot my mouth off."

"That wasn't exactly how we planned to tell you," Karen said. "I had a little speech all prepared, but then we got to talking about everything that happened and it just came out."

"Well, I, for one, am honored to have been part of this," Sly announced. "I think anyone getting married is reason enough for celebration." He raised his sweet tea in a toast. "Here's to many years of happiness."

"How about you, Sly?" Riley asked. "You never married?"

"Nope." He shook his head, his expression far away. "I came close once. Really loved that little gal, but my mama pitched such a fit I couldn't do it.

"I went to Mr. Louis about it," he went on, his voice soft and low, as full of longing as if it had been yesterday instead of decades ago.

"He told me he'd help me if I was determined to do it, but we both knew it wouldn't happen. I wasn't brave enough to go against my mama's wishes and break the law, so I joined the Army and went away for a while."

"Break the law?" Jake said. "How?"

"I know," I said. "Your girl, she was white, wasn't she, Sly? That's why you couldn't marry her."

"That's right, Miss Glory. It was a different world back then."

"It was before either of us was born," I told Jake. "But I heard about it. It took a long time for things to change, but eventually they did."

I looked over at Sly. "It was just too late for some."

Sly nodded. "Your uncle Louis, he understood. Offered to drive us up to Chicago or New York, one of them places, if we really wanted to go. Coulda got hisself in trouble for it, but he was willing. He was a real good man, Miss Glory."

"Do you mind my asking about this?"

Sly shook his head. "Ancient history, Miss Glory. Can't hurt me now."

"Why you? I mean, sure, he was a good man. And he didn't seem to have much patience for a lot of what went on back then. But why did he help you and not someone else?"

"Mr. Louis was a friend of my mama's," he said. "She worked cleaning houses with her little sister. They worked for Mr. Louis's daddy when Mr. Louis was a young man, and he took a shine to my aunt Sissy. You can bet his mama put an end to that right quick. Sissy got shipped over to cousins in Slidell, and Louis ran off and joined the Army.

"Sorta like me."

"I had no idea," I said, my head spinning.

"Course, all that happened before I was born," Sly said. "So I only know what my mama and daddy told me later on. They used to carry news about Sissy to Mr. Louis, right up to the day he died. I think helpin' me was his way of sayin' thanks."

CHAPTER THIRTY-ONE

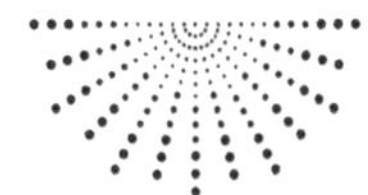

Sly's story explained a lot about Uncle Louis. He must have been one stubborn son of a gun to come back to Keyhole Bay after his stint in the Army.

"I don't know if I'd've ever come back here," Riley said. "Even if my mama and daddy were here. I'd've hightailed it west so fast you wouldn't have seen me go."

"West?" Jake asked. "I've been there. Not that much different from here, unless you're in one of the big cities. Otherwise it's the same; good people and bad, rich and poor, happy and miserable. From what I've seen, people are the same wherever you go."

"True, that." Sly nodded his agreement. "I saw a lot of places courtesy of my uncle. Uncle Sam. Good people and bad, wherever you go. Whatever you go looking for, that's what you're gonna find. And I found good people, generous and helpful people, everywhere I went."

I got up from my chair and walked over to Sly, and knelt down next to him. Tentatively, I reached out and put my arm around his shoulders, and gave him a one-armed hug. "That's because you're a good and generous man, Sly. Like goes to like, as Memaw would say."

Sly reached out with one callused hand and ran his fingers along my cheek. "Louis would be proud of you. I think he *is* proud of you. You're a good girl, Miss Glory."

"Thanks." I stood up and blinked back the tears that threatened to spill over. Sly had given me a fresh look at the only family I had in Keyhole Bay, and I was grateful. Uncle Louis and Bluebeard could be mighty annoying, but I was still glad to have them in my life.

"Speaking of Uncle Louis," I said to my friends, "have I told you about his latest antics?"

I launched into the story of the postcards, lightening the somber mood with the tale of his mess and of the epic pout that followed. "He was still pouting the next day," I said, "when Buddy McKenna came in. I think that was some kind of record, even for Bluebeard."

It was good to be among friends, people who knew about Uncle Louis, and be able to speak freely. I had kept the secret of my ghostly roommate for a long time, unwilling to admit it, even to myself. But now everyone in the room knew about Louis, and accepted his presence in my life.

Soon Karen and Riley announced that they had to leave. They thanked Jake for dinner, and a few minutes later we heard Riley's truck pull away.

Sly hugged me good-bye, a real hug. Somehow it felt right this time. Sly's connection with Uncle Louis made it feel like we were family, and I was happy to add another person to my little family circle.

"I'll see you later in the week," he said to Jake, "and I'll see you tomorrow."

"Lunchtime," I agreed. "And I'll be sure to bring a treat for Bobo."

We watched the T-Bird pull away, and Jake and I were left alone.

"Time for me to go, too."

"You're welcome to stay a little longer," Jake said. But when I didn't accept the invitation, he walked me to my truck and said good night.

"I'll stop by in the morning," he said, "and see if Bluebeard is still pouting."

"Probably will be."

I started the engine and drove the few blocks back home. I parked in the back and let myself in, checking the locks and alarms twice. All the talk about Andy Marshall had left me uneasy, and I still wasn't ready to accept the police's explanation of Bridget's death.

I peered through the dim light in the shop, but everything was in its proper place, and Bluebeard didn't even complain about me disturbing his sleep.

I was about to head upstairs when I noticed the box of postcards still behind the counter. I picked up the box and carried it upstairs with me. I could turn on the TV and finish resorting the cards before bed, and then I wouldn't have to look at the mess in the morning.

I found a sappy romantic comedy on a local channel and set to work on the postcards.

I was halfway through when I found another card with Bridget's precise printing. Like the first one, this one also said Edina, MN, on the address side. But where the first one had only a few letters in the message space, this one had two complete words.

Let's talk.

Who did she want to talk to, I wondered. There was only one person who might be able to tell me, but good manners told me it was far too late to call anyone, and especially someone I only knew casually.

Good manners, however, didn't prevent me from sending e-mail. Buddy might not get my message until tomorrow, but it could wait that long.

I grabbed my laptop and opened the e-mail program. Using the address on Buddy's business card, I typed in my question:

Who did Bridget know in Edina, Minnesota?

I set the computer aside and got up for a glass of sweet tea before I went back to my sorting.

To my surprise, the computer chimed with an incoming message just a few minutes later.

Just my dad, as far as I know. Why?

I debated how to answer him. If Bridget was actually sending a postcard to her father, offering to talk to him, then maybe she was trying to mend their broken relationship. Perhaps working with Buddy had somehow convinced her to reach out to her father, even if it was only a postcard.

But that wasn't something for an e-mail in the middle of the night. It was a message loaded with emotional baggage, and I wasn't going to trust it to pixels on a glowing screen.

Nothing critical. Just something she said. I'll tell you about it the next time I see you. Good night!

I closed the e-mail program and shut down the computer. If Buddy answered my e-mail, if he asked any more questions, I could honestly say I hadn't seen the message.

I thought about how I'd found Bridget's message while I finished sorting the postcards and got ready for bed.

Of all the things Bluebeard had said, all the clues he'd dropped, why this one?

I put the box of postcards, now carefully sorted again, at the top of the stairs so I would remember to take them back downstairs. The one with Bridget's message I left in the middle of the coffee table. I'd try to remember to give it to Buddy next time he was in the shop.

CHAPTER THIRTY-TWO

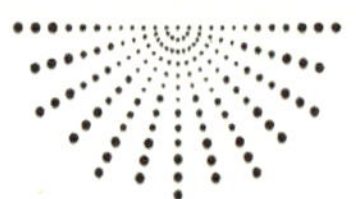

I floated in that half-dreaming state between the first soft beeps of the alarm clock and the "I have to be downstairs in fifteen minutes" freakout, savoring the last few minutes of peace and quiet before the onslaught that was a summer Monday.

The early morning warmth made me kick off the light blanket, but the slow whirring of a box fan kept the bedroom reasonably cool for now.

Although I didn't have to get up for another few minutes, my brain had already kicked into gear. Julie would be here with Rose Ann, so I could get out of the shop for a little while. There was a short list of absolutely necessary errands, and I considered how best to make use of my time.

The bank was a high priority after a holiday weekend. And groceries. No one who lived in Keyhole Bay went near the market on a summer weekend. My Friday morning visit had been problematic; Saturdays were impossible, and by Sunday the shelves were picked clean.

I remembered my date with Sly. I had promised to bring the truck for an oil change, and I'd said I would bring lunch. Which meant I either had to make something, or stop for takeout. But if I didn't get groceries, there weren't a lot of options in the making-something department.

Takeout it was.

I didn't like carrying around cash, so I'd go to the bank first, pick up lunch, get the truck taken care of, and swing by the store on my way back. That way

I didn't have to leave too early, and Frank and Cheryl should have restocked by early afternoon, which would make my shopping easier, too.

I lingered in bed a moment longer, pretending to think about what to wear. I knew I was stalling; my work wardrobe was jeans and sneakers. In the winter I wore T-shirts or polos, in the summer I wore T-shirts or tank tops. I could probably qualify for one of those wardrobe makeover shows.

I forced myself out of bed and into the shower. I was toweling dry when I heard my phone beep with an incoming text. I finished dressing and retrieved the phone on my way downstairs with my coffee.

"Coffee?" Bluebeard said the instant I appeared at the bottom of the stairs.

"No coffee," I answered. Why did he even bother asking? He got the same answer every day. I gave him some apple slices and part of a banana instead, and changed his water.

Slipping back behind the counter, I checked the phone messages. There was only one text, from a number I didn't recognize. I almost deleted the message unopened, but there was something vaguely familiar about the area code.

I turned on the computer and did a quick search. Area code 952 covered an area south and west of Minneapolis. That was why it looked familiar: I'd seen it on Bradford McKenna's business card.

Reassured, I opened the message. Sure enough, it was from Bridget's brother.

Found something I need to show you. Meet me at Bridget's.
Buddy

I glanced at the clock. Julie would be here in half an hour, but I didn't want to wait. I could get out to Bayvue and back before we opened, if I left right now.

I texted back, *On my way*, scribbled a note to Julie, and left it on the counter in case I wasn't back when she got here.

"Mind the store," I hollered to Bluebeard as I headed out the back, stuffing my wallet in my pocket. "I'm gonna go see what Buddy wants."

I was in the truck and on the road before it struck me. Buddy. Sure, Jake called Bluebeard "buddy," but I'd never heard the parrot use the word in reply.

Not until Buddy McKenna came to town.

Maybe Bluebeard wasn't talking to Jake. Maybe he was talking about Bradford McKenna, the "Buddy" I was on my way to see.

The traffic was still light this early in the day, and I was able to take the highway out to the county road and turn north toward Bayvue Estates. In a couple minutes the brick gateposts appeared on my right, and I turned in to the abandoned development.

I hadn't seen another vehicle since the smattering of traffic on the main drag, and the empty roads made the vacant lots and unpaved streets seem all the more deserted.

It felt like the main street of some Western movie, just before the big showdown, with brittle palm fronds in the dusty road instead of tumbleweeds. I almost expected to hear the lonesome whistle of a distant steam engine.

But this was the twenty-first century, I was in Florida, not the Wild West, and I wasn't heading for any kind of confrontation, just trying to help out the family of a friend.

I parked my truck in front of the house where Bridget had stayed and stuffed the keys in my pocket. I stepped carefully around the jagged edge of the concrete walk where the crew had apparently just stopped pouring and let the wet cement puddle and dry in a lump.

The front door was ajar when I reached the porch, and I pushed it open. "Buddy?" I called out. "You in here?"

A muffled voice answered, "Upstairs. C'mon up."

I walked through the entry hall and started up the stairs. "What'd you find?"

"Up here," he answered.

At the top of the stairs I turned down the hall past the sagging cabinet door. I pushed it closed, even though I knew it would just fall open again.

"Where are you?"

"Here," the voice, high-pitched with excitement, came from the back bedroom. The one with the unfinished closet.

But I didn't find Buddy McKenna in the bedroom.

Instead I found myself face-to-face with Lacey Simon. And she didn't look happy.

"Lacey? What are you doing here?"

"Trying to talk some sense into this, this Yankee!" She spat the last word. "But it doesn't seem to be working."

Who was she talking about? There didn't appear to me anyone else in the room. But just then a groan from the closet drew my attention. There on the floor was Buddy McKenna, blood pooling under his head.

I turned to run but Lacey was ahead of me, blocking the door, a length of cedar plank in her hand.

"Francis was too squeamish to take care of his own mess," she said. "But someone's got to clean up after him and his damned fool friends. It was good of you to come so quickly when I asked you to."

The outline of a cell phone bulged in the pocket of her shirt, and I guessed it was Buddy's. My stomach knotted as I realized *anyone* could send a text message.

I saw her swing and tried to duck, but it was too late.

The timber caught me in the temple and I collapsed on the floor.

I looked up at Lacey. I wanted to ask her why, but I couldn't decide which Lacey to talk to. There were at least three angry women looming over me.

And all three held needles.

Even my addled brain knew what came next.

A prick against my skin.

Heat sliding through my veins.

Darkness.

Eternity.

CHAPTER THIRTY-THREE

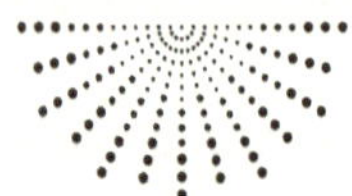

"You just couldn't leave it alone, could you?" the Laceys said, each of them waving her needle. "We all told Boomer it had to be an accident, had to be her own fault."

They filled the needles from identical bottles of clear liquid, pulling the fluid into the syringes. Tapping the side of the tube. "But you couldn't accept that and move on.

"I saw you, you know. Right after I was in your store. Couldn't wait to go running to your new best friend and tell him all about my business. We just needed a couple days, but the two of you wouldn't let us have it, would you? If you'd just waited a little bit, 'til I sold our stuff, we'd have been long gone. But oh no, not you. Not little Miss Busybody.

"So now I have to clean up another mess."

The needles came closer, and I tried to squirm out of the way.

I felt a hand grip my arm, roughly shoving my T-shirt sleeve toward my shoulder. A rubbery strap slid around my arm and pinched it tight. My fingers went numb, and I felt something poking the soft flesh on the inside of my elbow.

For an instant the three needles merged into one, its tip pressed against my vein.

Fueled by panic, adrenaline surged through me. I wrenched my arm away from the needle and heard a tiny snap, followed by a string of curses that would have made Bluebeard blush.

"I can't find another needle," the Laceys muttered, digging through identical black bags. "Maybe in the car . . ."

The echoing voices drifted toward the door. "Don't go anywhere," they said. "I'll be right back."

Go anywhere? It took all my strength and concentration to remember to breathe. How could I go anywhere?

But if I didn't, she would be back. With another needle, and another vial.

I tried to raise myself up on my elbow, but my arm didn't want to cooperate. Sharp pain stabbed me in the joint and I had to lay back down.

I straightened my arm and found pieces of the needles sticking out of the veins, the ends broken off an inch above my skin. Blood seeped from the veins that bulged around the broken needles.

I closed one eye, hoping I could figure out which needle was the real one. The three needles blended into two, but not one coherent image.

I dragged my other arm across my body, clumsy fingers grasping for the sharp points.

In the distance I heard a car engine start. Lacey was leaving. I could just take a little nap, then I could try again.

From the closet, Buddy groaned. I remembered the pool of blood. I might have time for a nap, but did he?

The double images refused to come together, and I closed my eyes against the nausea-inducing sight. If I couldn't see, I would have to rely on my other senses.

I ran my hand up my arm, reaching for the strap. I found a rubber tube, like the nurses used at the blood bank. I tugged on the short end, and was rewarded with a sudden loosening of the pressure on my arm.

The warmth of returning circulation flooded my arm. But there was still a needle to deal with. I ran my hand back down toward my elbow, feeling the slick of blood that covered my arm.

I was bleeding. A lot. Just like Buddy.

I shoved the terror into the back of my brain and slammed a lid on it. No time for panic.

My fingers slipped in the blood. Pain shot through my arm as my hand brushed against the needle, pushing it sideways. Instinctively, I drew my hand away, releasing the pressure on the needle.

Slowly, gingerly, I reached again. I inched my fingers closer, trying to find the needle without causing more pain.

At last I felt the fine metal against my fingertip. I squeezed my eyes tighter, and held my breath.

My hand trembled, and I clamped it into a fist to control the nervous tremor, then reached for the needle again.

The slender shaft was slick and difficult to grasp. I tried to pull on it, but my fingers slipped off. A second time, same result.

The pain didn't matter. I had to pull the needle out of my arm, if I wanted any chance of getting away from the Laceys.

I tugged at the bottom of my T-shirt, wiping off my arm. The needle dug into me, and I bit my lip to stifle the scream that rose in my throat.

On the third try I managed to keep hold of the needle, and I finally pulled it out. The sharp pain gave way to a dull ache and a heaviness in my arm, but the needle was no longer piercing my skin.

I rolled over, using my good arm to push myself to my knees. As I did, something dug into my thigh. I still had my cell phone in my pocket.

I grabbed for it, but I couldn't focus on the keys. I tried punching numbers, but all I got was a sharp tone that pierced my skull and a voice telling me to hang up and dial again.

I managed to stop the voice after some random button pushing, and began crawling toward Buddy. I didn't know how long we had before the Laceys came back, but I was sure it wouldn't be long enough.

Buddy's breathing was ragged, but at least he was still drawing breath.

That was the good news.

The bad news was that he didn't respond when I spoke to him.

I leaned closer, putting my mouth against his ear, and called his name. He moaned and shifted slightly.

"Buddy! You have to wake up!"

Nothing.

I had to leave him here. I couldn't wait any longer.

I managed to get to my feet, and staggered toward what I hoped was the door. I missed the doorway the first time, but made it into the hall on my second try.

I inched along, holding on to the wall for support. I had no idea how I'd get down the stairs, but I had to keep moving.

I heard running footsteps on the stairs. Lacey, several Laceys, appeared on the landing.

With an angry shout, they launched themselves in my direction. The cabinet door sagged open, hanging between us. I grabbed the door, leaned my weight against it, and leaped at the Laceys.

The door connected with a satisfying crunch, and bodies crumpled at my feet.

I didn't stop to try and sort things out.

I ran for the stairs, grabbing for the railing with my good hand. I touched a solid piece of wood, sloping away into the jumble of stairs that swam in front of my eyes.

I held on tight and let gravity pull me down, stumbling and bumping my way to the bottom.

The open front door was a blaze of light against the cool interior of the entry. I aimed for the light and kept moving, trusting I would find my way outside.

I staggered onto the porch and down the walk. I tripped over the jagged cement jumble I had avoided so easily before. I went down, banging my knee painfully against the concrete walk.

My truck, several trucks, sat at the curb, but there was no way I could drive. Even if I could manage to get in, and get the key in the ignition, I wouldn't make it to the county road before I drove into the ditch.

I had to stay on foot.

The bare lots around me offered no place to hide. I struck out across the unpaved street, heading for the swamp at the edge of the development.

Someone would miss me, and help would come.

Julie knew where I was. Somebody would find me. I just had to stay safe until help arrived.

But Buddy couldn't wait.

And I couldn't abandon him.

CHAPTER THIRTY-FOUR

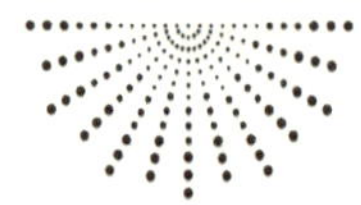

I made it to the tree line, and hunkered down behind a cypress knee. From my vantage point I watched the front of the house for a couple minutes. The door kept multiplying and then merging back into a single image, sometimes even holding together for several seconds.

Fatigue washed over me, buckling my knees. I tried to focus on the house, the door, but Lacey did not appear, and I worried what she might do to Buddy.

I had to keep moving.

I'd grown up here. I knew the area. All I had to do was stay behind the trees and head toward the county road.

Even if no one came along that road, it was only a couple miles to the highway. I was sure to find someone who could call for help once I reached the heavily traveled main road.

I staggered from one tree to the next, holding on to maintain my balance. I was still seeing double most of the time, and it slowed my progress as I dodged trees and roots that weren't there.

I tripped over a long branch hidden in the tall grass, and fell heavily against a tree, scraping the side of my face.

My left arm ached with a weariness that frightened me. I'd broken Lacey's needle, but not before she'd managed to inject part of the drug dose.

It wasn't a happy thought.

Using my good right arm, I dragged the branch out of the grass and used it to reach in front of me. I swung it from side to side, the way I'd seen blind people use their canes.

I didn't know exactly why they did that, but I guessed it would alert them to obstacles in their path. I hoped it would do the same for me.

I walked slowly, waving my makeshift cane, for what felt like hours. Each time I heard a noise, I stopped and listened, wondering when Lacey would catch up to me. How long before I felt that viselike grip on my arm, and the sting of the needle? How much time did I have left?

Even more worrisome, how much time did Buddy have?

At last, after an eternity of staggering through the trees, I came to the intersection with the main highway. I hadn't seen or heard a single car on the county road, and there wasn't a car on the highway either.

I wanted to turn toward town, but in order to do so, I had to leave the protection of the trees. Terror rooted me in place, refusing to let me move forward.

I gripped my stick in both hands, and forced myself out from the tree line. I limped toward the road, leaning on my makeshift cane.

A car came toward me. I fought the impulse to run and hide, fearful of who might be behind the wheel.

It wasn't until after the car sped past without even hesitating that I realized what they must have seen. A woman with a scraped-up face walking along a deserted road in a bloody T-shirt, waving a giant stick.

I tried to tell myself I would have stopped to see if she needed help, but the truth was darker and more unpleasant. I wouldn't have stopped, would have been afraid to stop.

But I would have called the police, and maybe they would, too. That would be enough.

The thought of calling the police worked its way through my addled brain, and I reached for my cell phone. Maybe I could focus enough to use it.

But my phone wasn't in my pocket. I checked every pocket, even those far too small to hold my phone, then checked them all again. But no matter how many times I patted and prodded every opening, there was no phone.

When had I seen it last? I knew it wasn't important; all that mattered was that I didn't have it. But it was a puzzle I couldn't leave alone, in the same way you can't ignore a stray thread on a shirt.

I started walking along the road in the direction of Keyhole Bay. Even if no one was willing to stop, I had to keep moving toward town, toward help.

Toward someone who could rescue Buddy.

As I walked, I puzzled over the phone. I'd had it when I left the store; slipped it into my pocket just before I got in the truck.

I remembered a voice, telling me to hang up and dial again. When was that? Had I tried to make a call while I was driving?

I watched two more cars zoom past, and hoped one of them would call the police.

Where the hell was my phone?

The voice had come after a piercing noise, a noise that shot through my brain like a hot needle.

Needle! I'd used the phone after I took the needle out of my arm. In the upstairs bedroom where Lacey had attacked me.

I knew where I'd seen the phone last, but that knowledge did me no good. If it was in that room, Lacey had it now, and I wasn't going back to look for it. All I could do was keep moving forward.

Perspiration stung my scalp, fat drops rolling down my neck. My T-shirt clung damply to my body, sweat mixing with drying blood and dirt from the swamp. I pulled on the neck of the shirt and wiped my face. I winced at the touch of the cloth against my scrapes. The feeling of momentary relief was quickly displaced by a fresh sheen of sweat.

I walked slowly, concentrating on just putting one foot in front of the other. Time didn't seem to make any sense. I didn't know whether I'd been walking for an hour or a week. It could have been either one.

Far ahead I could see buildings. I knew they were the motels and fast-food restaurants that dotted the fringes of Keyhole Bay, though I couldn't identify them at this distance. I had no clue how much farther I had to go. Half a mile? A mile? Two miles?

Could I even see two miles away? I didn't know, but the thought provided a welcome distraction. Anything was better than thinking about what could be happening in the empty model home in Bayvue Estates.

Double and triple images danced in the distance, and I abandoned the effort to make them merge. It hurt too much to force my eyes into focus, so I let my eyelids droop and my vision blur. The pain receded slightly.

I heard a car slow alongside me. Panic sent adrenaline surging through my exhausted body. Fight or flight, and I was too weak to fight.

I dropped my stick and tried to run, tried to focus on the field beside me. To find a path away from the attack I knew was coming.

But without the support of my stick, my legs refused to cooperate. My knees buckled, and I fell.

Hard.

I crawled, dragging myself along with my good arm. It didn't matter where I was going. I just had to get away.

"Glory!" I heard someone shouting my name.

I glanced over my shoulder, still trying to crawl away. The figure of a man, of several men, loomed over me. A hand reached down and clamped around my arm, pulling me to my feet.

A chill shot through me, and the world went black.

CHAPTER THIRTY-FIVE

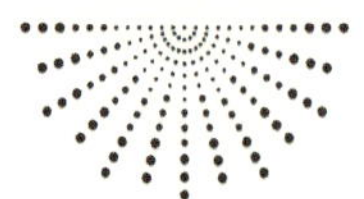

"Glory!"

I heard my name again, from a long ways away. Somebody was shaking me, telling me to wake up.

I didn't want to.

"Go 'way," I said, swatting at whoever was jostling me. "Want to sleep."

"I can't understand you," a man said. His voice was familiar, but I couldn't place it.

"Go 'way," I repeated as forcefully as I could.

"Glory, look at me!" It was a command, and somewhere deep inside, an obedient child forced my eyes open in response.

A broad, khaki-covered chest floated in front of my eyes, dozens of dark buttons dancing across the layers of fabric. I looked up from the chest to the face, closing one eye in an effort to bring his features into focus.

"It's Boomer, Glory. You know me."

Relief flooded my eyes with sudden tears.

Boomer was here. I was saved.

"Buddy," I said. My tongue felt funny in my mouth, and I tried again. "Buddy."

Boomer's face shifted and for a few seconds he had a single mouth, the corners turned up in a faint smile.

"Yep, I guess I am your buddy about now." He slid an arm underneath me, and raised my head slightly. "Can you sit up? We need to get you out of here."

He pulled me up. I grabbed at him, my fingers digging into his starched khaki shirt.

"Buddy!" I yelled. "Have to save Buddy!"

Boomer shook his heads. Head. I knew there was only one, in spite of what looked like two or three Boomers helping me to my feet. "That's a nasty bump you got there," he said. "How did you hurt your head?"

I raised my hand to my head, feeling for the bump he said was there. I didn't remember hitting my head on anything. I'd fallen and banged my knees, and my arm felt funny. But I couldn't remember exactly why; and I didn't remember hitting my head.

I leaned heavily on Boomer. He had one arm around my waist, and my feet barely touched the ground as we walked back toward the sounds of traffic on the highway.

Boomer put me in the passenger side of his cruiser and went around to slide under the wheel. He pulled out, headed back to town.

"Stop!"

This time he understood. He pulled abruptly back onto the shoulder, the car rocking to a sudden stop.

"Glory, we need to get you to a doctor," Boomer said, turning his head to look at me.

I squeezed my eyes shut and concentrated on forming the words he had to hear. "Must. Go. To. Bayvue."

I opened my eyes, silently begging him to hear the words I was trying to say.

He nodded, two heads bobbing his understanding. "Why?"

"Buddy. Danger. Needle." I had to work to produce each word as clearly as I could, to make my lips and tongue and teeth cooperate to form the precise sounds. "Hurt."

"But you need a doctor." He turned away, watching traffic.

"Go. Now. May. Be. Dead."

His head whipped back around. "Dead?" he asked.

"Maybe."

A siren, louder than I'd ever heard, stabbed into my skull. Colored lights flashed around me, and the car shot into traffic. The rear end squealed around in a high-speed U-turn, sending gravel showering across the road.

I was forced back into my seat as Boomer accelerated toward the county road. Whatever he'd heard, it had convinced him. Now all I could do was hang on and hope we got there in time.

Boomer flipped a switch on the dashboard, stabbed the brakes, and swung in a controlled slide around the corner onto the county road.

As he straightened out, he began yelling. "Need backup at Bayvue Estates. Code Three. Possible drug overdose. Request emergency rescue unit meet me there."

For an instant he swiveled his head toward me then immediately back to the empty road ahead of him. "And send an ambulance. I have one casualty, unknown how many more are at the scene."

Boomer cut the lights and siren as the brick gateposts appeared on our right. I thought we were going to fly right past them, but he swung wide and fishtailed into the deserted development.

I spotted my truck, still parked on the street. As we drew closer, the multiple images merged into one and held. I moved my head and they split apart again. But they had been one truck for several seconds.

I turned to look at the second house and held my head steady while my brain slowly pulled the image into focus. Buddy's rental car sat in the driveway alone.

Lacey's car was nowhere in sight, but I didn't remember seeing it when I arrived. Was it hidden, or had she actually left?

Boomer threw his door open.

Moving slowly, I unbuckled the seat belt Boomer had put around me, and opened the door.

"Stay there," Boomer ordered, reaching past me to pull the door closed. "I'll check it out."

"Wait."

He hesitated.

"Lacey might be here." The words came out slowly, but Boomer watched me as I spoke. "She had a needle." I gestured to the bruise on the inside of my elbow where the needle had broken off. "She tried to give me a shot."

Boomer closed his door and looked at me as though I was finally making sense. My efforts were paying off.

"Was there anyone else in the house?"

"Buddy McKenna," I said. "He was bleeding."

"McKenna? The McKenna woman's brother? That's who you were talking about." I half expected to see a lightbulb go off over Boomer's head. "He was here?"

"Upstairs. Closet in the back bedroom." A deep sadness welled up in me as I thought of Buddy left alone in that closet. "I couldn't wake him up."

"I know how that feels," Boomer muttered as he opened his door again. He slid out, crouching behind the open door.

He stayed there for a minute or two, then darted quickly toward the house, flattening himself against the front wall. I saw him turn his head, and heard his voice speaking softly through the radio in the car.

"There's a second victim reported to be upstairs," he said. "I'm going to check."

I could hear sirens coming in our direction, growing louder.

"Backup is on the way," the dispatcher said from the radio. "Hang on, you'll have help in two minutes."

I could see Boomer moving toward the front door, crouching down below the windowsills and sliding along the front of the house.

He reached the door just as the first car slid to a stop behind the cruiser where I waited. An officer in a protective vest, his gun drawn, jumped from the front seat and sprinted across the bare clay of the yard.

Together, the two men entered the house. Boomer provided cover for the armored officer, then followed him inside.

Another car pulled in ahead of Boomer's and two more officers spilled out. The radio crackled with questions and terse answers as the two men inside made their way through the house.

Repeated calls of "Clear" marked their progress as they checked for signs of life.

As Boomer radioed that they were starting up the stairs, a rescue unit slammed to a stop in the middle of the road. Two paramedics piled out and began pulling equipment cases from the back of the truck.

"Pool of blood in the upstairs hall, and blood on a cabinet door," Boomer reported. "But no one here."

I felt a grim satisfaction at their discovery. I remembered a solid thud of the cupboard door as it hit Lacey. I felt certain the blood was hers.

Payback.

I listened as they made their way through the bedrooms, calling out each time they verified a room was empty. They cleared the master suite, and the second bedroom, without seeing anyone. All that was left was the back bedroom.

The place I had last seen Buddy.

A familiar car lurched to a stop next to the cruiser, blue and red lights strobing from a portable flasher. A tall figure burst from the door.

Jake.

He threw open the cruiser door and pulled me into a tight hug.

"Are you okay?" he asked. "I got here as quick as I could."

"Yes," I answered, my face buried against his chest. "I'll be fine, just as soon as I stop seeing double."

Jake pulled back and immediately started inspecting my head. He found the lump on my left temple, gently pushing aside my hair and inspecting the injury.

"You need to see a doctor," he said. "Why did Boomer bring you back out here instead of taking you directly to the hospital?"

"I told him to."

"And he did what you told him, not what he should?" Anger tightened Jake's voice.

I started to explain, when Boomer interrupted me. "Second victim," he said over the radio. "Head wound. Possible drug overdose. I need the paramedics up here now!"

Jake released me. "Sure you're okay?"

I nodded.

He sprinted across the front yard and disappeared into the open front door. Seconds later I heard his voice on the radio. Calm and confident sounding, he repeated information from the paramedics to the hospital emergency room and the incoming ambulance.

But he didn't sound like a volunteer repeating the words of others; he sounded like someone in charge. Someone who knew and understood exactly what was going on. Someone with more training and experience than Keyhole Bay could ever provide.

The kind of person who read the things I'd seen on his bookshelf.

But there would be time to speculate on that later. Right now I wanted to know about Buddy.

The house was clear. Boomer had assured everyone of that in his last transmission. No reason I had to stay in the car.

I opened the door and got out. For the first few seconds the ground tilted and swung around me as I clutched the door frame to steady myself. But eventually the world righted itself and I was able to let go of the car.

Stepping with exaggerated care, I made my way to the front door and went inside. The staircase stretched in front of me, triggering memories of my last trip down it, clinging to the handrail and half crawling, half falling to the bottom.

I tried to grip the rail with my left hand, but my arm still didn't cooperate properly. Instead I leaned my good right arm against the wall and inched my way up.

I was still a couple steps from the top when Boomer found me.

"I told you to stay put," he said, taking my hand and helping me up the last two steps. "Don't you ever do what you're told?"

"I waited," I said. My words came quicker now, but I still had to concentrate. "Until you said the house was clear."

"That doesn't mean it was safe for you to go walking around," he answered. He turned my back to the wall and gently pushed my shoulders down, forcing me to sit at the top of the stairs.

"Is Buddy . . ."

"They're still working on him," Boomer answered the question I couldn't finish. "They'll get him stabilized before they take him to the hospital. But the paramedics seem to think he's going to make it."

That was the good news.

"And Lacey?"

Boomer shook his head. "No sign of her. But we have four states on the lookout for her car. She won't get far."

I nodded and closed my eyes. "Can I sleep now?" I asked.

"Fifteen minutes," Boomer said. "You almost certainly have a concussion. I'll see if I can find you some ice. And you have to wake up every fifteen minutes until the doctor says different."

I heard his rapid footsteps go down the stairs as I faded.

CHAPTER THIRTY-SIX

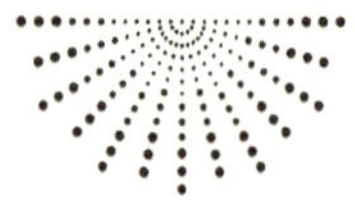

Sudden cold against my scalp jolted me back to awareness. Boomer held a towel to my temple, the ice inside it already beginning to melt in the afternoon heat.

Drops of cool water slid down my cheek and splattered onto my grimy T-shirt. I looked down and realized I couldn't tell what color the shirt had been when I put it on that morning.

Two men in navy slacks and crisp white shirts hurried past me with a stretcher.

They disappeared into a door at the end of the hall.

Much later they wheeled the stretcher out of the room. This time there was a body strapped to it, tubes and wires running from under the draped sheet to beeping monitors and bags of clear fluid.

As they neared the top of the stairs, I forced my way to my feet. I had to see for myself.

Buddy's face was nearly as pale as the stark white sheet. His eyes were closed, and he made a nasty gurgling sound with each breath. But he was breathing, and his eyelids fluttered as the paramedics rolled him down the hall.

They reached the stairs and stopped to maneuver the stretcher into position to carry it down. Buddy's eyes opened slightly, and he caught sight of me.

The tube in his throat prevented him from speaking, but his expression of relief matched the emotion that passed over me.

We were both alive. Something I wouldn't have bet on a few hours earlier. I hoped someday he could tell me what had happened in those hours. But for now we both needed medical attention.

The ambulance crew folded up the legs of the stretcher and made their way down the stairs. At the bottom I heard the legs click into place once again and the wheels clattered across the entry and out the door. A minute later the siren gave a chirp and the ambulance rolled away.

Jake emerged from the back bedroom with the paramedics, helping them lug their equipment back to the truck.

As I looked in his direction, I caught sight of the sagging cabinet door. A blossom of brownish dried blood marked the side facing the stairs.

"I did that," I said to Boomer, pointing at the door. "She was coming at me, and I hit her in the face with the door."

"I'd be willing to bet you broke her nose," he said, "judging by the looks of it, and that puddle on the floor. I'll be sure to add that to the bulletin."

"If she goes for medical help, we might find her that way."

The three men reached us and stopped. Boomer took the equipment case away from Jake. "I'll take this," he said. "You take care of her and I'll meet you at the emergency room."

He held out his hand. "Give me your keys," he said. "I'll see to it that someone brings your truck back into town."

The truck. "What time is it?"

Jake glanced at his watch. "Half-past twelve. Why?"

"Sly's waiting for me. He was supposed to change the oil on the truck today." I knew better than to even ask. There was no way Boomer would let me drive until I saw the doctor.

I dragged the keys out of my pocket and reluctantly placed them in his upturned palm.

"We'll take it to Mr. Sylvester," Boomer assured me. "But I suggest you call him so he doesn't worry."

"I would, but I lost my phone somewhere."

"Oh, yeah." Jake dug in his pocket and handed me my phone. Bloody fingerprints on the screen made clear when I had last tried to use it, and a shudder ran up my spine.

Jake grabbed it and stuffed it back in his pocket. "Never mind," he said. "You can use my phone when we get to the car."

He wrapped his arm around my waist and helped me down the stairs and out to his car. He retrieved his phone from the console, punched a couple buttons, and handed it to me. It was already ringing.

When Sly answered, he seemed relieved to hear my voice. "Miz Julie called here looking for you. Said you'd gone out to talk to that banker fella and she knew you were supposed to bring the truck by today. You okay?"

"I'll be fine," I assured him. "Had a little trouble, but it's taken care of. Sorry for missing our lunch date."

He laughed, and I could imagine the wide grin on his face. "Yeah, well, don't let that fella of yours know I'm beating his time. You be by later?"

"I don't know exactly. Boomer said he'd have someone drop the truck at your place and I can pick it up, but I don't know quite when. Might be tonight before I can get over there."

His chuckle died. "Sounds like more than a little trouble, girl. You *sure* you're okay?"

Jake held out his hand, gesturing at me to hand him the phone. I surrendered it reluctantly, afraid he'd reveal more than I wanted Sly to know.

"Sly, it's Jake." He listened a moment. "No, she's going to be fine. Bumped her head is all. Boomer and I both think she ought to be checked before she goes gallivanting around town."

Gallivanting? Did I actually hear Jake use that word? He was clearly starting to talk like a local. Next thing you know, he'll start saying "y'all."

"I'm taking her to the doctor now," he continued. "and I'll bring her by to get the truck as soon as the doctor says she's okay to drive."

He was silent again, listening as he pulled onto the county road. "I'll tell her," he said. "And I'll let you know when we're headed your way."

He hung up and tossed the phone back into the console. "He says for you to take it easy and not be in too big of a hurry about anything." He glanced over at me, then back at the road. "I didn't have to tell him that was completely useless advice, because you'll just do what you please anyway."

I started to protest, but he cut me off. "And don't try telling me any different. I know better."

Unfortunately, he did. I gave up trying to argue, and sat quietly the rest of the way to the hospital.

Typical summertime injuries crowded the emergency room. Kids with cuts and scrapes, teens with extreme sunburns, retirees with heat stroke, and a middle-aged couple injured by a fender bender.

But I didn't have to wait. As soon as the nurse heard my name, I was whisked out of the waiting room and into a bed. "Boomer told us to take good care of you," she said.

Jake stayed by my side, but discreetly turned his head as she cut away the remains of my T-shirt and covered me with a clean sheet. No one questioned his right to be there.

"How did you know what to do?" I asked him at one point. "You sounded like you were in charge up there."

For a long moment I didn't think he was going to answer, but then he said solemnly, "I was a paramedic once, in another life. I guess it's time you knew about that life.

"I promise I'll tell you all about it. After I get you home."

I fully intended to hold him to that promise.

A nurse cleaned up my scrapes and iced my bruises. They sent me for X-rays and scans of my brain. They bandaged my arm and checked my blood for signs of the drugs Lacey had tried to shoot into me. The tests stretched into late afternoon. I sat in my bed, the curtains drawn for a modicum of privacy, and tried not to eavesdrop as patients came and went in the beds around me.

Jake stayed until I shooed him out. "You still have a store to run," I reminded him. "You can't just close for the day in the middle of the summer."

"I can do whatever I choose to do," he replied.

He finally let me chase him out, but only after Linda and Karen arrived in response to his calls. "Somebody needs to take care of her," he told them, as though I wasn't perfectly capable of taking care of myself.

Still, I had to admit I kind of like him fussing over me.

Boomer came in while I was waiting for the test results, and asked my two protectors to give him a few moments alone with me.

"Go get a Coke," he said, and they agreed.

Once we were alone, he pulled a chair close to the bed.

"If you keep this up," he said, "I am going to have to just give up and put you on the force."

I shook my head, and instantly regretted it. "No," I told him, "you really won't. It's not like I *want* to do this."

"Then why, Glory? Why do you end up in the middle of these things?"

I couldn't very well tell him it was Bluebeard's fault. Bad enough I'd shared that secret with my friends. I didn't want to share it with the police chief.

Instead I asked a question of my own.

"How's Buddy? None of the doctors will tell me anything."

Boomer seemed just as happy to change the subject. He told me Buddy was doing well, and was expected to make a full recovery. They'd removed the tube in his throat and he was awake and talking, though he was still weak.

"Lacey shot him full of something she got from the pharmacy," Boomer said. "Probably the same stuff she tried to inject you with." He cleared his throat, and lowered his voice. "We picked her up a couple hours ago, and when I left the station, she was still talking. Trying to blame it all on Francis.

"You didn't hear any of this from me," Boomer continued, "because I can't tell you anything, but Lacey said Francis went out to beg Bridget to help him keep his job and the house. Bridget knew him from the bank, so she let him in. But when he asked her to give him a second chance she said she couldn't. Francis pushed her, she fell and hit her head, he couldn't wake her. Francis called Lacey in a panic, and she decided she had to clean up his mess. Her words."

I remembered her saying something like that at the house when she attacked me. "And her idea of cleaning up a mess was to shoot her full of drugs?"

Boomer shrugged. "She was improvising, and drugs were the one thing she knew. She thought she could pass it off as an overdose—that everybody would be willing to believe it—and it almost worked. She figured it would give them time to sell off anything of value and make a run for it."

"If I hadn't spent some time with her, I'd have believed it, too." I left out the part about the postcards and Bluebeard. That part was personal, and he already had all he needed to put Lacey and Francis away for a long time.

He hesitated, as though deciding whether to give me any more information. "Did you know Lacey and Francis had a boat?"

"Nope."

"Had it moored over near Port St. Joe. That's where Lacey was headed. Guess they were planning to head south." Boomer pushed himself up out of the chair. "Anyway, Buddy will be okay. We sent a unit out to pick up Francis, and I just got a call that they're on their way in with him in custody." He shook his head. "No job's worth that."

CHAPTER THIRTY-SEVEN

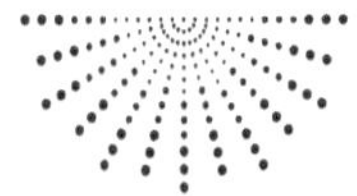

Julie agreed to work until I was better, insisting I stay upstairs and rest. Jake agreed with her, and he checked on me several times a day to be sure I stayed out of the store.

At night he brought dinner and told me stories of his days as a firefighter, paramedic, and fire captain in California.

There was a lot to tell, including the fire that killed one of his crew, and forced his retirement on a partial disability. No wonder he'd been worried about making the grade in Keyhole Bay's volunteer unit.

But even with the constant company of Jake and Karen and Sly and Linda, and a short outing to Karen's for our regular dinner on Thursday, I was getting stir-crazy. A week of enforced idleness had nearly driven me nuts. When the doctor finally agreed on Monday afternoon to allow me go back to work, I was overjoyed.

Jake brought me home after my appointment and we let ourselves in the back door. Julie was at the counter with Mandy, deep in conversation.

"We need more," Julie was saying as she inspected a shirt with a large picture of Bluebeard on the front.

"I'll need three days, and that's if we put a rush on it," Mandy replied. "I think I can get my boss to waive the fee for it, just this once."

Julie noticed me and waved me over. "Is that okay with you?"

"Is what okay?"

"A reorder. We need more shirts."

I shook my head. "Not until these are sold," I told her. I thought about the gamble I'd already taken with my Buy-Out-Peter Fund. "I can't commit any more money to untested inventory."

Julie waved a piece of paper. "I started taking orders last Monday, when Mandy brought the prototype, and people have been picking them up all weekend. We're out of a couple sizes, and low on the rest. Oh, and the mugs are nearly gone, too."

Stunned, I looked across the shop at Bluebeard. If it was possible for a parrot to look smug, he did.

Jake slipped his arm around me. "It's time to start talking price with Peter," he said. "Thanks to Bluebeard."

From his perch across the shop, Bluebeard ruffled his feathers and struck a pose. Just like the one on the shirts and postcards.

"Pretty boy."

This time he didn't mean Jake.

MENUS AND RECIPES

A cold supper usually consists of a variety of salads, along with bread and butter, a tray of pickles and olives, and sweet tea. While the salads require refrigeration, the flavors will be stronger and richer if the dishes are cool, not icy cold.

Glory's Childhood Cold Supper

Chicken salad can be spreadable for a sandwich or chunky for a main dish. Either way, the ingredients are similar: cooked chicken and vegetables in a creamy dressing. Although some versions use grapes, Glory's favorite recipe adds a bit of chopped apple for sweetness.

Chicken Salad

3 cups cooked chicken, chilled and cubed

½ cup each chopped onion, celery, and apple

½ cup toasted pecans

¼ teaspoon caraway seed

salt and pepper to taste

1 tablespoon lemon juice

¾ cup mayonnaise

There are several options for the chicken itself: grill or bake chicken breasts and/or thighs, roast a whole chicken (or buy one already cooked at the supermarket), or buy precooked breast strips.

Toss the chicken, onion, celery, apple, and pecans lightly. Stir the caraway seeds, salt, pepper, and lemon juice into the mayonnaise; pour over the chicken mixture; and stir to coat. Refrigerate, covered, until ready to serve. Garnish with additional pecans, if desired.

For a luncheon, serve a scoop of salad atop a leaf of butter or iceberg lettuce. Or like Glory, you can serve family-style from a large bowl.

Deviled eggs are a favorite in the South. While a dozen eggs may sound like a lot, these are very popular. And if you do have leftovers, mash them into egg salad for sandwiches!

Deviled Eggs

1 dozen eggs, hard-cooked

½ cup mayonnaise

1 tablespoon mustard

2 tablespoons sweet pickle relish

salt and pepper to taste

paprika, for garnish

To make perfectly hard-cooked eggs, refrigerate raw eggs for 3 to 5 days before cooking (they will be easier to peel) and bring them to room temperature. Place them in a single layer in a pot, cover completely with cold water, and bring to a rapid boil. When the water boils, remove the pan from heat, cover tightly, and let sit for 17 minutes (20 minutes for jumbo eggs). Drain and cover the eggs with cold water for at least 10 minutes. A trick for peeling eggs: after draining the cold water, leave the eggs in the pan, put the cover back on, and shake gently for 20 or 30 seconds.

When the eggs are cooled, cut them in half and scoop the yolks into a bowl. Mash the yolks with the mayonnaise, mustard, pickle relish, salt, and pepper. Fill the scooped-out whites with the yolk mixture, sprinkle with paprika, and chill.

Coleslaw is another Southern staple. It's a mainstay on BBQ platters and at picnics throughout the region.

Cole Slaw

½ head each green and red cabbage, shredded

1 carrot, shredded

dressing (recipe follows), or use your favorite bottled dressing

parsley for garnish

Toss the shredded cabbage and carrot with the dressing. Chill for at least an hour to allow the flavors to mellow. Garnish with parsley.

Coleslaw Dressing

¾ cup mayonnaise

2 tablespoons vinegar

½ teaspoon sugar

½ teaspoon celery seed

salt and pepper to taste

¼ teaspoon caraway seed, optional

Mix well.

Everyone has their favorite potato salad recipe. In the South there is a wide variety of pickles, most of which can be used in place of the dill pickles.

Potato Salad

3 pounds potatoes

3–4 boiled eggs

½ cup each of celery, onion, and dill pickle, chopped

1 cup mayonnaise

¼ cup mustard

salt and pepper to taste

paprika for garnish

Cook the potatoes until tender, but still firm. Cool, peel, and cube. Reserve one boiled egg, and chop the remaining eggs. (See "Deviled Eggs," above, for instructions on cooking eggs.) Mix the potatoes, chopped eggs, celery, onion, and pickles. Mix the mayonnaise and mustard with salt and pepper. And a tablespoon of pickle juice, if desired. Pour the dressing over the potato mixture, toss gently, cover, and refrigerate.

When ready to serve, slice the reserved egg to garnish, and sprinkle with paprika for color.

Macaroni salad and potato salad are very similar, though macaroni salad usually does not include boiled eggs. As a variation, macaroni salad may be made with Miracle Whip, a popular mayonnaise substitute with a sweeter, spicier flavor.

Macaroni Salad

3 cups cooked elbow macaroni

1/3 cup each of celery and onion, chopped

¼ cup chopped pimento, optional

½ cup mayonnaise or Miracle Whip

1 tablespoon vinegar

1 tablespoon sugar

salt to taste

Cook the macaroni according to the package directions. Rinse and run under cold water. Toss with the celery and onion. Add the pimento, if using. Whisk together the mayonnaise, vinegar, and sugar. Toss the macaroni mixture with the dressing. Refrigerate until ready to serve.

For three-bean salad, you can either cook your own beans or use canned beans. If you're trying to avoid heating up the kitchen, canned is the way to go.

Three-Bean Salad

1½ cups kidney beans

1½ cups garbanzo beans

1½ cups green beans

1 red onion, thinly sliced

½ cup vinegar

½ cup salad oil

salt and pepper to taste

If using canned beans, drain and rinse well under cold running water. Toss the beans and onion with the vinegar and oil. Add salt and pepper to taste. Refrigerate several hours, or overnight, to allow flavors to combine and mellow.

Fruit salad will depend on the season, and the region. Use whatever fruit is perfectly ripe when you visit your local grocery store. Better yet, seek out a local farmers' market for fresh, local produce. Experiment with different melons, such as yellow watermelon, Santa Claus, Crenshaw, or Persian melons. Red, black, or green grapes can also be added.

Fruit Salad

1 small watermelon

1 medium cantaloupe

1 medium honeydew melon

3 medium peaches

2–3 kiwifruit

1 medium pineapple

1 pint strawberries

½ pint blueberries

½ pint blackberries

dressing (recipe follows)

mint leaves, for garnish

Cube the melons, slice the peaches, and peel and slice the kiwis. Clean and cube the pineapple. Clean and hull all the berries—they can be used whole or cut into pieces, depending on size. Toss the melons and pineapple; gently fold in the berries. Arrange sliced peaches and kiwi on top, and drizzle with dressing. Chill. Remove from the refrigerator, garnish with mint leaves, and let stand about 20 minutes before serving.

Dressing

juice of 1 orange, about 2 ounces

juice of 1 lemon, about 1 ounce

juice of 1 lime, about 1 ounce, optional

1 tablespoon good-quality honey

Mix the orange and lemon juices (and lime, if using). Whisk in the honey.

We truly have no idea where these cookies originated, but they appear under many names in kitchens across the country. They're easy, tasty, quick to make, and require no baking—a real plus in a Florida summer!

Lunchroom Cookies

3 cups oatmeal

1/2 cup peanut butter

1/2 milk

2 cups sugar

1/4 cup cocoa

1/2 cup butter

1 teaspoon vanilla

1/4 teaspoon salt

Mix the oatmeal and peanut butter in a large bowl. Set aside. In a saucepan, combine the milk, sugar, cocoa, and butter. Stir frequently, until the mixture makes a syrup. Bring to a rolling boil and boil 1 minute, stirring frequently.

Remove from heat; stir in the salt and vanilla. Immediately pour the hot syrup over the oatmeal–peanut butter mixture. Stir. As soon as the syrup is mixed in, drop the batter by teaspoonfuls onto waxed paper. Allow to cool for at least 1 hour before removing from the paper. Store in an airtight container.

Homemade ice cream is a wonderful end to any meal. Sweet, creamy, flavored with fresh fruit. Who could ask for anything more?

Peach Ice Cream

4 cups fresh peaches (about 8 small peaches), peeled and diced

1 cup sugar

12 ounces evaporated milk

1 package (3.75 ounces) instant vanilla pudding mix

14 ounces sweetened condensed milk

4 cups half-and-half

Mix the peaches and sugar; let sit for 1 hour. Puree the peach mixture in a blender or food processor until smooth. In a large bowl, stir the pudding mix into the evaporated milk. Add the pureed peaches, condensed milk, and half-and-half.

Place the mixture in the container of a 4-quart ice cream freezer and freeze according to the manufacturer's directions. When the freezing is completed, place the ice cream in an airtight container in the freezer until firm and ready to serve.

The standard Southern beverage, sweet tea, is served at every meal. Southerners like their sweet tea, and most traditional homes will have a pitcher or two in the refrigerator.

Sweet Tea

6 cups water

6 tea bags—traditionally, plain black tea

1 cup sugar

mint sprigs or lemon slices for garnish, optional

Bring the water to a boil, add the sugar, and stir to dissolve. Steep the tea bags in the sweetened water to the desired strength, and serve in tall glasses of ice. Garnish with mint sprigs or lemon slices, if desired.

A grilled dinner is a tradition across the country on Independence Day. But instead of the standard burgers and dogs, try these recipes for an exciting change of pace. Add a big jug of sweet tea or a cooler of beer, and you have all the ingredients for a spectacular Fourth of July.

Felipe's Grilled Gala

Shrimp in lettuce cups, or lettuce wraps, are a cool spicy/sweet start to an evening of grilled goodness. The lettuce acts as a bowl or wrap, which makes these finger food.

Shrimp in Lettuce Cups

1 pound cooked cocktail shrimp

1 small cucumber, chopped

1 large avocado, diced

3 Roma tomatoes, diced

1/4 cup cilantro, chopped

1/4 cup white wine

1/4 cup olive oil

salt and pepper to taste

1 head Boston, Bibb, or romaine lettuce (see instructions)

Toss together the shrimp, cucumber, avocado, tomato, and cilantro. Mix the white wine and olive oil, add salt and pepper to taste, and pour over the shrimp mixture.

For lettuce cups, use Boston or Bibb lettuce. Wash and dry leaves and arrange on a plate. Place a spoonful of shrimp in each lettuce "bowl" to serve.

For rolls, use romaine lettuce. Cut the bottom off the lettuce, wash and dry leaves, and cut in half crosswise. Place a spoonful of shrimp mixture on each half leaf, fold up one end about a half inch, and roll up like a cigar. Use a toothpick to secure each roll.

Serve with plenty of napkins!

This simple marinated and grilled chicken is the perfect antidote to a summer of hamburgers. Served with grilled vegetables, it makes a hearty, and healthy, summer meal.

Grilled Chicken

3/4 cup white wine

3/4 cup melted butter

1 ounce lemon juice

5–6 cloves garlic, minced

2 tablespoons dried rosemary, or 2 sprigs fresh rosemary leaves

salt and pepper to taste, about 1/2 teaspoon each

2 chickens, 3–4 pounds each, quartered; or 6 pounds bone-in chicken pieces

Mix all the ingredients except the chicken; reserve about 1 cup for basting. Pour the remaining mixture over the chicken in a plastic bag. Turn and shake gently until the chicken is completely coated. Force out as much air as possible, close the bag securely, and allow the chicken to marinate for several hours in the refrigerator.

Place the chicken bone-side down on a hot grill. Baste with marinade, and continue basting frequently while cooking. Cook for about 10–12 minutes, turn and baste, and cook another 10–12 minutes. Repeat turning and basting until the chicken is completely cooked (meat thermometer reads 180° when inserted in thickest part of the piece). Total cooking time is about 45 minutes.

Vegetable skewers, with their variety of colors and textures, are an attractive addition to any grilled menu. Use or omit any vegetable that you prefer, or do each skewer with a single vegetable and allow your guests to help themselves to their favorites.

Skewered Vegetables

2 each medium red bell, green bell, and yellow bell peppers

2 small yellow squash

2 small zucchini

1 red onion

24 cherry tomatoes

24 mushrooms

1/2 cup olive oil

1/2 cup lemon or lime juice

1/4 cup water

1/4 cup Dijon mustard

2 tablespoons honey
2 tablespoons minced garlic
2 tablespoons chopped fresh basil leaves
1/2 teaspoon salt
1/2 teaspoon freshly ground black pepper

Prepare the vegetables: Remove the seeds and stems from the peppers, and cut into 2-inch squares; section the squash and zucchini into ¼-inch slices; peel the onion and cut into 2-inch squares; rinse the tomatoes; the mushrooms may be used whole, or halved if they are very large.

Mix the remaining ingredients, pour over the cut vegetables in a plastic bag, and marinate for 3–4 hours. Soak ten 12-inch bamboo skewers in water, or use metal sewers. (Be careful when handling metal sewers; they will get very hot!) Thread an assortment of vegetables on each skewer, place over a medium-hot grill, and cook 10–12 minutes, turning regularly and basting with marinade.

Eggplant does well on the grill. Be sure the eggplant is tender, but don't overcook it, as it can get mushy.

Grilled Eggplant

2 eggplants
1/4 cup olive oil
1/4 cup balsamic vinegar
1 tablespoon minced garlic
1/4 teaspoon each thyme, basil, dill, and oregano
1 teaspoon kosher salt, or to taste
1/2 teaspoon black pepper, or to taste

Slice the eggplants about ½-inch thick. Whisk together the remaining ingredients. Coat the eggplant slices with the oil and vinegar mixture (brushing works well), and grill on a hot grill, turning once, for about 15 minutes.

Tomatoes show up in lots of Southern dishes. They can be baked, broiled, fried, sliced, diced, made into sauce—or grilled. This basic recipe can be enhanced with herbs or spices such as oregano or pepper flakes, depending on your personal preferences, topped with fresh herbs such as basil or thyme, or garnished with grated Parmesan cheese.

Grilled Tomatoes

4 large tomatoes
2 teaspoons salt
1 teaspoon black pepper

1 teaspoon garlic powder

1/3 cup minced garlic

1/4 cup extra virgin olive oil

Cut the tomatoes in half crosswise. Mix the salt, pepper, and garlic powder; season the cut side with the dry mixture. In a small saucepan (you can do this on a side burner, or the back of the grill), sauté the minced garlic in olive oil and set aside.

Place the tomatoes cut-side down on a hot grill. Grill 3–5 minutes, turn over, top with the garlic and oil mixture, and grill for another 3 minutes. When the tomatoes are done, they can be topped with fresh herbs, bread crumbs, and/or grated cheese.

This grilled menu holds an array of vegetable dishes and aromatic chicken, a departure from the standard grilled meal. But we bow to tradition with the inclusion of the classic summertime dish: baked beans. And while a traditional cook would start with dried beans and spend a couple days cooking, this recipe takes a shortcut and starts with canned pork and beans, then improves them.

Baked Beans

3 15-ounce cans pork and beans

1 large onion, chopped

¼ cup brown sugar

¼ cup honey

¼ cup yellow mustard

¼ cup ketchup

1 ounce lemon juice

½ pound bacon, cut into small pieces

Mix all the ingredients except the bacon in a fireproof baking dish (a disposable aluminum pan works well). Sprinkle the bacon pieces on top. Cover with foil and heat on a grill for 1½–2 hours. All the ingredients except the bacon are already cooked, but the longer cooking time allows the flavors to blend and mellow.

After an excellent meal, this light dessert is a perfect finish. Sweet and juicy, it's like a little slice of peach heaven. Choose fruit that is still firm to the touch; too ripe and it will fall apart on the grill.

Grilled Peaches

6 medium peaches, ripe but still firm

¼ cup melted butter

¼ cup honey or brown sugar, optional

Halve the peaches and remove the pits. Peeling is not necessary but you may do so if you prefer. Brush the peaches with the melted butter. Brush on the honey or sprinkle with brown sugar, if you want a little sweeter dessert. Lightly oil the grill. Place the peach halves on the grill facedown. Cook for about 4 minutes. Turn. Brush on additional honey, or sprinkle with more brown sugar, if desired. Cook for another 4–5 minutes, until the peaches are soft.

Serve plain, or with vanilla or peach ice cream, yogurt, or whipped cream.

MURDER TIES THE KNOT

"THOROUGHLY ENTERTAINING."
—JULIE HYZY, *NEW YORK TIMES* BESTSELLER

CHRISTY FIFIELD

NATIONAL BESTSELLING AUTHOR

MURDER TIES THE KNOT

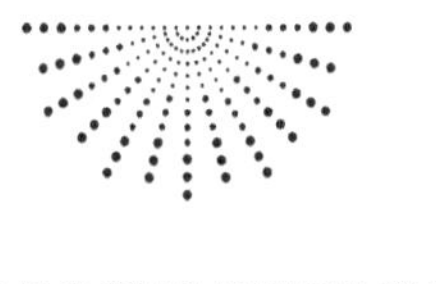

CHRISTY FIFIELD

DEDICATION

This one is for the fans, who make it all worthwhile.
And especially for Dru Ann, the patron saint of cozy writers.

ACKNOWLEDGMENTS

To the usual crew of crazies:
Colleen, first reader, friend, gym pal;
Jan and Jeri, sisters who really know how to celebrate a birthday;
and most of all Steve, who's kept me sane for the last thirty years.
Thank you all!!

CHAPTER ONE

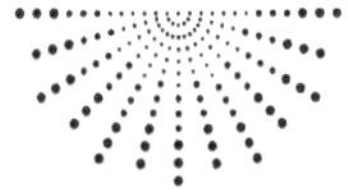

I stood in the center of my small living room, struggling to remain motionless. I wore a dark green satin dress that clung to me in an unfamiliar way, and tottered on a pair of matching heels far higher than anything I had ever owned.

The sliding door to my miniscule balcony was open a crack, letting in a cool, late afternoon breeze. It was early November, and in the Florida Panhandle that meant seventy degree days. The temperature was dropping and I would have to close the door soon, but for now I welcomed the slight chill. It helped soothe my nerves, and I wasn't the only one with an attack of nerves.

My furniture had been pushed back to clear the center of the room, and Keyhole Bay's radio star, Karen "The Voice of the Shores" Freed, paced like a caged animal.

"Glory! Stand still," Karen snapped. Normally I would find the contrast between her actions and her words amusing. But this wasn't a normal day.

I sighed, not even trying to hide my exasperation. Ever since I agreed to be her maid of honor, my so-called best friend had started channeling every bad bride I'd ever seen. And as the owner of a gift shop in the Florida Panhandle, I'd seen plenty of them on "destination" weekends, bossing their bridesmaids around and generally acting like what my memaw called "donkeys in horses' harness."

"Seriously, Martine?" Karen said, her chestnut curls shaking in disbelief.

"This poor woman is trying to mark the hem of your dress, and you can't stop fidgeting." She waved at her former and future mother-in-law, on her knees in front of me.

To her credit, Mrs. Freed just laughed. "Easy, Karen," she cautioned. "Glory already did this for you once, if you'll remember. Not many friends would do it twice."

Karen reached down and hugged the older woman. "And not many women would be lucky enough to get you for a mother-in-law. Twice." She took a deep breath and backed away. "I think I'll go get us some coffee, okay?"

Mrs. Freed nodded, distracted by the heavy green satin that pooled around my ankles. "Go on," she said around a mouthful of pins. "I'll be finished by the time you get back."

Karen shot me a last warning glance and hurried down the stairs that led from the small apartment to the gift shop below.

True to her word, Mrs. Freed finished pinning the hem and I was comfortably back in my jeans and polo shirt by the time Karen returned.

She carried a cardboard tray of paper coffee cups and a white bakery bag from Lighthouse Coffee next door. Setting the coffee on the kitchen table, she held the bag out to Mrs. Freed. "I really appreciate what you're doing," she said. "And Pansy says to tell you hello."

Mrs. Freed opened the bag and sniffed appreciatively. "Lordy, that woman knows her way around a cruller, doesn't she?" She took a shiny glazed twist and passed me the bag.

Still warm, the pastry was irresistible.

"Careful," Karen commanded. "You still need to fit into that dress."

"Do we really need to do all this?" I knew I was whining, but Karen's wedding was still six weeks away. A lot could happen in that time.

"Glory!" Karen's impatience with me was evident in her voice. "We had to book the church a year ago, and the florist wanted more than six months.

"Weddings take time," she said, as though that was a real answer.

"They don't have to," I argued. "People get married without all this," I searched for a description, and came up with one of Memaw's favorites, "fuss and feathers."

I knew better than to continue, but I couldn't stop myself. "It's only Monday. You and Riley could go to the courthouse tomorrow, get your license, and get married on Friday. Or we could get on a plane tomorrow morning, fly to Las Vegas, and you'd be married before suppertime."

"And my mother would never forgive me." She shook her head. "I did the no-fuss thing the first time I married Riley, remember? Maid of honor and best man as witnesses, with a justice of the peace. I think my mom was still holding a grudge when we got divorced. So we better do it right this time."

I followed Karen and Mrs. Freed down the stairs to the shop. It was time for my assistant Julie to leave, and I had to relieve her.

We all hugged Mrs. Freed good-bye, then Julie dashed out to retrieve her toddler from Grandma. Anita Nelson doted on Rose Ann, and one of these days she hoped to retire and keep her only grandchild full-time. But that day wasn't today, or likely very soon.

"Besides," I continued once Karen and I were alone, "your mother is three thousand miles away."

"Not for long," she shot back. "She decided she's needed, and she's planning to come for a month before the wedding."

"What about the latest stepdad? Doesn't he have a say?"

"That's the worst of it," she moaned. "He's coming with her! Remember she said he was some high mucky-muck in the Navy? He was in charge of that base up in Washington state or something like that. I figured that would keep them there."

I just nodded. No sense trying to get a word in while Karen was on a roll.

"Well, he might be transferring to Pensacola." She groaned. "Can you believe it? She wouldn't just be in the same state, she'd be in the same *county*."

Karen paced through the store, dodging around the merchandise shelves and T-shirt racks. I cringed as she waved her arms in distress, imagining a display of mugs and shot glasses crashing to the floor. To my amazement she managed not to knock anything over.

"@!^$#%%$#!!" The string of curses startled Karen, stopping her mid-rant.

"Sorry, Bluebeard," she muttered.

Bluebeard ruffled his feathers and fixed one beady eye on her. He ruled the roost, and we all knew it.

The parrot had been here longer than any of us, after all. I'd inherited him with my 55 percent of Southern Treasures. Along with him, I'd inherited the ghost of Great-Uncle Louis Georges, the previous owner of my shop.

Uncle Louis had definite opinions about how things should be, and he sometimes used Bluebeard to express his disapproval. In fact, you could say Uncle Louis specialized in meddling in my life. A lot.

"Sorry," Karen repeated, offering him a shredded-wheat biscuit from the tin underneath his perch.

The treat bought her a temporary reprieve from Bluebeard's glare, and she turned back to me.

"I do want her to be happy," she said. "Really. But can't she be happy somewhere far away from me? Isn't Admiral What's-His-Name enough?"

"Is he really an admiral?" I asked. I didn't think she'd ever told me anything about Stepdad Number Three, except that he was in the Navy.

"I don't know," she admitted. "She met him a few months ago, and the next thing I knew she called me from Hawaii saying they got married on the beach."

"So why can't you do the same thing?"

Karen rolled her eyes. "Haven't you been listening? I never had a 'real' wedding, according to her. She's had two—three if you count the one on the cruise ship—and she didn't want this one to be a big deal.

"Besides, if anyone is going to run off and get married, it should be Felipe and Ernie."

She had me there. Our friends couldn't get married in the state of Florida, though I hoped that would change someday. I raised one hand in surrender. "Do what you have to. I'll do my part." I thought for a minute before I continued. "But if I ever get married, Vegas is looking pretty good."

Karen's eyes narrowed. "Is there something you aren't telling me? Something I ought to know?"

I shook my head. "No."

"You sure?"

I shook my head again. My relationship with Jake Robinson had become closer over the last year, but wedding plans were a long way off. I wanted to survive Karen's wedding before I even considered the possibility.

And I'd meant what I said about Las Vegas; an elopement might be more my style.

CHAPTER TWO

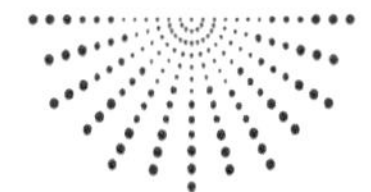

By Thursday morning, I had shoved Karen's question to a dark corner of my mind and slammed a heavy door on it. I didn't want to think about anything wedding related. I was spending the day with Jake, and I just wanted to enjoy our time together.

Julie was watching the store, and Jake had a clerk who could run Beach Books on a quiet weekday. We didn't often get the same day off, but we'd planned this one several weeks ago.

We headed north in my pickup. The truck was old, a 1949 Ford with a complicated history. Lovingly restored, the truck had once belonged to Uncle Louis, and had come "home" when my old Civic got torched. Elegant gold script on the doors and tailgate made it a rolling advertisement for my shop.

Besides, it was just darned cool to ride around in.

We took the back roads between the fields of scattered farms, and past the crossroads gas stations and tiny stores. Our pace was slow, but it felt right. Driving the vintage truck on the old farm roads felt like we'd gone back sixty years, as long as you ignored the occasional satellite dish and the signs that read "Speed Limit Enforced by Aircraft."

"Is the quilt supposed to be ready?" Jake asked as we neared the Alabama border.

"I'm not sure," I answered, watching for the brightly painted fence that marked the turnoff.

The fence stood out in an area of dusty split rails and sagging wire. I didn't know why the owner kept the posts and rails painted in rainbow hues, but I appreciated the landmark.

I turned off the two-lane highway onto a dusty road that wound through the trees. "Beth told me to check after the first of the month."

"You could have called her," he said.

"Yeah, but where's the fun in that?" I shot him a quick grin before turning my attention back to the winding dirt track. I tried not to think about what the dust was doing to my beautiful truck. I'd wash her just as soon as we were back in Keyhole Bay.

"Besides," I said, slowing for yet another curve, "this way I get to do some treasure hunting on the way back."

From the corner of my eye, I could see Jake's nod. "As long as I get lunch," he teased. He'd seen me stash a picnic hamper behind the seat before we left.

I laughed. "You had Pansy fill your thermos with coffee, and I know there were at least three muffins in that bag when you got in the truck." I gestured at the crumpled white pastry bag in the litter sack hanging from the radio knob. "I only ate one of them."

He quickly changed the subject. "Are you sure it's okay to just drop in?" He gestured out the windshield at the empty road. Trees closed in on either side, forming a shield for houses hidden down narrow dirt paths. The only evidence of human habitation was the occasional dilapidated mailbox at the side of the road. "Doesn't look like the kind of place where visitors show up unannounced."

"She's expecting me," I said, with more confidence than I felt. The truth was that we had settled on a date, but when I'd called Beth to remind her of my visit, I'd just gotten her voice mail.

She hadn't returned my call, or the two others I'd made in the last couple days. Which made me more determined to check up on her. I'd made a size-able deposit on the wedding quilt Jake and I had commissioned for Karen and Riley, and the wedding date was fast approaching.

I slowed to a crawl, watching for Beth's mailbox on the right. I spotted it, a tin box painted like a log-cabin quilt on a carved wood post, and turned down the washboard driveway.

Around a sweeping curve about a quarter mile off the road, we spotted the weathered cottage. I didn't see Beth's car, but since they only had one, it was possible her husband had taken it somewhere.

"What do they *do* out here?" Jake asked, swiveling his head to take in our surroundings.

The cottage, little more than a clapboard shack, sat in a clearing surrounded by scrub pine, live oak, and several other species of trees I didn't immediately recognize. A few yards from the cottage stood a low shed, several times larger than the house. The wide doors of the shed were closed and locked with a heavy padlock. Next to the shed, an oil drum hinted at the presence of a generator, a common sight in the backwoods where power lines didn't reach.

"Whatever makes them happy." I shrugged. "She sews and quilts for cash, and he makes furniture. They have a garden around back, grow a lot of their own food. I think they even keep a few chickens for eggs. They told me they wanted to get 'off the grid' and live off the land. All very romantic and idealistic." I smiled and added, "Which is great when you're twenty."

Jake chuckled. "You mean you don't want to go back to the land? Get away from it all?"

"From what?" I shot back. "Indoor plumbing? Air-conditioning? The best coffee in the Panhandle right next door?" I shook my head. "I was born in the twentieth century for a reason."

I looked toward the cottage, wondering why no one had emerged to greet us. Beth must have heard us drive up.

I stuffed the keys in my pocket and opened the door. "Maybe we better go find Beth," I said. "So we can get back to civilization and find you some food before you starve."

Jake followed me up onto the front porch. I knocked on the door and waited, but no one answered. I knocked again, and called out, "Beth! It's Glory Martine. You around?"

Silence.

We waited a few minutes more, knocking and calling without any response. We left the porch and walked around the cabin. Maybe Beth and Everett were out in the garden, though I couldn't imagine why they hadn't heard us, or answered our calls.

Something moved in the woods beyond our view, and I jumped. It was faint, little more than the rustle of leaves, but there was no wind. Undoubtedly an animal, probably a deer startled by our intrusion, or a cat looking for a way into the henhouse.

Whatever it was, I was getting spooked over nothing.

Finally, I had to admit the place was deserted. I even checked the front door, but like the shed, it was firmly locked, and curtains were drawn closed over all the windows.

We climbed back in the truck and Jake looked at me. He raised his brows in question, but waited for me to speak.

"She knew I was coming. We set this up several weeks ago." I tried not to sound defensive. "Something must have come up."

Jake nodded, one corner of his mouth quirked up in the hint of a grin. "Clearly," he said. "Looks like we aren't going to pick up a quilt today. So how about we find a place to eat and go gather some treasures?"

I was reluctant to leave without finding Beth, but I had to admit I had no idea where else to look. There weren't any close neighbors, and the couple had only been here a year or so, not long enough to make many friends in this isolated area. Besides, as Jake had pointed out, this wasn't a place to just go wandering onto someone's property.

Without a reason to stay, I started the truck, turned around in the hard-packed clearing, and headed back the way we'd come, along the dirt road. We hadn't seen another vehicle the entire time we were off the highway, which was probably just as well since the road was too narrow for two cars to pass each other.

We reached the county road and turned back toward the highway.

Once on the highway, we found a small park with just a few parking spaces and a couple picnic tables. Exactly what we needed. Jake hauled the hamper to a table near a stream and we unpacked our lunch.

The picnic hamper looked as old as the truck, but with the help of some very modern gel packs, it kept the potato salad and fried chicken properly cool.

Jake let out a low whistle as he took the chicken out of the hamper. "This is homemade, right?"

I bristled with fake indignation as I spread an oilcloth cover on the rough wood table. "Of course it is! Would I serve any other kind?"

He grinned and continued setting out our feast. In addition to the chicken and potato salad, I'd packed a small fruit salad, a jug of sweet tea, and fresh cookies.

"I have to admit," I said, putting the plate of cookies on the table between us, "these are Miss Pansy's cookies. I'm a good cook—"

"You're a great cook," Jake interrupted.

I shrugged. "Even so, my cookies don't come anywhere near hers. With something that good right next door, it seems foolish not to take advantage of her talents."

As we ate, we watched the sparse traffic speed by on the highway. "Where to from here?" Jake said, helping himself to another one of Miss Pansy's cookies. "I've never actually been treasure hunting with you before. I don't know how this works."

"There are a few places I usually stop," I explained as I collected the remains of lunch. "I've got a little network of folks who watch jumble sales and flea markets for me, and a couple quilters like Beth. I've spent years developing my contacts all over the Panhandle."

"And you're taking me to meet them?" Jake asked as he stowed the hamper back in the truck. "I'm honored."

"You should be," I answered, climbing back behind the wheel and starting the engine.

We wandered the back roads around the north end of the county, past tiny ponds and wide pastures, and along muddy creeks. Treasure hunting was one of my favorite pastimes, cruising slowly down an unmarked country road and stopping to visit with the suppliers who had become friends over the years.

There were stories of children and grandchildren, births and deaths, marriages and separations. We drank what felt like gallons of lemonade and sweet tea, and the pickup bed slowly filled with vintage kitchenware and knickknacks that would keep my shelves and my website stocked for several months.

The sun dipped low on the horizon as we headed south after a mostly successful trip. Jake took over driving once we were back on familiar roads, and I leaned back in the passenger seat, pleasantly tired from the day, glad I didn't have to cook dinner.

Thursday nights I took turns cooking with my three best friends: Karen, Felipe, and Ernie. For the past several months, we'd been including Jake and Riley, though we hadn't officially expanded our group. Tonight was Ernie's turn, and I was looking forward to good food and good friends.

All in all, a pretty great day. We'd be home in time to unload the truck and close up our shops before dinner. The only bad thing was that I still didn't have the quilt.

I'd tried to call Beth before we headed south, but once again it just went to voice mail. I told myself not to worry; cell service was notoriously spotty in the rural area around the border, and we still had a month or more before the wedding.

Everything would be fine.

CHAPTER THREE

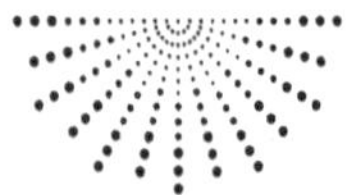

Jake stopped on the side street behind Southern Treasures and backed the truck into the parking area, carefully lining the bed up with the back doors. For a guy who could back a forty-foot fire truck down an alley, it wasn't even a challenge.

I unlocked the back door into the storage area. We carried in stacks of vintage spatterware and were headed back for more when Julie called for me to come up front.

Jake waved me away, saying he'd finish unloading, so I hurried up front to the retail area. Julie was waiting for me with a worried expression. "Bradley Whittaker's been looking for you all day," she said. "He won't tell me what it's about, just that he needs to talk to you right away."

Pansy Whittaker, the Miss Pansy who'd baked my picnic cookies, owned Lighthouse Coffee next door to my shop. Bradley, her oldest son, visited his mother regularly. I knew him well enough to say hello, but I couldn't imagine what was so important that he wouldn't tell Julie.

She was right to look worried.

"Tell Jake I'm next door," I said. "I assume that's where Bradley is?"

Julie nodded and I dashed out the front door.

Next door the shop was open, but there were no customers. The familiar smell of fresh-baked bread filled the small dining area. Bradley was behind the glass bakery case, deep in discussion with Chloe, the barista. He saw me come through the door and waved me over.

Chloe turned to look at who had come in. Her appearance sent a wave of shock through me. Her usual cheery expression was somber, and her red-rimmed eyes made it clear she'd been crying. She broke away and ran toward me.

"It's okay, Glory," she choked out between renewed sobs. "Everything's really okay."

I hugged her and patted her on the back, concern growing with every reassurance she sobbed out. Clearly everything was not okay, despite what she said.

"What? What's okay, hon?"

I looked over her head, buried in my shoulder, to Bradley. He was nodding, as though in agreement with Chloe, but I wasn't convinced.

He came a few steps closer, his expression serious. "Mom's in the hospital," he said. "The doctor is calling it a 'cardiac event,' whatever that is. Says he wants her to stay for a few days, have some tests."

Chloe pulled away and raised her tear-stained face. "We were making scones, like we do most mornings. She turned kind of gray and slumped over." She drew a deep, shuddering breath. "I thought she was—" She stopped, as though giving voice to her fears would make them too real.

"You did great, Chloe," Bradley said, smiling kindly at the distraught girl.

He looked back at me. "She called the paramedics and did exactly what they told her to. Wouldn't let Mom get up and go back to work, even though she tried."

I felt a smile lift the corners of my mouth. I could see Pansy doing exactly that. But a tiny eighty-something woman wouldn't have been much of a match for the sturdy young college student with a stubborn streak a mile wide.

Bradley apparently had the same thought, and a flash of amusement lit his eyes for a moment. "The doctors tell me they think she'll be fine, but she needs to slow down."

"I've been telling her that," Chloe sniffed. "But she won't listen to me. Thinks I can't manage without her."

"You can't, honey. Not as long as she carries all those recipes in her head," I reminded her.

Chloe gave me a look I couldn't fathom, but before I could ask her anything more, Bradley spoke again.

"I've spent most of the day with Mom," he said. "It took a lot of time and persuasion, but with the doctor's help, I have managed to convince her it's time to retire."

His announcement caught me by surprise. I'd begun to think Miss Pansy was going to work until the day she dropped over dead in her kitchen. Which she'd apparently come close to doing today.

"She had some reservations," he said without irony. "And she insisted I had to talk to you before anyone else.

"Miss Gloryanna, Mom would like to know if you're interested in buying Lighthouse Coffee."

CHAPTER FOUR

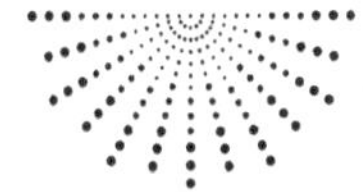

I knew the answer without any thought. Of course I was interested. What I didn't know was how I could possibly pay for it. Even with the money I'd put aside to buy out my cousin Peter's 45 percent of Southern Treasures, I wouldn't have nearly enough.

"Uh, well. Wow!" I stalled, trying to figure out how to answer Bradley. "I, um, I hadn't really thought about it," I lied. I'd thought about it, all right. Just not it terms of it happening anytime in this decade.

"Can you, um, can I take a little time to think this over?"

He frowned, and I hurried on before he had a chance to say no. "This is pretty sudden. There's so much to think about, like how I could even run both places, and how much Miss Pansy wants me to pay, and if I even know enough to run a coffee shop.

"But I guess if all you're asking is if I'm interested, well, then the answer has to be yes. Yes, I would be interested."

Chloe grabbed my arm and held on like a drowning woman clinging to a life ring. "I'll help, Glory! There's lots I can do, I promise! I can work for you and run the place and you won't have to do everything yourself. I'll even come in early and do the baking—"

"That's another thing," I interrupted her torrent of words to address Bradley again. "This place is worth a lot more if whoever buys it has Pansy's recipes."

Again the funny look from Chloe, but I dismissed it. The girl was still so shook up from the events of the day that there was no telling what was going on in her head.

"A few days," Bradley said. "But I'm afraid I can't wait much longer than that. Every day that goes by is a chance for Mom to change her mind and insist on coming back to work. And we are very much afraid that if she comes back, we will never get her out again."

His eyes misted up and he swallowed hard. "I know how much she loves this place, and how much she enjoys coming in here every day. I love my mom, and I hate like hell—pardon my language—to take that away from her. But if I don't, this place will kill her, sure as anything."

I nodded. "Give me the weekend," I said. "I should be able to give you an answer by Monday."

I put my hand over Chloe's, still clinging to my arm. "I'll talk to you tomorrow, okay? For now, you need to close up and go get some rest."

She shook her head. "I have to go see Miss Pansy first. She told me to mind the shop while she was gone today, and I need to let her know everything's being taken care of."

Bradley managed a weak smile. "She'll rest better knowing things are under control, even if she doesn't really believe us," he said.

"How about you?" I asked him. "Are you okay?"

"We all knew this day was coming," he answered. "Mom's nearly ninety, and the doctors say she'll see a hundred if she takes care of herself. We just have to convince her to do that."

His expression was still serious, but he looked calm and a lot less worried than Chloe. Of course, he hadn't been there when his mother collapsed, either.

"We're going to close up here and head for the hospital," he continued. "My brother's there now, with the rest of the family. Mom insisted I come back here and wait for you."

I nodded. "Please keep me posted on her condition," I said. "And tell her I send my love." A thought occurred to me as I headed for the door. "Is she here?" I asked. "Or in Pensacola?"

"Bayside Hospital in Pensacola," he replied. "Her doctor said they have the best cardiac unit in the area."

My heart was racing as I walked back to Southern Treasures. I accepted Bradley's assurance that Miss Pansy would be okay, but the rest of his news had my head spinning. How could I possibly buy Lighthouse Coffee while Peter still owned 45 percent of Southern Treasures?

Having my meddlesome cousin as a partner had its drawbacks. Like his continual attempts to tell me how to run the store. Peter had a master's degree, which he thought made him an expert on absolutely everything, including retail, which he'd never worked in his life. His degree was in mechanical engineering, and he held an important position—according to him—with a firm in Montgomery, a hundred miles from Keyhole Bay.

Even so, he thought he should tell me how to run Southern Treasures.

I'd worked in the store since I was a teenager. I'd laid off my last hired manager many years ago and I ran the place by myself. Peter got a check every month for his share of the profits, which I considered a clear signal that I was doing all right without his interference.

But could I buy Lighthouse and run it as a separate business? And if I somehow managed to find the rest of the money I needed, how would I ever get rid of my not-so-silent partner?

CHAPTER FIVE

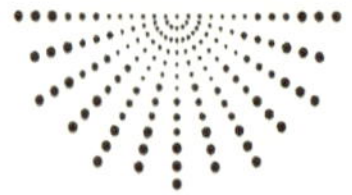

"I thought you were never coming—" Julie stopped midsentence as she caught sight of me. The bantering tone in her voice disappeared, and she came around the counter to put her arm around me.

"Glory? Are you all right? You look like you've seen a ghost. What did Bradley want that has you so upset?"

I tried to ignore her choice of words. I hadn't told Julie about Uncle Louis. She still brought Rose Ann into the store from time to time, and I wasn't sure how happy she would be, knowing there was a ghost living here.

"I'm okay," I said, shrugging out from under her arm. "But Miss Pansy's in the hospital."

Her hand flew to her mouth, and her blue eyes opened wide. "Oh my goodness! What happened? Is she going to be okay?"

Jake came through the door from the storage area just in time to hear her last question. "Is who going to be okay?"

"Miss Pansy," I said.

I locked the door and turned the sign from "Open" to "Closed" before I explained what had happened. "She collapsed this morning while she and Chloe were baking," I said. "Chloe called 9-1-1 and the ambulance took her down to Pensacola. To Bayside. Bradley said they called it a 'cardiac event,' and they say she'll be fine."

"You didn't hear the sirens?" Julie asked.

I thought for a moment. "I hear the sirens every time," I said. "Nearly every emergency call goes right down the road outside my door." I gestured toward the highway that formed the main drag of Keyhole Bay. "After enough years, it just becomes part of the background noise."

I shook my head. "I might have heard them this morning, but I can't remember."

Julie glanced at the clock. "I hate to run off, but if you don't need me, I better get going. Mom's expecting me to pick up Rose Ann. You'll keep me posted if there's anything we can do?"

I shook my head. "No reason for you to stay. I'll call you if I hear anything." I waved her toward the door. "You need to get home."

Once Julie was gone, I shooed Jake out to go close up the book store. Julie's mention of the time had reminded me we had plans for the evening. "Don't forget, we still have to be at Ernie's for dinner at seven."

"I'll be right back," he said, kissing me quickly before heading out the door.

I locked the door behind him and began the routine of closing up for the night. As I tidied the shelves and checked the stock, I thought about Bradley's —well, Miss Pansy's—offer.

"What do you think, Bluebeard?" I said as I cleaned his cage and gave him fresh water. "Do you think we ought to buy the place next door? Even if it means we can't get rid of Peter as soon as I hoped?"

"Buy it." The voice wasn't Bluebeard's, but Uncle Louis's.

The first time I'd heard that voice as an adult, it had scared me silly; but I'd eventually become accustomed to Uncle Louis's habit of using Bluebeard as his spokesbird. Now it held a strange kind of comfort.

Especially when he validated my own choices.

In the storeroom, I opened the small refrigerator to retrieve some cut melons for Bluebeard. He loved fruit, and I always gave him an extra treat when I'd been away for the day.

In the fridge I found the leftovers from our picnic. Jake had unpacked the hamper and put the food away. I smiled to myself as I dished out the leftover fruit salad.

Jake was definitely a keeper.

I shoved the thought away. There were a lot of other things I had to worry about right now. My relationship with Jake Robinson belonged back in that far corner, locked away for the time being.

The man himself was waiting at the front door when I returned. I let him in before I put the fruit in Bluebeard's cage.

I was rewarded with a head butt before the parrot hopped over to the bowl. "Buy it," he repeated, then turned his back on me and concentrated on the food.

"Buy what?" Jake asked as we made our way through the storeroom. He had spent enough time in the store to recognize the voice, just as I had. "What was he talking about?"

"Lighthouse," I said. "I'll explain when we get to Felipe and Ernie's," I promised. "That way you won't have to listen to the story twice."

Jake's car was parked on the side street behind the store. "I thought I'd offer to drive tonight since you had to do most of the driving today."

"Thanks." I climbed in the passenger side without protest. Truth be told, I hadn't been looking forward to more time behind the wheel, even if it was only five minutes each way.

Everything in Keyhole Bay was only five minutes from anywhere else in town. Except in summer, when the tourist traffic jammed the main drag and doubled or tripled drive time. Then the locals stayed off the highway, wound around back roads, and cut through residential neighborhoods that visitors didn't know existed.

As he pulled away from the curb, Jake teased, "How am I supposed to think I'm special, if you don't tell me first? How can I lord it over the rest that I already knew?"

"You think you're special?" I teased back.

"I do," he said. "Think about it. I know about Uncle Louis—who likes me, by the way. I helped you figure out how you could buy out Peter. I get invited to dinner with your secret club"—he pointed to the house as we pulled up in front of Felipe and Ernie's.

"It's not a secret club," I protested. "Just a bunch of friends who have dinner together once a week."

He parked the car and turned to look at me, his expression clearly skeptical. He leaned over and kissed me rather thoroughly. "And then there's that," he added.

I took a shaky breath. Yeah, there was that.

"Okay," I said. My voice quavered a little, and I laughed nervously, trying to lighten a suddenly serious moment.

"Bradley wanted to deliver a message from his mother. Miss Pansy wants to know if I'm interested in buying Lighthouse Coffee."

Jake gave a huge grin and started to say something. I held up my hand to stop him.

"He said I could have a few days to think about it, but only a few. I promised him an answer by Monday."

"Of course you'll buy it! Why wouldn't you? It's a wonderful opportunity." The grin returned. "Even Uncle Louis said so."

I shook my head. "I told Bradley I was interested, but there are a lot of things I need to consider."

I looked out in time to see Karen and Riley climb out of Riley's truck. They stopped at the back of the truck, looking expectantly at us.

"We can talk about this over dinner," I promised.

Jake took my hand and gave it a squeeze. "We'll figure this out," he said.

"I hope so," I said cautiously. I wanted to believe him, but I knew there were a thousand ways it could go wrong.

CHAPTER SIX

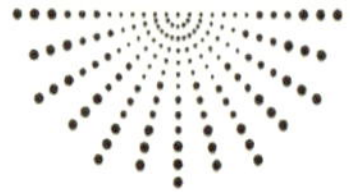

The heavenly fragrance of Ernie's cooking greeted us the minute Felipe opened the door.

Riley took a deep breath and sighed. "Oh, my! What's on the menu tonight? Smells wonderful, whatever it is."

Felipe welcomed each of us with a hug, collecting jackets, caps, and purses in the process. By the time he was done, the pile in his arms touched his chin.

Jake and Riley both offered to help, but he turned them down. "I'll just put these on the bed in the guest room," he said, disappearing down the hall.

The rest of us followed our noses to the kitchen. Ernie was the most committed cook in the group, and we always looked forward to his dinners.

"Whoa!" Karen stopped in the kitchen doorway. "What's that?" She pointed at a giant stainless steel range.

A grin split Ernie's face, his perfect teeth white against his dark skin. "Isn't she a beauty?"

He gestured toward the huge appliance like a spokesmodel on a game show. Dressed in jeans that looked like they'd been made for him and a white oxford-cloth shirt with the sleeves rolled up to expose the chiseled ebony of his forearms, Ernie had managed to cook something redolent of tomato and garlic while keeping his clothes spotless. With his slender build and elegant posture, he probably *could* have been a model.

"It's really . . . big," Riley said.

"Yep." Ernie's grin grew wider, if that was possible. "Went to an estate sale last week—a retired chef from up north—looking for inventory." With his partner, Felipe, Ernie owned Carousel Antiques. They carried high-end furniture and collectibles, and Ernie was a savvy shopper when it came to estates and auctions.

"This is in your kitchen," I pointed out. "I don't think that qualifies as inventory."

"You furnish your place with inventory from your store," he reminded me.

He had me there. Most everything in my small apartment had come in through Southern Treasures, sure. But I had plates and bowls, and the occasional lamp or kitchen chair.

"Not a bazillion-dollar stove," I protested.

"That's what made this so great," Felipe said, coming back from depositing the coats. "Nobody wanted to move this sucker."

"I could see why," Riley said quietly.

"But we do this stuff all the time. Have a regular crew we hire for the big jobs. So we were able to buy it for about ten cents on the dollar, and Ernie has his Christmas present early."

Jake whistled. "You ever want to get rid of it, the guys at the fire hall will take it off your hands." As a member of the volunteer fire department, Jake was always on the lookout for ways to improve the station.

Ernie had gone back to stirring the pot that was giving off the spicy, tomatoey smell of something decidedly Cajun.

He gestured at the steaming pot. "Tonight I made gumbo, the way my granny made it."

Ernie paused, looking at the simmering concoction. "Well, the way Granny would have made it if she'd had more than just what Pop-Pop caught that morning."

He stopped himself, as though he had revealed more than he'd intended to. "Anyway, this is chicken, sausage, and seafood. It still needs to simmer for twenty minutes or so. But if you're hungry"—he opened one of the many oven doors on his new range with a flourish—"we have boudin balls and fried okra."

He deftly transferred the bite-size pieces to a platter and placed it on the elegant teak dining room table. Their shop might tend toward ornate antiques, but at home both Felipe and Ernie were definitely midcentury modern, and the expansive dining room set was one of their treasures.

The sizzling bits of boudin sausage and cornmeal-dusted okra were an instant hit. We scooped them onto colorful pottery plates and added dipping sauces from the array Ernie provided.

Just like every other Thursday, conversation centered around the food for the next hour as we settled at the table and tasted the night's offering. Ernie kept the meal simple: steamed long-grain rice as a base for his spicy gumbo, sweet tea, and French bread and butter.

"Now I know we've had the argument time and again about what is and isn't traditional Southern cooking," Ernie said. "But it's been a while, and I want all y'all to think about this: We've been doing traditional every week for a couple years. A hundred meals or more."

There was a murmur of assent around the table. It was getting harder with each passing week to find new dishes, or new ways of preparing old ones.

"I hadn't thought about it that way," Karen said, nodding. "That's a lot of meals."

"I agree with Ernie," I said. "It's almost impossible to find something we haven't done several times already."

"I don't know what we want to do instead," Ernie said. "But Felipe and I have been talking this over, and we think it's time for a change."

"Maybe we can each try a different theme," Karen suggested. "Ernie likes to do Cajun and Creole—and judging by tonight's meal, I'd be happy to have him do more."

She glanced at Riley. "We could always do fish, depending on what Riley brings home from his latest trip." It was a safe bet; Riley owned a commercial fishing boat.

"We don't have to decide right now," Felipe said. "In fact, we don't have to make any decision. We can just do what we like for a while, and see what happens."

"Sure," I said. "As long as we don't let Freed go back to pizza." I grinned at my best friend. Her lack of kitchen prowess had been a running joke for years.

"You will notice," she said, "the quality of the food at Chez Freed has greatly improved over the years."

"I'll vouch for that," Riley said, drawing laughs from around the table. "You wouldn't believe what used to pass for dinner when we got married."

"The first time," he added hastily, in response to an elbow in the ribs.

"How *are* the wedding plans going?" Ernie asked.

Karen, always happy to talk about the wedding, launched into a story about her latest encounter with the caterer. But talk of the wedding reminded me of the missing quilt, and the missing quilter.

I couldn't very well tell the whole story in front of Karen and Riley—the quilt was a gift for them, after all—but I could tell my friends about the mystery that had dropped into my lap.

Again.

CHAPTER SEVEN

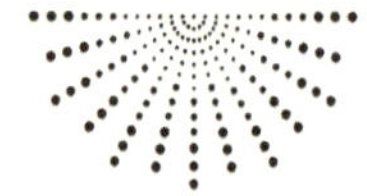

Karen went on with her story about the caterer, and her problems with the wedding cake. "I wish," she said with a sigh, "Pansy still did wedding cakes. I'd have her do it in a heartbeat."

Next to me, Jake groaned at the choice of words.

"What?" Karen said.

"Just, well"—Jake looked at me. "You want to explain?"

I nodded and quickly filled my friends in on the developments at Lighthouse Coffee. Karen flinched when I told them Miss Pansy had a "cardiac event."

"So," I concluded, "Bradley says they have convinced Miss Pansy to sell, and she wanted me to have the first chance at the shop.

"I really, really want to," I went on, "if I can just figure out how to make it work. The biggest hurdle is going to be the money."

That shouldn't have been news to them; they all knew that every penny I could pinch was going into my Buy-Out-Peter Fund.

Felipe and Ernie exchanged a glance, and I saw Ernie nod slightly. Felipe turned to me. "Southern Treasures and Carousel are two sides of the same coin," he said. "Ernie and I have been kicking around the idea of offering to buy out part of Peter's interest for a while now." He shrugged. "We already cooperate on buying inventory. You call me when something is too big for Southern Treasures, and we send people to you when their items don't fit our shop.

"Maybe it's time we talked about some kind of partnership."

Stunned didn't being to describe how I felt. Felipe and Ernie were among the best businessmen in town, and two of only a handful that I trusted completely.

"Maybe it is," I said slowly. "But I wouldn't want the business to interfere with our friendship."

Felipe nodded. "Agreed."

"I don't have much time," I reminded him. "Bradley wants an answer on Monday."

Jake chuckled. "You have your answer, Glory, and you know it. You want Lighthouse. The only question is how we do that and buy out Peter." He put his arm around me and gave me a reassuring hug. "All that's left is the arithmetic."

His use of the word "we" was still reverberating in my head when Karen spoke up. "So," she said, "do you want to do a wedding cake?"

The group erupted in laughter, the serious moment past.

I shook my head. "Isn't it more than enough that I am going to be your maid of honor? Again."

More laughter.

I glanced around the table at the friends who had become my family. As an only child, orphaned before I finished high school, I'd had to create my own family, and I was grateful for the warmth and support of the one they'd helped me make.

Our conversation spun on for another hour, sharing local news, gossip, and rumors. We talked about the Merchants' Association lobbying for more tax money to promote tourism while we cleared the table and loaded the dishwasher.

The question of whether Coach Bradley would retire when the football season was over was debated over dessert—an amazing bread pudding with warm caramel sauce that nearly put me in a food coma.

Ernie provided us all with copies of his recipes, a habit we'd developed when we started sharing dinners. Over the years I'd amassed a lot of recipes, and I'd used many of them.

"I'll definitely be trying this one," I told him. "Maybe it ought to go on the Lighthouse menu," I said, as though I owned the coffee shop already.

Ernie beamed. "I'd be honored," he said.

In between topics, I kept thinking of my missing quilter—but I couldn't find a way to bring up the subject without saying why I was looking for her; there just wasn't a graceful opening.

At last Riley yawned widely and reached over to rest a hand on Karen's back. "As much I am enjoying this," he said, "I was up early, and I'm running out of gas."

Karen nodded and rose from her chair. "I'm afraid I have to agree," she said. "I promised Riley we'd make an early night of it, since he was out of the house before daylight."

Ernie excused himself and returned a moment later with their coats and Karen's shoulder bag.

Ten minutes and many hugs later, they were out the door and headed for Riley's truck.

As soon as they were gone, Ernie turned to me, his brows drawn together in concern. "What's bothering you, darlin'?" he drawled.

"Who said anything was bothering me?"

"Um, you've been sitting there for the last hour looking like there was something you wanted to say. But every time you looked at Karen, you bit your lip. Like you didn't want her to hear whatever is on your mind."

"Is it that obvious?" I asked.

The three men nodded. I sighed.

"I, well, *we* had a strange experience today," I said, motioning to Jake to indicate he'd been with me. "I was supposed to see Beth. You remember the quilter, up north of Century?" Ernie waved for me to go on, though his expression told me he didn't remember Beth.

"We drove all the way up—it's practically to the state line—and she wasn't there. Her husband was gone, too. No sign of anybody around. Place all locked up tight."

"Of course it was locked up. It's out in the middle of nowhere," Jake said.

"That's not the point. The point is that she was supposed to be expecting me, and nobody was home."

Felipe shrugged. "I don't get it. You went to see someone and they weren't home. Why is that something you couldn't talk about in front of Karen?"

"Because of the reason we went up there. I commissioned a quilt for a wedding present for Karen and Riley. I couldn't very well say why it was so important."

Ernie shook his head. "You're overthinking this, Glory. I think you've caught some of Karen's wedding jitters." He gave me a reassuring hug. "I'll bet that gal just forgot you were coming. She'll probably call you tomorrow or the next day with some lame excuse, and expect you to go all the way back up there to see her."

"Happened to me just last week," Felipe said. "Ernie almost didn't get his range. The woman running the estate sale missed two different appointments with our delivery crew.

"I don't know what she was thinking," he continued. "Wasn't like anyone else was lining up to throw money at her. But she just 'forgot' twice."

The conversation turned toward difficult suppliers and troublesome customers, and I tried to put aside my worries about Beth and her husband, Everett.

And my missing quilt.

CHAPTER EIGHT

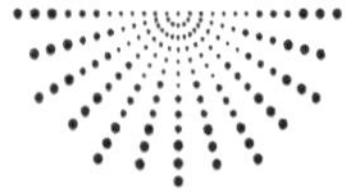

On the way home, I asked Jake, "Do you think I'm overreacting? Maybe Beth and Everett just flaked out?"

He shrugged. "I don't know. You said they weren't the type to do that, but how well do you know them, really?"

I thought about it. I had met the young couple several times, but our conversations had never gone much beyond merchandise costs and delivery dates. I might not know as much about them as I thought I did.

Jake took his eyes off the empty road long enough to give me a worried look. "Glory, you've managed to stay out of trouble for more than a year. I like that; so do the rest of your friends." He chuckled briefly. "Boomer *really* likes that."

"That's Sheriff Hardy to you Yankees," I said with a touch of irritation.

He shook his head. "We got to know each other pretty well, bailing you out of that last jam. He told me to call him Boomer," Jake said lightly, ignoring my jibe about being a Yankee.

I bristled at the implication I had needed rescuing. "I didn't need to be bailed out."

"Maybe not," Jake conceded. "But either way, why borrow trouble? Beth and her husband weren't home. There's nothing sinister in that. Is there?"

I stared out the side window at the darkened storefronts as we drove down the highway toward my shop. Jake had a point, darn it. "Still," I said, "something about the place didn't feel right." I couldn't explain what was wrong, but something didn't quite fit.

"How do you feel about Felipe and Ernie's offer?" Jake said, deliberately changing the subject. "Are you okay with just changing partners instead of being on your own?"

"It worries me," I admitted, following his lead. "I want to be rid of Peter, but it just seems like a huge risk. What if something goes wrong?" I thought about how I'd felt earlier. "This group is my family," I said. "Peter, his mom and dad and wife and kids, they're relatives. Karen and Riley, Felipe and Ernie…" I hesitated, drawing a deep breath. "…and you—you're my real family."

I stole a sideways look at Jake. His face was hard to see in the low illumination of the streetlights, but it was clear he was smiling.

"Getting rid of Peter isn't worth risking that."

"Okay."

Butterflies danced in my stomach and made my heart race. I'd known from the moment Bradley had made the offer that I was going to take it. As Jake had said earlier, now it was just arithmetic.

Jake parked at the curb and walked me to the front door of Southern Treasures. He followed me while I checked the alarms and the back door locks. Jake knew the ritual well; I'd installed the security system after Julie's drug-addled ex had broken into the shop, and I had maintained it faithfully ever since.

Okay. Maybe Jake had a point about me getting into trouble. But it wasn't like I went looking for it. Things just happened.

Strategically placed night-lights showed the way between the displays as we walked back to the door. Jake put his arms around me and pulled me into a warm hug. "I just want you to stay safe," he said, his chin resting against my head. He loosened his embrace and held me at arm's length. "Okay?"

I sighed. "I know."

Jake kissed me good night and waited on the sidewalk until I locked the door behind him.

A wolf whistle came from Bluebeard's darkened cage. He only stayed in the cage at night, with the door open and a blanket over the wire mesh to block the glow from the streetlights outside the big front windows.

"Bluebeard!" There were some things about having a permanent companion that weren't always perfect. A constant chaperone at the end of every date was one of them.

"Pretty boy," he said.

I made my way through the dimly lit shop and gave him a scritch. "Yes, you're a pretty boy."

"Not me," Uncle Louis's voice came clearly. "Your young man."

"He's not 'my' young man," I protested. It sounded weak, even to me.

"He should be."

Bluebeard turned and hopped back into his cage.

"Trying to $*&*%^#$%^ sleep here."

I took the hint and climbed the stairs to bed.

I called Beth several times on Friday, in between deliveries, occasional customers, and enough math to make my head swim. I tried to guess how much it would take to run Lighthouse Coffee, and what additional expenses I could handle.

I soon realized I needed real information, not guesses. A quick call to Bradley elicited a promise of recent financial statements, as long as I promised to keep them confidential.

Finally, with numbers buzzing in my head like a swarm of angry bees, I decided to go next door and have a little talk with Chloe. I didn't think I could make it work if she wasn't willing to stay.

I hung the "Back in 15 Minutes" sign on the door and stuck my phone in my pocket. Beth hadn't called me back yet, and I didn't want to risk missing her.

Chloe spotted me while I was still on the sidewalk and started a vanilla latte before I was through the door. She looked haggard, as though she hadn't slept the night before, which I realized was a real possibility.

"Do you have a minute?" I asked as I took the cup from her and handed over my punch card.

She glanced around the empty shop. "Sure. It's not like there's a rush this morning."

She poured herself a cup of coffee and joined me at a table in front of the window facing the street. From my vantage point, I could see if anyone approached the door of Southern Treasures.

Good manners, and genuine concern, dictated that I ask about Miss Pansy before I talked any business.

"She's sitting up and taking nourishment," Chloe said.

"I haven't heard anyone say that in years," I said. "It's something Memaw used to say."

Chloe studied her coffee cup as though the wisdom of the world was contained in the inky brew. "Miss Pansy says it a lot."

"Do they know when they'll let her come home?"

"Bradley called a little bit ago. Said she had a good night, but they want to keep her another night, just to be sure." She smiled briefly. "It sounds like he wanted them to make her stay, just so she'd rest for another day."

"I can believe that. I don't know what he'll do with her if she retires. That woman doesn't know the meaning of taking a day off."

I took another sip of my drink. It reminded me of Chloe's barista skills, and the real reason for my visit.

"Chloe," I said, "I need to talk to you about this place." I waved vaguely, taking in the entire operation. "If I'm going to buy—"

"Would you?" she interrupted with the first glimpse of her normal bubbly personality. "Would you really buy it? I really hoped you would, and that you'd let me stay." She paused to take a breath, but started again before I could stop her. "I love working here, Miss Glory. I'll come in and do the morning baking. I'll work whenever you need me—"

I held up a hand to deflect the torrent of words.

"That's what I came to talk to you about, Chloe," I said. "If I'm going to buy this place—and I'm trying to figure out how to do just that—I'm going to need someone I can count on to manage the bakery and coffee shop for me."

I remembered her promises from the day before, but I didn't want to count on that to make a business decision. I needed a commitment, not an emotional outburst.

"I know how to run a retail business, but I don't know how to bake, or make coffee, or a million other things. I need you for that, if you're interested." I smiled at her. "And I'd guess from your reaction that you are."

"I am very interested," she said. "Staying at Lighthouse, working for you, it would be really great, Miss Glory."

I offered her my hand. "Okay. If I buy Lighthouse, you've got the job. On one condition."

Chloe hesitated, her fingers just inches from mine. "What?" she asked warily.

"It's just Glory. Or Miss Martine, if you're talking to a customer. When you call me Miss Glory, it makes me feel about a million years old."

She ducked her head for a second. "My mama would pitch a fit if she heard me talk to one of my elders that way," she said. "But if you're my boss, I guess it's all right."

We shook hands, and the giddy smile returned to her face. "You really mean it? Really?"

"I need a baker," I said. "And you've been watching Miss Pansy for a long time. You're going to be my secret weapon in the bakery."

Her smile shifted, and I thought she was going to say something more, but she just nodded.

The door opened and a well-dressed couple in their sixties came in. Chloe hastily excused herself and rushed behind the counter, greeting the new arrivals. She spoke to them cordially and I left them chatting like old friends while she deftly made their drinks.

I checked my shop as I walked past. It was quiet. The only people I'd seen on the sidewalk were the couple that had just gone into Lighthouse Coffee.

I glanced at my phone, as though checking it every ten minutes was going to make it ring.

No joy.

CHAPTER NINE

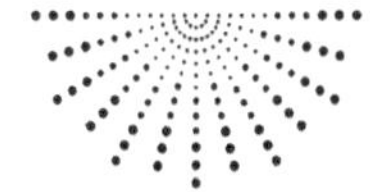

I hesitated at the door to Southern Treasures, but there was someone else I wanted to talk to, so I kept going. The Grog Shop, on the other side of my shop, belonged to Guy and Linda Miller.

Linda was like the older sister I never had. A young friend of my mother's, she'd been my babysitter when I was little, and my foster mother for the months following my parents' deaths. I trusted her advice, and Guy's, and I wanted to share my news with them.

The bell over the door announced my entrance, and Linda looked up from her book. Apparently her business was quiet too, and Linda was in her favorite place, a tall stool behind the counter with a cold drink and a fat novel.

She slipped a bookmark into the paperback before setting it down, then hopped out of her chair and came around the counter to greet me with a warm hug. Linda was good at hugs.

"Hey, stranger," Linda chided. "I haven't seen you in days. Where have you been?"

I thought for a minute. I hadn't been over to check in with Guy and Linda since Monday; a long time for us.

"Sorry," I said, returning her hug. "Been busy with wedding stuff for Karen, and then a buying trip yesterday with Jake."

I looked around for her husband. "Is Guy here? I have some news I want to talk to y'all about."

Linda's eyes lit up and I realized too late that the juxtaposition of my thoughts had her speculating in ways I hadn't intended.

"No, not that," I said hastily.

Her shoulders dropped and she sighed dramatically. "I can only hope," she said with exaggerated disappointment. "You know it's up to me, since your mom isn't around to ask when you're going to settle down."

I laughed. "Linda, I've been settled down for years. Running a business settles you down real fast."

She shook her head. "That isn't what I meant, and you know it." She turned her head and hollered toward the back. "Guy, Glory's here!"

A moment later Guy emerged from the storeroom, pushing a hand truck full of beer cases. I held the door of the walk-in cooler open for him, and the two of us quickly stacked the cases in the chilly interior.

Helping Guy stock the shelves had always been a favorite activity. I'd started helping in the store when I was a young teenager, far too young to actually sell beer or wine, but old enough to move cases and feel important. Guy's appreciation and encouragement meant a lot then, and helping him now reminded me of those times.

We emerged a few minutes later to find Linda waiting with a fresh pot of coffee. She held a mug out in my direction, but didn't fill it.

"News?" she said, keeping the pot just out of reach.

"Did you hear about Pansy?"

Linda nodded, but still didn't pour. "Of course we did. But I'm pretty sure that wasn't what you wanted to talk about."

"Ha! It is, too." I savored a brief moment of triumph before I continued. "At least it's related."

Linda relented and filled my mug. "Go on."

I cupped my hands around the mug, warming them from the chill of the walk-in. "Her son offered me the chance to buy Lighthouse."

Linda broke into a grin, and Guy nodded. "You are going to do it, aren't you?" he asked.

I exhaled, letting out a breath I hadn't realized I was holding.

"Yes." The giddy feeling that you get just before jumping off the high dive made me light-headed. "I'm not sure exactly how I can manage the finances, but if I can, then, well, yes."

"If you need help, you know you can always ask me," Guy said. He was a whiz with math. I'd always done my own books, and I was no slouch, but Guy could make numbers dance in ways I could barely follow.

"I will," I said. "Jake said the same thing."

Linda gave me a raised-eyebrow look that said as clearly as words that she was thinking about her initial assumption.

"Yeah, I told him. And Karen and Riley, and Ernie and Felipe. Last night was Thursday," I defended myself, "and we all had dinner.

"Besides, Bradley—you know Miss Pansy's son—made the offer just before I left for Ernie's house. I didn't have time to talk to anyone else."

"I'm sure that's the only reason," Linda said in a tone that clearly said otherwise.

"It is," I insisted.

Linda just smiled.

Guy looked from Linda to me and back again, then shrugged. He'd learned long ago to simply accept that Linda would eventually fill him in.

I drank down the coffee and handed the mug back to Linda. "Thanks," I said. "I better get back to the store."

She pulled me into another hug. "You'll tell us if there's anything you need?"

"Promise." I hugged her back and gave Guy a hug before heading to Southern Treasures.

The phone still hadn't rung.

Where was Beth? Where was my quilt? And why wasn't she returning my calls?

CHAPTER TEN

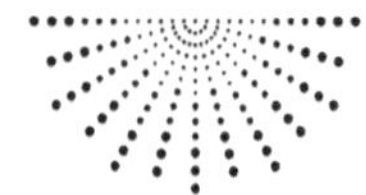

Karen called just as I was unlocking Southern Treasures.

"Want to nag some more?" I asked.

Her laugh came through the phone. "Just wanted to see how you're getting along. You seemed pretty distracted last night." Her voice rose at the end, turning her explanation into a question.

"It's just this thing with Lighthouse," I said, hoping she would accept my reassurance. It was the truth; I was preoccupied with the Lighthouse offer. Even if it wasn't the only thing on my mind.

"It's a big deal," she admitted, "but you know you want it. You've wanted it for a long time. Don't try to tell me you haven't."

"I have," I said. "I decided years ago that if Pansy or Guy and Linda, either one, wanted to sell, I'd be at the front of the line."

"So, what are you up to tonight?" she asked in typical Karen fashion. Her conversations swooped from one subject to another without warning, and I had learned long ago to go along for the ride.

"No plans," I said. "Why?"

"Riley's heading out before dawn again, so I'm batching it tonight. Thought you might want to grab some dinner if you didn't have plans."

"Sure." I checked the time. "I'm not supposed to close up for another hour. Want me to meet you somewhere?"

"I'm out running errands; I might as well swing by for you." I heard her rustling in her bag, a cavernous satchel she carried everywhere she went, followed by the crinkling of paper. "I still have to see the printer," she said, as though reading from a list. "And talk to the organist at the church." She sighed dramatically. "I should be able to make it there in an hour."

In the meantime, I started updating the website with new merchandise from our treasure hunt. I had only done about half the items when the phone rang.

I picked it up without looking, although I knew better.

It was Peter.

With a new scheme.

"Hi, Glory. How are you?" Peter tried to observe the niceties of social interaction, but I didn't really believe he cared a whit for how I was.

"Fine, Peter. And you?" Two could play this game.

"Doing fine. Job's great! Peggy and the kids are fantastic, getting ready for Thanksgiving with the family. You coming up this year?"

Every year he invited me to join his family at my aunt and uncle's home, and every year I declined. I would much rather spend the holiday with my friends in Keyhole Bay who were my family of the heart.

For an instant I entertained the wicked thought that I ought to accept his insincere invitation, just to see his reaction. But I didn't want to go to Uncle Andrew and Aunt Missy's for Thanksgiving, and I didn't want to deal with the fallout from accepting and then canceling.

But it was amusing to think about.

"I don't think so, Peter," I said with as much regret as I could muster. "It's a long drive, and I can't close the shop for more than a day or so."

"That's what you have employees for, isn't it?"

"But I don't feel it's right to ask her to give up her holidays, either." As far as Peter knew, I only had Julie; and I wasn't going to tell him anything different, at least for now. "Your boss doesn't expect you to give up your holidays so he can spend time with his family, does he?"

His indulgent chuckle told me what was coming. "Oh, Glory. You really don't understand corporate life, do you? We plan ahead for every holiday, so everyone gets their time off."

I told you he didn't understand retail.

My patience with his version of small talk was wearing thin. "So what did you call for, Peter?"

"Do I have to have a reason to call my only cousin? Can't it just be for a visit?"

"But you don't call just to visit, Peter. We aren't those kinds of cousins. So what did you call for?"

"Well…" he hesitated, and I knew we were getting to the real reason. "I saw something in the news this morning that I wanted to talk to you about."

I rolled my eyes. One advantage of talking to Peter on the phone instead of in person: he couldn't see my expression.

"Yes?"

"It was about this store somewhere up north. I didn't catch where, but you know how these things are, it happens one place and then everybody jumps on the bandwagon and then it's happening everywhere."

"Go on."

"There was this store, and they had a cat in the store. Not just wandered in, you know, but it lived there and the store owners kept it as a pet and fed it and all."

I bit my tongue, mentally urging him to get on with it.

"Anyway, the cat scratched a kid and the parents sued the store for keeping a dangerous animal on the premises. The insurance company had to give the family a big settlement to keep it out of the courts."

Like all my conversations with Peter, this one had reached the count-to-ten stage.

One.

Two.

"The owners were ordered to keep the cat out of the store, and had to pay a bunch of fines …"

Three.

Four.

"… for violating some law or other about animals in a public space."

Five.

I took a deep breath.

Six.

Seven.

Eight.

"I'm concerned about that parrot, Glory."

Nine.

"What if he hurts someone? What if he attacks a kid? We could lose everything, Glory. Everything."

Ten.

I remained calm. I told myself that Peter wasn't in the store, he didn't know how Bluebeard behaved, and he certainly didn't know about Uncle Louis. Nor was I ever going to share that with him.

If and when Uncle Louis decided to make himself known to Peter, it would be his choice. But I wasn't going to tell him.

"Peter, that bird has been in this store longer than I have. He is more than a pet, he's the symbol of Southern Treasures, and customers expect to see him when they come in.

"There is no way, *no way*, Peter, that I am taking him out of the store. This is his home, and it will be his home as long as he lives. And he has a name, Peter. His name is Bluebeard, not 'that parrot.'

"It that very clear?"

I wasn't actually shouting, but I had adopted a forceful tone. It got my point across.

"Y-y-yes," he stammered. "But Glory," he whined, "we could lose everything if someone got hurt."

"First, there is no law in Keyhole Bay against animals in public places. Second, Southern Treasures is private property, so that doesn't even apply. Third, Bluebeard is well behaved, and he has safe places to go if anyone is bothering him. Fourth, we are well insured, and my agent added a rider for Bluebeard many years ago."

I took another deep breath. "And last, *we* wouldn't lose everything. *I* would lose everything. *You* would still have your fabulous job and your beautiful home, and your retirement account. You would lose a small part of your investments. I would lose my home and my job.

"So if I am not worried about 'that parrot,' as you call him, then you shouldn't be either."

I bit back the rest of my rant. "I have to go now, Peter. The store needs my attention.

"Good-bye."

I hung up, my hand shaking as I put the cordless back in its cradle.

Peter had to go.

Now.

It was closer to two hours than one when Karen finally showed up. I had recovered from the anger Peter triggered, but I was more determined than ever that I had to buy him out.

"Sorry," Karen said when I unlocked the front door for her. "The organist took forever to find the right music, even though I'd told her several times exactly what we want."

I could only imagine what the poor woman had been through in the last hour. I had seen for myself how Bridezilla Karen told someone exactly what she wanted.

I grabbed my purse from behind the counter and followed Karen out to her car, locking the door behind us.

"How about Jake?" Karen asked, starting the engine. She glanced across the street at Beach Books.

"Some Merchants' Association thing," I answered. "Even for Jake, I won't go to one of those things."

"I know," Karen said. "'Not a boy, and not nearly old enough,'" she quoted my stock answer for why I didn't belong to the good ol' boys club.

"Someday that may change," I said. "But for now, I just can't spend time with a bunch of men who call me sweetheart because they can't remember my name."

"Hey," Karen said. "This is me, remember? I'm on your side."

I shook my head. "It's not about sides."

"Okay. I agree with you then."

"Better."

After a moment's silence, I asked, "Where are we going?"

"How about Neil's? Pizza sounds good to me."

I agreed, and a few minutes later we were seated in a high-backed wooden booth, sipping sweet tea and waiting for our pie.

"I've been thinking," she began. That always scared me. When Karen started thinking, it usually meant complications.

"Yes?" I said warily.

"It's the wedding. Sort of. I know it's kind of odd to be re-marrying your ex. But I think I'm really lucky; Riley and I figured it out while there was still time to do something about it."

I waited, wondering where this was going.

"But it makes me feel bad for the people who miss their chance. We were talking about Felipe and Ernie the other day, about how they couldn't get married."

"They could in several states, just not here. Yet. But things are changing."

"True," she said. "But this is their home. Anyway, that started me thinking about what happened to Sly. Did he ever tell you anything more?"

I shook my head.

Our friend Sly was nearing seventy. Last year he had told us the story of his lost love, a romance doomed by 1950s Florida laws forbidding interracial marriage.

But he hadn't given us details, and I didn't feel it was my right to ask. "He mentioned her name—Anna—but that's about it. It's so hard for him to talk about it. I just figured he'd tell me when he's ready."

"I know things were different when Sly met Anna," Karen said. "But just imagine if he'd met her now, though. Those laws are long gone. There wouldn't even be a question."

I still wasn't sure where she was going with all this, but I let her talk.

"So we know a first name, her approximate age, that she went to school in Keyhole Bay." Karen ticked off the items on her fingers. "We know she was white, and that she was still in town when Sly enlisted."

She stopped and thought for a minute. "Do you know when that was, exactly?"

"I think he graduated high school in 1962, give or take a year," I said. "But really, what does it matter? She moved away a long time ago. Sly said she was gone when he came back from the service."

"But what if we could find her?" Karen asked, leaning forward. "What if we could let Sly know what happened to her? I mean, not if it was horrible or anything. But if we could tell him where she went, what she did?"

"That's a terrible idea," I said without hesitation. "The few times he's mentioned her, it was clear he'd been badly hurt. Why bring all that up again? What's the point?"

Karen looked stunned. "I thought you were the one who loved solving mysteries," she said. "I figured you'd like the idea. Besides, if we find out something awful, we don't have to tell him anything."

"And if we find out she fell in love with someone else and got married and is living happily in some fabulous place? Is that supposed to make him feel better?"

"It might," Karen argued. "If he truly loved her, it would make him happy to know that her life turned out well, and that she was happy."

"Anyway"—I abandoned the argument for a minute—"why would you want to do this? Don't you have enough on your plate right now, with the wedding and your mother coming?"

"That's exactly why I need this."

I was about to ask her how another project would help when I heard our number called. I got up from the table, glad of the interruption, and retrieved our pizza.

I carried the box to the table. Neil's was primarily takeout and they expected leftovers, so even in the store, pizzas were served in a takeout box.

When I got back to the table, Karen was on the phone. She put her finger to her lips as she listened intently.

I sat down quietly and waited. Over the years, I'd grown accustomed to

Karen's "news face," the rapt expression that meant a hot story was in the offing.

"Be right there," she said.

She tossed her phone in her purse and reached to close the pizza box. "Take it home with you," she said. "I've got to go up to North County.

"Boomer's got two dead bodies."

CHAPTER ELEVEN

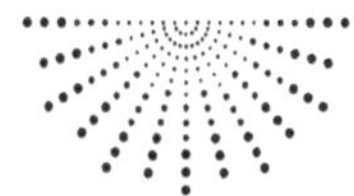

"Want some company?" I told myself the offer was just to keep Karen company on the late-night drive home. I didn't really think the bodies were related to Beth and Everett's disappearance. North county covered a lot of territory.

I didn't believe a word of it.

Karen shook her head, then reconsidered. "Are you sure?"

"Well, I could go home and obsess over my finances and not sleep, or I could ride along with you and maybe not obsess about my finances. What do you think?"

"Ride along it is, then. I'll stop and let you put the pizza away at your place since it's on the way."

Ten minutes later, the pizza was stashed in my refrigerator and we were on the highway heading north. Was it really only yesterday morning I'd driven this way? Of course, I'd been taking it easy on the back roads in my vintage truck. Karen was lead-footing it up the highway in a late-model SUV. Only the direction was the same.

We made the trip in a mostly silent forty minutes. I didn't want to tell Karen about Beth and Everett, and I couldn't think of a single other thing to talk about.

Karen was focused on the road and on the chatter coming from the police scanner she kept in her car. A local sheriff's patrol was at the scene, thanks to a call from a hunter who had found the bodies. Boomer was on his way, as was the coroner and a medical transport.

"I'll be there soon," Boomer said on the radio. "No sense creating a disturbance with the sirens and all. They ain't going anywhere."

Dr. Frazier, the coroner, acknowledged the instructions, as did the ambulance drivers. It sounded like we were only a few minutes behind them.

Karen's GPS chimed. "Turn left in one-quarter mile."

I strained to see the road ahead. We were close to the road I'd taken yesterday, but in the dark, it was hard to be sure.

"Turn left in five hundred feet."

Karen slowed for the turn. I saw a familiar fence, brightly colored posts and rails caught for an instant in Karen's headlights.

I told myself there were lots of places out in these woods, lots of people who lived out here away from big cities and small towns. It meant nothing.

My heart raced. I tried to speak, but my mouth was so dry I couldn't form words. I swallowed and licked my lips, but still nothing came out.

Karen dropped her speed on the winding, unlit dirt road. Out here, away from any city lights, darkness crowded in on us. Somewhere ahead we could see the faint pulsing of colored lights, signaling the presence of emergency vehicles.

My internal argument continued, but reasonable doubt had given way to unreasonable hope. Even that was soon dashed as we came around another curve and spotted the first of a string of emergency vehicles blocking the narrow road.

Karen stopped and shut off the engine. "I'll walk in from here. You can wait in the car."

I climbed out after her. I had no intention of sitting alone in the car in the dark, not knowing what was lurking in the woods.

"I'm coming with you." I was surprised the words came out as steady as they did. I felt like my entire insides were shaking.

"Suit yourself. But Boomer isn't going to be happy to see either one of us." She was already several steps ahead of me, following the beam of a heavy-duty flashlight she'd taken from the SUV and digging in her bag for her pocket recorder.

This was Karen at work: one of the most organized, focused, and determined individuals on the planet. Hard to believe she still lived and worked in the same small town where she'd grown up.

I trotted to catch up with her and her flashlight. I didn't relish the idea of stumbling around out here in the dark.

The first thing I noticed was the complete absence of onlookers. In town, the presence of a police car or an ambulance meant neighbors and passersby stopping to gape, trying to catch a glimpse of whatever was going on.

Not out here. There wasn't a single person eager for gossip or trying to snap a picture they could post, tweet, or sell to the highest bidder. The police hadn't even set a guard to prevent civilians from walking into their crime scene.

And yet, I felt like I was being watched. Like there was someone or something hiding just beyond the reach of the floodlights, watching everyone.

Animals, I was sure. Just like the day before. There was plenty of wildlife in the sparsely populated North County. I tried to guess what creatures might be around, distracting myself from the real reason we were here.

It could be a deer, or raccoons or possums, maybe even a fox or coyote, curious about the disturbance but careful to stay in the shadows.

We were nearly to the shed, a vague outline in the glare of the floodlights, when a sheriff's deputy stopped us. "Pardon me, ladies. This is a crime scene. I'm going to have to ask you to leave."

"Karen Freed. WBBY." Karen flashed a laminated card at the deputy. "Can I ask you a few questions?"

"Ma'am, I cannot answer any questions. And I will have to ask you to leave." He reached for Karen's arm, but she pulled away and tried to push past him.

"Stop!" His voice had gone from polite and deferential to commanding in an instant. "Don't move!"

"Freed!" Boomer's unmistakable growl came from somewhere in the glare. "I should have known."

Sheriff Barclay "Boomer" Hardy appeared, silhouetted against the floodlights, casting a long shadow in our direction. His imposing bulk was exaggerated by the lighting, his features obscured in the glare.

"Sheriff Hardy," Karen said.

Her words were formal and polite, but her tone was casual. We'd both known Boomer since we were teenagers and he was a rookie, and Karen crossed his path regularly in the course of her job.

"I know what you're doing here," he said. "But what are you doing with her, Miss Glory? I thought you'd decided to stay out of trouble?"

That final question sounded less like a question and more like a warning. Just because I'd been caught up in a couple bad situations. Now Boomer treated me like a troublemaker, even though I hadn't been the one making trouble.

"I just came along for the ride."

I crossed my arms across my chest, partially as a defiant gesture, but mostly to hide the fact that I was shaking. I was sure I knew who the two bodies were.

I was going to have to tell Boomer. Or I was going to have to withhold the information.

Either way, I was way up the creek and there wasn't a paddle in sight.

CHAPTER TWELVE

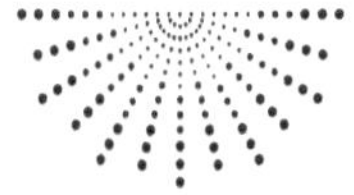

I braced myself for the barrage of questions that would follow my revelation. I didn't want to talk about Beth and Everett—the truth was, I didn't know that much about them—but I knew I would have to speak up.

"Do you know the identities of the victims?" Karen asked. She hit record and pointed the digital recorder at Boomer.

"You know I can't tell you anything until we notify next of kin," Boomer answered wearily. He'd had similar conversations with Karen many times over the years, but it didn't stop her from asking.

"And turn that damned thing off!" He glanced over at me. "Begging your pardon, ma'am."

I waved away his apology. He'd be saying worse in a few minutes, when I told him what little I knew.

"What can you tell us?" Karen forged ahead, the record light still blinking.

"We have two victims. Both male. Likely mid-thirties. That's all we have for now." He glared at Karen. "You didn't need to drive all the way up here and tromp around my crime scene for that. It'll all be in the record within the hour."

"My station manager says go, I go. He says ask, I ask. Just doing my job."

"And I'm trying to do mine." Boomer turned his back, clearly dismissing us.

"B-both male?" I stammered, finally able to corral my jumbled thoughts and form actual words.

"Yes." Boomer turned back and gave me a hard look. "What makes you ask?"

"I just, well, um." I stopped and took a moment to gather what little calm I could muster. "I know the people who live here."

There. I'd said it.

Karen whipped around and stared at me.

Boomer rolled his eyes and groaned. "Here we go again."

"No, nothing like that," I protested. "She's a quilter. Her husband makes furniture. I buy stuff from them for the shop. That's all."

"Do these people have names?" Boomer's sarcasm annoyed me, but annoyed was better than scared. Lots better.

"Beth and Everett." I dug through my memory for a last name. "Last name is Young, I think."

"You think? If you bought from them, what name did you put on the check?" More sarcasm.

"Paid cash. Always do. I get better deals if the money folds and they don't have to go to the bank, Sheriff. In any case, it's a man and a woman who live here, not two men."

"Could you identify the man?"

A chill ran down my spine. Did Boomer really want me to look at Everett's dead body? I didn't know the man very well, and it seemed somehow wrong for me to identify him.

But it might help catch his killer, and it definitely would make Boomer happier with me.

"I can try," I said. "I've only met him a few times, but I'll look if you want me to."

Instead of taking me to look at the two men, however, Boomer pulled a small electronic tablet from an inside pocket of his jacket.

"Don't look at me like that," he said to Karen. "You aren't the only one who knows how to run one of these things."

To me he said, "I have some photos on here—just faces, mind you. Nothing gruesome. They look like they're sleeping."

His voice was soft, his manner deferential. Far different from the man who'd been ordering us to leave a few minutes earlier. It was a side of Boomer I had rarely seen.

"Could you take a look and tell me if you recognize either man? You don't have to; I can't make you do this. But I would appreciate your help."

I swallowed hard and held out my hand for the tablet. Rather than hand it over, Boomer moved close to my side and held the display where we could both see. He kept the controls out of my reach.

"There are only two pictures you need to look at," he explained as he displayed the first photo. I could guess that there were many more pictures, none of which he wanted me to look at, and none of which I wanted to see.

Karen had crept up on my other side, silently moving to a vantage point where she could also see the display. Boomer ignored her and continued talking to me in a soft voice, asking if I knew the man in the photo.

The man was not familiar. Shaggy brown hair surrounded his thin face. His eyes were closed, but his mouth was open slightly. Sunken cheeks hinted at missing teeth, and the ones I could see were crowded into his narrow jaw.

I shook my head. "I don't know him," I said.

Boomer nodded and changed the display.

I didn't know this man either. His round face and blond pompadour were in sharp contrast to his companion, but there was nothing familiar about him.

I shook my head. "I'm sorry, Sheriff," I said. "I don't know him either. Neither one of them is Everett Young."

Boomer switched off the tablet and glared at me, the moment of deference gone. "And I'm supposed to believe you're just along for the ride?"

He shook his head. "I should have known better. I've got two dead bodies, your friends Everett and Beth are nowhere to be found, and you just happened to come along with Freed here"—he pointed a thumb at Karen without taking his eyes off me—"to what? Keep her company?"

"I am very sorry, Sheriff Hardy," I bit back a "sir" that would have laid it on too thick, even for Boomer. "Karen got the call while we were at dinner, and I offered to ride with her so she wasn't driving alone late at night.

"I didn't know we were coming here, and I didn't know that Beth and Everett aren't around." I looked at the house. If someone was in there, they would certainly have come out to see what all the commotion was about.

If they could.

The thought sent another chill through me, and I shivered.

Boomer saw my reaction and guessed what I was thinking.

"We looked in the house first thing," he assured me. "Nobody inside, and it looks like they've been gone a while."

The glare returned. "When was the last time you saw the Youngs?"

"Several weeks," I answered truthfully. The last time I had actually seen Beth was the day I paid the deposit on Karen's wedding quilt, right after Labor Day.

"How many is several?"

"It was just after Labor Day. I made a buying trip up this direction. Stopped in, had a glass of sweet tea, and picked up a couple little pieces. So probably nine or ten weeks."

A deputy approached us and signaled to Boomer. He stepped away and the two men held a whispered conversation intended to exclude us. When Boomer returned, it was clear he had something else on his mind.

"I still have some questions for you, Miss Martine. But right now there are other, more important things I need to do. I'll expect you in my office at ten tomorrow morning."

He nodded at us in dismissal. "The deputy here will see you back to your car."

"No need," Karen said. "I've got my flashlight."

The deputy, taking his cue from Boomer, led the way back to the road, his own five-cell flashlight casting a powerful beam into the darkness.

"No problem, ma'am. I'm glad to help you out."

I could feel Karen's retort building, and I dug an elbow into her side. "Thank you, Deputy," I said before she could make matters worse with a smart remark. "We're fine from here." I pointed in the direction of Karen's SUV. "We can see the car."

Karen managed to hold her tongue until we were in the car, safely out of earshot. But just barely.

She was on me before she even started the engine. "What didn't you want Boomer to know?" she demanded.

"Who says there was anything for him to know?" I countered. I was hoping the old saying was true, that the best defense was a good offense. "I just wanted to get us out of there before you managed to tick him off and get us invited to the station."

"Me? I wasn't the one who was all buddy-buddy with his prime suspects."

"I am not buddy-buddy with them. I know them, that's all. And what makes you think they're suspects? Just because they're not here doesn't make them suspects."

Karen started the engine. Emergency vehicles blocked the road ahead, and with no other choices she had to spend the next few minutes carefully going back and forth until she had managed to turn around in the single lane of gravel that passed for a road.

The tight maneuvers took all her attention, and I hoped the question of my relationship with Beth and Everett had been forgotten. But the second she was clear and headed back along the rough road to the highway, the interrogation started up again.

"You were holding something back, Glory. Something you didn't want Boomer to ask you about." When I didn't answer, she continued her speculation. "He asked you when the last time you saw them was."

"And I told him the truth. I haven't seen either one of them in several weeks."

Our headlights cut through the dark ahead of us, but they didn't penetrate into the woods alongside the road. I shivered, imagining what might be hiding just beyond the reach of our headlights.

Darkness crowded in on all sides, making the road feel even more remote. The woods seemed to close in on us as we bumped along the rough surface.

"That may be true," Karen said, her voice tight. She could feel the same isolation and vague threat I did. "But that isn't all of it."

She braked, moving even slower as she rounded a tight curve. I knew it was all in my imagination, but I half expected something—or someone—to step out in front of the slow-moving car, like the serial killer in a bad movie.

"You might not have seen them," Karen said, breaking into my cheap-horror-film fantasy, "but I'd be willing to bet you've talked to them since then."

We reached the highway at last, but instead of turning onto the pavement, Karen stopped dead and turned to look at me. "In fact, you were just up here. Yesterday. You and Jake came up on a buying trip. And if you were in the neighborhood visiting suppliers, what are the odds you went by your pals' place?"

I couldn't lie, not directly, and Karen knew it.

"You were out here. But you didn't see your pals. You wouldn't have told Boomer a direct lie."

"They aren't my 'pals,'" I insisted. "But yes, I was by here. They weren't home. Nothing to tell. But you saw how Boomer was, just because I know the people that live there. Imagine if I'd said I was out there yesterday."

"Yeah," she agreed as she finally turned onto the highway. "And I'm getting tired of posting bail."

CHAPTER THIRTEEN

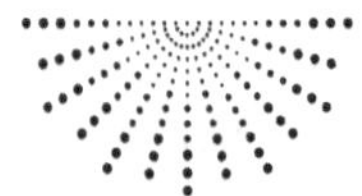

Karen turned up the volume on the scanner, and we listened to the chatter as we drove back to Keyhole Bay. I didn't volunteer any more about Beth and Everett, which wasn't difficult since I really didn't know much more.

"You want me to drive?" It was one reason I'd offered to come along. Sometimes I'd drive while Karen would call or text the station.

But not tonight. "No," she said, staring at the dark road ahead. "There isn't anywhere convenient along here to pull over and swap, anyway."

I didn't argue. Although there were several turnouts on the highway, none of them was well lit, and I didn't think either one of us was particularly interested in getting out of the car on the deserted highway.

"You wouldn't have had to post bail. Boomer could have insisted I talk to him, but there wasn't anything for him to charge me with."

"That wouldn't have stopped him," she said darkly. Karen had never really forgiven Boomer for arresting Riley's brother, even though we'd eventually proven Bobby was innocent.

"Maybe." When it came to me, Boomer seemed to run hot and cold. We'd found an amiable truce after Lacey Simon had drugged and nearly killed me over a year ago, but I'd also managed to stay off his radar since then.

Now I was involved in his business again, and if he thought I was interfering in any way, he wouldn't hesitate to break the truce. It wasn't a comforting thought.

I forced my thoughts away from Boomer.

"So, Freed," I said, reaching back to our earlier conversation, "what makes you want to track down Sly's old girlfriend? Why add that to all the things you've got on your plate right now?"

She sighed dramatically. "Because I have to have *something* to take my mind off this wedding and off my mother. Do you have any idea how stressful this all is?"

I bit back the truthful answer, that we were all very well aware how stressed she was because she was sharing it with everyone around her. "I can only imagine," I said instead. "But wouldn't another project just add to the stress?"

"I don't think so." She paused, as though searching for a way to explain it to herself. "See, the wedding and my mother and Stepdad Number Three, that's all stuff I *have* to do. It's not my choice, it's my mother's."

She held up her hand, palm out. "I *know!* I am a grown-ass woman—pardon my French—and I should be able to stand up to my mother and do things the way I want. But you know her, Glory. She doesn't hear what she doesn't want to."

That much was true. I'd seen her mother in action since we were in elementary school. Until two years ago, her Christmas cards had still been addressed to Mr. & Mrs. Riley Freed, even though they'd been divorced more than a decade. She didn't believe Karen and Riley should have ended their first marriage.

"I haven't even told you the worst of it," she continued. "The station manager told me today that he's giving me the month of December off as a wedding present. He heard my mother was coming, and he thinks he's doing me a big favor, giving me time for my family and all the last-minute wedding stuff."

She slammed her palm against the steering wheel in frustration. "I can't take a month off. I'll lose my mind; especially if I have to spend that month with my mother dictating wedding instructions the whole time.

"I *need* a distraction."

I sighed in resignation. "What do you want me to do?"

"I don't know. We need to do some research, see if we can find out more about her. There couldn't have been that many kids in Sly's graduating class, could there?"

"Keyhole Bay was pretty small back then," I said. "But who says they even went to the same school? The schools were still segregated back then, and if her family had a little money, she might even have gone to a girls' school somewhere out of town. I don't think that was all that unusual back then."

"It's a place to start," she said. "There are copies of the Keyhole Bay yearbooks in the library, and the *News and Times* publishes a list of the graduates every year. We can start with those, see how many Annas we find."

"I'll do what I can, but my boss didn't give me the month off. In fact, she's reminding me I have to get up for work in the morning."

Karen chuckled as we approached the streetlights at the edge of town. "You do work for a slave driver, Glory. And I bet she's only going to get worse when she buys Lighthouse."

"Undoubtedly," I agreed.

Karen pulled up to the curb in front of Southern Treasures. I reminded her of our pizza in my refrigerator, but she waved me off. "Riley's leaving for a couple days, and I won't eat it all by myself."

"And I will?"

"No. But I'm certain you'll have help." She looked pointedly at the closed book shop across the street. "Tell Jake to enjoy the pizza."

"I will."

She waited at the curb until I was safely inside the shop, then pulled away.

For once Bluebeard didn't swear at me for interrupting his sleep. I was kind of disappointed.

Boomer's office called the next morning and rescheduled my meeting with the sheriff. He'd been at the crime scene until after daylight and was out of the office for the rest of the weekend, giving me a reprieve until first thing Monday morning. It felt more like a stay of execution.

Late in the morning, Bradley stopped in the shop and dropped off a fat envelope of financial statements. We talked for a minute, but it was clear he was anxious to get going.

"Mom's still in the hospital," he told me. "But she's raising the devil with the doctors about going home. The doctor told her a couple days observation, and she's insisting it's been two days and she's leaving.

"I have to get back over there and try to keep her from breaking out."

Foot traffic was light, so I spent most of the afternoon staring at the numbers until I could close up and take them upstairs to do a more careful analysis.

Spreadsheets covered the table in my apartment, relegating the box of takeout pizza to the kitchen counter.

Jake rang the bell downstairs and I ran down to let him in.

Back upstairs, he grabbed a piece of pizza and sat next to me, listening intently as I pointed to the columns of numbers that I'd arranged and rearranged several times before he arrived.

"Southern Treasures is doing fine," I concluded. "Another six months—a year tops—and I'll have enough to get rid of Peter. Of course there's no guarantee he'll sell, but I think he will.

"Lord knows, I hope he will. If not, there may be bloodshed." I filled him in on the phone call from my dear cousin and his concerns about Bluebeard. "Of course I could tell him that Uncle Louis wouldn't let any harm come to any visitor to the store. But Peter's a perfect engineer—just the facts, ma'am—and he wouldn't believe me.

"Besides, it's up to Uncle Louis to choose who knows he's here. And he hasn't chosen Peter. At least not yet."

I pointed to another column. "These are the figures Bradley gave me for the last two years of operation at Lighthouse. The shop is turning a profit. He said the family could keep it, hire a manager, and still at least break even. But all of Pansy's kids have lives and jobs of their own, and even with a hired manager, there's a lot of work that *someone* will have to do."

I glanced up at Jake. "I know that all too well. I had someone else running Southern Treasures for several years before I took over. In some ways it's actually less work to do it all myself."

"So the shop can support itself," Jake said.

I nodded and continued. "If Chloe stays—and she says she will—I can promote her to manage daily stuff. A raise, sure, but nowhere near as expensive as adding a full-time employee. She'll do the baking that Pansy was doing, and I'll handle the administrative side."

"So the operation is covered, and it won't impact your cash flow from Southern Treasures."

I nodded. "There's still the question of the purchase price." I showed Jake the number Bradley had given me.

He gave a low whistle. "Yeah, that gets your attention."

"Yep, it does." I tossed my pencil on the table and grabbed a piece of pizza. Even leftover and reheated, Neil's was the best pizza I'd ever eaten.

"So what do I do?" I asked after I swallowed.

"Welllll," Jake said slowly, drawing the word out. "You have had a couple people offer their help."

I shook my head. "I've thought a lot about it, Jake. Felipe and Ernie are wonderful friends. I'd trust them to the ends of the earth, and I love them for offering.

"But like I said, I've thought about this a lot—*a lot*—over the last couple days. I don't want more partners, not even people as remarkable as those two.

I won't risk losing any of my friends over business. You should know that better than anyone."

He nodded. He'd put some of his own money in the Buy-Out-Peter Fund. An investment, he'd said. But I had insisted that he keep it in a separate account. I guess technically there were two Buy-Out-Peter Funds, but neither one was enough to cover what I was considering.

Jake turned back to the spreadsheets, as though something new might have emerged in the two minutes we'd looked away.

"Can you buy it on a contract?"

"I already talked to Bradley," I said, joining Jake's staring party. "He said Miss Pansy was willing to carry a note on the place, but her family doesn't want her to. They're afraid she won't let go."

I sighed. "So we're back to the same question we started with. How do I—"

I was interrupted by the ringing of my cell phone. Out of habit, I glanced up at the cat-shaped novelty clock on my kitchen wall. It was after nine P.M. on a Saturday, and my mother would have been scandalized that someone would call so late.

I checked the phone display. When I saw Beth's number, it dawned on me that I hadn't filled Jake in on last night's excitement.

"I've got news," I said to him. "But I have to take this first." I quickly accepted the call, before she could change her mind.

"Beth!" I said, making sure Jake knew who was calling. "Are you okay? We came up on Thursday, but you weren't home. Is everything all right?"

"I'm fine, Glory. We just needed to come up and see my granny. We should be back soon."

I hesitated, not knowing whether to tell her what had happened. It really wasn't my place, and I didn't think Boomer would appreciate my interference.

"How about the quilt?" I asked as I carried on my internal debate. "Is it ready?"

"Not quite," she said apologetically. "I thought I'd have time to finish it before we left, but we ended up leaving in a rush, earlier than we'd planned.

"I should be back in plenty of time to have it ready before the wedding," she promised. "It's put away in my cedar chest, safe and sound. Just needs a little finishing work when I get home."

Someone spoke to her in the background, and she relayed the message to me. "Everett says he'll drive it down to you once we're home, if you don't have time to come up and get it. Says since this trip was his idea, he'll take care of it."

"Then you'll be back soon," I said. That would be a relief; Boomer could deal with telling them what had happened while they were gone.

"I think so," she said. She sounded far less confident than I would have liked. If she didn't come home right away, I knew Boomer would somehow blame me, but I couldn't tell her why she needed to come back.

"Beth, can I call you right back? Will you be there? I need to check my schedule."

"No need, Glory. I can call you when I know we're headed back, and we can set it up then."

"I'd rather take care if it now," I said. It was a lame excuse, but I needed to talk to Jake.

"I'm kind of busy here," she said. "I just had a minute to call you about the quilt so you wouldn't worry."

"Well, can you just hang on a couple seconds then? I promise I won't be long."

"I guess so." She didn't sound happy about it, but she agreed to wait.

The instant I set the phone to mute, I told Jake about what had happened with Karen the night before and about our encounter with Boomer. "He had me look at pictures of both men," I said, feeling the same cold shiver up my spine that I'd felt when I looked at the pictures. "I didn't know either of them, but it was creepy to think they might have been out there when we were there on Thursday."

"Did you tell Boomer we'd been out there?" he asked.

I shook my head. "He asked when the last time was I'd seen Beth and Everett, and I told him. It was the day I went up and paid the deposit for the quilt. Which," I added, "I couldn't explain in front of Karen."

"Keeping Karen's wedding present a surprise may be the least of your worries. He didn't ask if you'd talked to them?"

"He didn't have time. He got called away, and told me to come to his office this morning."

"And?"

"And nothing. His office called, said he was back out at the crime scene this morning, and would I please come in first thing Monday morning."

"I think you better call him."

"Of course." I had no intention of getting in any more trouble with Boomer. Not for someone I hardly knew. "But I have to finish talking to Beth first, in case I can find out anything to tell Boomer."

Jake looked skeptical, but he didn't argue.

I took the phone off mute, fingers crossed that Beth would still be there, not sure what I'd do if she wasn't.

"Hello."

The single word let me breathe again.

"Hi, Beth. Thanks for waiting."

"It's okay," she said. "But I still don't know what else we needed to talk about."

"Well, do you have any idea when you'll be back?" I didn't want to tell her why. "I'm anxious to get that quilt. The wedding is only a month away." That much was a slight exaggeration, but it was basically the truth. It just wasn't the whole truth.

She hesitated, whispering urgently to someone in the background. I couldn't make out the words, but it sounded like she was asking someone else how to answer my question. Although she kept her voice low, it was clear she was disagreeing with whoever she was talking to.

I paced across the kitchen and stared out the window toward the tiny harbor that gave Keyhole Bay its name. Riley's slip would be empty, his boat *Ocean Breeze* still out fishing. Not that I could see anything but the occasional streetlight in the dark. I tried not to think about how long Beth was taking to answer my question.

Finally Beth finished her hushed conversation and spoke to me. "We aren't completely sure, Glory. We'll be here a few more days is all I know."

"Where did you go?" I asked in what I hoped was a casual tone. "You said you were visiting your granny?"

"Up north," she answered in a deliberately vague manner. She hesitated. "Um, Granny sounded sick when I talked to her the first of the week." The words came out in a rush, as though she might forget her story if she didn't hurry through it. "So we came up to check on her."

I didn't believe her, but there was nothing to gain by telling her so. "So you've only been up there a couple days," I said, fishing for more information.

"I think we left Tuesday." She laughed nervously. "You know how it is when you work for yourself, the days all run together. I should have called you earlier, but it kept slipping my mind—I've just been so busy with Granny."

"Is she okay?" I just wanted to keep her talking in the hope that she'd say something useful.

"She's fine. She said she was just tired when I called and I was overreacting. But after we drove all this way . . ." Her voice trailed off into an apologetic little laugh that didn't sound natural.

"Anyway, it should just be a few days. I'll call you when I get back and we can make arrangements about the quilt."

"Long drive, huh?" It was the best I could come up with, and it sounded silly, even to me.

"Yeah. Kind of. Anyway, I, uh, I have to go. I'll talk to you soon, okay? Bye!"

The connection went dead. I wasn't getting anything more out of Beth. Worse, I still had to call Boomer and I didn't have anything more to tell him, except that Beth was alive and somewhere supposedly visiting family.

I told myself that was his problem, not mine.

I wasn't convinced.

Trying to ignore what I knew Boomer's reaction would be, I dialed the sheriff's office. A female deputy answered the phone and informed me that Sheriff Hardy wasn't available. Did I want to talk to someone else?

No, I didn't. What I knew, or more precisely what I *didn't* know, was something for Boomer alone. I declined the offer and asked to leave a message for the sheriff.

The deputy tried to convince me I should talk to one of the other officers, but she finally accepted that I wanted to talk directly to Boomer.

She put me through to his office, where a recording told me Sheriff Hardy was unavailable and to please leave a detailed message.

I left my name and number. I told him I'd had a call from Beth Young, I'd see him on Monday morning, and I didn't have any other details.

Not that that would keep Boomer from harassing me.

CHAPTER FOURTEEN

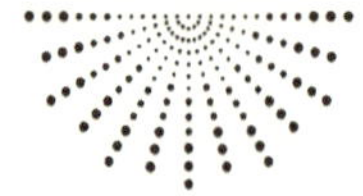

Monday morning started out great, but my upcoming meeting with Boomer cast a shadow over the day.

With Jake's help, I had worked out a plan for financing Lighthouse. I called Back Bay Bank—well, it wasn't Back Bay anymore, but everyone still called it that—and made an appointment to meet Buddy McKenna right away. Buddy swore I'd saved his life when Lacey Simon had tried to kill him, and maybe I had. With luck, he'd repay the favor.

I ducked next door to check on Miss Pansy. The aroma of fresh scones, sweetness and faint hints of citrus, cinnamon, and vanilla, tickled my nose and made my stomach growl. Behind the tall glass counter, Chloe was stocking the pastry case with freshly baked goodies—cookies, donuts, and cupcakes, as well as the scones—smiling like she knew a particularly good secret.

She looked up as I came in and the smile disappeared, replaced with an expression that looked to me like guilt.

What did Chloe have to look guilty about?

I instantly decided it didn't have anything to do with Lighthouse; she'd been an exemplary employee from her first day in the shop, according to Miss Pansy, and I didn't see any reason for that to have changed.

I didn't pry. Chloe wasn't usually secretive, and eventually she'd tell me what was on her mind.

"You made scones?" I asked, examining the display case.

She nodded. "Want to taste one? Tell me if they're okay?" She took one from the case and handed it to me without waiting for an answer.

"Is Bradley going to be in?" I asked before taking a nibble of the still-warm pastry.

She shrugged. "He doesn't have a schedule or anything, but he's been stopping in several times a day. Just checking in, he says, but I think Miss Pansy insists.

"I'm not sure what time he'll come in, though. Miss Pansy's supposed to be going home today. Is there something I can do?"

"Just tell him I came by." I took another taste of the scone, nodding my approval as I chewed.

She looked at me, her unasked question clear on her face.

"Very good," I told her when I finished my bite.

She thanked me, but I knew that wasn't the question she wanted to ask. I took pity on her. "Please don't tell Bradley—I want to do that myself—but I am going to accept his offer.

"In fact," I continued before she could interrupt, "I'm on my way to the bank to work out the financing.

"Just tell him I came by and I want to talk to him."

I left her to finish her stocking and headed back to Southern Treasures. I think I heard her whistling cheerily as I closed the door behind me.

Julie arrived early. She had Rose Ann with her, and an active toddler could be a handful in the shop, but she assured me her mother would be by within the hour to pick up her granddaughter. "She has a doctor's appointment," she explained, "but she'll pick up Rosie as soon as she's done. Until then, she has her playpen in the back."

"That's fine," I assured her. "It's been quiet. One thing I need you to do is check stock on the Bluebeard T-shirts and call Mandy with an order. There were several online orders for them this morning, so take care of those before you do the stock count."

"Will do."

The website sales had surprised me. When I finally got the website running at SouthernTreasuresShop.com, one of the instant hits was T-shirts with Bluebeard's picture on them. They were a steady seller in the shop, too, but the online sales had proven more popular than I could have imagined. They were my secret weapon in the Buy-Out-Peter plan.

Buddy was busy with another customer when I got to the bank, but he quickly excused himself. "Ms. Martine." He shook my hand warmly. "It's so good to see you."

"Please, Buddy, everyone calls me Glory. Or Miss Glory when they want to make me feel old."

Buddy chuckled. "You know I haven't got the hang of calling people Miss This or Mister That. The Yankee in me, I suppose."

As I followed him back to his desk, I asked after his wife and children back in Minneapolis.

"Doing fine," he said. "Wishing I came home more than one week a month. They spent the summer here, you know."

"I heard something about that," I said, taking the chair he indicated across the broad maple desk. "I'm just sorry I didn't get the chance to meet them."

"They came by the store a couple times, but you were out. Fell in love with the parrot, I can tell you."

"I have some kid-size Bluebeard shirts. You ought to take them each one." I thought about offering to give him the shirts, but with the reason for my visit, the gesture might well be misconstrued, or put Buddy on the spot.

"Great idea! I'll stop in before my next trip home."

"Be sure you do."

We chatted for another couple minutes, as required by good Southern manners, before we got down to business.

"So what brings you in today, Gloryanna?"

"I need a loan."

"You came to the right place. This is where the money is." He chuckled at his own joke before turning serious. "Sorry. Banking humor. What do you need it for?"

I gave him the condensed version of the offer from Pansy, and hauled out the sheaf of papers I'd put together for him.

"I have current statements for both businesses," I said, laying out the paperwork. "Cash projections. Business plans."

I shuffled a couple sheets to the top of the stack. "I think everything is here."

"Can you give me a minute?" Buddy asked as he pulled the pile toward him. "There's coffee, if you'd like a cup." He looked sheepish. "I should have offered earlier."

I declined the offer. I'd had most of a pot before I left home, and my nerves didn't need any more stimulants. I already felt like a piano wire stretched tight.

I waited, trying to contain my impatience, as Buddy leafed through the stack of paper. He stopped several times to jot a note on a pad, and twice he reached for his calculator.

After several minutes of silence, he looked up. "How long did you spend on this?"

"Most of the weekend," I admitted. "I'd have taken more time with it, but the Whittakers are anxious to move ahead before Miss Pansy has the chance to change her mind."

I grinned at him. "You've met her. You can understand why they want to move quickly."

"Yes, I can. But what I meant was that this is very well put together. Usually I'd have dozens of questions, but all the information I need seems to be here.

"There are just a couple things I want to go over before I take this to the loan committee."

My disappointment must have shown on my face, because he immediately began to reassure me. "Honestly, Gloryanna, this is a solid proposal. I can't promise anything, but as the interim manager and the leader of the transition team, I do have some influence, shall we say."

He took a couple pages off the top of the stack. "I think this should pass with flying colors, but let me show you the things I think will make it even stronger."

An hour later, I walked out of the bank with Buddy's reassurances still echoing in my head. He'd gone over the numbers that had had my head spinning all weekend, and given my business plan a thumbs-up.

I didn't have a loan approval, and I wouldn't for several days, but it didn't matter. I knew this was my future.

Even if the bank turned me down, I would find a way.

My next stop was the sheriff's station, and my interview with Boomer.

I was pretty sure my day was about to go to hell.

CHAPTER FIFTEEN

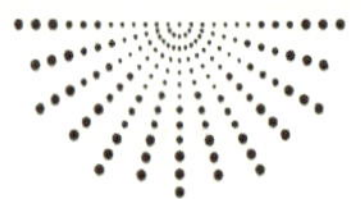

Boomer didn't look happy. "You didn't think I needed to know about that phone call?" he demanded.

"I called you as soon as I got off the phone," I replied. "You were out."

"And you didn't think it was important enough to talk to someone else in the office? You just left me a message and said 'See you Monday'?"

I lowered my head and avoided looking directly at the sheriff. I knew I'd been ducking him when I chose to leave that message, and he was making it quite clear he knew it, too.

"I just didn't have anything I could tell you." It sounded weak, even to me. And Boomer wasn't buying my explanation.

He let the silence build. I was sure he was staring at me, but I didn't look up. I knew if I did, he'd be able to see the real answer written all over my face.

At last he sighed with exasperation. "You didn't think the fact the Youngs were alive and well wasn't vital to this investigation? That knowing we were looking for live suspects, not additional victims, might be useful?"

"I told you Beth had called. You knew she wasn't a victim. But I don't think she's a suspect, either.

"She didn't tell me much else, and I'll bet you anything what she did tell me was a lie."

"When you find two homicide victims on the property and the people who live there are missing, chances are they're either victims or suspects. That's just the way it is.

"And how, pray tell, did you determine that she was lying?"

"It just didn't make sense." I paused, trying to remember her exact words. "She said her granny sounded sick on the phone, so they decided to go check on her.

"Who does that? You call a friend, or a family member who lives nearby, or even 9-1-1 if you think it's really bad. But who packs up and *drives* hundreds of miles because someone sounded sick on the phone?"

Boomer nodded in agreement. "No one," he said, his tone somewhat mollified. "But if you know where she went, you should have told me."

"I didn't. Don't. She just said it was a long drive is all. I guess I just assumed her idea of a long drive would be a day or more. But all she told me was that they went 'up north.'"

"And you hadn't seen her since right after Labor Day?" he circled back around to the questions I'd answered on Friday night.

"No, sir. I ordered a quilt from her for Karen and Riley's wedding gift, and paid the deposit. That's why I didn't explain on Friday, because Karen was there and I was trying to keep the gift a secret. But that's how I know for sure what day it was."

"And you haven't seen her or her husband since."

I shook my head.

"Have you talked to them?"

I'd been expecting that question since I arrived in his office. "Yes," I said. "I usually talk to her every couple or three weeks. Either I call her or she calls me. Usually about stock for the store, or occasional special orders. Like Karen's quilt. I do that with most of my suppliers."

"And they hadn't mentioned taking a trip?"

I shook my head. "We talked about business. It's not like we're best friends or anything. We're on a first-name basis, but I don't know much about her or her family." I thought for a minute. "In fact, now that I think about it, I don't know anything about her, except that she and her husband decided to come down here a year or two ago to get 'off the grid.'" I made finger quotes in the air.

We'd seen many people like the Youngs over the years, mostly in the northern part of the county. Young and not-so-young folks who thought they could get away from it all and live cheaply in the rural areas of the Panhandle. They wanted to grow their own food and live off the land.

Most of them lasted a few weeks, or months, before they went running back to whatever city they'd come from. Back to water that came from a tap instead of a pump, food from a supermarket, and a steady flow of electricity to feed their appliances and electronic gadgets.

Not that I blamed them. I was pretty attached to my version of civilization.

Boomer understood what kind of people I meant. I might have let him believe I didn't think much of Beth and Everett, which wasn't quite true. But it put me and Boomer on the same side, at least a little.

And I needed him to believe that, since I still hadn't told him about being out there on Thursday. And now was as good a time as any.

"There's something else I think you better know," I said.

His face clouded up and he gave me a curt nod. "Yes?"

"I was out to their place on Thursday."

Boomer opened his mouth, but I rushed ahead. There was an explosion coming, and I wanted to divert as much as I could.

"I was supposed to pick up Karen's quilt, so I couldn't really tell you in front of her, could I? There wasn't anybody home, which makes sense if they left on Tuesday. I did tell you she said she thought it was Tuesday, right? She didn't sound like she was really sure, but she said Tuesday.

"Anyway, I had an appointment with Beth on Thursday. Jake and I drove up, but nobody was there. We knocked, and looked around the cabin. Everything was locked up tight and the car was gone. We didn't see anyone, and there weren't any neighbors we could talk to, so we left."

Boomer made a face like he'd bit into a lemon, but he didn't yell. Which was better than I had expected. Instead he just looked at me and shook his head. "And is there anything *else* you think I should know about?"

"No."

"All right. You do have the same cell phone number we do, correct?"

I opened my cell phone and read the number I had for Beth.

"Same number," Boomer said. "Just wanted to be sure, since you seem to have a lot of information you didn't share with us."

"Have you been able to reach her?" I asked.

He hesitated. I think he wanted to tell me it was none of my business, but he didn't. Instead he sighed and shook his head. "She hasn't returned any of our calls."

"Maybe you can track down who her granny is, and find out where they went?"

"We're working on that. And on the identities of the two bodies we found." He looked back at the sheet of notes on his desk. "You sure you've never seen either of them before?"

"Not that I remember. They didn't look familiar. I don't know a lot of people in North County though, except the ones I do business with. And I don't know any of Beth's neighbors."

We'd been going around and around for more than an hour. My throat was dry, and I had answered the same questions with the same answers several times. I needed a drink of water and the restroom, not necessarily in that order.

All this fuss, and I wasn't even a suspect. I could only imagine how a real suspect would feel. I was beginning to think I should just confess to some random thing, so that we could get this over with.

Boomer asked a few more questions, but it was clear he didn't expect to get anything useful from me. He finally turned me loose with a final warning, reminding me for about the millionth time that I was to call him immediately if I heard from Beth again.

Or if I remembered anything.

"And Miss Martine," he said as I reached the office door, "please do not interfere with my investigation. I have a staff of trained officers. I think we can handle this."

I didn't necessarily agree with him; he'd been willing to believe Bridget McKenna's death was a self-inflicted drug overdose. But he'd also stood up to the feds when Bobby Freed was suspected in the murder of an undercover agent.

I went with the smart choice and didn't argue.

Back in my truck, I headed home. I needed to relieve Julie for lunch, I still hadn't talked to Bradley Whittaker, and I'd promised to call Jake as soon as I got back from the bank.

When I walked in the back door, I could hear voices up front. I hurried through the storeroom past Rose Ann's empty playpen, feeling guilty about leaving Julie alone well past her normal lunch break.

I needn't have worried.

Julie sat at the counter and Chloe stood across from her. On the counter between them was a white pastry bag from Lighthouse and two coffee cups.

"Glory!" Chloe spotted me and broke into a grin. "Bradley's back. I came over to get you, but Julie told me you were gone all morning, so since it was getting late I brought her a sandwich and coffee."

I wondered if there was more to this little visit, but even if there was, I didn't really have time for any more drama in my life. It made a strange kind of sense that Julie and Chloe would become friends.

Outwardly they seemed opposites: the classic pretty-blonde-former-cheerleader and the goth-chick-student-barista. But they shared amazing ambition, business sense, maturity, and the aura that they were determined to succeed on their own terms.

That final quality reminded me of me at their age. It could be why I thought Julie was my perfect employee, and I expected Chloe to be the same.

"Can you hang on a few more minutes?" I asked Julie. "Go ahead and eat if you want." Normally food wasn't allowed up front, but this wasn't a normal day.

"I can wait," she said, but I saw her eyeing the bag on the counter.

"If Chloe doesn't mind, maybe she can stay while I run next door and talk to Bradley. Chloe, could you stay a few minutes?"

Chloe grinned. "Sure, boss!"

"Not your boss. Yet." I smiled back, feeling giddy at the thought of what I was about to do.

Giddy, and terrified.

CHAPTER SIXTEEN

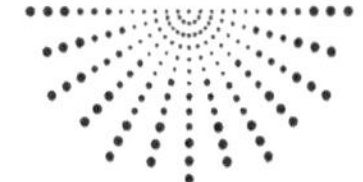

Bradley looked up at the sound of the buzzer when I opened the door to Lighthouse. A shadow passed over his face, and I realized he had been expecting Chloe.

"Chloe's covering for me," I said. "I hope that isn't a problem, but I wanted to come see you as soon as I got back."

"Not at all," he answered.

I glanced around the shop, verifying for myself that Chloe's absence wasn't causing an issue. A white-haired man lounged next to the front window, sipping a steaming cup, his attention focused on the newspaper spread across the table. The only other patrons, a young couple, sat at a table against the far wall, their coffee cups next to an empty paper plate. The woman daintily licked crumbs from her fingertips. I'd seen that same gesture from thousands of Pansy's customers over the years.

Was I crazy to think I could do as well?

I drew a deep breath and reminded myself that Pansy's recipes were part of this deal. Without them, Lighthouse was just another coffee shop. With them, the place was legendary.

I wanted to keep that legendary reputation.

Bradley waited patiently behind the register for me.

Moment of truth.

I felt like my head was a balloon, floating several feet above my body. My heart raced, and sweat ran down my back even though the weather was cool.

Bradley looked at me expectantly.

I stuck out my hand. "You've got yourself a deal."

He shook my hand with genuine warmth, and a relieved smile spread across his features. "I, *we*, are all delighted. Mom was starting to waver, but she said she'd made you a promise and she would keep it."

He continued to pump my hand, as though he was afraid I'd change my mind if he let go. "We've been so worried she'd insist on coming back to work if you decided not to buy the shop."

"I still haven't lined up all the financing," I reminded him. "But I did call my lawyer this morning and gave him the outline of your terms. He said he could have a contract drawn up and ready for signatures later this week."

Clifford Wilson had been our family lawyer for several decades before I was born. He'd drawn up Uncle Louis's will that left Peter and me Southern Treasures. Approaching ninety, I worried every time I called that I'd find him retired, and some stranger taking his place.

Fortunately for me, he was still in the office three days a week, and with the courtly manners of an earlier generation, had insisted he would have the papers drawn up overnight.

I protested, but he was insistent. His actual words were, "If Miss Pansy Whittaker is ready to sell, you best strike while the iron is hot. That little gal is stubborn as a mule, and if she takes it into her head to back out, you're going to need an iron-clad contract."

Mr. Wilson had known Miss Pansy her entire life, so he had a lot of evidence to back his opinion, and he brooked no argument. He said he would e-mail a draft the next day, I could send back any changes, and the contract would be ready on Wednesday or Thursday. He might have been born in another century, but he was up-to-the-minute when it came to his practice.

"I will look forward to that," Bradley said.

"I better get back to work," I said. "I'll send Chloe back over. Thanks again for letting me borrow her."

"She'll be working for you soon enough," Bradley said as I left.

I walked into Southern Treasures and found Chloe and Julie huddled at the counter, their attention focused on something Chloe was writing.

Julie glanced up at the sound of the bell, startled. She poked Chloe, who looked up and saw me. They both looked guilty, as though I'd caught them doing something they shouldn't be doing.

As I approached, Chloe hastily folded the paper she'd been writing on and laid her hand oh-so-casually on top of it.

"Glory," Chloe said, "we were wondering, are you going to invite us to

Karen's bridal shower? I mean, we feel like we're her friends, but you hadn't said anything to either of us, and we just wanted to know."

I furrowed my brow. "What bridal shower?"

Julie spoke up. "You're the maid of honor, right? One of the things you're supposed to do is host a bridal shower. At least that's the way my mama taught me." She stopped and a blush crept up her fair skin as she remembered I hadn't had a mama to teach me any of these things.

"No. I think I knew that," I admitted. "But since this is a second wedding with the same bride and groom, I guess I just didn't think about it."

Great, one more thing to add to my growing to-do list. I didn't know where I would find the time for party planning, but I supposed I would have to.

Chloe, however, was several steps ahead of me.

"I thought that might be it," she said. "And when Julie said she hadn't heard anything either, well, we were just talking about what we could do. That is, if you'll let us?

"Julie and I can handle the planning. I can take care of the food, and Julie says she knows all the games and stuff, and I think I can get Shiloh to help with the decorations. She left Fowler's, you know, and went to work at Flower Power, and she's really good at that kind of thing."

"Whoa! It sounds like you've got this all figured out, but I promised Bradley you'd be back to work. Can we talk about this later?"

"Sure! Just let me know when, okay?" She was out the door in a flash, and the shop was suddenly silent.

"So, you two were plotting while I was gone?"

Julie looked sheepish. "We were trying not to think about you talking to Mr. Whittaker, and we got to talking about the wedding and, well, it just kind of went from there."

"Seriously though, would you two actually be willing to do that for me?" The sense of relief at Chloe's offer was overwhelming, but I didn't want to overload my employee and my soon-to-be employee.

"Truth?" Julie said. "You've been so busy with the business stuff we figured you really didn't have time for this. And we'd love the chance to be part of it. I think Karen is amazing. I'd love to do this for her, and for you.

"And it was Chloe's idea, so I think she's good with it."

"Well," I felt like a huge weight had been dropped on me and then just as suddenly lifted off my shoulders. "If you're sure, I would be delighted to have your help.

"Now what do I have to do?"

"Nothing," Julie said. "Well, except we'll have you approve whatever we do, of course. And we will need your help to make sure we don't miss inviting someone."

I laughed. "This is Karen. Maybe we should just post a notice in the *News and Times* and invite the whole town."

Julie giggled, a lighthearted sound that I'd realized had been missing for a long time when we first met. It was good to hear her happy and relaxed, and I marveled at her resilience. She'd been through a horrible time with her ex, but she'd come out the other side stronger and more mature, with a beautiful daughter. She didn't just survive, she thrived.

"I'm sure anything you two come up with will be fabulous. And I'll be glad to look at the guest list when you have it ready."

"Thanks, Glory."

"No, thank you—you and Chloe—for thinking of this for me." I flashed on the impending arrival of Karen's mom and Stepdad Number Three. I could only imagine the dustup that would have ensued if there wasn't a bridal shower, and my gratitude grew even more.

"Did I tell you Karen's mom and stepdad are coming down for the wedding?"

Julie shook her head.

"Yeah, she thinks Karen needs her help, so she's going to be here for the month before." I lowered my voice to a whisper, even though we were alone in the store. "If you really want to help Karen, you'll distract her mom with shower plans."

"We can try," she promised.

With the bank, the sheriff, Bradley Whittaker, and the bridal shower all taken care of for the moment, I settled down to take care of some store business.

But as soon as I logged into the bookkeeping program, the bell rang over the door and I heard Jake's voice.

I'd promised to update him as soon as I got back, and I'd completely forgotten. I quickly shut down the computer, promising myself I'd work late to catch up on all the things I'd left undone while I worked on the proposal for the bank.

CHAPTER SEVENTEEN

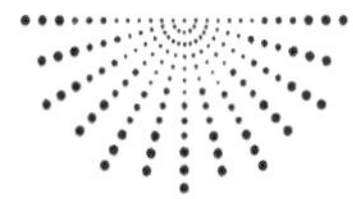

"Sorry," I said, giving Jake a quick kiss on the cheek.

A wolf whistle came from the front corner of the shop, followed by a cackling laugh.

"Bluebeard!" It did me no good to admonish him, but I still tried.

"He only does that because he knows it bugs you," Julie laughed. "He's like a two-year-old with feathers."

"I guess you'd know about two-year-olds," I said.

I turned my attention back to Jake. "I meant to call you, but Chloe was here looking for me for Bradley, and then we got caught up in some wedding stuff before I sent her back to work."

I glanced at the clock and decided I wasn't getting back to my paperwork before the end of the day, and there were some things I wasn't ready to talk about in front of Julie.

"Julie, if you want to take off, I can handle the rest of the afternoon. Doesn't look like we're going to be overrun with business."

She gave me a grateful smile. "Thanks. I'm sure my mom would appreciate my picking up Rose Ann a little early."

"Is she alright?" I asked. "You mentioned her having a doctor's appointment."

"Cellulitis," she answered. "She's doing okay, but I hate to leave her with Rose Ann when she's hurting. You sure it's okay for me to go?"

I assured her it was just fine, and she left quickly, as though she was afraid I might change my mind.

Alone with Jake, I filled him in on the visit to the bank.

"So Buddy's going back to Minnesota?" he asked.

"That was what he said. They'll be getting a permanent manager soon, and his transition team will be able to go home. At least until the next assignment."

I couldn't imagine a job that took me to a new city every few weeks or months. I'd been born in Keyhole Bay, lived here my whole life, and had no reason to ever leave. I liked knowing my neighbors and having lifelong friends like Karen and Riley.

"He said his family would like him to be home more, but they're getting used to the schedule. And I think he enjoys the work."

"But he'll be here long enough to get this application through, won't he?"

I nodded. "I sure hope so. Two years ago, I would have said I knew everyone on the loan committee and they knew me. But now that Back Bay's been sold, the new owners have brought in a lot of their own people."

Jake put his arm around my shoulders and gave me a reassuring hug. "Either way, Buddy thought it was a solid plan, right? It's going to be just fine."

"Just fine," Bluebeard echoed.

"You really think so?" I wasn't sure which one I was asking, but both Jake and Bluebeard answered "Yes" in unison.

"Now that we have that settled," Jake said, "what about your visit with the sheriff? I gather you didn't want to talk about it until Julie left."

"I didn't." I leaned against Jake, comforting myself with his presence. "It wasn't awful," I told him. "But it wasn't good, either. Boomer acts like he's halfway convinced I know more than I'm telling him. Even when I told him everything I knew and everything I *thought* I knew.

"And he keeps giving me the speech about not interfering with his investigation. Like I'd ever do that!" I pulled away, my voice rising as I released the indignation I'd held in check since I left Boomer's office.

I made the mistake of looking at Jake as I spoke that last sentence. He was biting his lip, trying not to laugh.

"No," he said hastily. "You wouldn't. At least not on purpose. But Glory"— he struggled to keep his voice serious—"you have gotten involved in several investigations in the past. You really can't blame Boomer for being concerned."

My anger vanished as quickly as it had come. "I hate it when you're right."

"No you don't," he said, pulling me close once again. "You already knew why Boomer was worried. You just needed to vent."

"Yeah. Still, I *did* tell him everything I knew. I even gave him Beth's cell number, which it turned out he already had."

Jake let me go and walked over to Bluebeard. He offered him a biscuit and scratched his head, and was rewarded with a head butt. "What do you think, old man? You think Boomer has reason to be concerned?"

The parrot bobbed his head as though agreeing with Jake. Then Uncle Louis's voice said clearly, "She can be a handful."

I sputtered. There wasn't really much of anything I could do when the two of them ganged up on me. "Just remember who gets you treats," I said darkly.

"You love me," Bluebeard replied and cackled again. That laugh was a new addition to his repertoire, a warped imitation of Rose Ann's high-pitched little-girl giggle.

"Yes, I do." I joined Jake in front of Bluebeard's perch. "But you can be a handful, too."

"You still love me." He cocked his head, staring at me with one dark eye. "I love you, too." Uncle Louis again.

It still unnerved me occasionally when Bluebeard slipped between his own voice and Uncle Louis's. I had accepted the fact that my great-uncle had never left the store he'd owned for many years. I had accepted his use of Bluebeard as his spokesbird. I had accepted, and even sort of appreciated, his interference with my personal life.

But it was still weird.

Jake suggested dinner when we closed up, and I agreed. "My place or yours?" I asked.

"Mine. I've got chili verde in the slow cooker, if that works for you?"

"Sounds good. Can I bring anything?"

"Just your appetite," he said.

After Jake left, I tried to settle back down to bookkeeping and inventory, but I kept coming back to my interview with Boomer. Had I told him everything? I couldn't think of anything I'd left out, but the feeling of guilt, the need to confess to *something*, persisted.

I wandered around the shop, straightening shelves that didn't need attention and restocking the few items that had sold during the day. Behind the counter, I found a neat stack of papers Julie had left, including a copy of the order she'd given Mandy for the Bluebeard T-shirts and copies of the packing lists for the shirts she'd shipped.

It was the reassurance I needed. In spite of my misgivings about Boomer, the rest of my life was moving in the right direction. Julie's competence once again validated my decision to hire her, and Buddy's confidence in my business plan reinforced my gut feeling that this was the right thing to do.

My spirits lifted, and I went back to work. Knowing dinner, and Jake, were waiting at the end of the day didn't hurt either.

As I worked, the thought of Beth and Everett kept tickling at the back of my brain. If I could just convince them to come back, Boomer would have to see that they were innocents whose only crime was being in the wrong place at the wrong time. Or not in the wrong place.

Beth had trusted me enough to call back, although she hadn't told me where she was or when she'd return. I just needed to come up with a reason for her to come back to Keyhole Bay and talk to Boomer.

Yeah, I thought as I forced my attention to the stack of invoices. *And maybe I should figure out world peace while I'm at it.*

CHAPTER EIGHTEEN

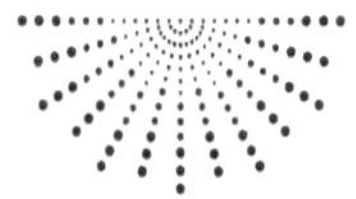

"You cooked," I said, getting up from my chair. "My turn to clean up."

Jake agreed, but he could only sit still for a couple minutes. Soon he was up from the wooden table in his kitchen and putting away leftovers while I ran water for the dishes.

I washed and he dried; a comfortable routine we'd developed over the course of many shared meals. I liked sharing the tidy kitchen with Jake, "accidentally" bumping into each other as we worked, and he seemed to feel the same; we'd discovered a lot of things we enjoyed doing together.

"Are you staying?" Jake asked, hanging his dish towel on the rack over the sink once the kitchen was tidy enough to meet his standard. He called it "squared away," a remnant of his years in the firehouse.

For several months I'd had an overnight bag stowed in the truck, but a few weeks ago Jake had casually suggested I just put my things in a spare cupboard. Now the question of spending the night didn't require planning and preparation. We just did what seemed right for the moment.

"Is that an invitation?" I teased.

"I guess it might be."

He gave me a kiss that left me a little breathless. An invitation, yes, but there wasn't any question whether I'd accept.

In the morning I slipped in the back door of Southern Treasures before the late autumn sun was over the horizon. I hastily reset the alarms and started up the stairs, walking softly at the edge of the treads, trying to avoid the squeaky steps.

It didn't matter.

I'd only gone up three steps when a loud squawk came from the shop. "Awk! Naughty girl, out all night!"

I sighed and continued up the stairs without worrying about making noise. "I'll be down to take care of you in a few minutes," I called out.

It was worse than breaking curfew as a teenager.

Fifteen minutes later, coffee made and a load of clothes in the washer, I came back downstairs to deal with Bluebeard.

"Coffee?" he asked.

Maybe he thought my guilty conscience would make me weak, but if so he was sadly mistaken. "No coffee for you. You know better."

He did—we had this conversation several times a week—but it didn't stop him from asking. Coffee was toxic for parrots, and no matter how much Uncle Louis missed his coffee, his host couldn't tolerate it.

Besides, I didn't feel particularly guilty. As Karen would say (and then apologize for her language), I was a grown-ass woman.

As though called by my thoughts, Karen appeared at my door a few minutes later.

"I stopped at Lighthouse for coffee," she said when I opened the door, "and I saw your lights were on."

I took the cup she handed me, abandoning my own mug of French press from upstairs. I was careful to put the mug where Bluebeard couldn't get to it. Not that I didn't trust him, but I didn't. Not where coffee was concerned.

I brought her up to date on my meeting at the bank, told her about my interview with Boomer, and moved on to Bradley Whittaker without giving her the chance to ask about Beth and Everett.

"So what are you doing out so early?" I asked as I finished the rundown of my Monday without mentioning Jake. "Early morning at the station?"

"No." She groaned. "I'm on my way to the airport. Stepdad Number Three had an appointment at the naval station. So, for my sins, I have to pick up my mother and bring her up here while his driver takes him out to the base."

She looked at me, a glimmer of hope in her eyes. "You wouldn't want to go for a little ride, would you? We won't be long, I promise."

"I wish I could help you out," I said. "But I've got a lot to do here before I open up."

"Naughty girl, out all night!" Bluebeard squawked.

I felt a blush creep up my face as Karen's eyebrows shot up. "Really?" she said. She gave me a knowing smile. "So maybe there *is* something I should know?"

I shook my head. "You know I spend time at Jake's, and he spends time here. And sometimes, well, you know.

"And when there's something to tell, you'll be the first to know."

"Me first," Bluebeard squawked.

"Well, you'll be the first to know after Bluebeard. I have no secrets from him, even if I try to."

I remembered there was something I needed to tell Karen, and it just might make her happier about her mother's arrival.

"I do have something that might be good news for you," I told her. "Chloe and Julie want to throw you a shower. Actually, they said as maid of honor it was my job, but they knew I was busy and they volunteered." I stopped and sipped my cooling latte.

The milky concoction reminded me of Chloe's barista skills. I was glad she wanted to stay.

"I don't need a shower," Karen said impatiently. "I still have the house we bought when we were married, and I think we have everything we need already, times two."

"But that's not the good part," I said. "They said they'd try to get your mom involved in planning the shower, and maybe keep her off your back a bit."

Karen looked like she wanted to cry with relief.

"It's not a done deal," I reminded her. "And there's no guarantee they'll be able to keep her distracted. But it might give you a break now and then."

"Right now, even a little break sounds wonderful. I don't know what I'm going to do with Mom here for the next month. I'm actually wishing Stepdad Number Three—do you think I should actually, like, learn his name?—has some huge emergency and they have to go back to Washington right away."

She threw her shoulders back and put her chin up, her chestnut curls tossing defiantly. "Okay, here I go. I can do this."

But as she went out the door, the defiant posture slumped and she looked so miserable, I reconsidered my answer.

Grabbing my wallet and keys, I stuffed them in my pockets and ran out the door after her.

CHAPTER NINETEEN

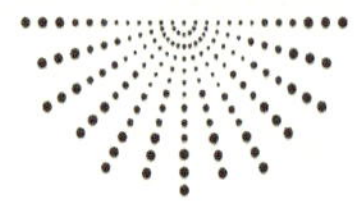

"Just this once," I said, as I slid into the front seat and fastened my seat belt. "And I'm already regretting it."

I glanced at the dashboard clock. "There's time, just barely."

We pulled onto the empty early morning highway and headed for Pensacola, the ever-present police scanner blinking silently in its cradle under the dash.

Karen was as silent as the radio, and I looked over at her. Her hands were white-knuckle tight on the steering wheel, her mouth drawn into a flat line of concentration. Or stress.

I searched for something to say, something to distract her from the family reunion that awaited her in Pensacola. I envied her that; I wished I had a mother to fuss over me. On the other hand, I'd seen firsthand how the relationship made them both crazy.

Karen was the only child of a single mom with enough maternal instinct for a dozen kids, and she'd suffered from the overabundance of attention throughout her childhood.

Her mom was Mrs. French when we were kids, and in my teens I'd heard her say that the name and the kid were the only things she got from her ex-husband. The ex-husband himself had taken on a legendary quality, having disappeared before Karen was a year old. He was one of the very few taboo subjects in Karen's life.

Now we were heading down the highway toward the only person guaranteed to make Karen even crazier than she'd been for the last few weeks.

Why was I in this car? Deliberately putting myself in the middle of this encounter went well beyond friendship. And I needed to stop obsessing about it and try to enjoy our last few minutes of freedom.

"Any luck tracking down Sly's friend?" I asked.

Karen shook her head. "A lot of the records from that time are only available on paper, and I couldn't get access over the weekend. I thought I'd spend some time this afternoon—until mother called and said they were coming in earlier than planned."

And there we had circled right back around to the subject I was trying to avoid.

"They aren't staying with you, are they?" I couldn't imagine Karen and her mother surviving thirty hours in the same house, much less thirty days, or more.

"No, there's some kind of visiting bigwig quarters at the naval base. They're expected to stay there. But instead of going there and getting settled in, Mom insists she has to come up here and—I don't know—start meddling, I guess."

Traffic was light and we made good time, arriving at the airport before the plane. Pensacola International was a small airport: a single terminal with twelve gates. We parked in the garage and walked across to the terminal.

Karen fidgeted, retrieving her e-mail and voice mail every couple minutes. She had an app for the airline on her phone, and she checked the progress of her mother's flight constantly. I wasn't sure whether she was hoping they'd arrive soon, or not at all.

"Are you expecting something?" I asked when she hit refresh on her messages for the fifth or sixth time.

"Boomer was supposed to have some preliminary information on Friday night's victims," she replied. "There was a rumor yesterday that there might be an identification coming. And he hasn't released the autopsy results, either. I know Dr. Frazier was called out Friday, so he should have something by now."

"They still haven't identified them?"

"You saw that place," Karen said. "Some of those neighbors aren't exactly neighborly, and some of 'em don't care much for any kind of law enforcement."

"Nobody likes to talk to the cops," I said. "That seems pretty normal to me."

"Are you really that innocent, Martine? Really?" She shook her head. "Did you look around when you were up there? Some of the locals have been out there for generations, and their means of support is the kind that doesn't exactly meet with official approval.

"There's a reason some of those guys stay deep in the woods."

"Oh!" I tapped my forehead. "Duh! You mean the 'shiners? I didn't think the sheriff paid them much mind."

"He might not, normally. But he's got two dead bodies. That changes things. He wants to talk to everybody that was out there, including you."

"He already talked to me," I reminded her.

"Yeah." She looked at her phone again, tapping the screen. Every movement screamed impatience. "They should be on the ground," she said, taking a conversational left turn. "Just a few more minutes."

I checked the time and mentally counted the hours to the West Coast. "How did they get a flight this early?" I asked, realizing it was still the middle of the night on the other side of the country.

"Flew to Houston yesterday," Karen said. "He has a brother or something there, and they were supposed to spend a few days with him. But there was some change in plans and the Navy wanted the Admiral—and no, I don't know if he's really an admiral, but I have to call him something, don't I?—they wanted him here first thing this morning.

"So here we are at this ridiculous hour." She glanced at her phone again and tapped irritably at the display. "I'm texting her to meet us at the luggage carousel. The app says it's number two."

Without waiting for my response, she took off for the baggage claim. I trotted to keep up with her as she moved through the near-empty terminal. Everything she did was rapid-fire this morning, and I wondered just how much coffee she'd had before she stopped at Lighthouse.

We arrived before the first bags came off the plane. We stood a few paces back from the conveyor, leaving room for the passengers, who soon began arriving. They mobbed the conveyor, snatching near-identical bags from the belt.

Where were all these people going at this hour of the morning? Some were vacationers, eager to get an early start on their trip, and the young men in Navy and Air Force uniforms made sense.

A group of men in pastel slacks and polo shirts bearing the name of a Houston country club claimed the golf bags a baggage handler brought out on a cart, and were whisked away by a uniformed driver who had been waiting with a card that read "Golf Trail Tours."

I was trying to figure out the rest of the passengers when I heard Karen's sharp intake of breath. "There they are." I think she meant to whisper, but nerves made her voice so loud that several people turned to look.

I looked in the direction she was facing. Sure enough, there was her mother, with her arm linked with the arm of a man in uniform. His dark uniform jacket sported enough ribbons and medals that he might really be an admiral.

Karen's mother looked older, but her carefully applied makeup, the expert streak job on her honey blond hair, and a figure that caused other women to look daggers at her, disguised just how many years she carried on her slender shoulders.

She still knew how to dress, something Karen and I had never learned from her. Simple oatmeal-colored capris and a bright turquoise camp shirt emphasized her tiny stature next to the imposing military man beside her.

I squeezed Karen's arm in what I hoped was a reassuring way and guided her toward her mother and her new stepfather, talking softly to her as we walked.

They caught sight of us when we were still several yards away, Karen's mom breaking into a broad smile at the sight of her daughter. Karen flinched, then pasted a big smile on her face and hurried forward to greet her mother with a hug.

When I caught up with them, Karen had already managed to extract herself from her mother's embrace.

"Gloryanna!" her mother exclaimed. She was the sort of woman who actually did exclaim. "It's so good to see you! Karen didn't tell me you were coming with her."

"A full-service maid of honor," I said lightly. I accepted a quick hug. "It's wonderful to see you, Mrs. . . ."

My voice trailed off as I realized I had no idea what to call her. She hadn't been Mrs. French since Karen and I were in our teens, and I didn't know her new married name. For that matter, I didn't know if she'd taken her new husband's name, though I suspected military protocols would dictate that she should.

"Please, call me Catherine. You're not a child anymore, and I'm certainly not as old as that makes me feel." She gave me another quick hug and linked her arms with mine and Karen's before turning to her new husband.

I took a look past the medals and ribbons to the man who was now Karen's stepfather. Ramrod-straight posture would have identified him as a career military officer, even without the uniform. Dark hair, just past crew-cut length with hints of gray at the temples, and brown eyes with fine lines at the corners that gave him the look of having a perpetual squint. His deep tan spoke of years on the water, reminding me of the veteran fishermen in Keyhole Bay.

"Karen, Glory, this is my husband, Captain Clinton Fontaine. Clint, this is my daughter Karen and her best friend, Gloryanna Martine."

"Ladies," he nodded, a slight tip of his head. He waited politely for Karen to offer her hand, then took it in both of his. "I've heard so much about you, I'm honored to finally meet you. If even half of what your mother tells me is true, you're pretty remarkable." There was a twinkle in his eyes, a hint that he understood his wife's exaggerations well.

He released Karen's hand and turned to me. "Catherine mentions you fondly, Miss Martine. She seems quite impressed with your accomplishments."

I shook his hand and tried to accept the compliment gracefully, always a challenge.

"It's Glory to my friends," I told him.

"Glory, then." He flashed a warm smile and excused himself to collect their luggage. "Stay here with the girls, Cat," he told Karen's mom. "I know you have a lot of catching up to do."

He walked over to the baggage carousel, where three bags circled the otherwise-empty belt. The two larger bags, in matching black-and-white houndstooth-check pattern, sported bright red bandannas tied to the handles. I could guess that those were Catherine's. The third bag was well-worn leather, smaller than the other two. Captain Fontaine deftly stacked the bags atop each other and wheeled them back to where we waited.

"Do you need your bags, Cat, or should I take them directly to our quarters?"

Catherine shook her head, gesturing to the hefty carry-on sitting at her feet. "I think I have what I need for today," she said. "You'll pick me up later?"

"Yes ma'am." He bent and gave her a kiss that had Karen and me both looking away. "The driver should be here," he said. "I'll call you when I'm through for the day."

He took the stack of luggage and strode toward the exit.

"My car's across the way," Karen said, grabbing her mother's bag. She staggered slightly as she added the heavy bag to the load of the carryall she toted everywhere.

I took pity on her. I took her mother's bag from her and slung it over my shoulder. I think Catherine must have been planning to go bowling later, judging by the weight of the thing.

We left the terminal just as Captain Fontaine was climbing into a dark sedan, a young sailor standing at attention, holding his door.

"I could carry my own bag," Catherine protested as we made our way across the street and into the parking garage.

"Mother," Karen said, "that bag would challenge an Olympic weight lifter. The only reason Glory can manage it is that she's used to heavy lifting."

"It's not that bad," I said, without much conviction. "And I'm not sure the comparison to an Olympic weight lifter is any kind of compliment."

The ride back to Keyhole Bay was almost as tense as the trip to Pensacola. Catherine immediately started quizzing Karen about plans for the wedding, and Karen's answers grew shorter and sharper with each question.

"Mom, for heaven's sake! Can we talk about something else, *anything* else, for just a few minutes? Tell me about Clint, or your new place in Seattle, or what you had for breakfast. Just don't talk about the wedding. Please."

"I just wanted to know what I could do to help," Catherine snapped. "And we don't live in Seattle. It's Oak Harbor, and it's a hundred miles from Seattle."

"Really?" Karen latched onto the subject like a drowning man grabbing a life ring. "I didn't realize it was so far out of town. Tell me what it's like."

Temporarily distracted, Catherine launched into a description of an island paradise that sounded too good to be true. She loved her new home, she said, and was glad to be out of the big city and back in a small town.

"And speaking of small towns," she continued, "what's going on in Keyhole Bay? It's been so long since I've been back here, and I've lost track of all the news."

"Well," Karen said, "the big news is actually about Glory. It seems that Pansy Whittaker is finally going to retire and Glory's buying Lighthouse Coffee."

"Glory! How wonderful for you. I told Clint you were a successful businesswoman, but I had no idea you were getting ready to expand. You must be so excited!"

"I'm not sure if excited is the right word," I said. "Terrified, maybe. It's a big undertaking and we're just in the preliminary stages. There's still a lot that could go wrong before it's a done deal.

"I don't want to jinx it by speaking too soon."

We were nearly back to Keyhole Bay when Karen's phone rang. She tapped the control on the dash, activating the speaker, and answered.

"Karen Freed. I'm driving and you're on the speaker with my passengers," she cautioned the caller.

"Freed." I recognized the station manager's voice. "Sorry to interrupt, but Sheriff Hardy will have a press release in twenty minutes. Can you get there, or should I send someone else?"

"I'll be there. I'm about ten minutes away. I just need to drop off my mom and Glory." She broke the connection and glanced over at her mother.

"You're going to have to entertain yourself for a little bit, I'm afraid. I wasn't planning on being off work until late next week."

"I understand," Catherine said. "But are you going to leave me at your house while you're gone, or what?"

Karen blanched at the thought of leaving her mother alone in her house. She'd come home to find the laundry done, the floors cleaned, and the entire kitchen rearranged. Not to mention whatever her mom might choose to snoop around in while she was gone.

Once again, the maid of honor rode to the rescue.

"Why don't you stay at my place?" I offered. "There are several breakfast spots within walking distance, or you can take a nap upstairs if you're tired. You must have had to be up at an unholy hour for that early flight."

I mentally reviewed the state of my apartment. I hadn't eaten at home last night, or slept in my bed, so it shouldn't be too bad. I hadn't even had time to change my clothes before Bluebeard and Karen started interfering with my plans.

"That's very generous of you, Glory, but I couldn't impose," Catherine's voice rose at the end of her sentence, inviting my reply.

Social convention dictated that she give me the opportunity to rescind the hasty invitation, but we both knew it was a ritual and I quickly repeated the offer.

"Not at all," I said.

"If you're sure?"

"It'll be fine, Mom," Karen cut in.

I'd run out of the shop so fast I hadn't brought my phone. "Karen, can I borrow your phone? I left mine in the shop."

She handed it to me, reaching for the control pad on the dash. "I assume you don't want us all to join in your conversation," she said.

"Thanks." Whether for the phone or the privacy, I wasn't sure.

I dialed Julie's number. It was still early, but Rose Ann usually had her up with the chickens, and today was no exception.

"Hi, Julie. It's Glory. I know it's your day off, but I wondered if you could come in this morning?"

"I don't have a babysitter," she said. "So I don't know how long Rose Ann will last in the store.

"And why are you calling from Karen's phone?"

"Don't worry about Rose Ann. I just wanted you to meet Karen's mother. They had a change in plans, and we just picked her up at the airport, which is why I'm using Karen's phone; I forgot mine. Anyway, I thought maybe you and Chloe would like to talk to her about the shower."

"I suppose I could do that, even with Rose Ann along. Give me time to get her fed and changed, and we'll be in."

"Thanks, Julie."

I hung up and handed the phone back to Karen. ""I think that will keep us busy for a while."

Catherine turned around, an expectant look on her face. "A bridal shower?" she asked.

"Yes." I hoped I sounded more enthusiastic than I felt. "Julie and Chloe offered to host, and they would love to have your help. Chloe works at Lighthouse, so we can go over and get a cup of coffee"—I hoped she hadn't noticed the discarded cups that revealed we'd already been there once this morning—"and I can introduce you to the girls."

"That sounds fine," she said. "But who's Rose Ann?"

"Julie's daughter. She's two."

"A baby!" Catherine was exclaiming again. "How wonderful! I can't wait to meet her."

I couldn't see Karen's expression, but I didn't need to. Grandchildren were one of the many contentious subjects between Karen and her mom. Catherine had made it abundantly clear that she was willing and eager to be a grandmother, but her only child wasn't sure she wanted to be a mother. Now, or ever.

A few minutes later, Karen dropped us off in front of Southern Treasures.

I made her promise to call me as soon as she could, to fill me in on whatever information the sheriff released. Beth and Everett hadn't been far from my thoughts ever since the station manager's call, and I was anxious to know what was going on.

I showed Catherine upstairs to freshen up and went back down to get the store ready to open.

CHAPTER TWENTY

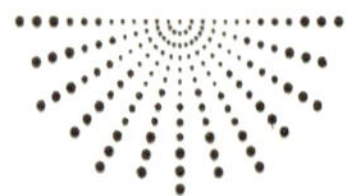

Catherine was still upstairs when Julie and Rose Ann arrived. "Thank you for coming in." I got a hug from Rose Ann, who trotted over to talk to Bluebeard. "Could you run next door and let Chloe know that Karen's mom, Mrs. Fontaine, is here, please? Ask her if she'd be available at some point to talk about the shower."

I had already heated my leftover coffee in the microwave, finished it, and was craving a mocha, but I forced myself to wait until Catherine joined us. Memaw would have been scandalized if I hadn't waited for my guest, no matter the circumstances of her visit.

"Leave Rose Ann," I told her. "I'll let her feed Bluebeard a treat. You know how much she loves that."

Bluebeard loved it, too. He had been charmed by Julie's daughter from the first day she'd come into the shop, and over the months, as she grew from infant to toddler, they had formed a mutual admiration society.

I helped Rose Ann get some grapes from the small refrigerator in back, and she carefully pulled them from the stems, putting some in a bowl for Bluebeard and popping a few directly into her own mouth.

"Hello, sweetheart," Bluebeard greeted her when she returned to his perch with the bowl of grapes. Normally he would greedily devour any treat, but with Rose Ann, he waited patiently as she held out each grape. He took the grape from her fingers carefully and gently, and thanked her for each one.

Still, I always supervised.

Catherine came down while we were feeding Bluebeard. She made a beeline for Rose Ann, every latent grandmother gene surfacing.

Rose Ann took the attention in stride. Having spent time in the store since she was a baby, she'd gotten used to strange women cooing over her.

"Chloe has a break in about twenty minutes," Julie said when she returned. "She said she'd be over then."

"Catherine." The name still felt strange on my tongue. She'd always been Mrs. French in my mind, and it seemed wrong somehow to address her by her given name. "This is Julie Nelson. She works for me, and she's Rose Ann's mom.

"Julie, this is Mrs. Fontaine, Karen's mom."

"Call me Catherine," she said immediately. "I'm so glad to meet you."

I asked Catherine what kind of coffee she'd like, and excused myself to call Chloe with our order. I told her to put the coffee and cookies on my tab, and she laughed and said, "Sure, boss!"

When I rejoined Julie and Catherine, they were having the kind of conversation you have after being away from a small town for a long time: who got divorced, who got married, what business closed or grew, who moved away, who passed away. It was a distillation of the last six years of the *News and Times*.

As I walked up, I heard Catherine's, "Matthew Fowler is still married? I thought she would have tossed him out years ago!"

"You should see the rock she's wearing," I said. "Oh, and the new Cadillac she got last year. You can't say Mr. Fowler doesn't pay for his mistakes."

"That hasn't changed," Catherine said. "He's been that way as long as I've known him."

"You worked for him, didn't you? I'd forgotten all about that until just this instant." I blurted it out before I thought about the implications of what I was saying.

Fortunately for me, Catherine didn't take offense. "Yes, I did," she said. "For about a day and a half."

I filed that away. As a struggling single mother, she wouldn't have quit a job on a whim. I wondered what the story was, but she didn't volunteer anything more, and I didn't ask.

A few minutes later, Chloe appeared with a tray of coffee drinks and a white pastry bag. She passed drinks around, including cocoa for Rose Ann, as I made introductions. "I cooled it down," she told Julie as she handed her the child's treat.

She handed Catherine a cup. "Nice to meet you, Mrs. Fontaine. Chai latte, right?"

The three of them spent the next half hour chattering about the plans for Karen's shower. I mostly stayed out of the discussion, watching the clock and wondering when Karen would call with whatever news the sheriff would release.

Chloe went back to work, leaving Julie and Catherine happily planning games and menus and color schemes.

Rose Ann started to fuss, and Julie put her down in her playpen. In a rare moment of two-year-old cooperation, Rose Ann promptly fell asleep.

She was still asleep as lunchtime approached, and showed no sign of waking. Julie suggested I take Catherine to get some food. "I can mind the store while you go," she said. "Besides, if Rose is sleeping, I hate to wake her. She's getting to the point where she doesn't want to nap, no matter how much she needs it."

I called Karen, and she agreed to meet us at a small cafe near the police station and courthouse. "Boomer's press conference has been delayed about six times so far this morning," she said. "I'd love some lunch, but I can't go far, in case he finally gets around to talking to us."

The cafe catered primarily to municipal employees and people with business in the courthouse. Most of the dozen or so tables were packed with local men, the steady hum of conversation a deep bass rumble beneath the clatter of plates and silverware in the kitchen. The smells of fried chicken and slow-baked beans made my mouth water. My stomach gurgled, reminding me I'd had nothing but coffee and one of Chloe's cookies all morning.

Karen fidgeted through lunch, checking her phone for messages every couple minutes. It made the conversation choppy, and it raised my anxiety level with the constant reminder that I still hadn't heard anything more from Beth and Everett.

When Karen's phone finally did ring, it startled all three of us. I jumped about a foot, and knocked over my water glass. Fortunately, it wasn't full, but I was busy cleaning it up while Karen was on the phone and I didn't hear what she said.

When she finished, she tossed the phone into her bag, put some bills on the table, and slung her bag over her shoulder. "I have five minutes to get back to Boomer's office," she said. "I'll call you as soon as I can."

She dashed out the door and down the sidewalk at a pace that would have left me breathless.

Catherine and I tried to relax and finish our tea, but between Karen's abrupt departure and my spill, we were both ready to leave. We added to Karen's stack of cash and went back out on the sidewalk.

I checked in with Julie and she assured me Rose Ann was still sleeping, so I took the scenic route back to Southern Treasures, letting Catherine rubberneck at all the things that had changed since her last visit.

When we drove past Fowler Auto Sales, she let out a low whistle. "He's done all right for himself, hasn't he?" She craned her neck to take in the expansive used-car lot and the repair bays. "Does he own all that?"

"Not as much as it looks like," I told her. "See that chain-link fence behind the service area? That's the salvage yard. Friend of mine owns the place and he flat refuses to sell, especially to Fowler. There's several acres back there that Sly says Fowler will never get his hands on."

"Sly?"

"His name's Sylvester, but I've never heard anyone call him that." That wasn't exactly true; Uncle Louis had called him Sylvester the first time he'd come in the shop. But I wasn't about to mention Bluebeard's job as spokesbird for my great-uncle.

"I think I remember him," she said slowly. "Had some kind of car repair. A fair man, as I recall."

"That's him. He's the one who sold me this truck." I told her a sanitized version of how I got my truck, leaving out the part about the arson of my old Civic behind the store.

My phone rang while I was parking the truck, and by the time I picked it up it had gone to voice mail. Karen's number showed on the call log. Finally, some news.

I didn't stop to listen to her message, just dialed her back, anxious to know what Boomer had to say. Catherine continued on toward the front of the shop as I stopped in the storage area to talk.

"I have some information," she said when she answered my call, "but you aren't going to like it."

"No surprise there. What did you hear?"

"The two victims have been identified. They were familiar to the police a couple counties over. Moonshiners. Killed by gunshots, and the sheriff is calling it homicide."

"We already knew, or guessed, most of that. What's the part I won't like?"

"According to Boomer, there are two 'persons of interest' who fled the area just before the bodies were found and are wanted for questioning. He didn't name names, but it sure sounds like your pals from North County. He didn't call them suspects, but he might as well have.

"Your friends are in trouble, Glory, and it's going to get worse real fast."

CHAPTER TWENTY-ONE

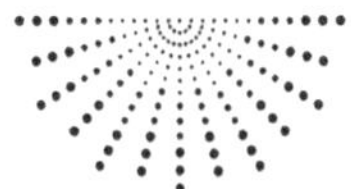

"But did they say when these guys were killed? I mean, I think 'my pals,' as you call them, left early in the week. If they weren't even here, how could they be suspects?"

"All they said about the autopsy was that they died of gunshot wounds. Nothing else. As press releases go, it wasn't much, and Boomer wouldn't answer any questions. In fact, he seemed unhappy about the whole thing."

I would have to call Beth again. She needed to realize that Boomer wouldn't just give up if she stayed away, not if he was calling her and Everett "persons of interest" and saying they "fled" the area. He'd already started looking for them, and after this announcement, I could expect the hunt to intensify.

I put aside the question of Beth and Everett for a minute, and asked Karen when she was going to come for her mother. "It's not that she's a problem or anything," I said. "But I just need to know what the plan is."

Karen always had a plan.

"Since I'm already here, I'd like to spend a little time going through the courthouse records. See if I can find anything about Sly's Anna. I expect I'll have better luck with the high school and the newspaper archives, but it's at least worth a look."

I couldn't imagine what she might find with the paltry information we had available, but there wasn't any harm in looking. Except that it meant I would be entertaining Catherine for a little longer.

Karen said she'd be by in about an hour, unless she hit pay dirt in her search. Then she'd call and let me know.

I finished my call and went up front to let Catherine know when Karen would be back. I found her deep in conversation with Julie and bouncing Rose Ann on her knee. She was clearly throwing herself into the surrogate grandmother role with enthusiasm. I probably should warn Karen, though I doubted Catherine's yen for grandchildren would be any surprise to her.

"Look who woke up all smiles," Catherine cooed as I walked in. Rose Ann rewarded her with a big grin. The kid was a charmer, no doubt about it, and she had never met a stranger. To her, everyone was just a friend she didn't know yet.

"I thought we'd go over and talk to Chloe," Julie said. "That is, if you don't mind?"

"Of course," I answered quickly. "You came in on your day off, and you covered the store half the day. Thanks again for doing that."

I assured Catherine that I had work to do, and I didn't mind her "deserting" me to go with Julie. The truth was, I hoped for a few minutes of privacy to call Beth and try to talk her into returning to the Panhandle.

I pulled out my phone, then set it aside as an older couple came in the store. Hand in hand, they wandered through, looking at the shot glasses, postcards, and T-shirts before stopping in front of the rack of vintage newspapers.

I had discovered a stash of newspapers buried in a far corner of the storeroom a few years back, mostly from the '40s through the '60s. On a whim I had put some samples in plastic sleeves and put them on display. They turned out to be wildly popular with the middle-aged-and older snowbirds that flocked to the Panhandle in the late fall and winter.

The couple flipped through the display, occasionally pointing out articles to each other. They looked as though they could have been newlyweds, their mutual affection evident in the attentive way they spoke to each other and the glances they exchanged.

They finally came to the counter with a couple child-size Bluebeard T-shirts and one of the old newspapers. "From the year we were married," the woman said as I rang up the purchase.

I glanced at the date. Nineteen sixty-six. "Congratulations," I said. My newlyweds had been married almost fifty years.

"Congratulations," Bluebeard echoed, getting a laugh from both of them.

They left, chattering about how they would have to bring the grandkids next time, and how those grandkids would love the parrot.

Sometimes I had the best job in the world.

Other times, not so much. I picked up the phone and dialed Beth's number. I didn't really expect her to answer, but I had to keep trying.

As I expected, the call went to voice mail. "Beth, you need to call me back. Right away. It's really, really important. I need to talk to you."

I figured she was getting calls from Boomer, and possibly from others. I could only hope that she would trust me enough to return the call. If not, after today's announcement, I was likely in for another session with Boomer, and I wasn't looking forward to it.

Karen showed up a few minutes later to collect Catherine. "They're next door," I told her.

"They?"

"Julie was here, remember? She covered the store while I met you for lunch. And she took your mom next door to talk to Chloe some more." I glanced up at the clock. "They've been over there almost an hour," I said. "What could be taking them that long?"

I tried not to worry about what they might be cooking up.

"And you should know that she's quite taken with Rose Ann," I added. "Just fair warning."

Karen groaned.

I quickly changed the subject. "Did you find out anything at the courthouse?"

She shook her head. "I didn't have much to go on. But you already knew that. I did find the birth records for the mid-forties, but that was the beginning of the baby boom. Do you have any idea how *many* kids were born in those years?"

"Lots?" I guessed.

"Lots," she agreed. "And without pinning it down to a single year, it's nearly impossible to sift through all those records and find the one we want."

Bluebeard had made his way across the room, hopping from one display rack to another. There wasn't really enough room for him to fly easily in the confined space, though he did occasionally take a spin around the warehouse. Now he sat near the counter where we were talking, his head cocked as though he was listening to our conversation.

"Baby?" he asked.

"Not Rose Ann," I told him. "Another Ann. Anna. From a long time ago."

"I know her?"

The question caught me by surprise. I supposed it was possible he did know her, but how do you question a parrot?

I could ask Uncle Louis about Sly. He'd befriended the couple, had even offered to help them elope. But even if he did know, I couldn't be sure he would actually tell me.

I was trying to frame a question when Catherine, Rose Ann, and Julie returned. In the hubbub that followed their entrance, any chance to ask Uncle Louis about Anna was lost.

Catherine was still entranced with Rose Ann. In her view, clearly, the child could do no wrong. Or maybe Rose Ann was on her good-behavior today.

Whatever the reason, Karen could see her mother was taken with the little girl. She leaned over and whispered, "I should have thought this through; letting Mom around a baby probably wasn't the best idea. But it's too late now."

Bluebeard stared at us, one dark eye sharply focused on Karen. He hopped closer, cocked his head, and said clearly, "It's never too late," before returning to his perch.

I knew from experience that it would be impossible to get him to explain what he meant. But I also knew he often wasn't referring to the current conversation.

I wondered, never too late for what?

CHAPTER TWENTY-TWO

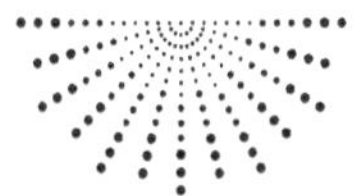

It took a while, but eventually I got Karen, Catherine, Julie, and Rose Ann out of the shop. There were delays as Catherine and Julie exchanged numbers so they could continue planning the bridal shower, and as Catherine said good-bye to Rose Ann.

Finally I had the shop to myself. I tried Beth's number again, and left another pleading message. I was beginning to wonder if she thought she could ignore me, too.

I left a final message as I was closing up for the day. "Beth, this isn't going to go away. The sheriff wants to talk to you, and he knows you went to visit your granny. If you don't come back, he *will* track down your granny, and someone *will* show up at her door looking for you. Is that what you want?

"I know Boomer, Beth. He doesn't just give up because you want him to. One way or another, you're going to have to come back and talk to him."

I hung up. I didn't know if anything I said would make a difference, but I had to try. I wasn't even sure why I felt it was my responsibility; Beth and Everett were adults and they were responsible for their own lives. But somehow I felt that I had played a part in whatever had happened.

Or it might just be the Boomer-made-me-feel-guilty thing.

My computer beeped, reminding me I had plans for the evening. I'd forgotten in the rush of Catherine's unexpected arrival, but Jake and I had promised to have dinner with my friend Sly. And if I didn't get moving, I was going to be late.

If it had been anyone else, I would have canceled. I was exhausted, and I hadn't even been upstairs since the previous morning. But Sly was special, and we hadn't seen him in a while. I went upstairs, changed, and was waiting when Jake arrived to pick me up.

"Sly said he wanted a steak," Jake told me once we were in the car. "He suggested Buccaneer Bay House."

I whistled softly. Bay House, as the locals called it, was the nicest place in town. "I may be underdressed."

Jake took a moment to glance over at my gray wool slacks and black sweater, accented with a vintage rhinestone brooch that would eventually find its way into the shop. "You look fine."

I tried to laugh, but all that came out was a nervous titter. Bay House was nice, but so were the prices. A dinner there could put a dent in my wallet, which I couldn't afford right now.

"He said he knows that place isn't in your budget. He's had a good week, he wants to celebrate, and dinner is on him. And, no, he wouldn't tell me exactly why there is cause for celebration. Insisted he'd tell us when we were both there."

A few minutes later, we pulled into the parking lot. Sly arrived at the same time, driving one of the dozens of cars he kept in the garages that dotted his junkyard.

Those garages were one of his best kept secrets. Most folks seeing a fenced-off junkyard assumed it was full of, well, junk. But Sly had been on that piece of land since he was a kid—his dad had owned it before him—and over the years he had collected and restored scores of vehicles.

Today's car was something from the mid-fifties, as near as I could tell. Sharp fins, hooded headlights, lots of chrome, and a slick two-tone paint job that looked like it just rolled off the showroom floor.

I couldn't identify the make and model, I just knew it was gorgeous; flawlessly restored, or kept in a museum for the last half century. Knowing Sly, I voted for restoration.

We walked closer and I could read the chrome script on the left side of the trunk. *Studebaker.*

"She's a real beaut," Jake said to Sly as we approached. "You do the work?"

"Yep." A wide grin split Sly's dark face. "Took me years to find that last piece of chrome." He gestured to the script on the right that read *President.* "Been hunting that one for a long time."

"Is that what you wanted to celebrate?" I asked, skeptical that a small piece of chrome was worth a dinner at Bay House.

"Partly," Sly answered with a twinkle in his eyes that told me there was a lot more to the story. "Let's go on in, and I'll tell you about it once I wrap myself around a rare rib eye."

Seated across from Sly, I had to fight the temptation to quiz him about Anna, the girl he had almost married. Karen had planted the notion in my brain, and now the idea of reuniting the sweethearts more than fifty years later seemed like the right thing to do.

Instead I pushed the thought away, reminding myself that there were a million ways this could go terribly wrong. A million ways I could make Sly's heartache infinitely worse.

Times had changed, certainly. A lot had happened in that fifty years, and interracial couples were much more common than they had been in the early 1960s. But a lot could happen to *people* in fifty years, too. How could we know if Anna would even want to see Sly after all this time?

And if she didn't, wouldn't that break his heart all over again? In the last couple years, I'd learned of his connection to Uncle Louis and I'd come to think of him as family. I wouldn't do anything to hurt him, and I wouldn't let anyone else hurt him, either.

We chattered through our salads, with Jake and me taking turns filling him in on my offer to buy Lighthouse.

"There's still the question of Peter," I said. "I can't get him out of there fast enough, but I have to be careful I don't overextend myself."

"But if the bank financing comes through for Lighthouse, you should be fine." Jake winked at me and squeezed my hand.

"That boy at the bank purely owes you, girl," Sly said. "Just 'cause he's a Yankee don't mean he shouldn't honor his obligations."

"But the bank doesn't owe me," I said.

"Oh yes they do," Sly said. "You found out who killed that purty little gal came down here to check on Back Bay for 'em. And you saved Buddy's life. I'd say they owe you plenty."

"Even if they do," I said, "that doesn't mean they'll give me the loan."

"If they won't," Sly said, his voice dropping to a confidential whisper, "tell 'em I'll guarantee the loan. Put up the yard if I have to, but my word should be good enough."

His offer, the offer of his home and his livelihood, brought tears to my eyes. I wanted to tell him I couldn't possibly let him do that, but I couldn't speak around the lump in my throat.

At that moment the waiter appeared with a heavily loaded tray. He deftly slid the plates off the tray and onto the table, serving my tenderloin first, then putting platters with monstrous rib eyes in front of both men. The steaks were so large that the accompanying mashed potatoes and creamed spinach were served on a second plate.

Sly dug in with gusto. The first bite went in his mouth, and an appreciative sigh followed. "Somebody back there"—he gestured to the kitchen—"knows his way around a good steak."

"It might be *her* way," I said with a grin. It was a running joke. Sly had always acted as though a woman could do anything she put her mind to.

"Well, whoever it is," he said after another bite, "they surely know how to do right by a piece of beef."

Conversation slowed to a crawl as we worked our way through the perfectly cooked meals, savoring the prime cuts served by Bay House. Their reputation as the best steakhouse in town was more than justified.

Finally Sly pushed his empty plate away and leaned back with a contented sigh. I had no idea where he found room for so much food, but I'd seen how hard he worked, and I knew he'd use up every calorie tomorrow.

"So what's the occasion?" I asked, pushing my plate away also. Unlike Sly, I'd have enough leftovers for another complete dinner.

"Couple things," he said. "First, like you said, was finding that little piece of chrome. It was the only thing left to make that car like new, and I been waiting a long time for that." He smiled and nodded in a self-satisfied way.

He stopped, drawing out the moment.

"And the other?" I prodded.

"I got a buyer for her. Wasn't sure, it had been a long time. But I called him today, told him I had that bitty piece of chrome, and he 'bout jumped through the phone." A grin flitted across his face, then he sobered. "So this is my last trip with her, one last night out on the town before she leaves for good."

The comment made me think of Anna again. But I couldn't ask about her, so I shoved the thought away.

I looked up to find both men watching me expectantly.

"What?"

"I think Sly has something more," Jake said.

I'd seen that expression on Sly's face once before. The day he'd sold me the truck that had belonged to Uncle Louis.

"Oh no," I said, shaking my head. "You aren't going to do this again. Uhuh."

"Do what?" he answered with feigned innocence. "Whatever do you mean, girl?"

"You know," I said accusingly. "Try to rope me into some deal to do with that car." Sly had sold me the truck, but he'd insisted that I pay him what he'd put into it, which was a small fraction of what the beautifully restored vehicle was worth.

"Me and Mr. Louis were partners in the President," Sly said. "He bought her from one of his customers, and I gave her a home while I worked on her. Put her in my name when he took sick, and made me promise to fix her up right.

"She's been in that garage near thirty years while I searched for parts."

"Which means she's yours, Sly. Uncle Louis gave her to you and you took care of her like he asked."

He shook his head. "That may be, but I'm a man as pays his debts, and I owe Mr. Louis more than I can say." He reached in his wallet and took out a piece of paper; a check. "I got a fair profit for my work, but it's only right that you get a little bit, too."

Though I tried to refuse, he gave me the check, taking my hand in his and placing it against my palm.

Curiosity got the better of me, and I unfolded it to look at the amount.

Five figures.

"No." I set it back on the table. "That's way too much."

"No it ain't," he said, shaking his head. "It's just a taste of what I got for her.

"Your uncle knew what he was doing when he bought that car. She's a rare model—one reason it took so long to find parts—and I got a fair price."

"But you stored her for almost thirty years," I protested.

"And I got a fair price for that. I'm telling you, that money's yours fair and square. You don't believe me, you check with Mr. Louis hisself."

It was the one argument I couldn't refute, and he knew it. If I went to Uncle Louis, he might or might not answer a direct question, and he might or might not make sense.

Sly knew he had me. With a triumphant flourish he opened the dessert menu. "I think I am ready for coffee and something sweet," he said, his tone clearly indicating the subject of the check was closed.

I picked at a small scoop of gelato while Sly devoured a slice of cherry pie and Jake had cheesecake. Jake offered me a bite and I took a nibble of the creamy cake, savoring the tang of the sour cream topping, but I was too full to do more than taste.

True to his word, Sly picked up the check. "It's my celebration," he said. "Only fair."

How could I even *consider* doing anything that might hurt this man?

CHAPTER TWENTY-THREE

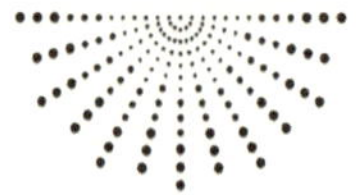

In the morning I took another look at the check. I thought about simply putting it away, not taking it to the bank. But that would only mean another argument with Sly down the road, when he realized the check hadn't been cashed.

The only remaining question was whether I owed Peter a percentage of the money.

When Jake stopped in before he opened Beach Books for the day, I posed the question to him.

"What do you think I should do? Technically, if this is for the car, it should be split between us, right?"

Jake looked at the check. "It's made out to you, not Southern Treasures," he pointed out. "And Louis split the store between the two of you, not his entire estate, correct? So who inherited the rest?"

I had to confess I didn't know. "I suppose I could check with Clifford Wilson. I'll be talking to him later today anyway, since he's supposed to have the final contract for Lighthouse ready this morning."

"You could probably just check the probate records at the courthouse, too," Jake suggested. "All that kind of thing is a matter of public record."

"If I have the time to go down there and dig through the records."

"True," Jake said. "Wilson might know, or be able to look it up more easily. Depends on what he keeps and what's in storage. Or destroyed."

I must have looked puzzled by his last suggestion. "Why would he destroy his records?"

"Glory, those files were closed more than twenty-five years ago. Everything was placed on the public record. Why would he keep them?"

"I don't know. I hadn't thought about it, just assumed that lawyers kept their records forever, I guess."

"They could be in storage," Jake said. "And he could even remember. From the way you talk about him, anything's possible."

"So you think the money should go to whoever inherited the rest of Uncle Louis's estate?" I went back to my original dilemma. "Whoever that is?"

Jake shook his head. "I think the money should go to you. That's obviously what Sly wants, or he'd have made the check to Southern Treasures. But if you're concerned about it, then I'd say follow the terms of Louis's will."

There was one other person who knew what those terms were, and he chose that moment to join the discussion.

"For you," Bluebeard said in Louis's voice. "For your mom, now for you."

"But what about Peter?" I blurted out. I knew better than to try and quiz Louis, but I still tried. "Doesn't he have a share of this?"

"Ask Wilson," the parrot said. He retreated across the room and into his cage, his way of telling me he was through.

I sighed and made a note to ask Mr. Wilson when I talked to him later in the day.

Jake had only been gone a couple minutes when the phone rang. I checked the display to make sure it wasn't Peter, and saw Beth's number.

I grabbed the phone. "Beth?"

"Glory, why are you hounding me?" Stress pulled her voice into a high-pitched whine. She sounded like she might burst into tears at any second.

"Beth, I'm so sorry. I didn't mean for you to feel like you're being hounded, but I know the sheriff is trying to reach you and he's getting pretty agitated. I was trying to warn you, to give you a chance to fix this before it gets any worse."

"Worse? I come up to see my granny, and you call and tell me the police are going to come track us down? How does it get worse than that?"

"Beth, listen to me." I stopped and let the silence stretch for several seconds. I had to be sure she was listening, not just waiting for the next opportunity to screech at me again.

I continued slowly and deliberately, trying to keep my voice low and forceful without sounding threatening. "Right now they just want to ask you some questions. But if you don't talk to them, if you continue to hide from them, the sheriff will get tired of playing games. He will decide that you have something to hide, and he doesn't like people who hide things from him."

On that score I had plenty of personal experience. Keeping anything from Boomer was a seriously bad idea.

"When he loses his patience, you will stop being someone he wants to talk to. Instead you will become someone he finds suspicious.

"And when he thinks you're suspicious, Beth, he will send officers with arrest warrants for you and Everett."

I stopped and let that sink in for a minute. Beth was stunned into silence, though I could hear her rapid breathing.

She had good reason to be afraid. She obviously knew way more than she had admitted to me. She and Everett had left abruptly, making up the story of a sick grandmother to cover their sudden departure, and it was obvious the sheriff wasn't buying it.

"There's only one way out of this for you. Come back here on your own and answer Sheriff Hardy's questions. If you do anything else, *anything* else, you will be sorry.

"That isn't a threat, Beth. I'm not hounding you. I am warning you. I know the sheriff, I know how he thinks, and I know how he runs his department.

"I'm trying to help you, whether you believe me or not."

I didn't have any other argument, so I shut up and let Beth think about what I had said. I clutched the phone so tightly my fingers started to cramp as I waited her out.

At last she let out a deep sigh. "Okay," she said quietly. "Let me talk to Everett. When we figure this out, I'll call you back. Just give me a little time to work things through."

CHAPTER TWENTY-FOUR

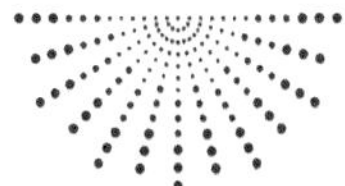

I paced through the shop, too agitated and nervous to sit still. I checked my e-mail and tried to review the new contract draft from Clifford Wilson, but I couldn't concentrate enough to read it.

I'd never been good at waiting, and this morning was worse than usual. I told myself it would be better once Beth called me back, once I knew they were coming home. But I knew it wouldn't be, not until they were back in Florida and safely in Boomer's office. Until then I would continue to worry.

Normally I would call Karen while I waited, or visit with Jake. But I was afraid to even use the phone for fear I would miss Beth's call.

I made a pot of coffee and drank two cups while I puttered about, fussing with displays and straightening shelves.

I kept up a running dialogue in my head, arguing that this wasn't a decision they could make instantly. Beth was convinced, but what if she had to persuade Everett? I hadn't told her why the sheriff wanted to talk to them, and judging by her reaction, I didn't think the sheriff had either.

None of my arguments did anything to diminish the growing tension that knotted my shoulders. I realized I was gritting my teeth so hard my jaw ached. If I kept this up, I'd be a complete basket case by noon.

Fortunately for me, Beth called back before I completely fell apart.

"Glory, we're leaving in a couple hours. We need to pack and get the car ready to go, and Everett needs a little nap before we hit the road."

"Okay," I said. "And?"

"It's usually a two-day trip. No matter how we figure it, we're going to have to stop for a few hours and sleep."

I waited, biting my lip to contain the questions that threatened to spill out.

"We should be back to Florida by about noon tomorrow. But there's one condition, Glory. One thing you have to do for us."

I waited, unwilling to agree to anything until I knew exactly what it was she wanted me to do.

"You have to come get us, Glory. We don't know this sheriff of yours, and according to the people we've met, he doesn't much like people from North County.

"We've got no reason to trust him, Glory. So if you really want us to come back and turn ourselves in, or whatever, you have to be the one. We'll turn ourselves in to you, and you can take us to the sheriff.

"Those are our terms. We will trust you to do right by us, and we'll come back. But only if you promise to come and get us when we get home tomorrow."

I struggled with my answer. Part of me wanted to tell her she was in no position to be setting terms. She was just lucky the sheriff hadn't caught up with her yet, and she ought to be grateful for the opportunity to come in on her own.

But another part of me understood her precarious position. She didn't know the sheriff, hadn't been around the area since she was a kid and the sheriff was a brand-new deputy, like Karen and I had. And she lived in a part of the county where most of the scattered residents preferred to keep their distance from any kind of law enforcement.

Add to that the stereotypical bad image of a small-town Southern sheriff, and it was no wonder she felt like she needed an escort to the sheriff's office.

I bit back my annoyance and accepted the proposed arrangement. I would meet her and her husband at their cabin no later than noon tomorrow.

I hung up and breathed a sigh of relief. In a little over twenty-four hours, I would escort Beth and Everett to Boomer's office and turn them over to answer his questions.

My part in all this would be over and I could go back to taking care of my business and buying a bakery. That would be plenty to keep me busy for the foreseeable future.

That, and getting rid of Peter.

Then it hit me. I had just agreed to drive to North County and pick up the Youngs tomorrow. On Thursday. When it was my turn to cook dinner.

I had a problem, and I cast about for a solution. I had planned to cook black-eyed peas and ham hocks with fried cornbread. The weather had turned cool, and it was the kind of warm, filling comfort food that fit the shorter days and chilly evenings.

But I couldn't cook an all-day meal if I was gone for several hours to get Beth and Everett. Sure, I could leave a pot simmering, but it would still need tending, and what if something went wrong and I didn't get back in time?

I kept coming back to the question of dinner as I read over the contract draft from Mr. Wilson. I still felt like I'd been punched in the gut every time I looked at the amount of money I was offering, but I was starting to feel a little less terrified each time I read the number. Eventually I would be desensitized.

Mr. Wilson hadn't missed a thing, as far as I could see. He had covered all the questions I'd brought up and several I hadn't thought of, and still kept it in language I understood.

I loaded legal paper into my printer and started printing the documents. The click as each page fed into the tray was like a countdown to the starter's gun at the beginning of a race; in just a few minutes, I was going to change my life forever.

With the contract printed, I signed the purchase offer and folded it into a large envelope. I wrote Miss Pansy's name on the outside and sealed it up.

"Well, Bluebeard," I said, tucking the envelope under my arm, "here we go."

"Go!" he repeated, and whistled shrilly. "Go!"

With his endorsement ringing in my ears, I walked next door and presented the envelope to Chloe. "Will you give this to Bradley when he comes in?"

"You bet, boss," she said with an excited grin, guessing at the contents of the envelope as she hefted it in her hands.

"Not yet," I cautioned. "There's still a zillion ways this can go wrong. I am not counting on anything until it's all done."

"Gotcha."

The smell of sweet apples and cinnamon tickled my nose and made my stomach growl. Chloe shook her head. "Don't you ever eat breakfast?" she asked.

I shrugged. "If I get busy in the morning, I forget," I said. "I've got so much on my mind right now . . ." My voice trailed off, and I eyed the array of pastries displayed behind the glass front of the bakery case.

"Let me fix you something," Chloe offered. "Any idea what you'd like?"

"The apple turnovers smell delicious," I said. "But I really don't need anything sweet right now. What would you suggest?"

She quickly ran through several options, and I settled on a slice of ham-

and-Swiss quiche with a fruit cup to take back to Southern Treasures with me.

I e-mailed Mr. Wilson while I ate, to let him know the contract met with my approval and had been sent to Miss Pansy for her signature. I also asked him if he could tell me who inherited Uncle Louis's estate, aside from Southern Treasures. I didn't go into detail, just asked if he remembered.

While I was thinking about it, I also called Buddy McKenna to tell him I had made an offer, contingent on financing.

"That's great, Glory," Buddy said. "The full loan committee meets on Friday, so I might have an answer for you that afternoon. But don't count on hearing before Monday. Sorry it can't be sooner."

I thanked him and hung up. More waiting. You would think with all the practice it would get easier, but it didn't.

And there was still the question of tomorrow's dinner.

Jake called to check in, and I told him about Beth's call. "She says she'll be home tomorrow, but she insists that I have to come and carry them to Boomer, that they won't come otherwise."

"Are you sure you want to do that?" Jake asked.

"I have to. The only way to get Boomer off my back is to make sure Beth and Everett get back here and talk to him."

"I don't like the idea of you going up there alone," he said. "Would you like me to come with you?"

I wanted to say yes, but it wouldn't be right to ask him to do that. It would mean closing up Beach Books and losing a day's sales. "No," I said. "I'll be fine."

"I'd still feel better if you didn't go alone." Jake kept his tone conversational. He knew better than to try and tell me what to do, but he still wanted to voice his objections.

"Really, I'll be okay. I just wish I didn't have to do it tomorrow."

"Tomorrow?" Jake thought for a minute. "It's Thursday. You'll have to miss dinner?"

"No. If they're home by noon, I should be able to make the drive and be back in plenty of time for dinner. But it's my turn to cook." I sighed. "I'm going to have to come up with something I can do quick, in case I get held up along the way."

"Let me cook."

I started to protest that it wasn't his responsibility, but he kept talking. "You've included me in a lot of your dinners over the last year or so, and I haven't returned the favor.

"Let me take care of dinner for tomorrow night. It won't be Southern—

maybe Southwestern—but that way you won't have to worry about it on top of everything else you have to do."

"You sure?"

"Absolutely. And we can eat at my place, so you don't have to worry about what time you get back."

The offer was too tempting to pass up, and I agreed to let him host my week. Another step in our relationship dance.

CHAPTER TWENTY-FIVE

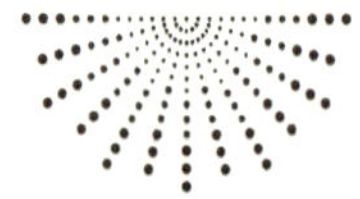

It was nearly closing time when Bradley Whittaker appeared at my door with a fat envelope in his hand. He made a ceremony of handing me the envelope and shaking my hand.

"Congratulations, Miss Glory. Mom's signed the papers. Soon you'll be the new owner of Lighthouse Coffee."

He shook my hand again. "And thank you, from all of us, for helping us get Mom to slow down."

Then he handed me another envelope, this one just as bulky, but sealed tightly with Miss Pansy's rather shaky signature across the flap.

I looked at him quizzically. "What's this?"

"That's her recipe file. She told me not to open it and to give it directly to you."

I thanked him and he left.

I immediately went to the safe, an old iron monster that lived under the stairs, and locked both envelopes inside. Whatever Chloe was doing in Miss Pansy's absence seemed to be working, and I didn't feel right about even opening the recipe file until the deal was complete. To do otherwise felt like cheating.

As I climbed the stairs, looking forward to a quiet evening alone, I ran through the mental checklist of my various projects. The immediate problem of tomorrow's dinner was in Jake's capable hands; if he could feed a ravenous firehouse crew, dinner for a few close friends wouldn't be an issue.

The purchase of Lighthouse was settled; all that was left was to wait for the bank to approve my loan. I could worry about what to do if they didn't, but there was, as Memaw would say, no sense in borrowing trouble. Besides, there wasn't anything I could do until I knew their decision.

The wedding still loomed ahead of me, but at least Chloe and Julie had taken over planning the bridal shower. All I would have to do for that was show up, bring a present, and foot the bills. I said a fervent prayer that they didn't get carried away with their plans. Or worse, let Catherine get carried away.

Even the question of Beth and Everett would be settled by early tomorrow afternoon, the plan already in place to take care of my part of the problem.

I hadn't paid much mind to the victims of the shooting; that was the sheriff's mystery to solve and I was determined to keep out of his way. I was sure he preferred it that way, too.

Still, it seemed curious that we had heard so little about what had happened out at Beth's place. The lack of information bothered me, and by the time I'd heated some leftover soup and eaten it with a few crackers, I decided to call Karen and see if she had heard anything.

Karen's phone rang several times without an answer. About the time I expected it to go to voice mail, Karen picked up, sounding harried and out of breath.

"Yes?" It wasn't so much a greeting as it was a challenge.

"Is this a bad time?" I asked. "I could call back later."

"No, no, no. Just hang on a second." She spoke to someone, and then I heard footsteps and the sound of a door closing, followed by a deep sigh.

"Okay, I've locked myself in the bathroom. I should be safe for a few minutes."

"What in the name of heaven is going on, Freed?" Karen wasn't the type to hide in the bathroom. From anything.

"My mother," she said, as though that explained everything. Which maybe it did. At the very least, it explained Karen's bizarre behavior.

"What is she up to now?" I tucked the phone between my ear and shoulder and started sorting laundry. I could tell I was in for a long-winded explanation.

"We're having a 'family' dinner." I could hear the quotes around the word family, even through the phone. "Just the four of us: Mom and Clint, Riley and me. I cooked, which naturally gave her an opening to suggest ways I could learn to be more domestic.

"Then, if that wasn't enough, she started quizzing Riley about his plans for the honeymoon. You *know* he wanted to keep it a surprise for me, and she won't stop asking him about it. He keeps telling her he's working on it, but she doesn't stop."

"I'm sorry, Karen." There wasn't much else to say. Catherine was unrelenting once she got an idea in her head, and she would pester Riley until she was satisfied with his answers.

Karen sighed. "I know she's just excited, but I wish she would calm down and let us take care of things our own way." Her breathing slowed, and I could picture her forcing her shoulders to relax as she tried to calm herself.

"Sorry to dump on you," she said. "But I feel better having got that off my chest." She laughed, embarrassed by her tirade. "But I'm sure that's not why you called.

"What can I do for you?"

"I was actually just calling to find out if you'd heard anything more about the men out at Beth's place. Boomer didn't tell you much yesterday, and I figured you'd be on his case until he gave you something more."

"I would be, if I didn't have my mother trailing along behind me. But she's been here since the crack of dawn; showed up before I left for work and said she'd just tag along and visit with me when I wasn't on the air. Like I didn't have anything else to do between broadcasts.

"I would have refused, but Clinton dropped her and took off for some terribly important meeting and I was stuck."

"So, no news?" I asked.

"Not a word. I called Boomer several times today, but all I ever got was that simpering idiot who calls herself his 'public information officer.'"

I knew the one she meant. Twenty years ago she would have been called a switchboard operator, before switchboards were replaced with phone consoles. Basically she answered the phones and routed calls around the office. Occasionally she answered basic questions. But lately she'd been "putting on airs" (to use one of Memaw's favorite phrases) and revising her title.

"Karen, what are you doing tomorrow? Is your mom coming back up again?"

She groaned. "Probably. Almost certainly, if I can't come up with a solid reason to keep her away."

"What if you weren't in town? If something work related took you out of town for the day, and you couldn't take her along? Would that work?"

"It might," she conceded. "But I don't have anything like that coming up. Unless you have something?" she said hopefully.

I told her about Beth's phone call, and her insistence that I come to get them. "I'm going to have to drive up there early, and be gone all morning. If you went along, we might be able to talk to Beth and Everett before they see Boomer."

"Your truck wouldn't be comfortable for three," she said, suddenly much cheerier. "You must need me to drive, since the SUV has room for everyone."

"You have a point," I said, as though the whole thing had been her idea. And it would be, by the time she told her mother the story.

"I can pick you up. We better leave early, just to be sure we're there when they get home. Wouldn't want to miss them and then have them change their minds or something, and back out."

I agreed, and we made a date for early in the morning.

I checked one more thing off my mental list, started the washer, and set to work on dessert for tomorrow night. Whatever Jake decided to cook for dinner, I had planned on pecan pie for dessert. I could still do at least that much.

CHAPTER TWENTY-SIX

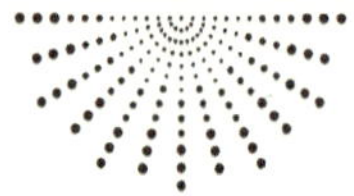

The drive to North County was uneventful, a welcome break after the commotion of the last few days. Karen was uncharacteristically quiet, the result, I guessed, of having spent the last couple days arguing constantly with her mother.

I hadn't called Boomer. I'd thought about it and even discussed it with Jake, but in the end I couldn't trust that things would go right. And if they went wrong, I didn't want to antagonize Boomer in the process.

Karen didn't ask for directions. She had driven this way just once, a week ago when the bodies were found, but she always seemed to remember a route once she drove it.

She slowed, and I caught sight of the colorful fence that was my signpost for Beth's turn. Karen seemed to hesitate, and I realized she had only been here in the dark.

"That's the corner," I said, answering the question she hadn't asked.

We bounced slowly along the narrow dirt road leading to Beth's cabin. As we neared Beth's driveway, a grungy pickup approached from the opposite direction. There wasn't room for the two vehicles to pass each other, but we managed to reach the driveway and pull off before the pickup went past.

We pulled up in front of the cabin. No car, and no sign of anyone else around. Karen sighed, and I started to apologize but she just shook her head. "It's quiet here," she said. "If we have to wait a little while, so what? I could learn to like this."

"No you couldn't," I said. "You'd go crazy with this much quiet. You barely manage as it is."

She started to protest, but stopped as we heard another car coming down the driveway.

I climbed out of the car, anxious that Beth and Everett see me since they wouldn't recognize Karen's SUV. I didn't want them to get scared off, now that we had come this far.

But instead of their tiny hybrid, what rounded the curve into the packed dirt of the parking area was the dilapidated pickup that we'd seen on the road.

It roared up to me and stopped abruptly, sending a cloud of dust swirling around my ankles. I instinctively stepped back, putting more distance between me and the unknown passenger and driver. The truck rose above my head, its big tires and jacked-up suspension hinting at off-road adventures that I imagined involved poaching and other unsavory activities.

The truck idled loudly in the surrounding silence, an unmuffled rumble with an uneven rhythm Sly could have cured in two minutes, though I suspected these were not the kind of guys who took their vehicles to an actual mechanic.

The passenger opened his door, the hinges squealing in protest. He jumped down, scuffed motorcycle boots sending up another puff of dust.

Dirty jeans, a T-shirt with the sleeves ripped off, and an oil-stained denim vest made his outfit a match for the heavy-set victim Boomer had shown me. His face and hair were more like the other victim: hollow cheeks, long hair hanging in dark wisps, a bandana tied around his head.

I backed up another step.

The driver left the engine running and came around the truck to stand next to his buddy. Taller and wider, he was dressed in the same dirty jeans and denim vest, minus the T-shirt. His white belly reminded me of the underside of a fish.

The truck's rough idle made me wonder if he didn't dare shut it off, but I didn't figure it was a good idea to ask about it. In fact, I thought it was probably a bad idea to talk to these guys at all.

Not that they gave me any choice.

"What you doin' out here, city girl?"

"Just waiting for my friends. They're supposed to be home here in a few minutes." I didn't bother to protest him calling me a city girl. By the standards of North County, I *was* a city girl.

"Seems a strange place for somebody with a fancy car to be waiting for a 'friend.'"

"I just buy quilts from the woman who lives here," I answered. Not the whole truth, but mentioning the sheriff seemed like a really bad idea.

"Calvin," the thin man poked his friend in the arm. "There's another gal in that car. Looks like she's messing with her phone or something."

Calvin looked over at the SUV, now covered with a fine layer of dust kicked up by the truck's arrival. Anger flashed across his face, quickly replaced by a bland smile that I was sure some girl had told him was cute. It reminded me of a shark.

He walked toward the SUV and I followed, with Skinny Guy bringing up the rear. I slowed to let him pass, not wanting either man where I couldn't see him, but he slowed even more, not letting me get behind him.

Calvin approached the driver's side window, which Karen had lowered, and bent down to look in the car. If he saw the police scanner, we were going to be in trouble.

"What you doing, little lady?" he asked. His tone was meant to be friendly, but he wasn't a good enough actor to disguise the menace that lurked under the innocuous words.

Skinny Guy stood next to Calvin, a goofy grin on his face, as though that would put us at ease.

I moved around to the passenger side and unlatched the door, ready to climb in if we needed to leave quickly. Calvin shot me a glance that told me he knew exactly what I was up to, and he found it amusing.

The thought didn't make me happy.

"Just waiting for the gal who lives here," she said. "We were supposed to meet her this morning, but it looks like we're a little early." She shrugged, as though being confronted by strangers on a deserted road was an everyday occurrence. She gestured at the thermos bottle in her hand. "Thought we'd just drink our coffee and wait for her."

On the seat beside her, out of Calvin's line of sight, her pocket recorder blinked its tiny red "record" light. She was saving the conversation.

I glanced at the scanner and realized none of the lights were on. In the darkened interior, it was nearly invisible in its holder, and a jacket was tossed carelessly in front of it, the dark navy blue fabric making the radio even less visible.

I was pretty sure the thermos wasn't what Skinny Guy had seen—her phone was in its usual place in the console, but it had been on the dash just a few minutes before.

"What about that phone my pal Donny says you were messing with? Don't think the cell service out here's very good. You might not be getting a signal."

"I wasn't," Karen answered coolly. "Tried to call and find out how long we'd have to wait, but I couldn't get through." She waved at the phone. "Have to try again later, or drive out to the highway or on in to Century. But really, she should be here pretty soon."

She waved the thermos again. "Want a cup of coffee? I think I have a couple clean cups here somewhere."

"No thank you, ma'am," Calvin said. I wasn't sure if she'd managed to distract him or not, but I got my answer at once when he said, "But I would trouble you to let me look at the phone. Donny and me, well, we don't cotton to having our pictures took, and I just want to be sure you weren't doing that.

"You wouldn't mind showing me what's on there, now, would you?"

My heart raced at his question. I was certain Karen was taking pictures to go with the recording she was making, and I didn't think either Calvin or Donny was going to look favorably on either activity.

"Well," Karen stretched her hand out for the phone, and began fiddling with it, as though she couldn't quite figure out how to display the photos she'd taken. "Dang! Just a sec, okay? I can't get this darned thing to work."

She fiddled a few more seconds. "Damnation!" Her hand flew up and covered her mouth. "Oh, my! Pardon my French, my mama would purely wash my mouth out with soap for that." She smiled at Calvin. "You won't be telling my mama, will you?"

Under normal circumstances, Karen's Southern belle act would have had me in stitches, but these circumstances weren't in any way normal.

All the while she was talking and smiling coyly at Calvin, she kept fumbling with the phone. Donny jiggled as he waited, nervous energy pouring out in each fidget and shuffle.

Calvin waited stoically, his face impassive, as Karen continued her fussing for another few seconds, drawing out the time as long as she dared.

"Got it!" she crowed triumphantly, just as though she hadn't been able to do exactly what Calvin asked in an instant.

She handed over the phone with a smile. "See, right there? I just took a picture of the cabin. It's the sweetest thing, out here where it's quiet and peaceful, don't you think? I wanted to show it to my boyfriend, 'cause it's just the kind of place I think we'd like to have.

"If I can ever talk him out of living in the city, of course."

Calvin took the phone and nimbly flipped through the images. I couldn't see the pictures from where I stood, but the expression on his face was enough. There weren't any pictures he cared about; certainly none of him or Donny, or anything else that might arouse his suspicions.

He slipped the phone in his pocket, and I saw Karen's right hand clench into a fist, hidden at her side. Outwardly she remained calm, her expression puzzled.

"Why would you take my phone?" She let a hint of outraged innocence color her words. "I *showed* you that there wasn't anything in there that concerned you! You asked me, and I showed you, nice as pie, and then you take my phone. Why would you do that?"

"Just bein' careful, ma'am." Now that he had the phone and was assured there weren't any pictures of him on it, he seemed to dismiss both of us. "Wouldn't want you doing anything foolish before we leave, now would we?"

He stood up and looked over the hood to where I stood on the other side of the vehicle. The door still hung open, but I had hesitated to climb in. I didn't want to be trapped in the car.

He waved toward his still-idling pickup. "Come on up in the truck. We'll carry you up close to the road, and then we'll leave the phone in the mailbox." He pulled it out of his pocket and waved it at her, as though reminding me he still had it. "You can pick it up and bring it back to your friend here."

He looked back down at Karen. "You just wait right here, okay? Your friend will be back in a jiffy, if you just do what we ask." He paused, then added, "Please."

As though that made it all right.

I looked at Karen, and she just stared back, like she was trying to say something. "It'll be fine," she assured me. "I'll wait right here, like they asked, until I hear them on the highway. Then I'll come and get you."

I swallowed hard and nodded. It wasn't like I had any choice.

I followed Calvin to the pickup, Donny bringing up the rear. The hair on the back of my neck stood up, imagining what he was doing where I couldn't see him, but I was afraid to turn around and look.

Calvin climbed into the driver's side, motioning for me to get in the passenger's side ahead of Donny. It would put me between them, a spot I didn't want to be in.

I hesitated.

"You need a boost?" Donny asked from close behind me.

That was enough motivation. I clambered onto the high running board and into the cab of the truck.

To my surprise, when Donny stepped up behind me, Calvin waved him away. "Git in the back, boy," he said. "No reason to crowd the lady here."

Donny didn't argue. He hopped into the bed of the pickup.

Calvin shoved the phone back in his pocket and put the truck in gear. He spun in a circle, sending another cloud of dust over Karen's SUV, and we bounced away down the driveway.

CHAPTER TWENTY-SEVEN

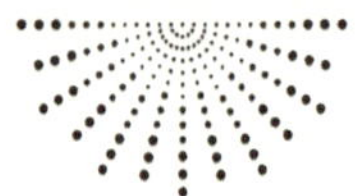

The driveway seemed longer than I remembered as we rumbled along. Adrenaline rushed through me, a combination of anger and fear. I gripped the armrest, trying to control the trembling of my hands.

I moved closer to the passenger door, gauging whether I could jump, and if I did what would happen?

Best case, I'd get away and the two men would give up and leave us alone. Yeah, and I'd find a pet unicorn and a pot of gold in the woods.

More likely one of them would go back for Karen while the other one chased me. I craned my head to look over my shoulder at Donny in the bed of the pickup. Sure enough, he was perched on the side and looked like he was ready to leap out at any moment.

Bad idea.

"Just sit tight," Calvin said. "Couple minutes, you do what we asked and we're gone, you're back in your fancy car, and your friend's come home to meet you."

He glanced over at me and I caught something in his eyes. An intellect that didn't quite fit with the rest of him, perhaps. It disappeared so quickly I wasn't sure if it was real or my imagination. I couldn't trust that my mind wasn't playing tricks on me.

We rounded a curve, and I saw the mailbox about ten yards ahead. Calvin stopped the truck and motioned for me to get out. "Just wait there," he said, once I was on the ground.

Donny hopped out of the back and reached for the phone. He stood on the running board, the phone in one hand, the other arm wrapped around the open window frame. He stared at me as the truck pulled slowly down the driveway, a warning not to move.

The truck stopped at the end of the driveway and Donny jumped down. He shoved the phone in the mailbox and ran back to the truck. As soon as the door closed, Calvin gunned the engine.

It coughed once as gas flooded in, then the engine roared, the tires grabbed, and the truck fishtailed onto the dirt road in a cloud of dust.

I immediately ran to the mailbox, grabbed Karen's phone, and headed back toward the cabin at a dead run.

Karen had turned around and come down the driveway to meet me. I threw myself into the passenger side and returned her phone.

I panted, trying to get my breath after the headlong rush back down the driveway. "What *was* that?" I shouted. "*Who* was that?"

Fear bubbled to the surface and I let loose with a string of curses that would have made Bluebeard proud.

Karen stopped the car and stared at me. "Glory?"

"Sorry," I whispered, still trembling. "I just . . ." I tried to laugh, but it came out more like a little sob. "I think Bluebeard might be a bad influence."

Karen punched buttons on her phone, muttering to herself. After several seconds, she gave a triumphant shout. "Got it!"

"Got what?" I asked. I had seen Calvin's reaction to the contents of her phone. There was nothing there to celebrate.

"Confirmation of my upload," she said. "I've got pictures of both those guys—not good ones, they were too far away and I was in a hurry—but I have pictures stored on the station's servers."

"But, I saw you—how?" I couldn't form an actual sentence, but Karen seemed to get my meaning.

"I deleted the pictures from my phone," she said. "But I had already sent them to the server. I wasn't sure, the service really is bad out here, but I checked and they're there.

"We have their pictures."

"So, what now?" I could think of several things. Most of them involved getting the heck out of there.

But what about Beth and Everett?

"And what were those guys doing here in the first place?" My voice was steadier, and my hands had stopped shaking, but I still worried that the two men might come back.

"Seems to me," Karen answered, "that we have two choices. We stay and wait for your friends, or we run away."

She looked over at me and cocked one eyebrow. "Ever known me to run away?"

I shook my head. The only time I had seen Karen run away was when she spilt up with Riley. Technically she didn't leave, but I considered changing the locks while he was at sea a way to avoid a confrontation when he came home.

She had always claimed that they had agreed to separate before he left. But I'd seen Riley when he came home, and he sure didn't act like a man who had agreed to a separation. He acted like a man who'd been locked out of his own house.

"Then we're staying." She backed slowly along the driveway, back to the clearing in front of the cabin, and shut off the engine.

In the silence that followed, I listened to the ticking of the engine cooling and the tapping of Karen's fingers on the display of her phone. She made occasional comments, talking to herself as she copied her photos and examined them for clues to the identities of our visitors.

After a few minutes, Karen reached over and flipped the power switch on the scanner. It crackled to life, clicking and squawking as it locked into a frequency, then settled into a low hum of carrier band.

"Those boys didn't want their picture taken, so I could just imagine how they'd have felt about a police scanner," she said.

"Or about having their conversation recorded," I answered.

"You saw that?"

"It was right there on the seat next to you."

"I was hoping you would and they wouldn't. Might have been kind of awkward the other way around." Sometimes Karen was a master of understatement.

I checked the time. Ten-thirty. Beth had said they'd be home by noon. I hoped they would be early.

While we waited, Karen filled me in on what little research she'd been able to do in her search for Anna.

"If my mother would let me," she grumbled, "I could track her down in a couple days. But Mom thinks we should be spending every spare minute together. Which means every minute, since Captain Clint has been tied up on base all day."

"So what you're saying is that this isn't getting you away from your mother after all?"

"No." Karen groaned. "But it gets worse. I think she's trying to wangle an invitation to dinner tonight. She's been dropping hints about wanting to meet my friends—besides you, of course—and getting to know the people that are important to me."

I didn't have any experience myself, but I still ventured an opinion. "That sounds like a pretty normal mom thing," I said.

"It is," she said. Her grudging agreement gave way to irritation again. "But I don't want to do it this way, to have her and Clint at our Thursday dinner. Especially not the first week they're here. If we do, then they'll expect to be invited every week."

"I hadn't thought of that."

"I have." She groaned again. "And I've given her every excuse I could think of. It's not at my house. I'm not in charge. The hostess isn't expecting extra guests.

"None of it is sinking in. She finally said 'Well, it's Glory hosting. I'm sure she wouldn't mind if we tagged along.'"

"I probably wouldn't," I admitted. "I don't dislike your mother, and I'd include the two of them if it made your life easier."

Heaven knows, right now I would do just about anything that made Karen's life easier and her less of a Bridezilla. But I had an ace in the hole, and I offered it to Karen. "Just tell her that I had an emergency and I couldn't cook." I waved at our surroundings. "It's the truth."

Karen shook her head. "She'd just offer to help."

"Tell her my boyfriend is cooking, and remind her how rude it would be for you to invite them to someone else's home. Someone they don't even know."

Karen thought for a minute and nodded. "Good idea. Especially the part about me being rude. She was always nagging me about my rudeness. Because having an opinion while being female is apparently the definition of rude."

Several minutes later we heard the sound of another vehicle, quieter than the pickup. Adrenaline surged through me, and my heart raced. Beside me, Karen had one hand on the ignition and the other gripped the steering wheel.

We both held our breath, straining to see what was coming at us.

CHAPTER TWENTY-EIGHT

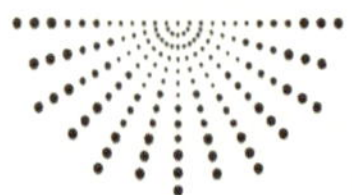

This time it really was Beth and Everett. Their usually immaculate hybrid looked dirty and tired, or as Memaw used to say, "Like it'd been rode hard and put away wet."

As soon as I recognized the car, I jumped out of the SUV and waved, making sure they knew it was me. After our latest encounter, I wasn't taking any chances.

The car stopped and Beth dragged herself out from behind the wheel. She looked thinner than when I'd seen her last, and she was already a slender woman. She wore an oversized man's flannel shirt and a long skirt that brushed the ground as she walked. In place of her usual sandals, she had beat-up sneakers, probably a concession to colder weather wherever they had been "up north."

I trotted across the clearing to meet her. "Hi, Beth. Listen, that's my friend that's getting married," I nodded toward Karen, "and she doesn't know anything about the quilt, so don't say anything, okay?"

"Sure, I guess," she said. "But I wish you'd tell us what this is all about."

Everett had climbed out of the passenger seat, rubbing his eyes as though he'd been napping while Beth drove. "Yeah, we kind of need to know what we're getting into."

I wanted to scream. They had insisted I come up here and get them. I hadn't understood their reasons, but I had agreed. And now they were getting cold feet? I fought back the anger at what they had already put me through, and forced myself to smile in what I hoped was a reassuring way.

"I'm really sorry," I said, "but I think the sheriff would rather tell you himself. And I don't think he'd take too kindly to me stepping on his toes like that."

I took Beth's arm and began to gently pull her toward the SUV. Everett followed along, hovering protectively but just out of reach, like he was afraid I was going to grab both of them and force them into the car.

I had to admit, the thought had crossed my mind.

"We probably ought to get going," I said, urging them along. "The sooner we get down to Keyhole Bay and you talk to Sheriff Hardy, the sooner you can come back home and relax."

Beth swiveled her head, taking in the cabin and the surrounding area. A shiver passed over her, just the faintest tremble, as she looked around.

Whatever she was planning when she got home, I could see that relaxing wasn't on the agenda. Both the Youngs were as tense as bowstrings, and it felt like they were close to snapping. I had to get them moving before that happened.

"I did have to close the store to come up here," I said apologetically, "so I do need to get back and open up again. I'm happy to help you out, but I really do need to get going."

I opened the back door of the SUV and helped Beth in, resisting the urge to shove her in and slam the door. Everett let himself in the other side, and I jumped in front, motioning Karen to drive.

She didn't need much urging. In fact, she was already rolling down the driveway while I was still getting my seat belt fastened.

Beth realized we were moving and yelled at me from the backseat. "There's stuff I need to do before we go," she shouted. "Wait!"

But we had already reached the end of the driveway and Karen turned down the narrow dirt road, going as fast as she dared over the washboard surface.

A couple minutes later we turned south on the highway, and I breathed a sigh of relief. We had Beth and Everett in the car, no one was following us, and we were headed for Keyhole Bay at slightly over the posted speed limit.

"This won't take long," I assured Beth, turning around in the front seat to look at her. "We'll go get this taken care of, get it out of the way, and you'll be back home just quick as you please."

I crossed my fingers, but I wasn't really lying. As far as I knew, the sheriff just wanted to ask them a few questions; and when he got their answers, I knew he'd have to let them go. It happened all the time; somebody got caught up in something bad through no fault of their own, and the sheriff got suspicious.

But Boomer was a fair man, and as soon as he believed you were innocent, you would walk away. I knew; I'd done it myself a couple times. This wasn't any different.

It was clear that Beth didn't entirely believe me, but she didn't offer any additional protest. Instead she leaned her head back against the seat and closed her eyes. The message was clear: she was through talking to me.

I was just as happy that she was. I didn't want to argue with her, I didn't want her to spill the beans to Karen about the wedding quilt, and I wasn't going to tell her about the dead bodies on her property. So there really wasn't anything for us to talk about.

The rest of the drive to Boomer's office was even quieter than the drive to North County had been. I had introduced Karen and the Youngs when we first got on the highway, but they had not spoken to each other once they acknowledged the introduction.

I wondered if Karen still thought this was better than spending the morning with her mother.

Fifty silent minutes later, Karen pulled into the parking lot of the sheriff's station and stopped, but she didn't shut off the engine. "I've got some research I need to do," she said. "Just call me if you get through here before I get back."

I understood what she was doing. She didn't want to walk into the sheriff's station with her recording and her pictures. She would take them and store them away before she came back. And she might actually stop and do some research into Anna while she was at it.

Either way, she was leaving me with the Youngs at the sheriff's station, and she expected me to call her with an update the minute there was any news.

Maybe I should have tried to convince her to turn her possible evidence over to Boomer. It might relate to his case, after all. But I knew without asking that it would be futile.

I got out and waited for Beth and Everett. I pointed them toward the door and followed behind them into the station.

CHAPTER TWENTY-NINE

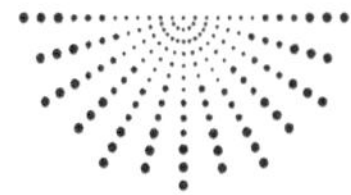

Taking the Youngs into the sheriff was the perfect definition of an anticlimax. After all the drama that went into getting them there, it was all downhill, excitement-wise.

I told the deputy at the desk that I had a couple people who needed to talk to Sheriff Hardy. She took their names and disappeared for a few minutes.

When she returned, she asked us to take a seat and indicated the row of hard plastic chairs along one wall. I remembered those chairs from the night Bobby Freed had been arrested. They were the most uncomfortable furniture ever created.

I stood.

I think Beth and Everett would have left if I hadn't been there and they hadn't been stranded without transportation. I could walk home if I had to, or call any one of a couple dozen people to pick me up. They were nearly an hour from home, and they didn't know anyone in town.

They waited, and so did I.

Boomer took his own sweet time coming out, like he didn't have a care in the world and he knew the Youngs would wait for however long he took.

He emerged in about ten minutes, looked around, and gestured to the Youngs. "You must be the Youngs," he said, smiling and extending his hand.

Beth took his hand and shook it like she was afraid not to, and Everett did the same. As timid and retiring as Beth was, Everett was even more so.

Normally friendly and a little shy, today he was so withdrawn, he was nearly catatonic.

"I apologize for keeping you waiting," he said, gesturing for them to come in the back with him. "I was on the phone and couldn't break away."

He turned back to me and his smile hardened. "I'll talk to you a little later, Miss Martine." I was dismissed.

I watched the door close behind him as he followed the Youngs into the inner sanctum of the station. I was left standing alone in the empty lobby, Boomer's warning ringing in my ears.

I escaped while I could. Boomer hadn't told me to wait for him, and I didn't see any reason to put that restriction on myself. As I saw it, I had done my duty and there wasn't any reason for me to hang around.

I went out the front door, turning north when I reached the sidewalk. A chilly breeze rattled the fronds of the palm trees in the parking lot and raised goose bumps on my arms, reminding me I'd left my jacket in Karen's car. I hurried along for a couple blocks before I pulled out my phone and called Karen.

"You're through already?" She sounded incredulous.

"I am. But Boomer just started with Beth and Everett. He kept us waiting, and then he took them into the back of the station and made it clear I wasn't included."

"Where are you?"

"A couple blocks away, headed toward the library. My jacket's in your car, and I'd like to get in out of this wind, but I didn't want to hang around the station. Where are you?"

"I'm on my way there now," she said. "I copied the pictures and the audio to my backup. I'm not sure what I'll do with them, but it seems like a good idea to keep them safe."

"Meet you there."

I hung up and covered the last three blocks to the county library at a fast clip. At least it warmed me up a little.

The gray brick building represented the largess of a nineteenth-century philanthropist. It sat in a place of honor in the downtown city park, an unchanged counterpoint to the waves of development that washed across Florida. I ran up the shallow stone steps to the entrance and tugged on the ornate wooden door. It swung open slowly, several hundred pounds of antique wood moving on well-oiled brass hinges.

The original brass coat hooks lined the vestibule. Library regulars, and there were several, had their favorite hooks. I spotted the forest green jacket of Naomi Parks, who ran a small motel out near Frank's Foods, and Linda Miller's favorite Fair Isle cardigan. She must have finished her last fat novel and be in the market for a new one.

Just then Linda herself came through the inner doors, a stack of books in her arms. "Hi, Glory!" She set the books on the shelf above her sweater and gave me a hug. "What are you up to? Shouldn't you be working?"

It would have taken too long to explain, so I just told her I was running a couple errands with Karen and we were supposed to meet back here. She naturally assumed it was wedding related and we chatted for a couple minutes about the upcoming event.

We were soon interrupted by Karen's arrival, and Linda said she'd better get back to the Grog Shop. "Guy will pitch a fit if I don't get back and get his lunch," she said with a chuckle.

We all knew better. More likely, Guy would have her lunch ready when she returned. After almost thirty years of marriage, that man still adored her.

Karen watched her walk out the door and turned to me. "If Riley and I can do half that well, I'll be happy."

I nodded in agreement.

"So what now?" I asked her. "The Youngs are going to be with the sheriff a while. Beth has my number, so I guess she'll call when they're through." I shook my head. "I don't know what they'll expect me to do.

"They demanded I come and get them, but we didn't talk about how they intend to get home. This is Thursday, and I do have a business to run, and a bunch of other commitments."

My voice rose as I thought about the corner they'd backed me into. "Do they think I am going to just drop everything and run back to North County to take them home? Did they even think about that?"

"Down, girl! We'll figure it out. Maybe they have friends down here they can stay with, or someone else who can drive them home. They're adults, they can take care of themselves. And if they can't, well, that's kind of Boomer's problem, wouldn't you say? He was the one that wanted them here as soon as possible."

She had a point, but I wasn't ready to calm down just yet. "But what if Boomer doesn't take care of it? What then? I'm the one that got them down here."

"You did them a favor, one they asked you to do. There's nothing to gain by worrying about it now." She reached for the inner door. "Now let's go see if we can find something about the elusive Anna before I have to go face my mother."

The library's main room boasted a high ceiling and a mezzanine level, with a third-floor reading room. The children's area took up a corner of the main floor, under the watchful eye of the head librarian. Popular fiction ringed the walls, and low cases for periodicals surrounded the central reading area. Along the back wall, a few computer terminals stood in carrels, available for public use.

As we climbed the dark wood staircase to the second floor, I trailed my hand along the intricately carved banister. The building had stood in this same spot for a hundred years, lovingly tended by a staff who cared about the books and the library itself. The care they took was evident in the condition of each post and rail.

The reference shelves ran all the way around the mezzanine at right angles to the walls, with reading desks spaced along the railing overlooking the first floor.

Karen made a beeline for a shelf halfway along the left side and started running a finger along the spines of high school yearbooks shelved there.

"We know Sly graduated in about 1962, give or take," she said, pulling books off the shelf. "So Anna, whoever she is, is probably no more than two or three years different. Younger, I would guess, wouldn't you?"

She gestured for me to hold my arms out and piled a half dozen yearbooks on them, then took another group off the shelf for herself. I followed her to a reading desk, setting my stack of books alongside hers.

"So we are looking for a white woman named Anna somewhere between 1961 and 1966 at the outside, most likely in '63 or '64." She shifted the stacks, separating the books for '63 and '64.

"One thing you might check," I suggested, "would be the Army enlistments for those two years. Sly did say he enlisted, and I'll bet you could find some records of exactly when.

"That might help narrow down the search."

"It might," Karen agreed as she sorted, "but since I don't have those records here, and these yearbooks *are* here, let's just focus on them for now."

I pulled over a second chair; we each took a book from 1963 and turned to the senior pictures. As I started turning pages, my heart fell. There were hundreds of black-and-white pictures, and that was just in one of the books for that year.

How did we hope to find a single girl among the hundreds of possibilities?

Karen sighed heavily, clearly thinking the same thing.

"We won't have time to go through these more than once," she said, gesturing to the daunting stack in front of us, "so we better have a system."

She pulled a camera from her bag and set it on the table between us. "Anyone named Ann, or Anna, or something similar, just take a picture of the page and move on. Faster than writing it down, and we can worry about sorting through the pictures later."

She set a notepad next to the camera. "We should keep track of which schools and which years we look at," she said. "In case we don't get through them all today."

There was something odd about the pictures, and it took me a couple minutes to realize what it was. "Karen," I whispered. We were alone on the mezzanine, but I still felt the need to whisper in the library.

"Yeah?" She looked up from the page she had just photographed as she turned the page.

"Everyone in these pictures," I continued whispering, "they're, well, *white*. Doesn't that seem odd?"

As soon as the words were out of my mouth, I realized what I was saying. "I just reminded you the other day that the schools were still segregated back then, didn't I? I forget how much has changed. I know we talked about how Sly and Anna couldn't get married, but it almost didn't seem real, you know?"

Karen nodded and gestured to one of the stacks of yearbooks on the desk. "Exactly. If you want to see Sly's picture, he's probably in one of those."

I nodded and went back to scanning the book in front of me. It was amazing how many variations of Ann I found. There was Ann and Anne and Anna, of course, but there were plenty of others. Annabelle, Annabeth, AnnMarie, Mary Ann, Annamaria, and even a Gloryanna. I dutifully photographed each one and moved on, aware of the afternoon slipping away.

I should have turned off the ringer on my cell phone, but I left it on. I expected Beth to call anytime and want a ride home, or something, and I didn't want to miss her call.

Not that I wanted to have to tell her no, but not talking to her was at least as stressful as dealing with the situation and having it done with.

I finished the first yearbook and started to reach for another, then stopped and took the 1961 yearbook off the stack Karen had pointed to. I was curious to see what Sly looked like as a young man.

I flipped to the index and ran my finger along the column of names, stopping at "Benjamin, Sylvester." There were several pages listed, and I turned to the first one. It was a grainy shot, a group of young men—boys, really— standing around a 1940s sedan. The caption said it was the auto shop class and listed their names. Sly's was among them, but the photo was too small and indistinct to make out much.

I looked at two more photos, similarly hard to see, before I found the individual photos in the class listings. I found Sly in the "Junior Class" section. His smile was broad and it was easy to see the man he had become in the picture of the boy he had been.

I put the volume back on the stack and took the 1962 book. He would have been a senior, and his photo would be bigger and easier to see. But I wasn't prepared for just how much I did see.

CHAPTER THIRTY

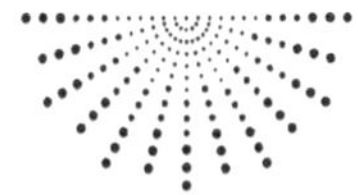

I found the formal senior portrait, but the young man who seemed to glare at the camera was a far cry from the cheerful boy of the previous year.

His hair was longer and wilder, a defiant burst of dark curls that formed a halo around his head. The broad smile had disappeared, replaced with an intent scowl that spoke of simmering anger. He looked like someone who expected trouble, maybe even welcomed it.

It was a side of Sly I had never seen.

I stared at the picture for several minutes, trying to imagine what had caused the change.

My guess would be the woman we were searching for, and once again I questioned the wisdom of our investigation. Had the intervening years worn away that anger? Or had they merely buried it where it could be resurrected by our interference?

Karen realized I had stopped turning pages. She slid over to see what I'd found. She glanced at the book, then took a second look. She froze for several seconds, staring at the picture, as though finally understanding the implications of what we were doing.

"Oh. My." Her voice was soft, without the usual self-assurance. "Oh," she repeated.

"Exactly," I said. "You still think this is a good idea? Messing around in Sly's life just to provide you with a diversion?"

"I, uh, I'm not sure," she confessed. She stood up and started replacing the books on the shelves. "I need to think about this."

She left the 1962 yearbook, open to Sly's picture, to the last. She closed it gently and placed it back in its appointed spot on the shelf.

Karen gathered up her camera and the notepad, and we left the library in silence. It wasn't until we had buckled ourselves into her SUV that either of us spoke.

"I'll drop you at home," she said. "I've got some things to do, and I have to spend some time with my mother if I want to escape for dinner tonight."

She left me at the front door of Southern Treasures, with a promise that I'd see her and Riley later.

A sign on the door told customers that we were closed for the day. I took advantage of the closure to go next door and check on Chloe.

Lighthouse was busy, a mid-afternoon rush of locals with a few tourists sprinkled in for good measure. Chloe was making coffee drinks and chatting up customers with her usual cheery attitude, and I hung back from the counter and watched until the line of customers had been taken care of.

"How are you doing?" I asked when I reached the counter. From my observation, she was doing very well indeed. But I wanted to know what she thought.

"Good," she said. "We're staying busy, and I have enough stock to last the rest of the day."

I glanced at the case. There were a few pastries left, and some quiche, as well as several loaves of bread, cake slices, and half a cheesecake.

"I'm impressed that you're staying on top of the baking with Miss Pansy gone." I spoke softly, my words muffled by the soft hum of conversation at the tables around the room. "You know, Bradley gave me her recipes. They're in my safe."

I glanced around. No one was paying any attention to us. "I don't own the place yet, and I didn't feel right about opening them up. But if you need them to keep things going, I'd be happy to give them to you."

Chloe hesitated. She glanced around the shop, then motioned for me to come around the counter.

I followed her to the doorway between the shop and the kitchen, wondering just what she was being so secretive about.

Once she was sure we couldn't be overheard, she looked at me sheepishly and bit her lip.

"I have a confession," she said.

My brain raced. What now? Didn't I have enough on my plate without trouble from my almost-new employee?

I kept my expression neutral and nodded for her to go on.

"I don't need the recipes," she blurted.

I probably looked as surprised as I felt. Pansy had guarded those recipes like they were the gold at Fort Knox. She carried them in her head, not trusting them to be written down where someone else could see them.

"I've been watching her for years," Chloe continued. "She doesn't know, but over time I have managed to figure out most everything she makes. I'd never tell her; the secret recipes mean a lot to her, but so far nobody has noticed any difference."

I thought for a moment. I'd had a couple things from Lighthouse in the days since Pansy went in the hospital. Everything had been excellent, just like always.

"You're right," I said. "I didn't notice, and I knew what was going on."

"See? But you can't tell Miss Pansy! Promise?"

"Of course. I agree completely. That's a very important thing to her. She didn't even let Bradley see the recipes; she gave him a sealed envelope to give to me."

Chloe grinned, relief evident in the lift of her shoulders. "Thanks, Glory. I knew I'd have to tell you and I wasn't real sure how you'd feel about it. I'm glad you're okay with it."

I glanced out to the shop where happy customers were sipping coffee and enjoying the food Chloe had prepared. "I'm more than okay," I told her. "I'm glad to know you can keep things going while we get this sale settled, and I don't have to worry about what kind of food we're putting out in the meantime."

She glanced out at the shop again. A couple of the customers were leaving. "I better get back out there," she said. "If you're really okay?"

I patted her shoulder. "You're doing a great job, Chloe. And I really am okay."

I watched her hurry out front in time to exchange good-byes with the departing customers and wish them a good afternoon. It was what every shopkeeper should do, make their customers feel like valued guests, but not everyone could do it with Chloe's apparent sincerity.

I tried to imagine running Lighthouse without her, and was instantly grateful I didn't have to go there. It would have made the entire enterprise a lot more scary.

Taking advantage of my freedom, I crossed the street to Beach Books.

Jake's offer to cook tonight was one big reason I had free time this afternoon, and the least I could do was check in and see if there was anything I could do to help.

Before I went inside, I slipped my phone out of my purse and checked, just in case. Still no word from Beth.

Jake greeted me warmly, reassuring me that dinner was under control. "I decided against Southwest," he said, "Lasagna's ready for the oven, and there's salad and garlic bread. Nothing fancy, but it was a favorite at the firehouse."

In the last few months, Jake had finally started to tell me about his life before Keyhole Bay. He'd been a firefighter and a fire captain in California until his retirement on a partial disability.

Little things, like cooking for the crew, and big things, like the tragedy that killed one of his men and caused the injuries that forced his retirement. It was a sign of our growing connection.

"I can't begin to thank you for that."

He leered at me, and suggested I might find a way. Fortunately we were alone, but I think I blushed anyway.

"So how was your trip up north?" he asked.

The question brought me up short. Had it really only been a few hours since Karen and I had driven up to get Beth and Everett? So much had happened, it seemed like days ago.

"Well, I think we might have met some of the Youngs' neighbors. You'll probably hear the story again tonight, but I know you won't want to wait," I teased.

I launched into the story of Calvin and Donny and our encounter at the cabin. As I talked, Jake's face grew darker, and a frown pulled his eyebrows down.

"And what did Boo—um, Sheriff Hardy—have to say about all this?"

I looked down, not able to meet his gaze. "I didn't tell him," I said quietly.

"What?" Jake acted as though he hadn't heard me.

"Ididn'ttellhim." I mumbled again.

Jake put his fingers under my chin and tilted my head up until he was looking me in the eye. "You did what?" he asked again.

"I didn't tell him."

"Some strange men accost you out in the middle of nowhere, in a place where dead bodies were found just a few days before, they steal Karen's phone, and they force you into their truck"—he paused for a deep breath—*"and you didn't tell the sheriff?"* He shook his head. "Are you two crazy?"

"I didn't get a chance to."

I tried to explain. "They didn't hurt us, just scared us a little. And they didn't even take the phone, they just checked to make sure there weren't any pictures and then gave it back.

"When we got to the station, Karen didn't stick around, and when Boomer finally came out, he just wanted to talk to Beth and Everett, and he made it clear I wasn't invited to join them."

I stood a little taller, and my voice steadied. "By that time, I figured I was better off getting out of there. Besides, what good would it have done? He probably would have made me talk to that self-important woman at the desk, and if she believed me, I would still be sitting there in some tiny room waiting for Boomer to ask me a million questions."

I took a deep breath and went on. "Besides that, they would have demanded that Karen turn over her pictures and the recording she made. I think you know how well that would have gone over."

"You still should have told him. And I thought you said there weren't any pictures. So what was there for Karen to turn over to the sheriff?"

I explained how she had uploaded the pictures to the station's server before removing them from her phone, and about her little digital recorder. "She got everything they said to her."

"Including them forcing you to go with them. That's evidence of at least attempted kidnapping, Glory."

"Maybe."

I didn't want to talk to Boomer, and Jake knew it. He let the subject drop for now, but I knew he'd come back to it later.

CHAPTER THIRTY-ONE

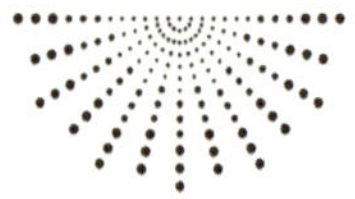

I got the evil eye from Bluebeard when I finally returned to Southern Treasures. He was used to having company all day, and he made his feelings about being left alone quite clear.

"Out all night, out all day," he chided. "Where have you been? I'm starved!"

He clearly wasn't starved. I had given him a breakfast of fruit and shredded-wheat biscuits before I left, and there were still several of the biscuits in his bowl. What he was, was spoiled.

"No you're not," I told him. I gave him a bit of apple and a piece of banana in penance for my absence. "You can have a treat, but you are not starving."

He muttered as he ate the fruit offering, the words indistinct to anyone who didn't know him as well as I did. "Language, Bluebeard!"

The muttering abated, but it didn't stop. It was part of his game, and I let him have his fun. I had become accustomed to his language and he was usually good when there were customers in the shop. But he expected a reaction and I gave him one.

"Bluebeard!"

He stomped back into his cage, still muttering as he went.

It had been a long and stressful day, and it would be a late night. I started upstairs for a nap.

From below I heard Uncle Louis's voice clearly. "People aren't always who you think they are."

To my surprise, I slept soundly for an hour. I had fully expected the phone to ring the minute I closed my eyes. Neither the store phone nor my personal cell showed any missed calls or messages, but I still checked voice mail on both, just in case.

Nothing.

I took a quick shower and dressed in jeans and a polo shirt. I called Jake to double-check if there was anything I could bring for dinner, but he said he had it all under control.

I took him at his word, but I still carefully packed up the pecan pie I'd baked the night before.

Fifteen minutes later, I was at his door. The instant he opened the door, the mingled aromas of tomato, cheese, and herbs hit me. My stomach grumbled, and I realized I hadn't really stopped to eat anything all day.

Jake helped me out of my jacket, and I took it and my purse to the bedroom. I told myself there was no significance to the action—everyone's coats and jackets would end up thrown on the bed when they arrived. But I did put my purse in "my" drawer of the dresser.

Back in the kitchen, Jake was laying out an appetizer of Caprese skewers. Grape tomatoes, mozzarella balls, and fresh basil leaves on frilled toothpicks, sprinkled with olive oil, balsamic vinegar, and a touch of sea salt and black pepper.

I popped one in my mouth and bit down. The tart tomato juice combined with the acid of the vinegar and the earthy flavor of fresh basil, all mellowed by the creamy mozzarella.

My taste buds, and my stomach, thanked me and demanded more. I quickly complied.

"Are those okay?" Jake asked. His back was turned as he pulled a bubbling baking dish from the oven.

"Mmm-hmmm," I answered, my mouth full.

He set the dish on the stove top and turned to look at me. He broke into a grin. "I'll take that as a yes," he said.

I reluctantly left the skewers behind and helped Jake set the table for dinner. When it was just the two of us we ate in the kitchen; but for the Thursday night crew we needed more room than the kitchen table provided.

In the living room, Jake had pushed the furniture back. We pulled the dining table into the middle of the room and opened it up to add a leaf.

"Expecting a crowd?" I asked when Jake added the second leaf, taking it from a square for four to a rectangle that would hold eight comfortably.

"Just six, I think. But you never know."

"What do you mean, 'you never know'?"

"Riley called early this morning. He said his future in-laws were still making noises about joining us for dinner."

"How early?"

"Probably nine, ten o'clock," he said as he headed back into the kitchen to bring the placemats and plates.

I followed him, coming back with silverware and a stack of glasses. "Then I think we have it covered. Karen and I were talking about it, and she was going to play the manners card."

"You know, 'It's just *rude* to invite extra guests to a dinner party without checking with the host first.'"

"That's one her mother will understand."

"But Riley did check with me," Jake said. "So that argument won't stand up."

"It will if Riley doesn't *tell* them he called you. And Karen will make sure he doesn't."

Jake shrugged. "Whatever works. I planned on leftovers for the freezer, so there's plenty of food either way. But Riley and I both agreed that it wasn't our place—either of us—to decide who to invite or not invite to Thursday dinners."

I filed that thought away for later discussion. Since Riley and Karen were getting married, and Jake and I were a couple even though we hadn't made any long-term plans, maybe it was time to make our Thursday get-togethers officially the three couples.

We finished setting the table, tossed the salad, and made a quick home-made vinegar-and-oil dressing. We'd just slid the garlic bread under the broiler when the doorbell rang.

As hostess, I answered the door while Jake watched the bread. It was Riley and Karen, without Catherine and Clint.

"Rude was a great idea," Karen said, giving me a hug. "Mom completely understood. Of course that only works for this week, but at least it's something."

"Next week is Felipe's turn," I said, thinking out loud, "and the week after is yours. Maybe you should just suggest that she meet everyone at your house in two weeks."

Karen made a face like she'd just bitten into a lemon.

"You know you're going to have to do it sometime," I said. "You might as well do it on your home turf."

"Maybe," she said. But she didn't sound convinced.

"So, have you heard from Beth?" she asked, turning the conversation away from her mother.

"No, and I'm starting to worry."

"Well, stop it. They're adults. You're not responsible for them. I bet they didn't even say thanks for you coming all the way up there, did they?"

"I don't know if *thanks* was the right response. I shoved them in the car and we carried them down to the sheriff. They didn't seem real grateful at the time."

Riley had disappeared into the kitchen while we were talking, and after we deposited the coats in the bedroom, we went in search of the two men. We found them deep in a serious discussion that stopped abruptly the minute we walked in.

I immediately realized what was going on. Riley wanted to surprise Karen with a honeymoon destination, as she'd told her mother. Riley thought California might be nice, and since Jake had lived most of his life on the West Coast, Riley had asked him for advice.

"Did you think any more about what we found at the library?" I asked Karen, drawing her attention away from the men.

She helped herself to one of the Caprese skewers and then motioned that her mouth was full. It was her way of ducking the question she didn't want to answer.

She was saved by the doorbell.

I went to let Ernie and Felipe in, and Karen followed along, still munching.

There were hugs all around, and exclamations over the smells drifting out from the kitchen. I shooed the new arrivals toward the kitchen while I ferried the last armload of coats to the bedroom.

By the time I returned, the crew was already carrying food to the table: the steaming pan of lasagna, a large bowl of green salad, the Caprese skewers, and a towering platter of garlic bread fresh from the oven.

We settled around the table and Jake brought out a couple bottles of wine. He poured samples for everyone, explaining that these were wines from one of the places he'd lived, a small town north of San Francisco in California's wine country.

I watched Riley's face out of the corner of my eye as Jake talked about the wineries. He was trying to watch Karen without being obvious, looking for her reaction to the talk of wine country. So that was definitely what he was up to.

Jake passed glasses around and answered a couple questions, but he didn't press the point. He'd seen Karen's reaction, and so had I. The idea appealed to her. That was all Riley needed to know.

We spent the next hour talking about food. The Caprese was well received, and I gave away one of Jake's secrets: he'd started a container garden in his sunporch and grown his own basil and grape tomatoes.

"It might not be traditional Southern," I said, "but the basil and tomatoes were grown right here in Keyhole Bay."

Which meant Ernie had to have a tour of the garden. He'd always had a few pots of fresh herbs in his kitchen—any real cook would, he said—but lately he'd been thinking about adding some other plants.

The two of them returned a few minutes later, Ernie looking like a little kid just bursting to unwrap a new toy.

Felipe rolled his eyes as his partner folded his tall frame into his chair. "You're going to want to turn our lanai into a truck garden, aren't you?"

"No, *cher*. Just a few pots of this and that. Really, you'll hardly notice." He squeezed Felipe's arm. "You'll see."

Felipe smiled indulgently. When it came to food, he'd never been able to say no to anything his partner wanted. He enjoyed Ernie's cooking too much.

While they were gone, the conversation had segued from the food to local gossip and personal news. Felipe asked about the Lighthouse plans, and I filled them in on the latest developments.

"Bradley even brought me Miss Pansy's recipes," I said. "She had sealed them in an envelope before she gave them to him, signed her name across the seal, and instructed him to give them directly to me. He looked more relieved to get rid of that envelope than he did about the contracts."

"Have you heard back from the bank?" Ernie asked.

I shook my head. "Buddy McKenna was very positive when he reviewed the proposal." I nodded to Jake and Ernie. "Thank you both for your help with that. I'm very grateful."

"Anything for you, *ma chère*," Ernie said with an exaggerated New Orleans drawl. "Anything at all." He glanced at Felipe, who was shaking his head. "Well, *almost* anything," he quickly amended, drawing a laugh from everyone at the table.

"So he's going to approve it?" Felipe asked.

"He doesn't have the final say. He said it was a good proposal and the numbers more than justified what I was asking for, but it has to go to the loan committee, and they don't meet until tomorrow.

"And even then, he said I probably won't hear until after the weekend." I was twisting my napkin into knots, and I dropped it on the table. "Not like I'm nervous or anything."

Riley jumped in to reassure me. "Normal reaction, Glory. Do you remember when I was trying to buy *Ocean Breeze*? I about lost my mind waiting to find out about the loan.

"I think that was the time I decked Bobby for some fool thing he did, and my dad said it was his own damned fault for crossing me while that was going on.

"First and last time I got away with thumping on one of my little brothers."

I did remember that. It was before he married Karen the first time, and the complications of buying the boat and setting up his fishing business very nearly scuttled the wedding. Which was part of the reason we'd ended up on the beach with a JP.

I very nearly told him that at least I wasn't planning my own wedding at the same time that I was worrying about the loan. I didn't because it suddenly felt awkward to make a direct reference to my wedding when I was sitting next to Jake, especially after my conversation with Karen last week put the thought in my mind.

Felipe and Ernie repeated their offer of the previous week, and I graciously declined. "There aren't many people I'd trust, and you're two of them. But I've thought about it and thought about it, and your friendship means too much to me to take a chance that anything could go wrong and damage that."

"It isn't just you guys, either," Jake said. "I've offered, and so has Sly. She's turned us both down."

"Speaking of Sly," Ernie said, "how's he doing? I haven't seen him in a while."

"Seems fine," Jake said. "We had dinner with him Tuesday night. He'd finished a restoration on an old Studebaker, found a part he'd been looking for for years, and wanted to celebrate."

Karen shifted uncomfortably in her chair, and Ernie turned to look at her. "Something wrong, girl?"

"I don't know," she said slowly. "I don't think so, but I started something and now I'm not sure if it's the right thing or not.

"It's kind of a long story, you sure you want to hear it?"

Jake picked up the wine bottle and passed it around the table. "Let's freshen our glasses, and I'll take the plates to the kitchen," he said. "Then we definitely want to hear it."

Ernie helped Jake and me whisk the dirty dishes and leftovers into the kitchen. I knew what was coming, and I told them just to leave everything on the counter. I didn't want to give Karen time to change her mind about sharing her latest investigation.

We returned to the living room, settled into our chairs, and the men turned expectantly to Karen. She looked at me, her expression pleading for my help in explaining what she'd done.

"Go ahead," I said, waving her on. "This was your idea."

"Okay," she said, fidgeting. She didn't know where to begin, and if I didn't give her a little push, we could be there all night.

"Do you all remember," I cut in, "the day Karen and Riley told us they were getting married again? The Fourth of July? Sly was with us that night, and he told us about the girl he almost married."

Nods all around.

"Well, Karen thought we should try to find this woman and find out what happened to her."

They all turned to look at Karen.

"And did you?" Trust Felipe to cut to the chase.

"It hasn't been that easy," Karen said, finally speaking up. "We didn't know much except a first name and a guess as to how old she was. And that she was white, of course."

"But why?" Riley looked genuinely puzzled.

Karen sighed and looked around the table. "My mother was coming, the wedding plans were making me crazy, the station manager decided to do me a big 'favor,'—she wiggled her fingers, making air quotes around the word— "and give me the month off.

"I wanted a distraction."

"You couldn't read a book?" Ernie drawled.

"I don't know why I came up with this," she said. "All I can say is that it seemed like a good idea at the time. It had nothing to do with me or the wedding. It was just a puzzle that I could try to solve, and maybe if I found out something about her, I could share it with Sly."

She waved her hands in front of her face, brushing away the startled reactions. "Not if it was anything bad," she said quickly. "I wouldn't ever tell him anything unless I thought it would make him feel better about what happened to her."

"I would hope not," Riley said.

"It started out as a lark, just something to do when I needed a break from all the wedding stuff. But then this afternoon, well"—she gestured to me— "you tell them."

"This afternoon we met at the library after I left the Youngs at the sheriff's station."

"Sheriff's station?" Riley said. He turned to Karen. "You didn't tell me anything about going to the sheriff's station."

"I didn't go," she protested. "Glory went."

"And she didn't tell Boomer anything she should have," Jake said darkly. "But we'll come back to that." He waved at me. "Go on."

"Karen suggested we take a look at the yearbook collection, see if we could find anyone fitting what we knew about Sly's girlfriend."

"And did you?" Felipe again.

Karen shook her head. "No. And yes. We found so many possibilities in a single year that it purely overwhelmed us. But that wasn't the real problem."

The four men swiveled back to me, waiting for the rest of the story.

"I found Sly's photo," I said. I knew that wasn't enough of an answer. I took a swig of wine, trying to swallow the lump in my throat at the memory of those pictures.

"Actually, I found several. Some clubs and so on, and his picture from his junior year. He looked a lot like the man we all know; he was smiling and he looked happy. You could see in his eyes that he was the same guy.

"But then I looked at the picture in the next year, when he was a senior. It had to have been taken just a few weeks before he left Keyhole Bay and enlisted; he told me he joined the Army right after he finished high school."

I hesitated, and Jake put his arm around my shoulders. "So what was wrong with that picture? Why does it have you so upset?"

"It was the way he looked, Jake. Angry. Like he was expecting trouble, or maybe even looking for trouble. Something had taken away his smile, but it wasn't just that. He had turned into someone else in the year between those two pictures. Someone we don't even know."

"It wasn't even the anger," Karen said. "It was like he was looking out at the world and daring anyone to tell him what to do."

"And yet that's exactly what he did," Jake said. "He let the world tell him what to do, and he did it and never looked back." He shrugged. "Not to say I wouldn't have done the same thing, given the times."

"How do we know that?" Karen asked. "He might have looked for Anna, he just didn't tell us. And maybe he didn't find anything. He's not a trained investigator or anything. All we know is that he hasn't seen her since he left Keyhole Bay to join the Army."

"What are you going to do about it now?" Riley wrapped a protective arm around her and spoke softly. "Are you going to give up on your search?"

"I really don't know. All I know is that it changed from a diversion for me into something a lot more complicated. It's Sly's life we're talking about, and it isn't my place to interfere.

"The problem now is that after just a few hours of looking, *I'm* real curious to know what happened to Anna. I wonder where she went and what she did, whether she married someone else, and if she even remembers Sly. I don't know how you could forget your first love"—she reached up and squeezed Riley's hand that rested on her shoulder—"but what if she did?"

She sighed. "Whatever I do, it isn't my place to carry any tales to Sly."

CHAPTER THIRTY-TWO

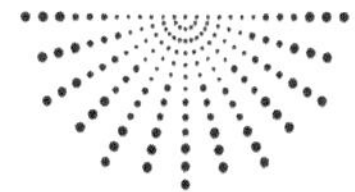

I helped Jake clear the rest of dinner and serve dessert in the lull that followed Karen's story.

"I didn't plan a fancy dessert," Jake explained as we carried dishes to the table. "Since I was pinch-hitting, I'd planned spumoni ice cream and cookies from Lighthouse. But Glory brought a pecan pie.

"I don't know how well that goes with lasagna and garlic bread, but I know which one I'd rather have."

"You never did explain why you ended up cooking tonight," Ernie said. "Not that I'm complaining, mind you." He patted his stomach and grinned. "That was a mighty fine meal."

"It was my fault," I said, sitting down and taking a bite of pie. "I had an emergency and had to go up north this morning."

"Does this have something to do with the trip to the sheriff's station?" Riley asked, looking at Karen.

She nodded, but left it up to me to explain.

"I told you last week about my suppliers up north that flaked on me. Well, they seem to have gotten themselves in some trouble, and they asked me to help out."

"I don't remember anything about that," Riley said.

"You and Karen were already gone. You had an early trip the next morning, so you left before I told these guys about my problems with my quilt lady." I hoped the explanation would remind the others why I hadn't told the story in front of Karen.

"Turned out they'd gone to visit family. At least that's what they told me. In the meantime, the sheriff found two bodies near their cabin, and he really wanted to talk to the people who lived there.

"I found out about the bodies when I went up there with Karen. Her station manager called while we were at dinner and I just went along for company, but Boomer wasn't inclined to believe me. Especially when he found out I knew them."

"With your history, can you blame him?" Felipe said.

"No, I get it. But I've stayed out of his business for a year and a half. You'd think that would buy me a little credibility.

"Anyway, I talked to Beth. I didn't tell her why she had to talk to Boomer, just that he would track her down if she didn't come back. She said they would, but only if I picked them up. So Karen and I went and picked them up this morning."

I stopped, and Karen didn't add anything, but Jake wasn't letting me off the hook. "There was a bit more than that, Glory." He didn't look happy. "A bit you really ought to share with Boomer."

"We ran into a couple of the neighbors while we were there." Karen jumped in before I could say anything more.

I looked at her. The reason she spoke up was written across her face: she hadn't told Riley about our adventure.

I wasn't about to be the one who told him.

"Yeah," I agreed. "Couple guys pulled up while we were there. I think they were looking for Everett, but I wasn't real sure. They were only there a few minutes, though."

Jake started to say something, but I caught his hand under the table and squeezed. Hard. I'm not sure he knew why exactly, but he got the message.

"So what's the latest with your mom and the captain?" I asked Karen, eager to change the subject.

She jumped at the change in topic and launched into a long tale of her woes with her mother. "The only saving grace is that Julie and Chloe have got her so distracted with this shower that she forgets to bug me for minutes at a time."

"Doesn't Clint help?" Jake asked, playing along with the change of subject.

Karen shook her head. "Whatever Mother wants, Clint's more than happy to give her. He thinks the sun rises and sets on that woman.

"I suppose I should be happy for her, and I am. I just wish she didn't have to run my life, too. And he's so busy with whatever the Navy's got him doing we hardly see him."

"We are going to have to include them in dinner while they're here," I reminded her. "Maybe we ought to figure that out while we're all together."

It was Felipe who solved our dilemma. "I've been thinking about that," he said. "I know you said you and Riley were spending Thanksgiving with your families, but Ernie and I were thinking of doing a traditional Thanksgiving spread at our place next Thursday, since we're loosening up on the menus. Why don't you invite your mother and her husband to join us then?"

"Really? Are you sure?" Karen's smile of relief nearly split her face in half. "That would be amazing, if you're serious."

Within a few minutes, we planned the meal and Karen texted her mother an invitation. We each offered to bring something, but Ernie turned us all down. "I can't wait to really use all the capacity of my new range," he said. "It's Felipe's turn to cook, but I think we're going to do this one together."

"That actually ties in to something I've been thinking about," I said. "Now that Riley and Karen are getting married, and Jake has proven he can actually cook, maybe we ought to consider officially changing the group from the four of us to the six of us."

I saw Felipe and Ernie nodding, but Jake spoke first. "I'd be honored to be included," he said. "It's a pretty exclusive club, and I would truly appreciate you letting me in."

Ernie reached across the table and shook Jake's hand. "We'd be honored to have you."

"Thanks," Jake said. "How about you Felipe?"

"After that meal, how could I say anything but yes?"

"I'll gladly ride your coattails," Riley added.

"We're counting on you for fish," I told him. "I still wouldn't know how to cook grouper properly without you."

The evening was winding down, and Jake went to retrieve the coats from the bedroom. Riley offered to help and the two men walked down the hall.

They were gone several minutes, their absence covered by the general chaos as the four of us—the original crew—made quick work of finishing the clearing up.

By the time Jake and Riley returned with coats and jackets, Riley lugging Karen's heavy bag, the dishes were stacked by the sink, the leaves were out of the table and it was pushed back against the wall, and the living room furniture was back in its proper place.

"Leave the dishes," I told Ernie as he started to run hot water in the sink. "Jake and I can take care of them."

Though it went against his tidy nature, Ernie managed to walk away from the chore, and soon we were saying our good-byes.

Once we were alone, I asked Jake what he and Riley had been talking about.

"The honeymoon," Jake said. "As if you didn't know."

"I knew that much." I slid a stack of plates into the hot, soapy water. "I'll wash, since you cooked. But you have to tell me what Riley's planning. Something tells me it involves California wine country."

"That obvious, huh?" He picked up a dish towel and started drying plates as I propped them in the drainer. "You don't think Karen noticed, do you?"

"No." I tried to reassure him. "I only figured it out because I knew you and Riley had been talking about it. I don't think she suspected anything."

"Good. Riley would kill me if he thought I gave it away."

"So *is* that what he's doing?"

"I think so. It's just a matter of timing. It's fun to go during the harvest, though that won't be until late summer. If they go now, it could be chilly, but there's still a lot to see and do. I've been helping him find some fun stuff."

He stacked the dried plates in the cupboard and went to work on the silverware. "Like the B&B made out of train cabooses."

"Cabooses?"

"Yeah. Instead of a bedroom, you get a caboose. They're all separate, so there's lots of privacy, with a central dining room for breakfast.

"It's north of the Bay Area. I got to know the owner when I lived up there. Nice guy, and a heckuva cook."

"That sounds like something that would definitely appeal to Riley, especially the food," I said. "And Karen. She likes things that are a little bit different."

"This definitely is. Anyway, there are a bunch of wineries in the area, so Riley's trying to put together a wine country honeymoon and I'm happy to help him out."

We finished the dishes, and Jake picked up the second wine bottle. "There's enough here for a nightcap," Jake said. "Unless you're in a hurry to get home."

I wasn't.

CHAPTER THIRTY-THREE

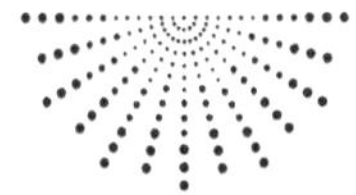

I crept out before dawn the next morning, leaving Jake snoring softly. He stirred in his sleep as I took my purse out of the dresser drawer, but he didn't wake up.

I wasn't that successful with Bluebeard.

"Out all night." He wolf whistled. "Again."

I rummaged in the refrigerator and found some cut-up fruit. The faint light of a false dawn wasn't enough to turn off the streetlights that shone through the front windows as I made my way through the shop.

"I brought you some fruit," I said, dumping the berries and melons into his dish. "But I give up on trying to let you sleep."

He gobbled down several pieces of fruit before stopping to give me a beady-eyed stare. "Out all night."

I stared back. "Are you waiting up for me? Is that why you're awake when I come home?"

He turned his head and went back to the fruit. He emptied the bowl in a few seconds, then stomped off into his cage.

"Trying to #&#^*^$% sleep here," he squawked.

"I give up," I said and headed upstairs to make coffee.

Short on sleep, I thought I would have to depend on the coffee to keep me going. Too early to open up, I carried my mug downstairs and checked the website for orders. More Bluebeard T-shirts, some mugs, and one of my regulars inquiring about the new spatterware pieces I'd listed.

I filled orders as the sky lightened from gray to peach to pale blue. By the time the sun was fully up, I had packages ready for pickup, I'd e-mailed confirmations to each customer, and I was ready for another mug of coffee.

When I came back downstairs with my refill, Bluebeard was out of his cage and surveying the world from his perch in the front window.

"Coffee?" he said when he saw me come through the door with a mug in hand.

"No, Bluebeard. You can't have coffee." I kept thinking one day he'd stop asking since he always got the same answer. But given that we'd had this same exact exchange several times a week for the last six or seven years, it didn't seem likely.

I unlocked the front door and turned over the sign. I truly wished I would be able to stay in the shop and have a normal workday. I hadn't had one of those in a while, and the idea appealed to me. A lot.

I was working on my inventory when the computer chimed with an incoming e-mail. I finished the item I was working on and flipped over to the e-mail window. There was a message from Clifford Wilson, with the subject line "Will of Louis Georges."

I thought of Sly's check, still uncashed. It was in the safe, along with Pansy's recipes and the purchase contract for Lighthouse Coffee. All related, and all likely to be influenced by what was in Mr. Wilson's e-mail.

My hand shook slightly as I clicked on the message. It popped up, a lengthy block of text couched in Mr. Wilson's careful legalese. I read it slowly, then read it again to make sure I understood exactly what he said.

He apologized for taking so long, saying he had consulted his original files to be sure he answered completely accurately. There had been several specific bequests, including the ownership of Southern Treasures and the disposition of family heirlooms. My Uncle Andrew had received stock in Back Bay Bank, and the rest of the estate had gone to my mother.

That meant, he explained, that anything that wasn't specifically listed in the will belonged to my mother, and as her only heir, it belonged to me.

Which meant the check in the safe was truly and legally mine. I could do whatever I wanted with it, and Uncle Andrew and Peter had no right to it.

The legal right to the money was settled. But the question remained: what would my conscience let me do with it?

I wrestled with the dilemma as I worked through the morning. Customers came and went. The delivery driver dropped off an order and picked up the outgoing packages. I made another pot of coffee and drank most of it.

And the whole time, I thought about what to do with Sly's check. I could keep it all, or I could give Peter half, or I could give him a smaller portion since I wasn't obligated to give him anything at all.

I could even use it to boost the Buy-Out-Peter Fund, an option I found particularly ironic.

Shortly after noon, Karen showed up at the shop. Her grim expression drove all thoughts of Peter from my mind. "What's wrong?" I said, pulling her into the back of the shop.

"I just came from a press conference with Boomer and Assistant District Attorney Morris." Her voice was controlled, but I knew she was angry. "Morris made a big show out of it, called every news outlet he could get hold of.

"Glory, he's charging Everett Young with the murder of those two moonshiners, and he's charging Beth as an accessory."

I stared at her with my mouth open, too stunned to speak.

"Why?" I asked when I finally regained some semblance of control. "What in the world does he think he's doing?"

"He's gunning for his boss's job," Karen said grimly. "He thinks he's 'cleaning up the county' with this hard line, and thinks that it will appeal to the voters."

"And what happens when the voters find out he's got the wrong guy?"

"He's not thinking that far ahead, Glory. He saw a chance to get some press and he grabbed it. It has nothing to do with what's right or wrong, just what he thinks will advance his career."

I couldn't stand any more. I dashed behind the counter and grabbed my wallet and keys.

"What are you doing?" Karen asked.

"I'm going down there and give Boomer a piece of my mind. Maybe several pieces.

"He got me to talk Beth and Everett into coming back. I even went and carried them to the station—well, you did, but only because I talked them into it—and then he charges them with murder? What kind of a Judas goat does that make me?"

"Don't bother." Karen grabbed my arm and kept me from running out the door. "There's nothing Boomer can do. Once the DA's office files charges, it's out of his hands."

She eased her grip, like she was testing whether I'd run away, but I waited to hear her out. "You said he was there."

"He was. But I got the feeling the whole thing was a surprise to him. And he was not happy about it. He looked like he'd bitten into a sour lemon when that jerk made his big announcement."

"So Boomer doesn't think they did it."

"I didn't say that. I said he was unhappy about the big press conference and the announcement. Knowing Boomer, at the very least he's waiting for more evidence before he makes up his mind."

"That's not what you said when he arrested Bobby," I reminded her.

"No, and I still think he jumped the gun on that one. But he had the feds breathing down his neck. I think he was trying to keep Bobby in Keyhole Bay, and that was the only way he could think of to do it."

"What do we do now?" I asked.

"Nothing," Karen replied. "It's hard for me to admit that, but there isn't a thing we can do right now. The ADA says there will be an arraignment and a bail hearing this afternoon, but he's already made it clear he'll oppose bail. He says they don't have any 'ties to the community' and that makes them a flight risk."

"Right," I said bitterly. "Especially since they just came back from wherever they were of their own accord."

"You know what he really meant."

"I do. He's reminding everybody that they aren't from around here. They're outsiders, so they can't be trusted." I threw my keys back on the counter in frustration. "Sometimes I hate this place!"

"He's wrong, Glory. We both know that, and I think Boomer knows it, too. This will eventually sort itself out, but there isn't anything we can do today.

"Tomorrow, after the dust settles a little, you can go down and see if Boomer will allow you to visit Beth. I doubt you'll get to see Everett, but he might at least let you talk to her."

"And say what? 'Sorry I got you arrested'? How do you think she's going to react to that?"

"You could offer to find her a lawyer, or whatever else we can do to help."

"We?"

"Yeah." Karen looked sheepish. "The truth is, I feel like I'm responsible, too. I went up there with you, and I was part of the plan to get them back here. So, yeah. I want to help."

Karen's offer, well intentioned though it was, only served to depress me more. Usually she knew what to do, who to call, where to apply pressure to get what she wanted. This time all she could say was "Wait," and waiting wasn't one of my better skills.

"What about the pictures you took? And the recording? Isn't that evidence?

Those guys were out there, sniffing around the place." Against my better judgment, I made a suggestion. "Maybe we should take them to Boomer and get him to follow up."

"And just how do we explain that we didn't report it when it happened?" Karen was always reluctant to turn over anything to the sheriff; I shouldn't have expected this to be any different. "Besides, all it shows is that a couple guys confronted us while *we* were sniffing around instead of calling to tell the sheriff that Beth and Everett were coming back. I couldn't really see faces or vehicles or anything useful, and no matter what they show on TV the sheriff doesn't have a magic computer that can change that."

We talked for a few minutes longer, both of us trying to come up with something positive we could do, to no avail. Karen left, saying she had to cover the bail hearing, and she promised to call me if she heard anything more.

I was still reeling from the news when Jake showed up an hour later. He flashed me a big grin as he came through the door.

"You didn't have to leave so early," he said as he walked toward the counter. "I was going to cook breakfast."

"You were sleeping so soundly," I said. "I woke up way early and remembered that the loan committee was supposed to meet today. After that, there was no way I could get back to sleep. I didn't want to wake you up with my tossing and turning, so I decided to get back here and get some things done."

"I'm always happy to wake up if you're there."

He looked at me, a frown creasing his forehead. "Glory, what's wrong? They said you wouldn't hear about the loan until after the weekend. Did they call?"

I shook my head. "It's Beth and Everett. Karen was here a little bit ago. They're being charged in the deaths of those two moonshiners Boomer found up on their property."

"That's ridiculous! What is Boomer thinking?"

"It's not Boomer." I sighed. "It's some assistant DA who's out to make a name for himself. Karen says he's trying to take over his boss's job, and he jumped on this case as a way to make some headlines."

"What an idiot! He's going to get plenty of attention, sure. But he'll get even more when he has to let them go. Especially if a smart lawyer gets hold of them and they decide to sue the county."

"Wow, I hadn't even thought of that."

"One of the joys of being a civil servant."

I was sure there was a story behind that remark, one that I wouldn't like any more than Jake did. But this wasn't the time, and I made a mental note to ask him about it later.

"Karen said there isn't anything we can do today, not until after the bail hearing and the arraignment. Apparently this guy isn't letting any grass grow under his feet. Karen's gone to the courthouse to report on whatever he does.

"She'll call when she knows anything."

The phone rang and I grabbed it, expecting to hear Karen's outraged report on the latest machinations of Assistant DA Morris.

Instead I got Peter.

"Are you okay, Glory?" he asked as soon as I said hello.

"Yes. Why wouldn't I be?"

"Mother just called me," he said. "She wanted to know if I had talked to you, if you were all right."

Peter's mother, Melissa, was a prune-faced gossip who delighted in borrowing trouble. Aunt Missy—it rhymed with prissy for a reason—took every snippet of bad news she heard and made it her mission to share it far and wide. I had no idea what her latest rumor was, and I certainly wasn't in the mood to be patient with Peter's ill-concealed glee at my potential misfortune.

"I can't imagine why she thought I wouldn't be," I snapped.

"She heard about the murders, Glory. There were two men killed right there in your county, and she was worried that you might know them." His tone grew increasingly patronizing as he went on, "You know, you do have something of a reputation for getting yourself into trouble, Gloryanna. You've had several run-ins with the law, and Mother says you've had your name in the paper far more than any lady ought."

"Peter," I lowered my voice and spoke slowly, a tactic that usually stopped him. "I am fine. Those two people were found miles away from me, practically across the border into Alabama. They were probably closer to you than they were to me."

"Maybe so, but I haven't been in trouble with the law, now have I?"

"Peter," I growled.

This time he didn't catch the warning in my voice, and he plowed ahead. "You have to realize we worry about you, Glory. You're down there all alone, without any advice from your family, and we worry about you."

Under normal circumstances, this was the point at which I would start counting to ten. But I had barely gotten to one when Peter made the worst mistake of his life.

"I know you need my help with the store, and I'm sorry that I can't just leave my job and come down and help you, but—"

"Shut up!"

"What?" Peter's indignant shout answered my angry one.

"Just shut up, Peter. Right this very minute.

"Stop talking and listen to me. Very carefully, because I am only going to say this once, and if you ever bring it up again—ever!—I will never speak to you for as long as I live."

I waited for an instant of stunned silence and then continued. "Are you listening?"

"Yes, but—" The whining had started.

"No buts. Just listen.

"You have one chance, right now, to apologize for your attitude. I run this place, I work hard, and I do a good job. Your insistence on offering me advice will stop, as of now, because I am going to buy your interest in the store.

"You have always complained that your 'investment' in Southern Treasures doesn't provide an adequate return." I stopped short of reminding him that he hadn't *invested* a penny in Southern Treasures; he'd inherited it, just as I had. The difference was I'd spent years working in the store.

"Well, this is your chance to take that 'investment' and put it somewhere you think is better." I wanted to tell him where he could put his investment, but I resisted. There were some limits on my anger. "Put it someplace where you can make the kind of return you think you deserve."

"You can't do that!"

"Oh, yes I can. I will. You *will* sell to me, Peter."

"No," he said scornfully, defiance replacing the whine. "You can't buy me out because you can't possibly have enough to pay me what my share is worth."

I thought about the money I'd been saving, and the fund Jake had put aside to help me make Southern Treasures all mine.

Sly's check was still in the safe, and I no longer had any dilemma about its ownership. It was mine, and I was going to use it to do the one thing I wanted most in the world.

"Peter," my voice didn't waver, though my insides were shaking like a bowl of jelly, "I recently had the bank assess the value of Southern Treasures, and I know *exactly* what your share is worth. To the penny. I'll be glad to send you the report they gave me, along with a cashier's check for forty-five percent of the total on that report.

"In return, I want full ownership of Southern Treasures."

Peter began to sputter incoherently.

"Take it or leave it," I said coldly. "But the longer you make me wait, the lower my offer will go. My banker tells me that all those years of below-market wages should make my value much higher than the fifty-five percent I inherited. The longer I have to think about this, the more I think I just might have to take his advice.

"Call me back when you decide."

My hands were shaking so badly I couldn't hang up the phone. Jake took it from me and placed it back in its cradle, then helped me into the tall chair behind the counter as my legs threatened to give way and topple me to the ground.

"Bravo!" From across the shop, Uncle Louis's voice shouted his approval, whistling and flapping his wings. "Bravo!"

I looked up at Jake as the reality of what I'd said hit me.

"What have I done?"

CHAPTER THIRTY-FOUR

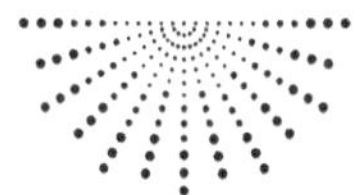

"Exactly the right thing," Jake said. "Bluebeard thinks so too, don't you, old man?"

The parrot had left his perch and made his way across the shop to sit on the counter in front of me. "Absolutely."

"Thanks," I said, addressing both of them. "I think I scared him a little. I know I scared me."

"Heck, you scared me," Jake said with a laugh. "Remind me not to ever make you mad."

"I've put up with so much from him, I just couldn't take any more. Especially when he told me I couldn't possibly have the money to buy him out."

"But that wasn't what started this, was it?"

"No. What started it was him telling me I needed his help with the store. He has never understood what goes on here, and he's made no effort to actually learn. I just had to get him out of here. I'll deal with the fallout later."

Jake offered to stay a while longer, but I shooed him out and sent him back to take care of his own business. I did promise to call him if I heard any news.

Eventually Karen called. As she'd predicted, the assistant DA had argued against bail, and the judge agreed. Beth and Everett were in jail for the foreseeable future.

"They didn't even have a lawyer," Karen told me. "Oh, some young public defender showed up about halfway through, but he didn't even know what the charges were, much less anything about his supposed clients.

"It was all just for show."

We agreed to meet the following morning and try to see Beth at the jail, in the hope there would be something we could do. I didn't realize I hadn't told her about Peter until after I hung up. No matter, it could wait.

When I finally closed up for the night, I was feeling restless. I hadn't been home much in the last few days, and I'd been looking forward to an evening alone, but I wasn't ready to settle down quite yet.

I needed to move. I grabbed a jacket, stuck my wallet, phone, and keys in the pockets, and picked up a bag full of reusable grocery sacks. A walk to Frank's Foods and back would take care of my restlessness and alleviate the problem of my empty refrigerator.

One of the downsides of having Jake cover my Thursday dinner was the lack of leftovers. Usually I could count on enough food to carry me through the weekend after one of my Thursday nights. But this time the food was in Jake's freezer, not mine.

It was only a few blocks to Frank's, just far enough to work some of the tension out of my back and shoulders. I was feeling more relaxed by the time I reached the market, glad I'd decided to walk instead of drive. I might not be able to carry as many groceries, but that wasn't even the point.

I wandered through the store, trying to decide what I wanted for dinner. It was just me tonight and I wanted comfort food, something warm and familiar.

I went for an old favorite: canned chicken noodle soup and grilled cheese sandwiches. I needed a couple cans of soup, a package of cheese slices, and a loaf of white bread. Nothing fancy, tonight's dinner was more about familiarity than fancy.

I wandered through the produce section, selecting fruit and vegetables to share with Bluebeard, careful to limit myself to what I could readily carry home.

After the turmoil of the last few days, it felt good to do something normal, and I made a leisurely circuit of the entire store. I ran into Cheryl, Frank's wife, next to the dairy case as I searched for the proper sandwich cheese.

We talked for a few minutes, catching up on the things normal people talk about. I didn't have to talk about murder or arrests or meddling partners. I didn't have to think about who might hear us, or what tales they might carry back to the sheriff.

Normal.

Frank rang up my groceries and I swiped my debit card and punched in my PIN. We chatted as he filled my shopping bags, arguing lightheartedly about whether tomato or chicken noodle was best to accompany a grilled cheese sandwich.

It was exactly the kind of outing I needed, and when I left the store, I was carrying a couple heavy grocery sacks, but my mood was considerably lighter.

The trip also reminded me why I loved living in a small town. I'd run into friends in the store, stopped for a minute to say hello and exchange pleasantries. There hadn't been a single conversation that was terribly important, but they were all important; every one was a reminder of the connections we all shared.

Bluebeard greeted me with his usual litany of complaints about being gone, but it quickly turned to wheedling when he realized I was carrying grocery bags.

I let him carry on, trying to guess what was in the bags and what might be for him, but I still brought the full bags up the stairs to my apartment. As I put away the groceries and cut up some fresh vegetables for him, I could hear a steady stream of pleading and sweet talk floating up from the shop below.

I finished prepping the produce and took several small containers to the downstairs refrigerator. I could have kept everything upstairs, but I liked the convenience of having Bluebeard's food close at hand.

I gave him his treats, taking time to reassure him I wasn't going out. "I just want a quiet night at home," I told him as I scratched his head. "I want to have dinner, maybe read a book, and turn in early. I don't want to think about any problems, or worry about anyone except you and me."

"No worry," he echoed back. "Don't borrow trouble."

Someone else had said the same thing just a few days ago, and I searched my brain for the memory that hovered just out of reach. I was in a car, north of town, so it had to be Karen or Jake. But trouble had already found me when I was with Karen.

Jake. Jake had said the same thing to me when Beth and Everett weren't home.

"Great advice," I said. "But it didn't work out so great the last time."

I shut down the lights, checked the alarms, and went upstairs to grill a cheese sandwich, heat some soup, and lose myself in a made-up world for a couple hours.

Julie was in early the next morning, and I filled her in on the last few days as we got the store ready to open.

"How's your mom?" I asked.

"Getting better," she said. "Doctor told her they caught it early, and she's responding really well to the medication. She even said she could keep Rose Ann all day today, though I think that might be a bit much for her."

I nodded. "I'm going with Karen first thing this morning, but I should be back before noon. If you need to get home and relieve your mom, it shouldn't be a problem."

"Thanks. More wedding stuff?"

"I wish."

Julie did a double take at my answer. I had made it clear that Karen's constant wedding errands and projects were trying my patience, so if I would rather be doing wedding preparations, something was seriously out of whack.

I quickly explained about Beth and Everett, and the turmoil that I'd been drawn into. I was just finishing up when Karen arrived.

"I have something to tell you both," I announced and waited until I had their full attention.

They looked at me expectantly.

"I had a call from Peter yesterday," I went on, my voice squeaking with the remembered tension of the phone call.

"Spit it out, Martine," Karen commanded. "We haven't got all day."

I swallowed hard and concentrated on speaking calmly. "I told him I was buying him out, that I wanted full ownership of Southern Treasures."

"Sure did!" Bluebeard chimed in from across the room. "Told him good!"

Julie glanced over at Bluebeard. "I swear, that bird has a bigger vocabulary than some people I know." She turned back to me. "What did he say?"

"He didn't take it well. He said a lot of things, but the worst was that I couldn't have enough money to buy him out." I felt my anger rising again, just thinking about how smug he'd been. "Like he knows anything about my finances! He might spend every penny he makes, but I've been saving for a long time, and I do have enough."

Julie had taken a half step back, and Karen was holding out her hand, her palm toward me. "Down, girl!" she said. "I just hope you gave him a dose of that."

"Oh, I did. Believe me, I really did. And I told him the longer he waited to accept my terms, the worse they would get for him."

"Good for you!" Karen beamed her approval, then glanced at the clock and back at me. "We better get going," she said. "Boomer agreed we could have a few minutes with Beth, but I got the distinct impression that he didn't think the ADA would look too kindly on our visit.

"We need to get over there before Morris gets wind of it and tries to keep us out."

CHAPTER THIRTY-FIVE

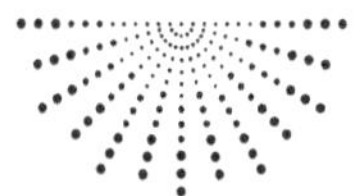

At the sheriff's station, Deputy Fuentes, a solid woman with dark eyes and slicked back black hair, checked our IDs and then led us into the back. She ran a wand over both of us. "Standard procedure," she explained, and locked Karen's bag and my purse in a secure bin and handed us the key to claim our property on our way out.

She showed us to a small room with two narrow, barred windows and a sturdy table bolted to the floor. Two chairs sat on each side of the table, with a large mirror behind one set of chairs. I was sure the mirror was placed to allow someone in an adjoining space to observe the room, but there wasn't much we could do if Boomer had decided to eavesdrop on our conversation with Beth.

"Sheriff Hardy is out this morning," Deputy Fuentes said, "but he left instructions that you were to be allowed ten minutes with the prisoner. No more. I'll bring Mrs. Young in and lock the door." She showed us a button on the underside of the table. "If you need help, just push that and an alarm will sound. Otherwise, if you want anything before I come back for you, use the call box by the door."

She had said this was all the usual process for visits, and for the first time I really understood that Beth was in jail charged with a crime, and being treated like an accused criminal instead of an innocent bystander.

"Do you understand everything I told you?" Fuentes asked before opening the door.

Karen and I both nodded.

"Good," she said. She opened the door and went out. It closed behind her with a solid *thunk* as the latch clicked into place.

I have never been claustrophobic, but when that door shut with the sound that made it very clear we were locked in, I had to battle a momentary feeling of panic.

For one brief moment I felt as though I was the prisoner and I might never get back out.

I looked at Karen and it was obvious she had the same reaction. "It's creepy, being locked in here," she said, as if talking about her fears would make them less powerful.

I just nodded, not trusting my tightened throat to speak.

A minute later the door opened and Beth Young came in. She wore a shapeless gray jumpsuit and slip-on plastic sandals. The jumpsuit was that marvel of modern clothing, one size fits all. Just not very well. I supposed her undergarments would be the same poor fit, but after another glance, I was pretty sure they simply didn't exist.

That was the first thing on my checklist then. Some clothes that fit, maybe even some of her own, if it could be arranged.

We said our wary hellos and took seats at the table, Karen and I on one side facing the mirror, and Beth with her back to it. Judging by the way she studiously ignored the mirror, I could guess that she'd been through this once already and been forced to sit on our side of the table.

Karen fiddled with her tablet. Fuentes had checked it over thoroughly and allowed her to keep the device instead of a pen or pencil. There was no outside connection available, but she could use it for notes.

Beth didn't look happy to see us.

"Are you okay?" I asked. It was a stupid question. The woman was in jail and her husband was charged with murder. How could she be okay?

"I've been better."

I fumbled for the right words, finally settling for the simplest. "Beth, I am really sorry. I had no idea Boomer would do this, or I wouldn't have been so eager to get you back here. I really thought you would answer a few questions and he'd send you home. I never imagined this would happen."

I didn't think she was going to accept my apology, and I could see that she didn't think she would, either. But I hadn't reckoned with Karen's power of persuasion.

"Beth, we all got taken in by this. I won't say they lied to us"—I noticed that she didn't specify *who* lied—"but we were certainly misled.

"I don't expect you to necessarily believe that; I certainly wouldn't if I was in your position. I don't really expect you to trust us, either. But I hope you will let us help you if we can."

She tapped the pad and started typing. "I'm going to make a list of what you need so we can try to figure out what needs doing first, okay?"

Beth nodded, still skeptical, but at least she was listening.

"First off, did you get a lawyer?"

Beth shrugged. "There was a public defender at the hearing thingie yesterday."

"I was there. I saw him," she said. Her tone left no doubt of her opinion of his legal skills. "They assigned you some kid who just got out of law school and has probably never tried a case, much less a serious felony.

"No, what I meant was, have you been able to find a *good* attorney?"

Beth shook her head. "We don't know any lawyers down here. Haven't had any need of one. And even if we knew a good one, we couldn't afford him anyway."

"Doesn't matter," Karen said firmly. "You'll get a public defender, but they have to provide you adequate counsel, which that bozo certainly is not.

"I know a couple people," she went on. "I'm sure they can see to it that you get someone qualified to represent you."

Beth didn't look convinced, but I knew better. Karen wasn't the type to tell you she "knew people" just to impress you. It wasn't her style.

But she did have contacts. Not always the top dog, but always someone with knowledge and influence, the kind of person who sometimes found it useful to let information "leak" to the press. She was honest and she was discreet. It made her friends in high places.

"I'm not promising you any special favors or preferential treatment," she went on, choosing her words carefully for the benefit of whoever might be watching. "I'm just saying some of my friends will be interested in making sure you have a proper defense; that no one cuts any corners or stacks the deck.

"This is a serious case, and they're going to take it very seriously."

"Is there anything you need in here?" I asked. "If we brought you some of your own clothes, something that fit, do you think Boomer would let you have them?"

"I don't know," Beth said. "He did tell me that he didn't have any women's sizes, I had to take the smallest men's size he had. It's a bit large."

That was an understatement. The baggy garment hung off her and the pant legs were rolled up several times to keep them from dragging along the ground.

"I can bring you some jeans and a couple T-shirts," I said. "I think you're a bit smaller than me, but they should be a better fit than that jumpsuit."

"A hairbrush," she said quietly, running her fingers through her long, straight hair. "All they have here are flimsy plastic combs. And a clip, or some rubber bands, something to tie it back a little."

"Okay," Karen typed her instructions. "We can get that here, unless you'd rather we went up to the cabin and brought you your own things."

"No," she said. Her voice changed from hesitant to authoritative. "That's such a long way to go."

"What about the cabin?" I asked. "Is there someone to take care of things while you're gone?"

"Don't worry about that," she said firmly. "Really. I know you're trying to help, but there just isn't that much that needs doing. I've already called Granny, and she said she'll take care of things."

She rose from her chair, and it was clear our visit was at an end. "I think I'll go back now," she said. "Could you call Deputy Fuentes, please?"

We were back in the car with our reclaimed property when Karen spotted a sharply dressed man parking in one of the reserved spaces at the front of the lot.

She slid down in her seat and turned away from him. "Is he going into the building?" she asked me.

I turned my head, but she snapped at me, "Don't look at him, just tell me if he pays any attention to us."

"And how do I do that without looking at him?" I asked. I kept facing forward, straining my eyes to the side to see if I could follow his movements.

"He's going in," I said, relaxing my neck a little as the man turned his back to us. All I could see was an expensive suit, a BMW with custom plates, and the back of a haircut he definitely didn't get in Keyhole Bay.

In Keyhole Bay, you went to the barbershop that had been in the same spot with the same barber since the '70s, or you went to the beauty school in what used to be the five-and-dime. A haircut like that came from a much bigger city with pricey salons.

"Is that Morris?" I asked.

"I think so," Karen said. "I didn't get a good look, but I didn't want him to see me."

"You two have a history?" Karen had friends in high places that could prove valuable, but she also had friends in low places, and that sometimes brought her into conflict with the authorities.

"Not yet." She started the car and backed out, pulling slowly past the Beemer on her way out of the lot. "That's his car, all right. Look at the license plate."

I read the letters aloud. "M-O-R-L-A-W. Charming. He certainly doesn't have any problem telling you who he is."

"Or what he stands for," Karen said, pulling into the light Saturday morning traffic. "Except he doesn't stand for much, of course."

"But you said he was using this case to go after his boss's job; doesn't that mean he's one of those 'tough on crime' guys?"

"Not necessarily. I did a little research on ADA Morris, talked to a couple people who have lots of business in the courthouse." By which she meant local bail bondsmen, though she'd never say so publicly. "He's new to the area—"

"I wondered," I cut in. "I didn't recognize the name."

"No, he moved here a couple years ago from down near Orlando. Politically very ambitious, and the field down there was crowded, so he grabbed at the chance to be a big fish in a small pond, and maybe snatch a few headlines in the process. Wanted to raise his profile for a run at something bigger.

"Word is he's being groomed for a Senate run at some point, and this will look good on the CV."

"CV?" It wasn't a term I was familiar with.

"Curriculum vitae. It's kind of like a specialized résumé, with lots of additional information. But lately it seems like the politicians are using the term, incorrectly I might add, to make themselves sound more important."

"So this is a guy from five hundred miles away, trying to make headlines by charging Everett with murder, basically saying he's guilty because he's 'not from around here,'"—I drew in a deep breath—"and he's not even from around here himself?! Is that about the size of it?"

Karen nodded, her mouth in a grim line. "That's about the size of it," she agreed. "The guy's an opportunist. He's part of a big family firm down south that specializes in estates and trusts and real estate investing. No criminal work, unless one of their regular clients gets caught with his hand in the company cookie jar. And no civil work either, except when some millionaire wants to jettison his wife for a newer model."

"And you wonder why people hate lawyers."

"I don't wonder," Karen replied. "I know."

I let it drop. "Have you found out anything from the pictures you took?"

She shook her head. "Zip. I showed them to a few people I know, but nobody recognized either of them. As I said, the quality is so poor that I don't think they'd be any help to Boomer."

"How about the recording?"

"Garbled," she answered. "All that trouble, and we got nothing."

We pulled up in front of the shop and she let me out. "Got time for coffee?" I asked.

"Wish I did. Mother's waiting for me to go shopping with her. She insists I need clothes for the honeymoon, even though I have no idea where I'm going or what I'm doing."

I didn't take the bait. I wasn't about to even give her a hint of Riley's plans. "Just take whatever advice she gives you," I told her. "I'm sure Riley gave her some guidelines."

Karen rolled her eyes. "You know how much I love taking fashion advice from my mother. We're two completely different body types; she hates every-thing I like, and vice versa. And you want me to take her word for what I need to pack?"

I shrugged. "Suit yourself. But I do think she's talked to Riley and will know what kind of things you need."

"It's a vacation," she said. "Jeans. Sneakers. A couple T-shirts and maybe a bathing suit. What's so hard about that?"

I didn't argue. Actually, from what I'd heard so far, she was probably right. But Riley was determined to make this trip special, and I suspected she'd need something a little more fancy than T-shirts and jeans. Either way, I'd leave that fight to her mother.

CHAPTER THIRTY-SIX

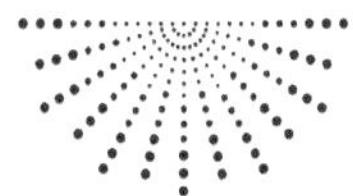

Business was brisk on Sunday, a nice change from the slow days. Several times I had customers lined up at the counter, while Bluebeard did his best to entertain those who were still browsing the aisles.

I noticed two clean-cut men who came in, wandered for a few minutes, and then left without buying anything. Not that that was unusual—I got my fair share of lookie-lous—but these two weren't locals, and they didn't fit any of the usual tourist categories.

There was something about them that drew my attention, perhaps because they seemed intent on not being noticed. I even wondered if they were a couple, but not openly so. I rejected the idea; Felipe had taught me to recognize far more than most people did.

It occurred to me that they might be shoplifters, casing the place to see if it was a worthwhile target, which it wasn't. I kept most of the smaller valuables in the locked case up front, and everything else was either too big or too inexpensive to be worth stealing.

That seemed the most likely explanation, and as soon as I could I made a call that would start the phone chain, alerting other merchants in town in case the duo found someplace that looked more enticing. It might be nothing, but a reminder to be extra vigilant just might save a friend from losing inventory.

When I closed for the night, the register held a nice stack of bills, and I'd rung enough credit card sales to see me through the next week. Combined with the online sales, it made for a good week in spite of all the distractions.

I settled Bluebeard for the night and set the alarm. I felt uneasy as I checked and double-checked the sensors, like someone was watching me. I told myself it was just a reaction to the two strangers and the stress of my visit to Beth. Still, I checked the alarms a third time before heading next door for a six-pack of microbrew.

"Hot date?" Linda teased as she rang up the beer.

"With Sly," I told her. "Which reminds me. I need a couple pieces of beef jerky"—I pointed to the case next to the register. "Low sodium, please. It's for Bobo."

Linda put two pieces of jerky in a small bag and handed them to me. "For Bobo, no charge," she said, and sighed. "I wish we could have a dog, but Guy's right: we're in the store all day and it wouldn't be fair to the dog to be left alone like that."

"You could always bring him in with you."

She shook her head. "Not here. Too many people and no place to hide. At least Bluebeard can get up out of reach of little hands if he needs to."

I took the beer and jerky and cut through the storeroom and out the back to my truck. One of the advantages of being friends with the owners.

It was nearly dark as I drove to Sly's, streetlights winking on as the light drained from the sky, and I saw few other vehicles on the short drive. The empty roads and the deepening twilight made me feel like the last person on earth.

I pulled into Fowler's parking lot and drove around the back to the gate in the chain-link fence. Sly had left the gate open and I pulled through into the junkyard.

I was climbing out of the truck when Bobo bounded out to greet me. After the eerie feeling of emptiness, I welcomed his joyful greeting.

I patted his head and scratched behind his ears, and he rewarded me with a yelp of pure doggy joy. He was too polite to jump up, Sly would never allow that. But he leaned into me and rubbed his head against my leg.

How different from our initial meeting. I had come upon him unexpectedly the first time I ventured into the junkyard. He had appeared out of nowhere, alert for the sound of an intruder. I'd frozen, staring at an immense black dog with a head the size of a basketball. If basketballs had a mouth full of sharp teeth.

Bobo was Sly's early warning system when strangers came in the yard, and he was usually all that was needed to keep out those who didn't belong there.

Fortunately for me, I belonged.

Sly was a few steps behind Bobo. He greeted me with a hug and grinned at the beer in my hand. "You sure know how to make an old man happy," he said, leading the way back to the cinder-block house, hidden among the rows of cars and trucks that filled his yard.

"You're not that old," I chided him as I followed along. I did some quick mental arithmetic, based on the pictures we'd found in the library. "Heck, I'll bet you aren't even seventy yet, are you?"

"Few months away. Like I said, an old man, old enough to be your grandpa."

"That's not that old. And you're barely older than my dad would have been, nowhere near old enough to be my grandpa." It was only a slight exaggeration.

Sly didn't have an answer to that, and I accepted my win with gracious silence.

From the outside, his house looked like a plain block-wall structure, with a few windows and a nondescript, wooden front door. The kind of place you would expect to find a not-so-old bachelor and his dog.

But once inside, the décor of the house was completely unexpected. Wicker and chintz and lots of plants. Every time I came in, I was struck by the contrast between the cozy, comfortable interior and the harsh exterior. Sort of like Sly and Bobo.

A small fire crackled in a Franklin stove and the front room was warm, in spite of the evening chill. A medley of homey aromas drifted in from the kitchen.

I took my usual seat on a wicker settee and Sly lowered himself into the leather recliner that was his favorite spot, with Bobo at his feet.

We had fallen into a routine over the last several months. Every few weeks, Sly would invite me to dinner. Usually we'd eat at his place, unlike out celebration at the Bay House; I'd bring the beer and a treat for Bobo, and we would spend a quiet evening catching up on whatever we were doing. I wasn't exactly checking up on him, but I was the nearest thing to family he had, and I cherished that role.

"Meatloaf and potatoes in the oven," he said. "And succotash simmering. Should be about ten minutes, we'll be ready to eat."

I took the small, plastic bag out of my purse and handed it to Sly. "For Bobo," I said. "I made sure to get low-salt."

Bobo was instantly alert, his sensitive nose picking up the smell of the jerky the moment Sly opened the bag. "You know you only get a little bit." He shredded one piece of jerky into several smaller pieces.

"Sit."

Bobo obeyed instantly, his eyes glued to the bit of dried beef. Sly lowered it to the floor in front of the dog. Bobo remained still, though I could see the effort it took for him to maintain control.

"Okay."

The word was barely out of Sly's mouth before the meat disappeared into the mass of teeth. A second later, Bobo looked up in anticipation of more beefy goodness.

Sly put Bobo through his paces, giving him several small pieces of jerky before sealing up the bag. "That's all you get for now," he said. He patted Bobo's broad back and put the remaining jerky in the drawer of a small side table.

"No sense tempting him by leaving it out. He's a good dog, but even a good dog has his limits.

"Sort of like people." He gave me a look that said he was waiting for me to tell him what was going on.

"What?" I sounded defensive, even to myself.

"Somethin's up with you, girl. You're all tensed up, like you been pushed past your breaking point. So what gives?"

"How can you tell that? I haven't said or done anything since I got here except drink a little beer and watch you give Bobo treats."

"Mostly because you're looking like this is the first time you've relaxed in quite a while. Which means you've got something on your mind. So tell me what it is."

A timer rang in the kitchen, and I was literally saved by the bell. But not for long.

In just a few minutes, we were seated at the kitchen table with our dinners in front of us.

Sly speared a bite of meatloaf and looked up at me before he put it in his mouth. "Now, tell me what's going on."

Some of it was easy, and some he had even heard already. He knew about Beth and Everett being charged, and he had already heard all about Morris. "He may be from down south," Sly said between bites, "but he's still no better than a carpetbagger."

I nodded in agreement, my mouth full. I swallowed and continued my story. I told him about going to the jail, and how adamant Beth had been about our not going up to the cabin. "It wasn't like we were going to snoop," I said. "Okay, well, maybe a little, but only to try and find evidence that would help clear them of these bogus charges."

"And she didn't trust you to do that? Were you really surprised? You were the one who handed her over to the sheriff. I can see where that would make a body a mite unhappy with you."

"But I didn't know he was going to arrest her. I know she didn't do it, and I would swear Boomer knew that, too. I figured if they came back on their own, that would make it easy on everyone involved. Besides, you know how cranky Boomer gets when people don't want to talk to him."

"Yep." The single word implied far more than it said.

I gave him a sharp look. "Have you been talking to Jake?"

"Ain't saying I did, ain't saying I didn't."

"Which means you did.

"I know I should have told Boomer about those men, but he never gave me a chance. He didn't want me around while he was questioning Beth and Everett—didn't even thank me for going up to North County and carrying them back—so I left, and I haven't had a chance to talk to him since."

"Have you tried?"

"I was at the station just yesterday. He wasn't even there." It was a weak argument, but it was all I had.

"And you didn't try very hard to see him."

I shook my head in surrender. "I know I should talk to him, but now that the ADA's already filed, nobody's going to want to hear what I have to say anyway."

Bobo barked at the front door, and Sly excused himself to let the dog out. "Something got him riled," Sly said when he returned. "Likely a possum or a raccoon. He doesn't much care for other critters in his space."

"There was something else I wanted to talk to you about," I said, taking the opportunity to change the subject. "It's that check you gave me."

"Nothing to talk about. It's yours, fair and square. I told you that."

"Yes, you did. But I wasn't sure what to do with it. Seemed to me like maybe it didn't all belong to me, that part of it should go to Uncle Andrew, or to Peter."

"Those two don't have any claim on that money," Sly interrupted. "They got their share years ago."

"Well, I had to make sure of that. Just for my own peace of mind. And I did. I heard from Clifford Wilson on Friday. He told me the terms of Uncle Louis's will, and that anything that would have gone to my mother would come to me."

"Good. So cash the dang thing and do something good with the money. Something you'll enjoy."

"Actually"—I paused, drawing out my announcement—"I already have. I'm doing the one thing I want most in the entire world."

Sly looked impressed. "Good for you! What did you do?"

"Well…" I backpedaled. "I haven't done it yet, but I am working on it.

"I told Peter I'm buying him out. And that check will make a huge difference in paying him off and getting him out of my hair."

Sly grinned so wide, I though his face might split in half. "That is about the best news I have heard in a month of Sundays," he said. "Mr. Louis would be so happy to know you did that."

"Oh, he was." I told Sly about Peter's call, and about Bluebeard's approval. "Jake said I did the right thing, and Bluebeard said 'Absolutely,' so I think he was pretty happy."

Sly got a faraway look on his face. "He was a great man, your Uncle Louis. I never met a more righteous man in my life, aside from my own dad, God rest his soul."

We talked through the rest of dinner, and over the peach tarts Sly had baked for dessert.

"What about Lighthouse, you haven't told me where that deal stands. Have you heard from the bank yet?"

I shook my head. "Buddy told me the loan committee would meet on Friday, but not to expect an answer until after the weekend. He said I had a great business plan and it should go through just fine, but it's hard not to worry."

"Nothing to worry about. I'm glad to help you out if there's any problem." He thought for a minute. "I could probably just make you the loan myself and get more than what the bank's paying on my savings."

I sat back, startled. Sly had offered to guarantee my loan, even offered the yard as collateral. That I understood. But to make the loan himself, he had to have a lot more money put away than I thought.

"I don't need much," he said with a shrug. "My daddy left me this place free and clear, and business been good over the years. I started putting something aside every week.

"It adds up."

I let out a low whistle. "I guess. I appreciate it, Sly. And I'll keep it in mind. But I really have to believe what Buddy said. I won't need it.

"Besides, what would happen if you needed it? If you wanted to take a trip, or buy another car? Or a boat?" Boats were popular around Keyhole Bay, all kinds and sizes.

Sly picked up the plates from the table and stacked them in the sink.

"Don't need none of that. Got me plenty of cars, and if I want to fish, there's a perfectly good pier." He started the water running, his back to me. "As for travelin'," he said in a voice so low I could barely hear him over the rush of the water, "I did plenty of that with Uncle Sam. Now everything I want is right here at home."

Somehow I didn't quite believe that last part. There were things he still wanted, but he'd made peace with not having them. It was an uncomfortable reminder of the pictures I'd seen at the library.

For Sly, peace had come at a cost.

Bobo scratched at the door, wanting in. Sly glanced over at Bobo's usual resting place as though just realizing the dog was still outside.

"He must have found something that purely needed chasing," he said. He opened the door and Bobo came in. His fur was matted, and he had a couple scratches. Clearly he had tangled with something while he was out, though we hadn't heard any sounds of a fight.

Sly grabbed a towel and cleaned him up, though Bobo didn't seem at all concerned with his condition. He endured the cleaning with a nonchalance that clearly said, "You oughta see the other guy."

"What have I told you," Sly said to the dog as he took a tube of ointment out of a drawer and applied it to the scratches, "about fighting above your weight class? What?

"I told you don't do it. I said fight someone your own size. But did you listen? You did not. And who gets to clean you up when you do this? I do."

Sly capped the ointment and patted Bobo's head. "I swear," he said, turning back to me. "That dog would take on a Florida panther if one wandered into the yard."

Considering that there hadn't been a panther sighting in the Panhandle in my lifetime, I didn't think it was something to worry about.

There was still plenty of wildlife that was common, though, and he'd obviously encountered something.

CHAPTER THIRTY-SEVEN

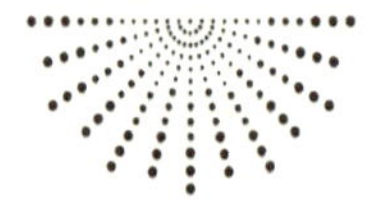

I was still thinking about what might be out in the yard when Sly walked me to my truck a little while later. Bobo had tried to follow me out, but Sly ordered him to stay and closed the door behind us. "No sense letting him run off and find something else to mess with tonight."

I could imagine unseen eyes watching us in the dark, tracking our progress by the beam of Sly's flashlight and the perimeter lights.

I thanked Sly for dinner and clambered quickly into the cab of the truck. "I'll lock the gate," I offered, but Sly turned me down.

"I'd just have to come out and check it later," he said. "Can't sleep unless I make sure everything's closed up proper."

I drove out through the gate in the chain-link, secretly relieved that I didn't have to get back out of the truck in the dark. It was silly, but after Bobo's encounter, it felt as though the night was full of eyes, all watching me.

The feeling intensified on the drive home, finally spooking me to the point that I parked under the streetlight in front of the store instead of pulling around to my usual spot in the back.

I could move the truck in the morning. In the daylight.

Bluebeard woke up the instant I put the key in the front door. "Who's there?" he called loudly. "Who's there?"

"It's just me, Bluebeard," I answered. I locked the door and reset the alarm. "I'm home."

I understood his agitation. Changes in routine distressed him, and normally when I went out at night, I would park in back and come in through the warehouse door. The only time I used the front door was when someone else dropped me off.

"Don't do that," he said.

I didn't bother to ask him to explain; he never did. Instead I murmured something noncommittal that he could take as agreement if he wanted to, and went about my business.

I wasn't ready to settle down, and I thought I would do a little work downstairs.

The minute I turned on the overhead light, however, I felt exposed. The large front windows afforded anyone passing by a view of the store and a view of me. Combined with the eerie sensation that someone was watching me, I quickly became too uncomfortable to stay in the store.

That, too, would have to wait for daylight.

By morning my fears seemed as foolish as they had seemed real the night before. Jake came by early, with lattes from Lighthouse Coffee and a biscuit for Bluebeard.

"How was your dinner with Sly?"

I accepted the coffee gratefully. "Good." I sipped the sweet drink and felt the warmth slide down my throat. "You know, I'm going to lose a steady customer once I buy this place"—I gestured with the cup. "I won't be able to have you buy me coffee anymore."

I took another sip. "Which will be soon, I hope."

Jake grinned. "Well then, enjoy it while you can."

"You know, Sly did say something that caught me by surprise. He told me he could loan me the money to buy Lighthouse, and he'd make more off the loan than the bank was paying him."

Jake whistled, impressed. Whether by the offer itself or by the amount of money involved, I wasn't sure.

"He said he'd inherited his place free and clear, and when I suggested he might want to spend some on himself, maybe even travel, he said he already had everything he wanted right here."

"I know how he feels," Jake said.

"Really?" I was headed into dangerous territory, but caution wasn't on my agenda lately.

Jake nodded and counted off on his fingers: "A job I love, a great volunteer unit to belong to, a comfortable house, wonderful friends, amazing weather all year…" He paused as though trying to remember what else. "Oh, yeah! And you."

It made me laugh. I gave him a hug, happy that he had included me in the list of everything he wanted.

"But that's why I don't believe him completely," I explained. "He says he has everything he wants, but he's all alone. And don't tell me he has Bobo. It's not the same thing."

Jake was quiet for a minute, thinking. When he spoke again, his voice was low and I had to strain to hear him.

"You resign yourself to certain things, and you learn to be okay with them. Over time, okay becomes content, and eventually you are almost happy. And you tell yourself your life is just fine.

"And that works until you meet somebody that changes everything." He leaned down and kissed me lightly.

"Hey, break it up!" Bluebeard's squawk interrupted the moment, and we both jumped.

"Yes, sir!" Jake snapped, tossing a salute in the direction of Bluebeard's perch. "At once, sir!"

Bluebeard cackled, the high-pitched laugh that imitated Rose Ann's toddler giggle, and preened, reminding us that here at least it was all about the parrot.

Jake said he needed to get back to work, and I walked out with him to move the truck around to the back.

"I wondered what this was doing at the curb," Jake said as I unlocked the door.

"I got spooked last night. It was dark and the street was deserted. I didn't want to park around back in the dark, so I left it out front. But I need to move it before the parking patrol comes around."

When the highway is also the main drag, parking is sometimes at a premium. As a result, the Merchants' Association funded a year-round position for a parking enforcement officer.

We didn't call her a meter maid—for one thing, we didn't have any parking meters in Keyhole Bay, and she took her job seriously. Very. Seriously. Enforcement would start in half an hour. If the truck was still in front an hour after that, there would be a warning, complete with instructions to the municipal lot a block off Main Street; and in another hour, I'd find a pricey parking ticket on the windshield.

"Maybe we should think about putting a high-intensity floodlight on your parking area," Jake suggested. "With a motion sensor, you wouldn't have to leave it on all night."

"Good idea," I said. "There's one on the back of Lighthouse since Pansy comes in so early." I stopped and corrected myself. "Chloe comes in so early." I shook my head. "That's gonna take some getting used to."

"I'll watch the door until you get back," Jake said. He stood on the sidewalk, sipping his latte while I drove around the block, parked the truck in my spot at the back, and came back through the warehouse to the front of the shop.

I waved through the window and he waved back, glanced up and down the quiet street, and crossed back over to Beach Books.

Just another autumn Monday in Keyhole Bay.

I normally wasn't much of one for watching the clock, but nothing was normal for me right now.

I didn't know what was going on with Beth, hadn't heard anything from her since our visit on Saturday, even though Karen had dropped off a small bundle of clothes at the jail on Sunday afternoon.

The bank was supposed to call today, but I had no idea when.

And then there was the question of Peter. He could go in any direction, from complete cooperation to complete obstruction, and I honestly couldn't guess what he might do.

I got my answer shortly after lunchtime, when Peter's phone number showed up on my caller ID.

I wasn't sure I wanted to talk to him, but I knew we were going to have to resolve the issue. And as much as I might not want to talk to him, I wanted this settled more.

"Southern Treasures, how may I help you?"

"You can stop acting like you don't know who this is." Peter's superior tone instantly raised my hackles, but I waited him out, and he finally continued. "I really don't think there's anything you can do to help me."

I literally bit my tongue, holding it gently between my teeth, to avoid telling him I knew he was beyond help. I realized that was quite the opposite of what he meant, but it didn't stop me from putting my own spin on his gibe.

"But there is something I can do for you." He sounded a little deflated, as though he was trying to goad me into an argument and I was refusing to play. "I've been thinking about our last conversation, and I think it's time I pulled my investment out of Southern Treasures and put it somewhere more lucrative. Put it into something that will provide an adequate return for my family.

"I'm sure you'll understand that, won't you?"

I understood all right. I understood that Peter was taking what I'd said, taking my demands that he sell me his share of the business, and acting as though it was all his idea.

My brain said *I understand you are once again dismissing my concerns as though they are of no value.* But what my mouth said was, "Of course. I'll have my attorney draw up a contract for the sale. At fair market value, of course, with a consideration for my services over the last three years.

"I'm sure you'll understand."

The yelp at the other end of the line told me Peter understood exactly what I'd just said. I allowed myself a moment of "gotcha" before I explained. "He tells me I've been undervalued about twenty thousand dollars a year for several years. But that seems like such a huge amount, how about we say five thousand a year for the last three?"

It was all an elaborate bluff. Buddy had advised me that my proposed salary in my business plan, consistent with my current earnings, was well below the market and I should be drawing a much larger salary. I'd used that information as leverage in my battle with Peter.

And it worked.

"Fine," he snapped. "Market value, less fifteen grand. But I want a copy of that appraisal. My financial advisor will need it to plan for the tax consequences of the sale."

My brain said *I'm not impressed,* but my mouth agreed to send a copy of the appraisal.

I ended the conversation and hung up the phone before my brain took control of my mouth and said several things that would probably kill the whole deal.

I reminded myself that I really didn't care all that much what Peter said or thought, as long as he sold.

Bottom line? That was all I needed.

Southern Treasures was all mine. And I had a long list of things that I had to do immediately.

But first I had to tell Uncle Louis.

Bluebeard had been napping in his cage when the phone rang and hadn't bothered to come check on my conversation. But when I called his name, he hopped out, looking around for the cause of the commotion.

"We did it! Peter's selling!"

Bluebeard leaped from his perch and flew to the top of the ceiling, moving around the hanging fluorescent fixtures. There really wasn't room for him to fly inside the shop, and his movements were ungainly, but there was no other way for him to express his excitement. He shrieked and squawked as he dodged obstacles in his flight path, finally coming to rest on the counter where he did a little hoppity dance, bobbing his head and spreading his wings.

I gave him some pets, then put a couple almonds and a pecan in his cage as a treat. He hopped across the racks and into the cage, happily settling down to the challenge of opening the nuts for the tasty treat inside.

It was his favorite way to celebrate.

I e-mailed Clifford Wilson and asked him to draw up another sales contract, this one for my purchase of Peter's interest in the business. I outlined the terms, including the fifteen thousand as consideration for my work in the shop, and asked him to let me know as soon as the papers were available. I wanted to move as quickly as possible, before Peter changed his mind.

I also e-mailed Peter a confirmation of our conversation and reiterated the terms we had agreed on. I might have even implied that I had a recording of the phone call, though that was certainly subject to interpretation.

I called Karen, but only got her voice mail. I glanced at the clock and confirmed my suspicion—it was time for her regular news broadcast. I left a message, telling her Peter had agreed to sell, and to call me when she had time.

There were other people I needed to call, and many more details to tend to, but one person deserved to know more than anyone. I locked the door behind me and dashed across the empty street to Beach Books.

Jake looked up as I burst in the door, caught sight of the giant grin on my face, and ran over to give me a hug.

"They approved your loan!"

I hugged him back, then disentangled myself and stepped back. "Even better!"

Jake looked puzzled. "What could be better than that? Did you win the lottery?"

I laughed out loud. "It feels that way."

"So, what? Come on, you've got me dying of curiosity."

"Peter just called. He agreed to sell me his share of Southern Treasures. And I got him to agree to a fifteen thousand dollar kicker to make up for all the years I've worked."

Jake's eyebrows shot up and he gave me another hug. "Fifteen grand? You actually got him to go for that? Man, you are good!

"We need to celebrate!"

"Wish I could, but I'm still waiting on word from the bank. But I had to tell you, since you're going to have some of your money in this deal."

"I consider it a sound investment," Jake said, his voice shifting from jubilant to serious. "You'll make it worth my while to invest in Southern Treasures."

"And you won't try to tell me how to run my business," I reminded him.

"No way. I've seen what happens when a man tries that."

"Just remember that," I teased as I headed for the door. I waved as I walked out. "I'll talk to you a little later."

I went back to the shop, intending to make a few more calls. I certainly wanted to tell Sly, and Guy and Linda. Julie would need to know as well.

But before I could pick up the phone, an older woman came in and marched up to the counter.

"Are you Gloryanna?" she asked. Her direct approach marked her as a Yankee as surely as her flat Midwestern accent.

"Yeeees," I drew the word out, tentative.

"I need to talk to you." She stuck out her hand. "I'm Althea Stevenson, Beth's granny."

CHAPTER THIRTY-EIGHT

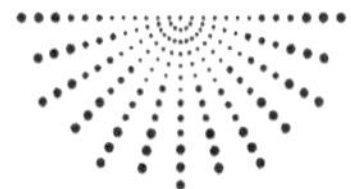

"Gloryanna Martine. I'm glad to meet you," I said, shaking her hand. The skin on the back of her hand was loose, as though it was too big for the tiny bones underneath, but her grip was as firm as her voice. She might be a small woman, but she had enough grit for a linebacker.

I liked her immediately.

"What can I do for you, Mrs. Stevenson?"

"For starters, you can explain to me what kind of trouble that granddaughter of mine and the fool she married have gotten themselves into. And how we're going to get them out of it."

I started to protest that I barely knew Beth and Everett, but she continued talking a mile a minute. "No question whether he did it or not. Boy couldn't hurt a fly. I mean *really* couldn't hurt a fly. I've seen him carry one outside and let it go instead of swatting it like he ought to. The only way he could kill someone is to talk them to death."

I'd never thought of Everett as much of a talker, and my skepticism must have shown on my face.

"I know, I know. Normally the boy won't say *boo*. But every once in a while, he decides something is real important, and then he won't shut up about it. Talk 'til you think you're going to die of boredom."

"He is charged with murder," I said.

"Charged isn't convicted," she said. "And I'm telling you, I know he couldn't do it."

"You know it. I know it. But there's an assistant district attorney that says he did."

I saw Bluebeard peek out of his cage, then retreat back inside, like a turtle pulling into his shell. Sometimes he preferred the role of an unseen observer.

"Then he's a fool, or a liar," Mrs. Stevenson shot back. "Or both. If he's a politician, I'd say both."

I couldn't argue with the truth.

"So this fool charges Everett with murder, based on what? The fact that the two guys were found near his house? He wasn't even home. He and Bethie were at my house."

"Where is your house? I don't think Beth ever said."

"Dearborn. Outside Detroit. It's almost a thousand miles." She winced and her tough exterior cracked for a minute. "And right now I am feeling every one of them."

I excused myself and ducked into the back to get the coffeepot and a couple mugs. "You look like you could use a cup of coffee," I said, offering her a mug.

"That I could. It was a long trip." She took the mug and held it out for me to fill. "Black's fine," she said, anticipating my next question.

"You fly?" I asked. I poured myself a mug and took a sip.

"Drove. Didn't have time to mess with schedules and rental cars and all the rest. Beth and I tossed our bags in the car and drove all night."

"Beth?"

"Sorry." She gulped coffee. "My sister-in-law. My granddaughter was named for her. Never had any kids of her own, so my Meg named her youngest after her favorite aunt."

She drained the mug and set it on the counter. "So what do we do?" she asked.

I told her there wasn't much we could do. Karen was already working her magic where the public defender was concerned, and once they had a competent lawyer, he could petition for another bail hearing.

"About the best thing would be to find out who really did it. But that's not really a job for amateurs," I said, conveniently failing to mention that I'd been involved in several investigations that were solved by an amateur, namely me.

I wondered if my history had anything to do with Mrs. Stevenson's visit. "Why did you come to me, anyway?"

"Because Bethie said you wanted to help. You were the only person she knew down here, and she said you'd been kind to her.

"Thanks, by the way, for the clothes. She told me she hadn't even realized how much that jumpsuit depressed her until she was able to take it off. We'll replace everything, of course."

"No need. I have a whole wardrobe of jeans and T-shirts, so plenty to spare." I remembered how defeated the baggy jumpsuit had made Beth look. "She just looked like she could use some regular clothes. So you're welcome."

It struck me that she'd come in alone, but she'd said her sister-in-law had driven down with her. "Where is the other Beth?" I asked. "Isn't she with you?"

"She's back at the motel. She did a lot more of the driving, so I told her I'd come see you and let her get a little nap before we went back to see Bethie.

"She used to live around here when she was a kid, and I think she's a little overwhelmed. Lots of things she recognized, but lots that's changed, too."

She snapped her fingers. "One other thing Bethie asked me to tell you. That quilt of yours is still at the cabin, far as she knows, but even if she could get it, the sheriff wouldn't let her have the tools she would need to finish it off.

"Beth and I are both pretty fair quilters, that's where Bethie learned it, so we'll go get it and finish it up in time for your friend's wedding."

It was a generous offer, considering how much this woman had on her plate already. "I would appreciate that," I told her. "But I know that you have a lot of important things demanding your attention right now, and I would understand if you can't get it done."

She huffed impatiently. "It needs to be done. We'll do it. It's how it has to be.

"Now I need to be going. Lots to do." She tapped the mug. "Thanks for the coffee. I'll be in touch."

She was gone as abruptly as she had appeared.

The final piece of my Monday fell into place shortly before closing time.

Buddy McKenna called me. We exchanged greetings, but for once I did away with the required pleasantries. It was apparently my day for blunt conversations.

"I have news," Buddy said.

I lowered myself into the tall chair behind the counter. I didn't trust my legs to hold me up.

"Go on."

"You're approved. Your application sailed through the loan committee, one of the easiest I've ever seen, and we got confirmation on all the reports this afternoon.

"It will take a couple days to fund and there will be some papers to sign, but the money is yours.

"Congratulations, Gloryanna. You just bought a coffee shop."

I thanked him and managed to hang up the phone before I got the shakes. Between Peter and Buddy, this was one of the most dramatic days of my life.

I picked up the phone again and dialed Jake's number.

When he answered, I said, "*Now* we can celebrate."

"I'll be right there."

"No," I said. "Meet me at Lighthouse. I can't wait to tell Chloe. And Bradley."

CHAPTER THIRTY-NINE

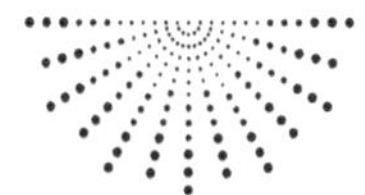

"We got us a coffee shop," I told Bluebeard before I left. "I have to go tell Chloe I'm her new boss!"

Next door I found Jake, waiting for me on the sidewalk. He looked like he was about to burst. "I didn't dare go in," he said, reaching for the door. "This is your news to share, and I would have totally blown it."

I laughed, giddy with the excitement of the day.

Once inside, I struggled to maintain my composure as Chloe waited on a couple stragglers, picking up bread and dessert at the end of the day.

I managed to tamp down my excitement until we were alone, but then I couldn't contain myself any longer. "I got it!" I hollered to Chloe. "I got the loan!"

Chloe rushed around the counter and grabbed me in a congratulatory bear hug, then just as quickly she released me and stepped back in confusion.

"I totally want to congratulate you, and you know I'm kind of a huggy person, but now that you're my boss, I think that's totally inappropriate, isn't it?" She struggled with the thought for a few seconds, then leaped forward and hugged me again. "But just this once," she said, nearly squeezing the breath out of me. "I can't help myself."

Bradley Whittaker came out from the bakery, a puzzled look on his face. "What's all the commotion?"

Chloe released me and turned to Bradley. "Glory got the loan, and she'd going to buy Lighthouse."

Bradley's smile was a mix of relief and regret. "That's good," he said. He offered me his hand. "Congratulations, Miss Glory. I know Mother will be happy, too."

"I hope so," I said. I shook his hand with both of mine, glad we had reached this point so quickly. "It will be a couple days for the funds to come through at the bank, but we can sign the final offer and acceptance any time, and you'll have your money by the end of the week."

We made a date for Wednesday afternoon. I offered to come to the house, but Bradley said his mom wanted to come back in, to say good-bye to the place. It was even possible I would have my money by then.

Chloe promised to keep up as she had been. "We can work out schedules and so on next week," she said. "After the dust settles a bit."

I sighed, a deep breath of relief that dissolved into happy giggles. "And I can finally open that envelope of recipes with a clear conscience."

Bradley looked at me, shocked. "You haven't opened the envelope? Then how?" He stared at Chloe. "How did you?"

She looked sheepish, like a kid caught with her hand in the cookie jar. "You must never, *ever* tell your mother," she said solemnly. "She would be crushed, and I would never hurt her. But I have been coming in early for years to help her with the baking, and I've learned how to make most everything in that time." An anxious frown creased her forehead. "You won't tell her, will you? Promise you won't."

Bradley smiled. "I couldn't. You're right, it would upset her terribly." He raised his right hand, index finger pointed toward himself, and drew an X across his chest. "Cross my heart."

I double-checked our meeting time on Wednesday, and Jake and I went back to Southern Treasures.

"This really does call for a celebration," Jake said. "What would you like to do? Anything you want."

I pretended to think over his offer. "Anything? How about dinner in Paris?"

"Too late," he said. "It's already after midnight there. But we might be able to make it in time for breakfast. Is your passport current?"

I held up my hands in a gesture of surrender. "You got me. Paris is out. I guess I have to think of something else."

Jake waited as I considered my options. There were a couple decent dinner places in town, and Pensacola was only a short drive away. Even the glossy casinos of Biloxi were just a couple hours away.

And I didn't want any of it. Not while Beth and Everett were still in jail. It would feel wrong to celebrate my good fortune when they were stuck behind bars, and I had helped put them there.

"Do you mind if we just stay home?" I asked. "We can call Neil's for a pizza, or get some drive-thru burgers, or I can cook for us, but I want something quiet tonight. Just us."

Jake nodded. "I wouldn't mind at all. But are you sure you don't want to call the rest of the gang over?"

He had good reason to be skeptical. I was usually the one who pulled together impromptu dinner parties and picnics, who organized events for out little group, and who always wanted to include my new friends when I got together with my old friends.

But tonight was different. Tonight, if I admitted the truth, I was afraid. I didn't want a celebration, I wanted comfort and reassurance.

I nodded. "I'm sure." I wasn't sure I could explain why, so I fell back on a reasonable, if less complete, explanation. "I'm just tired. This has been an unbelievable roller coaster the last few days, and I need a break. Besides, there will be plenty of time to celebrate on Thursday night."

I stretched and wiggled my shoulders, feeling some of the tension of the last week fall away. "I'll call people tomorrow. This was supposed to be our early Thanksgiving, and I will truly have a lot to be thankful for."

We climbed the stairs to my apartment and rummaged in the cupboards and refrigerator, coming up with the ingredients for a tuna-noodle casserole.

The creamy, hearty casserole was exactly the kind of comfort food I wanted. We found an old movie on television and settled down on the sofa with our feet propped up and plates on our laps.

Perfect.

Jake insisted on helping with the cleanup when we finished the movie. He scrubbed vigorously at the sticky bits in the baking dish, until I finally stopped him. "Let it soak," I said. "Otherwise you could be here until morning."

"Would that be such a bad idea?" It was a serious question, and he let it linger unanswered for several seconds. "Of course, you might think I was just after you for your money, now that you're the successful owner of two businesses."

"I don't know about successful," I said. I slid a small bowl of leftover casserole into the refrigerator. It could be dinner the next night. "And I only own one-and-a-half businesses. I still have a partner in the other one." I nodded at him, acknowledging his stake in buying out Peter's share of Southern Treasures.

"Not a partner," he said. "An investor. I put my money into a business I think will earn me more money, and I let you run it your way. That's the difference between an investor and a partner, to my way of thinking.

"I give you my money to do what you do best—run a gift shop. In return, you give me back part of the profits. It's the lazy man's way to make money."

I could talk about Jake all day and the word "lazy" would never be spoken. He worked harder than most men I knew, volunteered with the fire department several shifts a week, and helped run occasional disaster preparedness classes.

"So you're saying this isn't going to work for you."

"Of course it works for me. Why wouldn't it?"

"Because"—I waved my hand around the kitchen, now immaculate after Jake's attention—"you are clearly not a lazy man."

"I aspire to be. Isn't that good enough? I would be very happy to sit around reading books and drinking coffee all day."

"No you wouldn't. You barely made it through the movie, and it was less than two hours. When was the last time you sat in one place all day? I bet you can't even remember."

He had a ready answer, actually named a date, and he had an explanation. "You were in the hospital. Again. I spent two days there, most of it in the chair next to your bed."

"Okay," I said, quickly conceding the point. "So you can sit still for longer than an hour. Under duress. But you know that isn't what I meant.

"You're not the sitting-around type. You're a guy who gets up out of his chair and does things. You will never be content to be a lazy man, however you define it."

"So I will just have to keep myself busy with my own work, and keep my nose out of yours. I promise I will not interfere unless you ask me for my help."

"And no unsolicited advice?" I prodded.

"No unsolicited advice.

"We can do this, Glory. I really believe we can do this and still be friends. Because I respect what you have accomplished, and believe in what you will accomplish.

"And because you will always be more important than any amount of moncy."

Now how is a girl supposed to resist a declaration like that?

CHAPTER FORTY

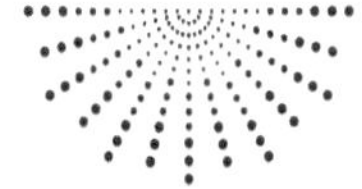

I took advantage of Julie's presence on Tuesday morning to get out of the shop for a little while without feeling guilty.

After coming to an agreement with Peter and getting approval from the bank, there were a ton of details to think about.

I managed to get a few minutes with Clifford Wilson, but only because I sat in his waiting room for forty minutes and snuck in between clients.

Mr. Wilson was his usual gracious self, but I knew he was short on time and I condensed my agreement with Peter to a couple sentences, giving Mr. Wilson a sheet with the figures on it for reference.

"He agreed to those terms," I said when I handed over the paper. "I just need that turned into an iron-clad purchase agreement. I'll have a cashier's check drawn to go with it as soon as you have it ready."

"You have that much in cash?" He cocked his head in a tiny salute. "You're doing better than I expected."

"I had an unexpected windfall, and a friend is investing some cash. Put that together with my savings—and that fifteen thousand dollar bonus—and I have enough."

"That windfall wouldn't have anything to do with the question you asked about Mr. Louis's will, would it?"

"It would. I know you have another client due any minute, so I'm going to get along. I'll tell you the whole story when we have a little more time."

I made my exit, waving at the receptionist on my way through the outer office.

Ten minutes later, I was sitting across the desk from Buddy McKenna, talking about his boys while we waited for the loan documents to finish printing.

"I'm going home in three weeks," he said. "For good. The new, permanent manager should be starting on Thursday, and I'll be showing him around town, introducing him to our business customers. I'll give you a call early next week to set up a time, if that's okay."

"Certainly, though I'll hate to see you go. I was kind of hoping you'd get to stay on, and bring your family to Keyhole Bay with you."

He shook his head. "We have a nice house in a wonderful neighborhood. Most of our family's in the Twin Cities. It's home for us, and eventually I'll move back to a desk job where I get to go home every night instead of one week a month."

"Well, before you go, be sure you stop by the store. Now that you won't be manager here, I'd like to give you those Bluebeard shirts for the kids as a gift."

"Thanks." He glanced over my head and I turned to look. The senior loan officer, a new man brought in during the transition, was headed our way with a stack of papers. Barbara, the bank's on-site notary, was next to him, her book and stamp in her hands.

The ritual of signing loan papers always took longer than anyone would expect. There was something about the act of signing a document promising to repay a staggering amount of money that made time slow down.

I signed my name about a million times, and signed Barbara's book a million more. I wrote slowly, carefully forming each letter, as though I expected to be graded on my penmanship when we were through, all under the watchful eyes of the senior loan officer.

When the signing was done, the loan officer shuffled the papers into several piles and assembled the piles into groups. He placed one set in a large envelope and offered it to me. "These are your copies," he explained unnecessarily. "Keep them in a safe place. I would suggest, if you don't have somewhere secure on your premises, that you talk to Mr. McKenna about a safe deposit box."

"I have a safe," I said. "I think it will be adequate."

"A pleasure to meet you, Miss Martine." He gathered up his remaining papers and rose from his chair. "If there's anything else I can do, please don't hesitate to call."

After he was gone, I turned to Buddy. "Is that it?" I whispered. "Am I through?"

Buddy nodded. "I'll call you as soon as the funds clear," he said. "And I'll see you sometime next week with the new manager."

Pleased with my productive morning, I moved on to the next thing on my list: checking in on Beth. I had sent over clothes and talked with her granny. But I hadn't talked to her directly since that first meeting on Saturday morning.

I'd packed a small bag with a few toiletries and some chocolate for her. Deputy Fuentes took the bag, glanced inside, and made a face. "Mostly we're not supposed to let prisoners have outside supplies," she said. "But since we don't really have provisions for females, I am going to let this pass. If anyone asks, I'll tell them it was just 'woman stuff,' and they'll shut up so fast you'll feel the breeze when their jaw snaps shut."

"How is she?" I asked. "Can she have visitors?"

"Her granny's back there with her, and they're limiting her visitors to family and her lawyer for today, so I'm afraid not. In fact"—she checked the clock on the wall—"her granny's time is almost up. You know, if you want to check on her, you could just wait until Mrs. Stevenson comes out and ask her."

I took her suggestion, but chose to stand rather than sit in those miserable plastic chairs. I would rather do almost anything than sit in those chairs.

Ten minutes passed, then twenty. I went back to the desk and asked Deputy Fuentes how much longer.

"They're in the middle of a conference with the lawyer, so I have to let them have all the time they want. I didn't realize he was in there with them when I told you to wait. I'm really sorry."

"It's okay. I'd appreciate if you let Beth know I came to see her, though. And if you could, tell Mrs. Stevenson to give me a call. I would like to know how it's going."

"After you had to hang around because of my mistake?" Fuentes said. "You got it."

Julie and Chloe were in the shop together when I got back, bent over pages of paper spread across the back counter.

"Hi, boss!" Chloe said. "I came over on my day off so Julie and I could settle some of the stuff for the shower."

"Get everything squared away with Bradley after I left?"

She rolled her eyes at me. "He was totally fine. Said he had wondered how

I'd managed. Thought maybe Miss Pansy made up some mixes for me, or had batters or something stashed in the freezer.

"As if we would ever serve anything that wasn't made fresh from scratch that day! I told him his mother would never have done any such thing, and I wasn't about to change that."

"Has anyone talked to the relief barista?" I asked. "I hardly know the girl, but I expect I'll keep her on. Actually"—I pointed to Chloe—"that will be your decision as manager."

"I did tell her Miss Pansy was selling, and that you'd told me you weren't making any changes. But that was all I said. I just wanted to tell her before the rumors started flying and she heard about it from somebody else."

"Good idea. Just keep me posted on what you decide." I turned back to Julie and the lists. "So what kind of trouble are you two cooking up for me?"

"We talked to Karen and her mom, separately and together. At first Karen said she didn't want a shower, they had everything they needed, most of it two times over. Her mother said the shower was a lovely idea and she should let her friends spoil her a little. They went back and forth for a while, and we just tried to stay out of it.

"Karen finally agreed to a party, but she was insistent on no gifts. We're still trying to come up with something that we can do for her, but we haven't got any ideas we like yet."

"The other thing we haven't settled yet," Chloe said, "is the food. I told Julie I could do most of the food, but we have to decide if we're going with tea and sweets, or cocktails and savory. I'm more a cocktail kind of girl, but I don't know about the rest of you. Or Karen."

"Of the two, I'd say Karen's more cocktail than tea. But not by very much. And a lot depends on who you want to invite. There are a few people around here who won't attend if they know we're serving alcohol."

"And a few that won't show up if we aren't," Julie muttered. Like every small town, Keyhole Bay had its very own problem drinkers, and I suspected at least a couple of those were on their guest list.

"Which is another reason to go with the tea and sweets." I looked from Julie to Chloe and back again. "I think we'd all vote for cocktails and savory finger foods, but I would not be able to relax and enjoy it, knowing the potential for problems." They nodded their understanding. "So we're agreed? Sweet?"

"Yeah."

"You're right."

The replies weren't wildly enthusiastic, but at least we had an agreement.

I left them to their planning and went back to work. It didn't seem to matter how few or how many people came through the store, there was always something out of place, a shelf that needed restocking, or merchandise that had to be priced or re-priced. It was a constant process, one that was never really finished, and I could always find something that needed fixing.

And it would only get worse when I took over Lighthouse.

Althea Stevenson showed up a couple hours later with another woman. She was a sturdier version of Mrs. Stevenson, her dark hair showing the first faint streaks of gray, and dark eyes that missed nothing.

"This is Beth Stevenson, my sister-in-law," Mrs. Stevenson introduced her companion. "The one I told you Bethie was named for. Beth, this is Bethie's friend Gloryanna. She's the one who sent her the blue jeans."

"Thank you so much for doing that, Miss Gloryanna. It was very thoughtful of you."

I thought I detected a hint of the South in her soft voice and the way she slipped into calling me Miss Gloryanna, and remembered that Mrs. Stevenson had said she'd grown up in the area.

"I am glad I was able to help in a small way," I said. "I hope you'll let me know if there is anything else I can do.

"Just how is Beth doing, Mrs. Stevenson? And Everett, is he holding up okay?"

The two women both started to answer me, then stopped and looked at each other. "Please, call me Althea."

"And me Beth. It's just easier."

"Then you must call me Glory." I smiled at Beth as I said it.

"We've been dealing with this for decades," Althea said. "Our husbands were brothers and they spent a lot of time together. We decided long ago that first names were better than confusion, even if it didn't fit Beth's idea of proper manners."

I had to smile. "I understand how you feel, Miss Beth. If my mama was still with us, she would purely skin me alive if she heard me call one of my elders by their Christian name."

Althea blinked and turned to Beth. "You weren't kidding, were you? All these years you told me stories like that, and I always thought you were exaggerating."

"Told you," Beth said. She was looking around the store, almost as if it was familiar to her. I wondered if she had ever been in before; Althea had said she lived here as a child.

"You've never been down here before?" I asked Althea.

She shook her head. "Beth came up north and married Milt's brother Will, but somehow we never came down here for a visit. Always some reason or another."

"To be fair," Beth said, her attention pulled back from her inspection of the store, "Mama and Daddy preferred to visit up north anyway. Always looked forward to coming up to our place."

"But you *did* grow up around here?"

"Lordy, yes. That's how Bethie and Everett got that place to live on. My daddy bought bits and pieces of land all over. Said it was a solid investment. Laughed at his own joke every time he said it, too.

"Anyway, when they said they wanted to try living off the land, I offered to let them stay in the cabin. Didn't think they'd last very long—no offense, Thea."

"None taken. I didn't expect them to make it a month." Not exactly the warm and fuzzy kind of grandma I'd envisioned, but her candor was part of her charm.

"Deputy Fuentes told me you were in with the lawyer," I said. "Was this one better than the first one, I hope?"

We'd lost Beth to an inspection of the store again, but Althea answered me immediately.

"You better believe it. He had read the charges, knew what the problems were, and he asked good questions. He's not going to get Everett released right away, but at least he's working on it." She glanced around, looking for Beth. "We better get going," she said, addressing Beth more than me. "Still a lot to do this afternoon, and not much afternoon to do it in."

After they left, Julie, who had kept a discreet distance while we talked, came up to my side. "That one gal sure took an interest in the place," she said.

"She grew up somewhere around here," I told her. "Probably just reminds her of someplace she used to go."

Her interest reminded me of the two men I'd seen in the store a few days earlier. I'd been meaning to ask Julie if they'd come in again, but when I asked, she said she hadn't seen anyone that looked like who I described.

We hadn't had any calls from the merchant alert links either, but I still couldn't shake the feeling someone was watching the store.

CHAPTER FORTY-ONE

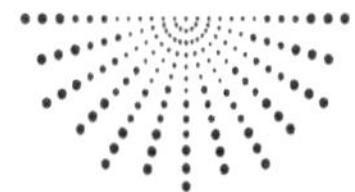

Althea Stevenson took me at my word and called late the next morning to ask a favor.

"We're going up to the cabin," she said. "We're going to stay up there, even if it means a long drive to see Bethie. Our motel isn't all that cheap, and we'd rather save our money for important things, like lawyers.

"The problem is that we haven't been over to the jail yet today, we still have several errands to take care of here, and I think once we get up there, we will be too busy to drive back down this afternoon. But I hate to leave Bethie alone, with no one to check on her.

"I know you have a business to run, but is it possible you could go over for just a little while and check in on her?"

"I'd be glad to," I said, and meant it. It would only take a few minutes, and I still carried the guilt of my part in getting Beth and Everett put in jail. It hardly atoned for what I'd done, but at least it was something.

I locked up shortly after noon and hung the clock sign in the window with the hands pointing to one o'clock. I hoped I would be back well before then, but I always erred on the side of caution.

I parked in the lot, taking a wary look around for the Beemer with the custom plates. It wasn't in any of the reserved spaces at the front of the lot, and I couldn't imagine someone who drove a car like that passing up the opportunity to flaunt his success.

Deputy Fuentes wasn't at the desk, but she came in while I was talking to a Deputy Hicks, according to his nameplate.

"She's on the sheriff's approved list," Fuentes said, waving at me. "Ten minutes. I'll take her back."

I checked my bag and followed Deputy Fuentes to the same interview room where we'd met Beth on Saturday. She locked me in like before and promised to return with Beth in a couple minutes. "She might want to freshen up to see a visitor," Fuentes explained.

While I waited, I thought about Deputy Fuentes's behavior. She hadn't asked permission, or waited for someone to give her the authority to act. She had done what any other deputy—correction, what any *male* deputy— would have done. She assumed she already had the authority and acted on it.

It was a little thing, one that could easily have gone unnoticed. But I was always wondering where our next group of leaders was coming from, where would we find the people who would replace the good ol' boys network.

Fuentes was somebody to watch.

Beth was surprised to see me. "When the deputy said I had a visitor, I expected it was Granny."

She looked very different than she had at our first visit. For starters, she was wearing clothes that fit.

"She asked me to stop by. She and your aunt Beth were busy, and then they were going up to the cabin, so she wanted me to make sure you were okay." I suddenly felt very self-conscious, not sure what to say. "I, uh, is there anything you need? Anything I can do?"

She shook her head. "Not unless you know how to get me out of here. Otherwise there isn't much anyone can do.

"What are they going up to the cabin for, anyway?"

"You didn't know?"

She shook her head. "They didn't say anything."

"I just assumed you knew. They checked out of their motel this morning. They're planning to stay up at your cabin, well, your Aunt Beth's cabin, I guess. Said the motel wasn't all that great and it was costing too much."

"They can't stay there!" Beth jumped up from the chair she had been sitting in and pounded on the locked door. "You have to let me out!" she yelled. "I have to stop them!"

She whirled around to look at me. "You have to make them come back. They can't stay there. It isn't safe!"

"What do you mean, it isn't safe?"

"There are some bad people up there. If they can't scare you off, they find other ways to get rid of you. Please, Glory, please go get them."

"Tell the sheriff what you know, Beth. He can send deputies after them."

"My lawyer told me not to."

I started to ask her what was more important, her granny's safety or what her lawyer told her to do, but the stricken look on her face told me she'd already thought of it on her own.

"I'll talk to him," she said, "but I don't know if he'll listen to me, or believe me."

She hung her head. "I couldn't blame him if he didn't; I didn't tell him the truth to begin with.

"But you could talk Granny into coming back here before anything happens, couldn't you? Just tell her I need her. I just need a little time to convince the sheriff.

"Besides, they only just left, didn't they? Maybe you could even catch up to them before they get there." Desperation and hope battled for control of her voice. "You have to stop them!"

She whirled back to look at the door. "Where are they?" she demanded. "They should be here by now!"

I reached under the table and pressed the alarm button Deputy Fuentes had shown me on my first visit.

Instantly the room was filled with the deafening blare of a Klaxon horn. Within seconds the door burst open.

The Klaxon cut off abruptly when the door opened.

Fuentes crouched in the doorway, her service revolver steady in her hand as she swept it across the room. Behind her, Hicks stood, his weapon also at the ready.

"It's okay!" I shouted. "But Beth needs to talk to the sheriff. Now! She's got something to tell him."

Fuentes made one more visual sweep of the room. I hadn't moved from my chair, my hands in plain sight on top of the table. Beth stood on the other side, her hands over her head.

Fuentes signaled Hicks to stand down. He backed up, still covering her as she slowly holstered her weapon, keeping a watchful eye on both of us. "You sure you're okay, Miss Martine?"

"Absolutely. I just needed to get someone for Mrs. Young. Like I said, she needs to talk to the sheriff right away."

"Wait here," she pointed at Beth. "You"—she gestured to me—"come with me."

I followed her into the hall. Hicks closed the door behind us and moved down the hall where he could still watch us.

As soon as Hicks backed away, Fuentes whirled around. Her eyes flashed with anger, but she kept her voice and demeanor under control. "I showed you that button for emergencies. Not for every whim that a prisoner takes it into their head to act out."

"Believe me, she was truly agitated. I thought she was calming down, but she was about that close"—I held up my thumb and forefinger a hair's breadth apart—"to a complete meltdown.

"She's afraid her grandmother and aunt may be in danger, and she's willing to spill everything she knows, or even thinks she knows, to protect them.

"Get Sheriff Hardy in there while she still wants to talk."

Wariness had replaced anger in her expression. "I can try," she said. "But the sheriff is out of the office and I'll have to track him down. I'll get her back to her cell—they're usually calmer there than in interrogation—and try to get him back here as quick as I can.

"In the meantime, I think it would be wise for you to leave."

On that we agreed 100 percent.

Back in the truck, I considered my options.

I could do nothing, and wait for Boomer to handle the situation. If Althea and Beth were actually in danger, his men would be the best qualified to deal with it.

I could wait and see if Boomer showed up quickly. If he didn't, then I could decide if I needed to do something myself.

Or I could do the thing I knew I was going to do as soon as Beth said it. I could drive like a bat out of hell to North County and hope I caught up with Althea and Beth before they got to the cabin.

I started the engine and pulled out of the parking lot.

If I hurried, I should be able to get back in time for my meeting with Miss Pansy.

CHAPTER FORTY-TWO

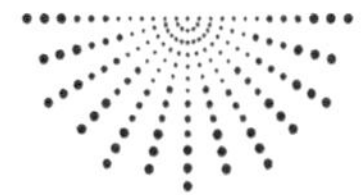

Normally, a mission like this needs an accomplice. And normally, my accomplice would be Karen. But since this all started with her wedding quilt —and since I still hoped to salvage that surprise out of this disaster—I couldn't call her.

I could call Jake, but it wouldn't be right to ask him to close Beach Books and go on a wild-goose chase with me.

That's all it was. The panic-fueled imagination of a frightened woman. But I'd do it because it might help calm Beth's fears.

I had pretty well resigned myself to making the trip alone when I thought of one person who might be up for a little adventure.

I turned toward the junkyard behind Fowler's. Even if Sly couldn't go, it only took me a couple minutes out of the way.

To my surprise, Sly not only agreed to go with me, he offered to drive. "Bobo loves car rides," he said. "If we take one of my cars, there's plenty of room for him to go along."

He climbed in the cab and directed me through the yard to one of the garages hidden deep in the maze of vehicles and parts. Bobo was already there, waiting for us with undisguised doggy glee.

Sly opened the garage door and gestured for me to pull the truck inside.

The inside of the garage, like the inside of Sly's house, was completely at odds with the exterior. Two vintage muscle cars were parked side by side behind the other two doors on a concrete floor that looked as clean as if it had been freshly poured. Rolling tool chests that would have put Fowler's service department to shame stood against the walls, and a series of hooks near the doors held an array of crisp coveralls.

Sly grinned knowingly at the stunned look that passed over my face. "I'd say that's how most folks would react, if I let folks in here. But you're only about the third person's ever seen my workshop."

"I'm honored," I said. "This is truly amazing."

"That there's the spot where your truck lived for a lot of years 'fore I sold her to you. We'll just leave her in her old space while we're gone."

He flipped a couple of switches and the garage door closed and another garage door opened, this one behind the sleek black Mustang. I wasn't sure of the year, but I would have bet it was in the 1960s.

Sly opened the car door and Bobo streaked for the opening. He leaped inside, planting his rump in the middle of the backseat. He was ready for whatever adventure lay ahead.

Sly got behind the wheel, I slid into the bucket seat on the passenger side, and soon we were on the highway heading north.

Sly slid the Mustang through traffic with a deftness born of long practice and an intimate knowledge of his vehicle. He had a light touch on the clutch and brake, a heavier foot on the accelerator. We quickly left the traffic behind and had the road to ourselves.

He grinned and opened up the throttle a bit more. The engine went from a purr to a roar in the blink of an eye. His grin grew bigger, the look of a man who purely enjoyed what he was doing.

In the backseat, Bobo yelped happily and mashed his nose against the tiny open slit at the top of the window. This wasn't the first time these two had done this, and Bobo seemed to be enjoying it just as much as Sly.

Sly held his speed for another couple minutes, then let off the gas and coasted back to within shouting distance of the speed limit.

"A car like this needs to open up once in a while," he said. "But I know if I keep that up for very long, I'll end up having a little chat with one of Keyhole Bay's finest."

We continued north at a little over the speed limit. While Sly drove, I filled him in on all the latest developments.

"I was going to save the news for tomorrow night, to tell you all at once. But really I've been dying to tell you since we got in the car."

I told him about Peter's phone call, and how I had bluffed him into taking less money.

He laughed. "You did good. You been working in that store a long time and he's been getting the benefit. 'Bout time he made up for that."

"Thanks. But that isn't all the news. The bank called Monday afternoon and my loan was approved. That's one of the reasons I'm in a hurry. I have an appointment this afternoon to meet Miss Pansy at Lighthouse and sign the final papers."

"You want me to go a little faster?" he offered with a wide grin. "I could, you know."

"I'd love it," I said, and meant it. The car hugged the road through long, sweeping curves and purred along the straight stretches, hinting at barely contained power. I would love to see it let loose. "But getting a ticket would take more time than staying close to the limit."

Sly nodded in agreement. "So why exactly are you going up here?" he asked. "You just told me you needed to go to North County and you wanted company. It don't make no never mind, but I'm curious what's so important."

I explained Beth's fear for her granny and aunt, and how agitated she'd become. "I don't think there's anything to be worried about. But I said I'd come in the hope it would calm her down. It didn't fix things, but it helped. And once I said I'd do it, I couldn't go back on my word."

"You won't have to. We'll get you up there, you can talk Beth's granny into coming back, and we'll be back in time to meet Miss Pansy. Now I might just have to go direct to Lighthouse.

"Just to get you there in time, of course," he added innocently.

"Suuuure."

"You just keep watch and tell me when I need to turn."

"It's hard to miss." I described the brightly painted fence and the narrow road leading off the highway.

I looked around, getting my bearings. "In fact, we're almost there."

CHAPTER FORTY-THREE

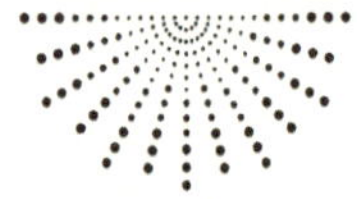

Sly spotted the fence about the same time I did and signaled the turn at the same time I pointed it out.

"Take it easy through here," I cautioned as he left the pavement for the hard-packed dirt. "It's so narrow that if another car comes along, one of us will have to pull into a driveway to let the other one pass. And it's not a very good road."

As if to underscore my words, the Mustang bumped through a deep pothole, bouncing us in our seats.

Sly grimaced at the insult to his pristine ride. He slowed even more and tried to steer around the worst of the ruts and divots in the roadway.

Fortunately, we didn't meet any other cars on our trip down the tree-lined road. This area had been logged once, and it likely would be again, but the fast-growing hackberry and oaks had filled in along the road, shielding the cabins and mobile homes that dotted the roadside. I was certain the privacy provided by the trees was no accident of nature. These were people who wanted to be left alone.

I described Beth's mailbox as we bounced along. "Should be just a little ways up here, on the right." I spotted the carved post and patterned box.

"Right there."

Sly made the turn and we crawled down the driveway. I recalled the last time I'd been down this driveway, in Karen's SUV, then coming back out in Calvin's massive pickup truck.

A shiver passed through me.

"You still think it's nothing?" Sly said.

"Yes," I said with more conviction than I felt. "I'm just spooked from my last visit out here."

Beth and Everett's hybrid was still there. A dusty compact was parked next to the porch, the Michigan plates a clear signal that Althea and Beth had arrived.

Now all I had to do was convince them to come back to Keyhole Bay.

We climbed out of the car, and Sly left the window down for Bobo. "Stay," he said when Bobo crawled into the front seat. "No sense letting him scare the ladies," he explained. "You remember how you felt the first time you saw him."

"I was in his territory," I reminded him. "He had every right to object. But I get your point." I reached through the window and gave Bobo a pat. "We'll be right back."

We climbed the steps to the large porch and I knocked on the door.

From somewhere inside, an exasperated voice shouted, "I told you they weren't here. Go away!"

"Althea," I called out, "it's me, Gloryanna. Beth asked me to come up here."

I glanced nervously around the clearing, wondering if the other visitors, whoever they were, had decided to hang around. The feeling of being watched returned full force, and I stepped closer to the door, as though looking for shelter from the prying eyes I imagined were watching from the woods.

The door swung open, taking me by surprise. I stumbled, then caught my balance.

Althea snapped, "Are you coming in or aren't you?" She swiveled to look Sly up and down before she included him in her brusque invitation. "I guess you better come in, too, if you're with her." She stomped away, leaving the door open.

"How could we say no?" I whispered to Sly, and led the way into the cabin.

I'd been here before, when I'd come to pick up quilts and small pieces of furniture. They had filled their home with handmade pieces from Everett's wood shop and wall hangings from Beth's collection of vintage quilts and needlework. The house was always tidy when I arrived, even when freshly baked cookies or bread showed they had been working in the kitchen shortly before.

Today the place was a mess. Furniture out of place, wall hangings crooked or knocked to the ground, dishes strewn across the table and counters, clothes spilled from drawers and closets.

It looked like someone had ripped the place apart.

We followed Althea to the bedroom, and I felt a knot in my stomach. If someone had robbed the place, it was likely the cedar chest had been rifled. The wedding quilt was, in all likelihood, gone for good.

From the doorway, I could see that the lid of the chest was closed. I took a step closer and spied deep gouge marks on the front, around the lock. But the chest appeared to be intact, the contents safe.

It was small consolation in light of the destruction.

Sly lingered in the doorway when I entered the room, as though he was uncomfortable invading the private space of the couple who lived here.

As I surveyed the damage, he made an odd, strangled sound, like his vocal cords had ceased to function.

I whipped around, worried that he might be ill.

He stared straight ahead, his eyes wide. He looked like he had seen a ghost.

"Anna?" he whispered, unable to get enough breath to speak.

Maybe he had seen a ghost.

I spun around, looking in the same direction.

Beth Stevenson stood in the doorway of the closet, her arms filled with a tangle of clothes and hangers, her mouth frozen in a tiny O.

"Anna?" Sly said again, his voice still soft, "Annabeth?"

I looked from one to the other. The pieces clicked into place, and I remembered one of the pictures we'd seen in the high school yearbooks. A girl with barely contained dark curls and a sweet smile. We'd snapped a photo and moved on.

A girl named Annabeth.

A girl who had stopped being Anna and become Beth.

"Sylvester?"

Her question answered all of mine. Somehow, without intending to, we had found Anna.

CHAPTER FORTY-FOUR

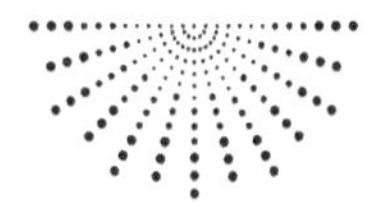

The two of them stared a moment longer as Althea and I stood rooted in place, too stunned to speak.

"You know him?" Althea asked, breaking the silence.

"That's Anna?" I asked a split second behind her.

"Yes."

"Yes."

Althea looked at me for an explanation I wasn't prepared to give her. It wasn't my story to tell.

When no one volunteered to explain, she shook her head and went back to work. "If we're going to stay here, we need to get this place cleaned up." She gave a disgusted grunt. "If this is my granddaughter's idea of keeping house . . ." Her voice trailed off into another grunt.

"It isn't." I jumped in, grateful for something to fill the awkward silence. "The house is usually tidy, everything put away, everything in its place.

"I don't think Beth left it this way."

"They did leave in a hurry," Beth said softly.

"No," I said. I forced back the panic that had been clawing at my insides since I first walked in. "They wouldn't have left this kind of a mess, no matter how big a hurry they were in.

"Someone's been here. They were looking for something"—I gestured to the spilled clothes and the marks on the chest. "I don't know if they found it, or if they got scared off, but I don't think we should hang around.

"That's what Beth sent me up here for," I said to Althea. "She wants you and her aunt Beth to come back to Keyhole Bay. She doesn't think you're safe up here."

I looked around the room. "I thought she was exaggerating, until about five minutes ago. Now I don't know. But I do know we shouldn't take any chances.

"Let's get what we need and get out of here. You can talk to Beth and decide if you want to come back."

I looked back to Sly. He and Beth—Anna—had moved within a few feet of each other and were talking quietly, haltingly, oblivious to the rest of us.

I wanted to give them their privacy, but I didn't want to stay in that house a second longer than we had to.

"Sly, Beth, um, Anna, um, whatever your name is." I was snapping, rushing, adrenaline making my voice sharp and stretching my nerves tight. "We need to go. Now."

Sly turned to me, hurt in his eyes. "I'm sorry," I said, instantly contrite. "I think I caught Beth's case of nerves. But I really think we should get out of here."

"And I think you ought to stay a while."

The voice, deep and gravelly, came from the hall outside the bedroom. Heavy boots clomped on the bare wood floor, and two men stood in the doorway.

Sly shot a look at me that clearly asked, "Are these the guys that gave you trouble?" I shook my head just a fraction of an inch. I didn't know either of them.

They stood one behind the other, each nearly as wide as the doorway. The man in back was slightly taller, but other than that, they were nearly identical—heavily muscled, stern-faced, bandanas covering their hair.

Worn black leather pants and jackets made them look like bikers. I hadn't heard motorcycles, but that meant nothing.

Sunglasses wrapped around their faces, hiding their eyes. I could imagine the cruelty in those eyes that went along with the voice, but I couldn't see them.

It was, if anything, even more frightening.

I tried to think, to find a way out. We outnumbered them, but three senior citizens and I didn't seem like much of a match for the two muscular men who were, I imagined, staring us down.

Besides, they had us trapped. There was a single, small window in the bedroom. But even if I could get to it and get it open, there was no way four of us could escape before the men could get across the room and grab us.

I could see Sly making the same calculations and coming to the same conclusions. I knew he should naturally be the leader; he was the toughest and strongest, but I wanted the two men to underestimate him.

Which they would do if a woman seemed to be in charge.

"What do you want?" I demanded. I was pleased my voice didn't waver, though my insides were quaking. "We just came to pick up some clothes and we found the place trashed.

"Did you do that?"

"What if we did?" The shorter man swaggered forward a couple steps, making room for the taller one to follow him into the room.

It had been crowded before with four of us in there. The addition of two more, large men at that, made it nearly impossible to move.

But if we couldn't move, neither could they. And we were smaller. Two of us could fit through a gap that would stop either of them.

I saw Anna clasp her hands behind her back. I wasn't sure what she was doing, but she seemed to be concentrating on something.

Althea moved close to her sister-in-law and laid her head against Anna's shoulder. The women whispered to each other and the tall man growled at them. "Nobody said you could talk."

"She's scared," Althea said in a submissive voice I had not heard from her. "We all are. I was just trying to keep her calm, poor thing."

"Women," he spat the word. "Just shut up. Nobody talks." He pointed at me. "Except her."

Okay. I was the spokesman. Spokeswoman. Whatever happened was going to be up to me.

"Tell us what you want," I said. "Maybe we can help you find it. Or help you find out if it's even here. It's a small place, it shouldn't take long.

"You get what you want, you're on your way, and everyone's fine and happy. You don't find it, at least you know it isn't here. Either way, nobody has to get scared or hurt."

I thought of Calvin and Donny, how they had done exactly that. I hoped these two were as reasonable.

"It's not a *what*," the big man said. "It's a *who*. We need to know where those two hippie-dippy freaks went, and we need to talk to them.

"Think you can fix that?"

Didn't these guys watch TV, or listen to Karen's newscasts, or read a newspaper? I dismissed the newspaper, but I still found it hard to believe they hadn't heard of Beth and Everett's arrest.

I had to turn that to our advantage.

I looked from one man to the other, trying to keep their attention on me. Whatever Anna and Althea were up to, I wanted to give them every advantage.

"Look, whatever happened out there"—I gestured to the woods beyond the cabin—"two guys ended up dead. Or hadn't you heard?" I was pretty sure they knew exactly what had happened, but I wasn't about to let them know what I was thinking.

"You think those two would stick around? My guess is, they hightailed it out of town about two steps ahead of the sheriff.

"These two old gals came to me, said the girl who lived here promised them some old clothes for some charity project," I rolled my eyes, "and they wanted me to help them get the stuff from the house.

"I'm a nice lady, I try to help, and this is where it gets me? I don't know where those two went, and I doubt anyone in this room does. But we'll help you search for clues."

I gestured to the other three, huddled together against the wall nearest the door. "Won't we?"

They all murmured their assurances.

"Where do you want us to start?"

The two men looked at each other, and I took the opportunity to sneak a peek at my companions. They had moved closer to the door while I distracted the men, maybe close enough to make a run for it.

Go, I mouthed and made a tiny shooing motion with my hands.

Sly looked as though he wanted to argue. I glared at him.

He was responsible for Althea and Anna. I could take care of myself.

I hoped he got the message.

"Well?" I challenged the men, drawing their attention back to me. "Where do we start? In here?"

I moved toward the closet. My path took me directly toward the window, and I made a show of pausing in front of it.

I got what I wanted.

Both men moved toward me, the smaller one taking a shortcut across the bed. He didn't realize the hippie-dippies still had a waterbed. It didn't make for solid footing.

He slipped, sprawling face-first across the bed.

The taller one grabbed me by the arm and pulled me against him. "What are you trying to pull?" he shouted, his face inches from mine.

I couldn't look at my friends, couldn't draw attention to them. I hoped they had used the distraction to escape.

A scream of pain from the bed told me otherwise.

The biker and I both turned.

Sprawled across the bed, the shorter man was staked to the gushing water bed with a metal rod driven through his leg and into the mattress.

Water and blood welled around him, sloshing onto the floor as he thrashed around, trying to pull the spike out of his leg.

My brain finally registered what had happened.

A wire coat hanger.

A flash of memory, Annabeth with her arms full of clothes.

And hangers.

The biker dropped me and reached to pull the hanger from his accomplice's leg.

I sprinted for the door, following my friends' mad dash toward the cars.

A hand grabbed my arm, tossing me to the ground. A heavy boot filled my vision and I had a moment of sick clarity, knowing it would land in my midsection, and knowing more blows would follow.

In the distance I heard Sly's shout. "Bobo! Cantaloupe!"

A black blur streaked across the dirt.

The boot hovered for an instant.

It moved out of my sight, accompanied by a thud that shook the ground.

Hands grabbed my arms, pulling me toward the car. Tiny hands with loose skin.

I was shoved into the backseat of the Mustang and we roared out of the yard and bounced over the washboard driveway.

As I sorted out the jumble of arms and legs, I realized Althea and Annabeth had managed to shove me in the back seat between them, with Sly at the wheel.

"Bobo!" I screamed at Sly. "Where's Bobo?"

"He'll find us," Sly said between clenched teeth.

He threw the car around a tight curve without slowing down. In the back, the three of us tumbled together, another tangle of arms and legs.

"Anyone behind us?" Sly shouted over the roar of the engine.

"Not yet," Althea shouted back. "But I can't see around the curves in the road."

"Not far to the highway," Sly answered grimly. "They won't be able to catch this baby once we're on pavement."

CHAPTER FORTY-FIVE

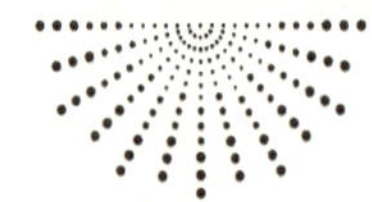

We rounded another curve and found a dark SUV coming straight at us. It reminded me of the car I'd seen Captain Clint climb into at the airport, and for one insane moment I imagined Karen's stepfather charging to our rescue.

A siren shrieked, and Sly spun his head, looking for a driveway. He slewed to the left, across the path of the oncoming vehicle, and slammed to a stop in a clearing barely big enough for the car.

I cringed as I heard branches scratch the sides of the Mustang. I hoped the damage could be repaired.

Two more SUVs sped past, followed by a patrol car.

Sly backed out and headed back the way we'd come, once again taking it easy over the bad road.

We slowly wound around the curves, Sly watching warily for vehicles coming our way.

"Bobo's gonna be looking for us," he said.

We eventually caught up to the SUVs, stopped in the middle of the road, angled every which way, and completely blocking the road. The sheriff's cruiser was pulled in behind them.

Sly stopped, then backed up until he was able to park the Mustang in a pullout about twenty yards away.

We waited, though we weren't sure what for. Within a few minutes, Bobo came trotting down the road, looking unharmed.

I would have sworn that dog was grinning.

He gave a happy yelp when he spotted the car and covered the rest of the distance at a dead run. Sly reached over and swung the passenger door open. Bobo leaped inside and greeted Sly with a big doggy kiss, obviously happy and excited to see his master.

Sly looked far more relieved than his casual assurance that Bobo would find us would have indicated. I knew how he felt.

We couldn't see much beyond the cluster of SUVs, and I wanted to know what was going on. I clambered over Althea and pushed my way out of the car.

"I'm going to walk a little closer," I told Sly.

"Not alone, you aren't," he said. He climbed out of the car, then turned back to his other passengers. "You ladies just stay here where it's safe," he said.

He looked at Bobo. "Guard," he commanded. The big dog yipped in reply.

"Let's go."

We took our time approaching the cluster of vehicles, making sure we were visible. We kept our hands in plain sight and our posture as relaxed as possible.

Even so, we were stopped by a stern-faced man with a crew cut and a badge that he flashed so quickly we couldn't read it. "This is a crime scene," he growled. "Authorized personnel only."

From behind him I heard an exasperated, "Martine! What the hell are you doing here? Pardon my French, but why can't you stay away from my crime scenes?"

"Hey, Sheriff. Mr. Benjamin and I just came up here to help Beth's granny get some things." I smiled, all innocence.

"Well, you just get right back to your vehicle." He took us each by the arm and started marching us back toward the car. In the distance I could hear voices shouting for somebody to "Stay down" and "Show me your hands."

I was pretty sure I knew who they were talking to.

"You are going to come to the station and answer some questions, and you are going to do it right now," he said. "There are a couple messed-up boys back there. One of them looks like he's been bit." He glanced over at Sly. "You know anything about that, Mr. Benjamin?"

"I believe I might, Sheriff."

"Then you don't want to talk to anyone but me," Boomer said. "You get in your car and you head for the station. I will be right behind you, just to make sure you don't get lost. You hear?"

Sly smiled and nodded. "Sure do, Sheriff." He looked over at me. "Miss

Glory, I do think it would be in our best interest to do as the sheriff asks, don't you?"

"Sure."

We climbed in the car, rearranging ourselves so Annabeth could ride up front with Sly. Bobo settled down between me and Althea, worn out from all his adventures, and we drove back to the highway.

True to his word, Boomer's car soon fell in behind us. Sly held the Mustang to the speed limit as we headed south with our escort.

"You know my car is still parked up there," Althea said at one point.

"Don't worry about it," Sly said over his shoulder. "I would be happy to take you ladies back up to get it when you're through."

The conversation reminded me of Karen driving Beth and Everett to meet with Sheriff Hardy. Except they hadn't come back for their vehicle; they'd gone to jail.

I kept that thought to myself.

CHAPTER FORTY-SIX

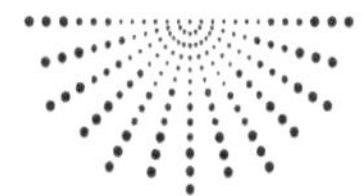

I missed my appointment with Miss Pansy. Bradley was alarmed when I told him I was at the sheriff's station, but I reassured him I was just a witness and would be home soon. We agreed to meet the next afternoon.

"How is Miss Pansy doing?" I asked. "Was it difficult for her to be back in the shop, knowing she wasn't going back to work?"

To my surprise Bradley just laughed. "She's already got a million projects started at home. Says she doesn't know how she ever found time to work so much. I think she's going to handle retirement just fine."

I hung up, relieved. I had been afraid that somehow missing the appointment would mean Miss Pansy would change her mind.

Boomer kept me cooling my heels in one of those blasted plastic chairs while he talked to each of the other witnesses, making me wait until last.

When he finally called me in, it was completely dark outside and the sodium vapor lamps in the parking lot cast a dull yellow glow over the cars parked there.

"Sit down," Boomer said wearily. I took the chair across from his desk, grateful at least that we were in his office, not the stark interview room where I'd talked to Beth that morning.

"Just tell me your version of the story," he said. "I've heard what the others have to say."

I started with my visit to Beth that morning. "I said I'd go because I thought it would calm her down. I really didn't expect any trouble. Sly, Mr.

Benjamin, offered to drive, and I took him up on it. Almost wished I hadn't; I think his car got pretty banged up."

"He says he can fix it pretty easy," Boomer said with a dismissive wave. "Go on."

"We got there, went in to talk to Mrs. Stevenson and Mrs. Stevenson"—it sounded funny to say it that way, but neither one of us even cracked a smile. "Then those two guys busted in, demanding to know where the two hippie-dippies were."

Boomer's mouth twitched at the description.

I shrugged. "Didn't sound like they knew Beth and Everett had been arrested, so I tried to distract them so the others could get away.

"I was the youngest and probably the fastest. Figured my companions might need a head start."

Another twitch. Maybe Boomer was starting to relax. Maybe he even believed me.

"Anyway, it worked. Mostly. They got away, but the big guy caught up to me." I shuddered at the memory of a huge motorcycle boot suspended over my body. "I think he was going to stomp me, when Bobo attacked him."

From there the memories were a jumble, but I told him as much as I remembered. "We parked the car and started back to see what was going on, and that's when the crew cut guy stopped us, and then you told us to come to the station.

"And here we are."

I sat quietly for a minute as Boomer scowled at a legal pad in front of him. "Anything else?"

I shook my head. "No. But what were you doing up there? And who were all those other guys, the ones with the SUVs?"

"Now, Miss Glory," Boomer started, then stopped. He tossed his pen on the desk and leaned across it, looking me in the eye. "Just who do you *think* they were? Big black SUVs. Crew cuts and knife-crease khakis. What does that look like to you?"

"Military," I shot back. I'd lived my whole life close to several bases. I knew what a military man looked like, and I knew what military investigators looked like. "But why?"

"I don't know. Officially. But the rumor is that several of the boys down at one of the bases, not saying it was the Navy, you understand. Several of those boys got themselves real sick on moonshine."

"They get shore leave, they get liquored up. Nothing new."

"This wasn't the usual," Boomer said. "Now mind you, this is only a rumor, right?"

"Of course," I answered. I resisted the urge to give him a big wink.

"The booze was bad, cut with something that poisoned some of those boys. I've heard that one of 'em died, and I've heard they just got real sick. Those Navy boys—oops!—those military boys can be real closemouthed."

"But what does any of this have to do with us? What does it have to do with Beth and Everett?"

"That's why I was there. After your little pal threw her fit in interrogation, Deputy Fuentes called me. Convinced me I needed to talk to Mrs. Young.

"She talked her head off, and I believed her. Put out a BOLO for your truck so we could stop you."

I thought of the patrol car that had passed us on the road. "I wasn't driving," I said. "We were in Sly's Mustang."

Boomer nodded. "I know that now. Anyway, Mrs. Young said they chased some moonshiners off the property when they first moved here. The husband even helped them move their still, if you can believe that. Those boys showed up a couple weeks back, trying to warn them off the place. Said a new crew was moving in, trying to take over, and the new guys were likely to come around looking for them. Asked them not to tell 'em where they'd moved the still.

"The way they described them to her, they sound like those two you met today.

"She says they heard a bunch of yelling in the woods later that day, got scared, and ran off back to Michigan."

He paused and glanced around like he was looking for eavesdroppers. "She identified the two victims as the men who warned them."

"That explains what you were doing there. But what about the other guys?"

"I think they were watching the place. I can't be sure, but it's the only way they could have been there that fast."

He sat back and steepled his fingers over his stomach. "I don't think those boys in the SUVs are going to be interested in anything you four have to say about what happened this afternoon. In fact, I am almost sure they would prefer you just forget everything that happened out there."

"Out where?" I asked with feigned innocence.

"Exactly," Boomer answered.

He nodded at me. "One more thing. Is it true that little gal, the one named Beth, is it true she stabbed one of them guys with a coat hanger?"

It was my turn to nod.

"That's a woman I wouldn't want to cross."

"Me neither." I stood up and stretched. "Is that all? Can I go home now?"

"Go," he said. "You know, you got lucky today. At least this time I'm not talking to you in a hospital bed, which is an improvement. But it would be even better if I didn't have to talk to you at all. If you get my meaning."

I nodded and walked out.

Jake was waiting in the lobby, looking worried. "Sly called me," he said. He wrapped his arms around me and pulled me close. He looked down and said, "At least I'm not picking you up at the hospital this time."

I wondered if he'd been talking to Boomer.

CHAPTER FORTY-SEVEN

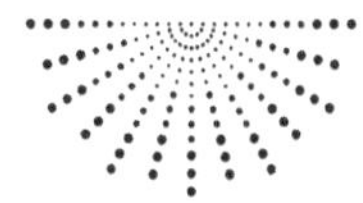

By the middle of Thursday, I had a cashier's check for the purchase price of Lighthouse Coffee. The amount was the largest single transaction of my life, even larger than the check I had written for Peter that morning.

Jake met me at Lighthouse when Miss Pansy came back in, and we gathered around a table: Miss Pansy, Bradley, Chloe, Julie, Jake, and me.

The little ceremony of signing the sales contract and handing over the check was a solemn moment. It represented a major change for all of us, including the two young women who served as witnesses.

"Thank you," Miss Pansy said when I handed over the check. "I am so happy to know the place is in good hands."

"That would be Chloe," I told her. "You taught her well, and I am lucky to have her. Thank you."

When the paperwork was done, I handed Miss Pansy a plastic card. It was one of the gift cards from Lighthouse Coffee. "It's good forever," I told her. "Anything you want, any time you want, you're my guest."

"I pay my own way," she said crisply.

"Yes, you do. And you've earned this fair and square. You take it. It's my way of making sure you come by now and then and say hello."

"Well, when you put it that way"—she slipped the card in her pocketbook. "Bradley, we need to get home. I've got work to do."

"Yes, ma'am." Bradley was on his feet instantly, escorting his mother out to the car parked at the curb.

We watched her go, and I doubt there was a dry eye in the place. I know mine weren't.

I turned to Chloe. "All right, you are officially in charge. I'll stop by in the morning to check in, but it's up to you now."

Jake promised to pick me up at six thirty for dinner, and I went back to Southern Treasures. Julie stayed behind to talk to Chloe for a few minutes.

I walked into Southern Treasures and stopped, looking around. It was exactly the same store it had been this morning, and yesterday, and last week and last year.

And yet it was completely different.

It was all mine now, along with the shop next door. And someday Guy and Linda would retire and I would buy the Grog Shop. It was what I was meant to do, I was sure of it.

Bluebeard whistled at me from his perch. "You did it, girlie. You by gum did it!"

"I did, didn't I?" I walked over and scratched his head, ruffling his feathers. "We're going to be retail moguls, you and me. This calls for a celebration."

"Coffee?"

I laughed. "You know better. How about a banana?"

I was still floating when Jake knocked on the front door. I let him in and we said good night to Bluebeard.

"I'm taking your best girl out to celebrate," Jake said.

"Your best girl," Bluebeard repeated.

Jake tilted his head like he was thinking, a gesture so like Bluebeard it was comical. "You're right," he said, taking my hand. "She is my best girl."

When Ernie answered the door, he grabbed me in a hug that took my breath away. "I heard you had another one of your adventures," he said. "Girl, this has *got* to stop!"

"It's not like I try to get into these things," I protested. "Stuff just happens to me."

He waved away my defense. "Well, it had better stop happening, is all I'm saying."

We followed him into the kitchen. Felipe was stirring gravy, and a perfectly roasted turkey sat on the counter, resting.

The table was already set for eight, with a cornucopia centerpiece that was as period as the sleek table. It looked like a centerfold from a 1950s *Better Homes and Gardens*.

"Eight?"

"Captain Clint and Catherine, remember?" Ernie said. "We called Sly, but he said he was busy, catching up with an old friend. Might you know anything about that?" He arched an eyebrow at me, clearly expecting me to know everything.

I did my best to look innocent.

I waited for Karen and Riley to arrive with Captain Clint and Catherine. Some kind of detente appeared to have been achieved, and the two couples seemed to be getting along better.

Or maybe they were just better actors than I gave them credit for. Clint was cordial and pleasant, though he kept disappearing to take urgent calls on his cell phone.

"Something's going on down at the base," Catherine explained. "We almost had to cancel. Which would have been a crying shame, to miss a meal like this."

She was right about that. Ernie, with Felipe's help I'm sure, had filled the table with a traditional Thanksgiving feast. It was all there, from turkey to oyster dressing to cranberry relish.

Clint came back from his latest phone call and I caught him staring at me. Something in his expression told me he knew more about my little incident with the crew cuts than I thought.

Might not be the time to tell everyone the details of that little adventure.

There was plenty of other news to share, and I managed to keep the conversation on my business dealings and off my latest run-in with the law.

"What about your pals in the hoosegow?" Riley asked. "Karen said she heard they were released late this afternoon. What's up with that?"

"I guess they caught the right guys," I said lightly. Clint caught my eye. I smiled sweetly. "I don't know any more than you do. In fact, I hadn't even heard they'd been released." I glanced at Karen. "Did they have a big press conference? Did Morris announce their release?"

"Ha! He hasn't shown his face in public since the word came down that the charges were being dismissed. I tried to reach him for a comment, but his office says he's 'unavailable' and won't be back in until after the holiday.

"They're claiming he had a family vacation scheduled for this week, but nobody believes a word of it. He's likely hiding out somewhere, trying to figure out just how badly he's tanked his career." She smiled, and it wasn't a pretty sight. "Karma can be cruel."

"I do have one other bit of news," I said. "If we're through talking about dear Mr. Morris."

"With any luck," Karen said, "I will never have to talk about Mr. Morris again for the rest of my career."

"From your lips to God's ears," Felipe said, crossing himself. He'd been raised a Catholic, and old habits die hard.

"So spill already, Martine," Karen said impatiently.

I looked at Jake and he nodded. He already knew. "I know who Anna is."

Stunned silence, broken at last by Ernie. "Is that what Sly meant by 'an old friend'?"

"Yes. Beth Young's granny came down here with her brother-in-law's widow. The two of them are pretty much best friends. Aunt Beth is the one who owns the property where Beth was living. And yes, it is incredibly confusing for both of them to be named Beth. Also for both of the women to be Mrs. Stevenson.

"Anyway, when Sly and I ran into the two of them, he recognized her and she recognized him. They've got fifty years to catch up on, so I think that might take a while."

"How did Sly take it?" Karen asked. "Is he okay?"

"He seemed genuinely pleased to see her, and it looked to me like she felt the same way. I got to talk to her a little bit. Did you know how they met? She came into Southern Treasures while he was there doing odd jobs for Uncle Louis. She told me they used to meet there and just talk when they couldn't be seen together anywhere else in town.

"I don't know how things will go, but at least they each know what happened to the other, and I think that's a good thing."

I looked around the table, at the family I'd made out of my favorite people. "Yeah," I said. "Today I have a lot to be thankful for."

CHAPTER FORTY-EIGHT

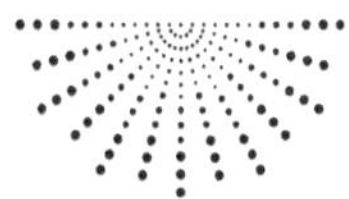

I stood in the church vestibule, dark green satin skimming over my body and brushing the toes of my high heels.

I was steadier than I'd been a few weeks ago, thanks to hours of practice, walking around my apartment, feeling foolish in stiletto heels and blue jeans. But at least I knew I could make it down the aisle without tripping over my own feet.

Jake stood next to me, keeping me distracted until the bridal march began and he had to take his place with the groomsmen. As maid of honor, I would walk with Bobby, Riley's brother and best man.

I fidgeted, unable to stand still.

"It'll be fine," Jake said, wrapping his arm around my shoulders. "Everyone knows what to do. And in very short order, Karen and Riley will be married again and headed for their honeymoon."

"Did you get everything worked out?" I asked him for about the thousandth time.

"Plane tickets to Las Vegas, hotel reservations, rental car reserved, hotel reservations in wine country, and a flight home Christmas Eve. It's all set.

"Are you sure she doesn't suspect?"

I shook my head. "She's still fussing over what to pack, but with Catherine and Julie's help, I managed to get everything she might possibly need."

I sighed and shifted again, trying to stay balanced in the narrow heels.

"Though I really think we could have started with the plane tickets several months ago, and skipped all this."

The church was full of people. Friends of the bride. Friends of the groom. Friends of their parents. Riley's people alone filled several pews; he had a big family.

Karen's side didn't have many relatives, but the pews were packed with her friends and co-workers. In the front pew, Clint sat patiently, waiting for the best man to escort Catherine to her seat.

Two uniformed Navy officers came in and one of the ushers stepped forward. "Friends of the bride's family," the taller one said. The voice was familiar, though I couldn't immediately place it. "The Captain is expecting us."

The usher, one of Riley's brothers, nodded. "He told us a couple of his team would be here. Asked me to seat you near him."

"Thank you."

I gasped, finally placing the voice. The tall officer turned, looking for the source of the sound. A tiny grin lifted the corners of his mouth for a fraction of a second.

"You all right, ma'am?" Calvin asked before he and Donny followed the usher to their seats.

In the small office at the side of the vestibule, Karen waited with her escort. She had asked Sly to walk her down the aisle. Her father had been MIA a long time, and she wasn't close with any of the stepdads.

She was getting to know and like Clint, and had even offered to switch. It was a peace offering to her mother, but Clint was a pretty smart guy. He declined, saying she should have her old friend do the honors, if she just saved one dance for her new stepdad.

Next to Clint, Anna waited for Sly. She'd delivered the finished quilt on one of her many trips down from Beth and Everett's place, where she'd been staying the last few weeks.

The organist ended the number she was playing, and then the opening notes of a Baroque canon drifted softly from her instrument.

That was our cue.

"See you soon," Jake said and kissed me good-bye.

He took his place in line, linked his arm with one of the bridesmaids, and followed the procession down the aisle. Moments later, I linked arms with Bobby and followed along.

We reached the front of the church where Riley waited, then turned to watch Karen make her entrance.

She was a beautiful bride.

I'd promised myself I wouldn't cry, but I'd known when I did that it was impossible. Two of my best friends were getting married. Again.

Sly and Karen reached the front of the church. He took Karen's hand from his arm and placed it in Riley's outstretched hand, then kissed her lightly on the cheek and stepped back to join Annabeth in the front pew.

As he passed Clint, the captain stuck out his hand and shook Sly's. I could see him form a silent "Thank you."

I took Karen's bouquet, holding it as she held Riley's hands and focused on his face.

The minister began his speech and the first part of the vows. I swallowed hard around the lump in my throat, knowing I had one more part to play.

The minister had come to the point where he asked, "Who gives this woman in marriage?"

On this point Karen had been adamant. She was a grown woman who had already been married to Riley once.

"I do," she said.

She expected the ceremony to proceed, but her family and friends had other ideas. With Riley's approval, we'd added one more item.

"And who comes to support this gift?"

Across the church, people stood. Sly and Anna. Felipe and Ernie. Chloe. Julie, holding Rose Ann. Catherine and Clint. Linda and Guy. Riley's parents and brothers.

We spoke in unison.

"We do."

MENUS AND RECIPES

Menus and Recipes

Ernie's Cajun Roots

Chicken, sausage, seafood gumbo

Gumbo, like so many home-cooked dishes, varies with each cook. As Ernie said, it often depends on what kind of fish or shellfish or sausage was available. The heart of the gumbo is the roux, and the trinity (onion, bell pepper, and celery) and okra are staples of every gumbo recipe. From there you can pick and choose the meats and seasonings you prefer, adding hot sauce, herbs, and spices to please your palate. Ernie's recipe is a good place to start.

1 pound boneless skinless chicken breast

1 pound smoked sausage, sliced 1/4 inch thick

1/4 cup vegetable oil

1/2 cup flour

5 tablespoons margarine

1 large onion, chopped

8 cloves garlic, minced

1 green bell pepper, chopped

3 stalks celery, chopped

1/4 cup Worcestershire sauce

2 teaspoons salt

1/2 teaspoon black pepper

1/2 teaspoon dried thyme

2 teaspoons file powder
1/2 teaspoon Cajun seasoning blend
1/4 bunch flat leaf parsley, coarsely chopped
4 cups hot water
5 beef bouillon cubes
14 ounce can stewed tomatoes, with juice
1 pound sliced okra, fresh or frozen
4 green onions, sliced
1 pound cooked shrimp
1 pound lump crabmeat

Season chicken with salt and pepper. In a heavy skillet, heat oil over medium-high heat. Cook chicken just until browned on both sides, it will not be cooked through, but will finish cooking in the broth. Remove from pan. Brown sausage and remove from pan.

Reduce heat to medium, sift the flour over the hot oil, add 2 tablespoons margarine and stir continuously until mixture is brown. This takes about 10 minutes, and constant stirring is essential. Set the roux aside to cool.

In a Dutch oven, melt remaining margarine over low heat. Cook onion, garlic, bell pepper, and celery in margarine 10 minutes. Add Worcestershire, seasonings, and parsley. Cook another 10 minutes, stirring frequently.

Add hot water and bouillon cubes to vegetables, whisking constantly until mixed. Bring to a boil, reduce heat, cover, and simmer 45 minutes. Add tomatoes, chicken, sausage, and okra, replace cover, and continue simmering for 1 hour.

Add green onions, shrimp, and crabmeat. Cook just until shellfish are heated through. Garnish with chopped parsley and green onion and serve over steamed rice. Serves 8-10.

Boudin balls

Boudin is a spicy pork sausage, especially popular in Louisiana. You can buy it ready-made (at least you can if your store carries it), or you can make your own. Either way, it's a great way to start your evening.

1 pound. boudin sausage, homemade or purchased
1 cup cracker meal or crushed crackers
2 eggs
1/2 cup milk
1 teaspoon. salt
1/2 teaspoon black pepper
1/4 teaspoon cayenne pepper
Oil for frying

Form sausage into golf-ball-size balls, set aside.

Mix the cracker meal (or finely crushed crackers) with seasonings and divide into two shallow bowls. In another bowl whisk together the eggs and milk. Roll the sausage balls in the first bowl of crumb mixture, coat with egg mixture and roll in the second bowl of crumb mixture.

Refrigerate prepared balls for 1 to 2 hours before frying.

Heat the oil to 350 degrees in a deep fry pan (or use a deep fryer) and fry until golden brown. Drain on paper towels and serve warm with remoulade or tartar dipping sauce.

Boudin

1 1/4 pounds pork butt, cubed

1/2 pound pork liver

1 quart water

1/2 chopped onion

1/4 cup each chopped green bell pepper, chopped celery

1 teaspoon chopped garlic

2 teaspoons salt

1 teaspoon cayenne pepper

3/4 teaspoon ground black pepper

1/2 cup finely chopped parsley

1/2 cup chopped green onion (green part only)

3 cups cooked medium grain rice

Place water in a large saucepan. Add pork butt and liver, onion, bell pepper, celery, garlic, 1 teaspoon salt, 1/4 teaspoon cayenne, and 1/4 teaspoon black pepper. Bring to a boil. Reduce heat and simmer 1 1/4 to 1 1/2 hours, until meats are tender.

Remove from heat. Drain, reserving the broth.

Using a food processor or meat grinder, process the pork mixture with parsley and green onion. Combine meat mixture and rice in a large bowl with remaining salt, black pepper, and cayenne. Mix in 1/2 cup broth. Continue adding broth in 1/2 cup increments until mixture is a firm paste. Be sure all ingredients are mixed thoroughly.

Rest the mixture until it cools enough to handle, and proceed as above.

Fried okra

Fried okra is as common as French fries in Southern restaurants, and maybe even more popular. These bite-sized pieces will disappear as fast as you can fry them up.

1 pound. fresh okra pods

1 cup milk

1/2 cup flour
1/2 cup corn meal
1 teaspoon salt
1/2 teaspoon black pepper
Oil for frying

Clean okra pods, remove stems, and slice into approximately 1" pieces. Put the milk in a bowl and set the okra pieces to soak. Sift the last 4 ingredients together and put in a paper sack (a plastic bag or a bowl will work as well).

Working with a few pieces at a time, shake the okra pieces in the bag to coat with the flour mixture. When you have finished shaking all the pieces shake them a second time to insure a good coating.

Heat the oil to 350 degrees in a deep fry pan (or use a deep fryer) and fry the okra in small batches until golden brown. Drain on paper towels, sprinkle with salt, and enjoy!

Bread Pudding with Caramel Sauce

Bread pudding is a great way to use bread that's slightly stale, and some recipes even suggest drying fresh bread before starting your pudding. The custardy goodness topped with warm caramel sauce can be topped with whipped cream or ice cream, but it's also delicious all by itself.

7 cups white bread or egg bread, cut into 1 1/2 inch cubes
1/2 cup golden raisins
1/2 cup melted butter
4 whole eggs
1 cup granulated sugar
1/4 cup light brown sugar
1 teaspoon grated nutmeg
2 teaspoons vanilla extract
2 cups half and half
2 cups whole milk
Caramel Sauce
1/2 cup butter
1 cup light brown sugar
1/4 teaspoon salt
1 teaspoon vanilla
1/2 cup evaporated milk

In a buttered 13" x 9" pan, place bread cubes topped with raisins. Drizzle with melted butter, but do not stir.

In a large bowl beat eggs and blend in sugars, nutmeg, milk, and half and half. Pour egg mixture over bread and let it soak in. Gently push bread down into liquid if it tries to float. Sprinkle with additional nutmeg, if desired.

Bake at 350 degrees for 40-50 minutes, until puffy and golden. If it browns too quickly, cover loosely with foil.

Cool.

Melt butter in a saucepan and add brown sugar. Bring to a boil, remove from heat, and whisk in remaining ingredients. Serve warm over squares of cooled pudding.

Glory's Pecan Pie

What can I say about pecan pie? It is, quite simply, the quintessential Southern dessert. Rich, buttery, filled with the dark, nutty goodness of pecans, a small slice will satisfy any sweet tooth. Glory's kitchen is small, so she often resorts to refrigerated crusts for convenience and time savings, and you can do the same. The pecans are the star of this show, so make sure they're the best you can find.

4 eggs

1 cup sugar

1 cup corn syrup

1 teaspoon vanilla

Dash salt

1 cube butter, melted and cooled

2 cups chopped pecans

9" pie shell

In a bowl, whisk eggs. Add sugar, corn syrup, vanilla, salt, and butter. Mix well. Stir in pecans.

Prepare your favorite pie crust, or use a ready-made pie shell.

Pour filling into unbaked crust and place on a baking sheet to guard against spills. Bake at 375 degrees for 35 minutes, or until a knife inserted 1" from the edge comes out clean.

Cool before serving. Refrigerate leftovers (as if there are going to be any!).

From the Secret Files of Miss Pansy and Lighthouse Coffee

Quiche

A quiche can be just about anything you can dream up. Eggs and cream create a rich custard base for whatever savory add-ins you can imagine. The meat and vegetable combinations are limited only by your imagination. And it's a great way to use up those leftovers that aren't quite enough to be a meal on their own. Start with this basic ham and cheese, and see where you wind up! As with the pecan pie, use your favorite pie crust recipe, or buy a ready-to-bake shell—though Miss Pansy would never allow such a thing in her kitchen!

1 9" unbaked pie shell
1 1/2 cups shredded cheese (any variety, use your favorite)
1/2 cup chopped cooked ham
4 large eggs
2 cups heavy cream, or half and half
1/4 teaspoon salt
1/4 teaspoon pepper

Spread cheese and ham in bottom of unbaked pie shell. In a medium bowl, beat eggs with cream, salt, and pepper. Pour over ham and cheese. Bake at 325 degrees for 45-50 minutes, until knife inserted in center comes out clean. Let stand 10 minutes before cutting and serving.

Scones

Scones come in many varieties, but Miss Pansy's favorites are the traditional biscuit-like ones. They can be plain, served with berry preserves, flavored with lemon or orange zest, or baked with a handful of currants or dried cranberries added.

2 cups flour
4 teaspoons baking powder
3/4 teaspoon salt
1/3 cup sugar
4 tablespoons butter
2 tablespoons shortening
3/4 cup cream
1 egg, beaten

Combine dry ingredients in a large bowl, mixing well. Cut in butter and shortening, using a pastry cutter or a fork.

In a second bowl combine beaten egg and cream. Add to dry ingredients and stir.

Turn dough out on a floured board and knead 10-12 times. Pat dough into a circle and cut in wedges. Bake at 375 degrees until brown, about 15 minutes.

Serve warm with berry preserves.

Pecan Tassies

These tiny tarts are like miniature pecan pies, and they fly out of Miss Pansy's pastry case every time she bakes them.

Cream Cheese Pastry
2 ounces cream cheese
2/3 cup butter

3/4 cup sifted flour
Filling
1-1/2 cups brown sugar
2 tablespoons soft butter
2 teaspoons grated orange peel
1 teaspoon orange extract
Dash salt
2 eggs, beaten
1-1/3 cup coarsely broken pecans

In food processor, process flour, cream cheese, and butter until it forms into a ball. Flatten into a disk, wrap in plastic and refrigerate for at least 1 hour.

Remove chilled dough from refrigerator and divide into 24 portions. Flatten each portion into a circle and line ungreased mini muffin cups, pressing into bottom and sides.

Set aside 1/2 of pecans. Place remaining 1/2 equally in pastry-lined cups. Mix remaining filling ingredients thoroughly and fill each cup about 2/3 full. Top with reserved pecans.

Bake at 350 degrees for about 25 minutes, or until set.

Cool, remove from pans, and serve.

AFTERWORD

I want to thank all the readers who have made these books possible. Being able to tell the stories of Glory, Bluebeard, and all the rest of the crew, is an absolute blast!

I hope you have enjoyed your visit to Keyhole Bay, and that you'll return for our next adventure in MURDER BUYS A LEMON, and MURDER TAKES A CHANCE (coming soon!).

In the meantime, my sincere thanks for your support, and for being a fan of me and my work. You are what makes this all worthwhile.